Praise for *Heart of the Highland Wolf*

"Refreshing and new, with fun, wit, and lots of sex appeal."

—*Book Loons*

"A high-powered romance that satisfies on every level... *Heart of the Highland Wolf* embraces the best of what romance has to offer with characters that jump off the pages and into a reader's heart."

—*Long and Short Reviews*

"Exciting, romantic, and utterly satisfying! *Heart of the Highland Wolf* is a book with a lot of heart... well-drawn characters, and a fascinating, suspenseful story line."

—*Over the Edge Book Reviews*

"Fast paced and completely and utterly fascinating... The chemistry between the characters was brilliant."

—*Royal Reviews*

"A wonderful romance with mystery, action, and violence along with a passion that just won't quit... The dynamics of the wolf pack is so well written that you can actually believe in its existence."

—*Eva's Sanctuary*

"This novel has it all... Hot doesn't even begin to describe it."

—*Love Romance Passion*

Praise for *Legend of the White Wolf*

"No one does tales of the wolf better than Terry Spear."

—*Genre Go Round Reviews*

"Spear's latest novel is bursting with romance, suspense, and heart-pounding excitement... *Legend of the White Wolf* will leave you howling for more!"

—*Love Romance Passion*

"Hooked me from the start, with its action and mystery woven together against the backdrop of a scenic Maine winter. This book has it all; fantasy, suspense, and romance with a touch of the paranormal to boot."

—*Literary Escapism*

Praise for *To Tempt the Wolf*

"Where this book truly shines is the werewolf society and the group dynamics amongst them. The sparring between the alpha leaders is top-notch and it's fascinating to see how wolf habits transcend into human behavior."

—*Medieval Bookworm*

"Chilling suspense and sizzling romance meet in this page-turner. The dark, sexy alpha hero will capture you—body, mind, and soul."

—Nicole North, author of *Devil in a Kilt*

"Do not attempt to start reading this book unless you have a full two hours to sit and be held spellbound... With absolute fascination and intrigue, I was held captive and unable to put this book down... with a quick slash of the pen, author Terry Spear will have you caught up and panting for more."

—*The Romance Studio*

"A paranormal romp that sizzles! Action-packed romance and suspense-filled plot add up to pure magic. I couldn't turn the pages fast enough. Terry Spear is a great addition to the paranormal genre!"

—*Armchair Interviews*

Praise for *Destiny of the Wolf*

"Terry Spear weaves paranormal, suspense, and romance together in one nonstop roller coaster of passion and adventure."

—*Love Romance Passion*

"A werewolf tale that will have you believing they live among us! This is a definite keeper on my shelf!"

—*Paranormal Romance Reviews*

"What I love most about these werewolves is that they read books about werewolves... The thought that some werewolf out there is reading this book added a whole new dimension of delight for me..."

—*Armchair Interviews*

Also by Terry Spear

Heart of the Wolf

Destiny of the Wolf

To Tempt the Wolf

Legend of the White Wolf

Seduced by the Wolf

Wolf Fever

Heart of the Highland Wolf

Dreaming of the Wolf

A SEAL IN

WOLF'S CLOTHING

TERRY SPEAR

Published by Sourcebooks Casablanca, an imprint of Sourcebooks, Inc.
P.O. Box 4410, Naperville, Illinois 60567-4410
(630) 961-3900
FAX: (630) 961-2168
www.sourcebooks.com

Printed and bound in the United States of America
RRD 20 19 18 17 16 15 14 13 12 11 10

*I salute those serving our country
in all branches of the armed services
and my son, Blaine Spear, who worked hard
to become an Eagle Scout, served as a
Civil Air Patrol cadet, and is now an
officer in the U.S. Air Force.*

Chapter 1

OF ALL THE DAMN TIMES FOR HIS SEAL TEAM LEADER, Hunter Greymere, to take a mate and fly off on a honeymoon to Hawaii, why did he have to do so now?

The problem wasn't only with the assassin, should he arrive here and target Hunter's sister, Meara, since Hunter was gone, but also with the fact that Meara was on the prowl for a mate. Finn Emerson had discovered that when he read the advertisement for cabin rentals that was lying on the white marble breakfast bar in Meara's cabin.

He would have been wryly amused if the situation wasn't creating even more difficulties for him. Glancing down at the counter, he reread the advertisement.

Cabin rentals with single occupancy located on Oregon coast. Great for rugged adventurers looking for a wilderness escape. No nearby shopping, theaters, or restaurants. Strictly a roughing-it getaway. For a special fee, management will provide a select menu. Cabin availability limited, so sign up now.

Meara Greymere, Owner and Manager

As he considered each point in the advertisement, Finn shook his head and slipped a bug into Meara's phone.

Single occupancy? After searching the five unoccupied cabins, Finn had found that each had two bedrooms and a living area furnished with a fold-down couch for additional guests.

Rugged adventurers? From what Hunter had told Finn, Meara had been searching for a mate for some years now, and he assumed she wanted only alpha males to rent the cabins.

Cabin availability limited? Yep, limited to five alpha males, if she could ensure she only rented to alphas.

Meara Greymere, Owner and Manager? What had happened to Hunter in the equation? Finn knew Hunter wouldn't have given Meara total control over the rentals.

As to the special fee for a select menu, he just wondered what—or more appropriately, who—she would be offering.

Finn spied a notebook sitting next to the phone and flipped it open. A woman's handwriting listed guests due to arrive this week—with abbreviated notes beside their names.

Joe Matheson, investment broker—sounded sexy, first arrival.

Hugh Sutherland, thrill seeker—rugged voice.

Ted Greystalk, bank president—promising.

Caesar Silverman, dive-shop owner—sounded wet and wild.

Finn snorted. He didn't think she liked Navy SEAL types much because he and Hunter were SEALs. So why would the owner of a dive shop be appealing? Maybe she covertly *was* impressed with SEALs but refused to admit it, and the diver reminded her of a SEAL.

Rocky Montana, independently wealthy—mysterious.

The guy sounded like he was a wrestler or something. But the "mysterious" bothered Finn most. A man with something to hide?

Five other names had been crossed out and had merited comments like "not rugged enough," "sounded way too controlling," "by own admission, strictly loner wolf," "too old sounding," "strictly human," and "mated!"

She had another list of eligible and ineligible wolves for the following week.

Finn slapped the notebook closed and set up a hidden camera in the living room, wedging it between books in the bookcase. He would have a couple of his buddies run background checks on each of the men to see if they could turn up anything. Because *lupus garous* lived so long, they had to change their occupations and locations after a time to avoid suspicion, so the background checks might not turn up much.

That was fine. Finn would interrogate the men thoroughly in person anyway. He smiled a little. He'd prove to them that none had what it took to turn Meara's head.

Still, Finn couldn't believe Hunter had left a couple of sub-leaders in control of the pack and Meara in charge of the cabins. So who the hell was in charge of Meara?

The worst-case scenario was that Meara would get stuck with a wolf she wasn't interested in mating due to a poor choice on her part. From what Hunter had told him, she'd always been headstrong and hard to heel, and Finn figured the years hadn't changed her. Besides, she was always picking up the wrong kind of men.

Finn stalked down the plush ivory-carpeted hall to her bedroom—a nicely appointed room with a queen-sized bed covered in an olive-colored silk comforter and pillows, all trimmed in gold. The walls were a marbleized olive color, and all the wood was rosewood, making him feel as if he were in a cozy woodland den. On the walls hung pictures of redwoods from the California forests Meara and Hunter had called home for more than a century. Finn wondered if Meara ever got homesick, or if she'd adjusted to living on the Oregon coast. He still couldn't believe they'd been forced to move because of some damned arsonist.

Used to living out of a duffel bag, Finn was surprised to feel an uncharacteristic pang of longing for an ocean-view cabin, comfortable, homey, and appealing for every season. He had a place of his own with an ocean view a couple hours south, having thought he might live there if he ever wanted to set down more permanent roots, but he rarely stayed there, renting it out to others for most of the year. Or using it as a safe house on occasion.

His home didn't feel like his own place, having been decorated by an interior decorator. Nothing there was his personally. It was just a spot to drop in when it was vacant, once in a blue moon, and he wasn't on a mission.

Meara's cabin had a different ocean view, and it was warmer somehow, filled with her enticing scent and smaller, homier than his place. A rosewood-framed collection of pictures of her family—Hunter, her parents, and her uncle, who had owned the cabin resort before giving it to Hunter and Meara—sat on the dresser. A silver-plated hairbrush engraved with her grandmother's name rested beside the pictures. A tube of lip gloss next to that made Finn think of Meara's moistened lips—succulent, full and petulant, and damned ripe for kissing. He scowled at himself for even going there and glanced out the window.

He could imagine a summer day like today with a refreshing, cool ocean breeze blowing through the open windows, or a wintry landscape where the pines were dusted with snowflakes while he ran through them in his wolf coat, or spring wildflowers filling the woods, or the leaves turning crimson, burnt orange, and brilliant yellow on a fall day.

He shook his head at himself. When had he become an old man?

He stripped out of his clothes and dumped them next to his duffel bag. If any of these vacationing wolves thought they had half a chance of making a play for Meara without Hunter around, they'd soon learn that they'd have to deal with another alpha male.

The situation could be a lot more serious than that—not that selecting the wrong mate wasn't serious enough, since *lupus garous* mated for life and lived long lives. Finn didn't know if, in an effort to get to Hunter, the assassin would attempt to grab Meara.

Finn snatched his cell phone from his belt and tried to call Hunter one last time. According to one of Hunter's sub-leaders, Chris Tarleton, Hunter would be flying out with his mate to Hawaii any minute now and he'd probably already turned off his cell phone. Hell, Finn had to warn Hunter to watch his back. If he'd only known sooner that Hunter had moved his *lupus garou* pack from Northern California to the Oregon coast, Finn might have caught Hunter before he left. A few months had passed since their last contracted mission, and Finn

had just assumed that Hunter and his pack were still living in the same place they had for years.

The phone rang and rang. *No answer*. Finn would
have to keep trying to reach him. For now, Finn needed
to stake the territory as his own until Hunter returned.
Finn extended his arms and summoned the quick and
painless transformation into his wolf form, welcoming
the stretching of muscles and tissue. The softer fur covered his skin close to his body, while the coarser outer
coat added a protective layer. He dropped to stand on
all four paws before loping down the hall to the kitchen
where a wolf door was his ticket to the outside.

Once outside, he raced across the slate-gray patio,
then dove into the woods surrounding the oceanfront
cottage and ran along a trail already marked by Hunter
and a female, probably his mate. By the time the two of
them returned from Hawaii, their scent markings would
be two weeks old, and another werewolf coming into
the area might think it was unoccupied, allowing him to
stake a claim to the territory.

Finn loped through the northern pine and Douglas
fir forests, scent-marking the area surrounding each of
the five rental cabins. Waves crashed below the cliffs,
and the Pacific Ocean breeze shook the pine branches
as the clean air filled his lungs. He paused briefly at
the cliffside to take another heady breath and watch the
foaming waves crest and fall against the beach. He could
never get enough of the sea.

But instead of striking from the direction of the sea
and returning there after accomplishing his clandestine
mission, as he would have done while serving as one
of the elite U.S. Navy SEALs, Finn was sticking to the

land this time. Nothing about *this* operation would be clandestine. Finn wanted the assassin to know he was here protecting his own, if whoever it was decided to make a hit on anyone else who had been with the team.

Hunter had been like a brother to Finn while they'd served as SEALs, and Finn owed it to Hunter to keep him safe—and Hunter's sister also, knowing that she could be a target and Hunter wasn't here to protect her. Not that Meara would see it that way once she learned why Finn was here, he suspected.

Finn leaped over a fallen tree on a pine-needle path farther away from the ocean, breathing in the scents of pine and fresh water trickling by in an ice-cold stream. Neither could mask the distinct smell of another predator. A cougar. And farther in the distance, its potential prey, an elk.

Finn paused, twisting his ears this way and that, listening to the sounds of the ocean, the water in the stream, and the birds twittering and singing to one another, but he could detect no other sound of animals, human or otherwise, traversing the land.

Despite this not being *Finn's* territory, he was leaving fresh markings and *making* it his territory until Hunter returned home. Finn scratched the ground again with his paws to help ensure that any newcomer would know Meara had not been left alone without protection.

Finn loped back toward the house, satisfied he'd left enough of his scent to warn anyone who intended to get close to the territory to back off. He glanced at the drive in front of the wood-frame cabin. No vehicle there yet. From what Chris Tarleton had reluctantly told him, Meara should be returning from the airport in about an hour.

Chris definitely didn't sound happy to hear that Finn was back, nor that he was looking out for Meara's welfare. Finn wondered what interest Chris had in Meara. A pack sub-leader's interest—as in she was the leader's sister, and if she was in trouble and Chris didn't watch out for her, he would be in trouble? Or something of a more personal nature?

Baby-sitting Meara wasn't what Finn had in mind, either. But the assassin had already attempted to kill one of their SEAL team members and was suspected of going after another. Finn had the sneaking suspicion that the assassin intended to go after each of them. Fortunately for them, the assassin was batting zero, and with the SEALs aware of the menace, whoever this was would have a devil of a time succeeding now.

Finn ran around the pine trees surrounding the house to the back patio of Meara's cabin. He'd checked out the cabin farther down the coast and found it was Hunter's and Tessa's. Meara's sweet scent permeated this cabin. And here's where he'd stay until he could reach Hunter and apprise him of the situation.

Butting through the wolf door with his nose, Finn entered the kitchen and headed for the master bedroom to dress. If he had judged the time right, Meara would be arriving soon. He'd have a fight on his hands from the outset. *Guaranteed*.

Although thrilled for her brother and his mate and their new beginning, Meara was trying not to show how excited and anxious she was to see Hunter and Tessa off quickly on their flight. Meara impatiently waved as they headed to the waiting area past the security check station, and once they were out of sight, she booked it out of there.

Now was her chance to throw out the red carpet for the prospective bachelor alpha males who had leased the cabins. If none of the men this week appealed to her, she had a new batch of bachelor males coming the next week.

They were her cabins for now. The guests were all hers, too. When Hunter and Tessa returned, Meara intended to convince them to let her be in charge of renting the cabins permanently while they ran the pack. She would insist that would keep her well-occupied and happy, since she'd been none too happy to move here from the redwoods of California in the first place. Damned arsonists. If she could get away with it, she'd locate them and... well, they wouldn't be setting any more fires. Not unless they did so in hell.

Thankfully, Hunter had two sub-leaders, Chris and Dave, to watch over the pack while she was given the job of maintaining the cabins. That meant the sub-leaders would be occupied as she actively looked over her mate prospects. Two weeks. That's all the time she had without her brother interfering and saying no to anyone she might be interested in. Not that she'd totally listen to him. But she hated how he always made her doubt herself about the men she'd been intrigued with. And once she'd hooked up with them?

Yeah, as much as she hated to admit it, Hunter had always been right. In every case, they'd been the wrong sort for her. But she was determined to get it right this time. *Without* his brotherly advice!

Of course, if none of these men were suitable, she'd keep looking. But she didn't believe she'd ever have a more perfect opportunity to be out from under Hunter's watchful eye than now.

In her excitement, she rushed home to ready herself for her first guest's arrival, exceeding the speed limit just a little on the winding road. But she had to be prepared.

Let's see. Snacks, drinks. Maybe dinner, even though it wasn't part of the paid "meal plan." But a light meal — she'd made the perfect homemade German potato salad, just in case — and conversation might go a long way toward quickly finding out as much as she could about each of her prospective guests.

What would be the best way to entertain the male arriving tonight? A midnight, moonlit swim? The Pacific Ocean in these parts was cold any time of the year, but she was up for anything a potential mate might enjoy trying. A moonlit stroll in the woods? A run in their wolf coats? Dinner on the patio with glasses of red or white wine, the moon and a sprinkling of stars glowing overhead?

Getting too cozy too early would be a mistake. She loved to run and she loved adventure, so curling up on the couch to watch a movie wasn't what she had in mind. Later, sure. But she had to know he'd want to do fun, adventurous activities. Not just lie around watching TV while she cooked meals for him. If he also cooked, so much the better. And if he didn't mind vacuuming? Even better.

Okay, that was getting a little too domesticated right off the bat. But she did hate vacuuming. And if he liked to vacuum, that would definitely work for her.

As soon as she reached the coast and her rustic

redwood cabin, she parked and got out of the car. But something didn't feel right. The blinds were still closed in the four windows facing the road, and the front door was shut like it should be. Everything seemed in order, but... she could have sworn one of the blinds in her bedroom had moved just a hair.

As wolves, well, part-time wolves anyway, she and her kind could see like wolves could. And catching a glimpse of movement that a human might not notice was one of the perks of being one of the wolf kind. Still, had it been her imagination? Maybe a trick of the pine branches dipping and rising in a graceful dance to the coastal wind's tune and casting shadows across her bedroom window? As she watched the interplay of light and shadows, she thought that might be the case.

She sniffed the air and smelled the scent of pine trees; the salty, fishy ocean breeze; a hint of sour seaweed; and even the smell of an elk. *And*, she narrowed her eyes as she shifted her gaze to the north, a *cougar*. He wasn't anywhere in sight, but she could smell him a few miles through the woods just the same. It was *their* territory. Not his.

But then she took another breath and frowned more deeply. Hell, a wolf had left his scent markings in the area. She sampled the air some more. *Male*. Had to be an alpha, or he wouldn't have been so bold. Had to be a *lupus garou* for the same reason. If it was the guy renting the cabin who was due to arrive soon and he'd gotten here early, she'd give him an earful. He was just a visitor unless she decided otherwise. And he had no business marking the territory with his own scent. Talk about having balls.

She looked quickly around. Where was he? There was no sign of a vehicle. No one sitting on the wicker settee on the front porch. No sign of a soul.

The scent markings warned her, though, that an alpha male was claiming this territory. She thought then he must still be running around in the woods in his wolf form. *Fine*. As soon as he showed up, she'd let him know in no uncertain terms what a mistake he was making.

Meara entered the main cabin that their uncle had given to her and Hunter. Now that her brother had moved into Tessa's home further down the coast, this place was all Meara's. But immediately she got a whiff of a male werewolf who had been *inside* her place. She stood stock still, lifted her nose, and sniffed the air with deeper purpose. A male wolf she didn't recognize had been in her home. *No...* the scent seemed vaguely familiar, but... she frowned. *Finn Emerson?*

No, he wouldn't be here when Hunter wasn't.

She glanced around the room, listening more than anything, although she scanned the living area, neat as usual, magazines on the table all about fishing and hunting—the kind of stuff she thought guys might be interested in, although she liked the subjects, too. As a young girl, she had been much more interested in wilderness camping and hiking, playing tug-of-war with the guys, and wrestling with them, than in playing with dolls or shopping with the other females when she grew older.

The bookcase against the wall was filled with knickknacks, photos of the giant sequoia trees that reminded her of home, nature books, and her treasured werewolf romance books by Julia Wildthorn, but nothing appeared out of place. She could hear her heart beating spastically.

She wasn't easily scared, but her innate wolf sense warned her to be wary. A wolf of a man had invited himself in when she was gone, and the door had been locked.

She swung around to look at the wolf door. He'd marked the territory and then let himself into her house in his wolf form?

Then she reconsidered. Sure, he would have left and returned as a wolf, but if he'd first arrived as a man, he most likely would have used a lockpick.

She thought she heard a couple of footfalls in her bedroom. Her eyes widened and her heartbeat quickened. *Great.* Her rifle was under the bed, easily retrieved if someone broke into her place when she was sleeping. But right now, it did her no good.

She backed toward the patio door that led to a small stone patio, the cliffside walk to a small beach below, and another walk that wrapped around to the front where her car was parked. Her plan was to make a quick getaway and call the pack for help.

But she backed right into someone solid who hadn't been there seconds earlier. She screeched and jumped several feet away, whipping around in terror to see one hunk of a male specimen. He was definitely a wolf type, a virile, dark-haired man with almost-amber eyes tinged with green. From the way his casual clothes hugged his chest and biceps, he had a body worth taking a second and third look at. His hair was cut military short, and because of his rugged appearance and the way he had moved so stealthily, he reminded Meara of Hunter's SEAL team members.

But he wasn't anyone she knew. And he didn't have the same scent as the other male wolf she'd smelled.

The stranger's lips curved up slightly, capturing her attention.

"Hey," he said in a deeply persuasive voice, putting his hands up to show he was unarmed. His wolfish gaze raked over her in an admiring manner that told her he was already interested in her. "Didn't mean to startle you, but the sign outside said this was the office, and I've got a cabin reserved for a week. Unless I've got the wrong place. I'm Joe Matheson." He lowered his hands slowly, as if to prove he wasn't going to harm her, and stretched his right hand out to shake hers.

Even though she'd heard him say the words she'd wanted to hear and the notion was finally sinking in that he was supposed to be here and was the first of the male guests scheduled to arrive, she couldn't shake the sudden chill she felt in her bones. Because?

She glanced back in the direction of her bedroom down the hall. She'd thought she heard footfalls in her bedroom. But now she imagined that had just been the sound of the ocean and the wind in the trees. After moving here from the redwoods in California, she didn't think she'd ever get used to how the Oregon coast sounded.

Except...

She lifted her nose and smelled. The faint scent of another male wolf still lingered in the air. She didn't think Finn Emerson would come here while Hunter was away and then *stay*, but she wondered: had he, and if so, why?

Chapter 2

MEARA COULDN'T HELP FEELING ANNOYED WHENEVER Finn showed up, knowing he meant to convince Hunter to go on another dangerous mission with him. She wasn't convinced that *he* was the wolf who had entered her home without permission earlier, but that didn't matter. Any thought of Finn instantly made her hackles rise.

She looked down at Joe Matheson's outstretched hand and then, not entirely free of her concern about the presence of another wolf, she offered her own. "Meara Greymere" she said, smiling. "I was expecting you. I was going to fix a drink and something to eat. Would you care to join me, Mr. Matheson? And then I can show you to your cabin."

She wanted to ask her guest to accompany her down the hall to see who the intruder was, if he was still here and hadn't climbed out her window, but she had to do it covertly without alerting him.

"Call me Joe, if you don't mind. I'm on vacation. I don't want to be a bother, but I flew in from North Carolina, and you know how they don't feed you on many flights these days. Pretzels, if you're lucky. And they don't sustain a body for long."

He gave her a sexy grin, and she thought about just how little the pretzels would do for a body like his.

"I'll need to find a place to pick up some groceries for the rest of the week so, yeah, a meal would be nice. Thanks."

She motioned to a seat at the bar but glanced around for a piece of paper and a pen to scribble a warning note about the possible intruder. "Any preference?"

"Anything you want to fix is fine with me."

She pulled out a can of tuna to make a salad so that whoever might be hiding in her home would think she didn't realize it. But as she stared at the can, she thought better of fixing a salad. Her brother hated them. This guy probably wouldn't want to eat rabbit food, either.

"Steak? Chicken? Fish?" she asked, again looking around for something to write a note she could pass to Joe.

"Chicken," he said.

She spied her notebook on the bar near the phone, but she remembered having taken notes on her prospective guests. She didn't want to flip it open and worry Joe might catch sight of it. She couldn't recall what she'd written about him, but she thought she'd said something about him sounding sexy. And he did. Even more so in person. But she didn't want him knowing that.

Her groceries notepad was sitting on the coffee table, though. Before she could skirt the counter to get it, she saw Joe staring in the direction of the bedrooms. Had he heard someone also? She planned to make it sound as though she didn't believe anyone was down the hall. Then when the intruder least expected it, she'd take Joe with her to investigate. But she didn't want Joe to alert the man that they were on to his game, if he was there.

"Homemade potato salad to go with the baked chicken?" she asked, hoping he'd go for the potato salad since it was one of her favorite dishes that she made from an old family recipe.

He shifted his attention back to her. "Potato salad sounds pretty good."

"So what do you do when you're not on vacation?" She hoped she sounded subtle enough—she still was doing her mate investigation, despite whatever was going on down the hall—as she grabbed the notepaper and pen, shoved them in her jeans pocket, and returned to the kitchen.

"I'm a business consultant," he said.

She seasoned the chicken thighs with lemon and pepper spice, set them in a baking dish, and started cooking them. Once the chicken was cooked, all she'd have to do was take out the glass bowl of potato salad, and the meal would be done. She'd sprinkled the potato salad with paprika to make it more visually appealing and because she loved the subtle, spicy taste.

Afterward, she pulled the pen and notepaper out of her pocket and scribbled a really quick note as she said, "Business consultant."

That didn't say a whole lot about him, but that's all he had told her when he'd called to reserve the cabin.

He smiled and waved a hand at her notepad and pen. "Taking notes?"

She glanced up from her note writing and could have kicked him. How was she going to secretly slip him a note if he was going to tell the world what she was doing? "I just noticed I'm nearly out of baking potatoes so I'm adding them to my grocery list." She hoped he hadn't seen the bin full of potatoes and would say something about it, too.

She had tried not to sound peeved, but his lifted brow indicated he was amused by the terseness in her voice, and she wondered if he thought he'd guessed that what she was doing had nothing to do with writing a grocery list. Just a list of what she found appealing in him. She gave him an annoyed look. "Did you want something to drink? Wine? Beer?"

He shook his head. "Don't drink anything hard."

"Oh. Water? Tea? Soda?"

"I'll have water."

Before she could slide the note to Joe, he asked, "Is Hunter around?"

Her fingers stilled on top of the note on the counter, and she stared up at him. "You know Hunter?"

This was so not good. If he had been friends with Hunter, he'd surely tell her brother what she was up to. And Joe wouldn't be a viable candidate for a mate. But she didn't remember meeting him before. Why hadn't she met him if he was a friend of Hunter's?

"Sure. So… is he around?" Joe raised his dark brows in question. He had a hard, angular face, made more severe by his short-cropped hair. But his eyes and mouth gave her the impression that he was smiling covertly.

She felt uneasy. As if she suddenly had a spy in her midst. Someone who would reveal what she was up to before she could get away with it. On the other hand, if he didn't know that Hunter was off on his honeymoon, maybe he hadn't been in contact with her brother for a while. She'd forget making any moves on this guy, no matter how delicious he looked, send him to his cabin, and work on guest number two instead when he arrived the next day. She really didn't want to get involved with one of Hunter's friends. Who knew what Hunter had said to them about her behind her back?

"He's off on his honeymoon with his mate, Tessa," she said, nonchalantly.

"Oh. I didn't realize he'd finally found a mate. So where'd they go?"

"Hawaii."

"Hmm."

Their kind normally didn't bother with honeymoons. Joe had to think it odd, but she'd leave her brother to explain to his "friend" what made Hunter's relationship with Tessa so different.

"And he left you alone? To manage the cabin resort?" Joe asked, his tone a little dark.

At first, she thought he was questioning her ability to manage the cabin resort by herself. And her hackles rose at that. But then she suddenly felt somewhat vulnerable, thinking that he'd meant she was here alone with no one to protect her from someone who might wish to do her harm.

"We have a pack," she said firmly. "As I'm sure you know. Since you're a friend." The pack didn't live that close by. What if this guy was bad news and another was in the bedroom or guest room right this very instant, or what if the two of them were in cahoots? "How do you know Hunter?"

"When your parents were pack leaders, Hunter and I went down to Mexico for about a month."

"Oh." She remembered that Hunter had left to get away from Dad, who had been quite authoritarian when he ruled the pack. But she didn't remember Hunter saying anything about going with a friend. And her brother had never revealed exactly where he'd ended up, either. About that time, she'd moved in with a girlfriend in another pack to get away from her dad, too. She guessed that's when it had been. *If* what this guy claimed was on the up and up.

But then she wondered why Joe hadn't kept up with her brother. Why didn't he know about her brother's mate?

She filled a glass with ice and water, and handed it to Joe. "So what mischief did the two of you get into?" If he said something she didn't believe, she'd recognize he was lying about knowing Hunter.

"If Hunter didn't tell you, I'm *sure* not going to." He winked at her with a silly smirk on his face, as if he hid a wealth of misdeeds that Hunter and he had gotten into when they were younger.

She believed that Hunter would have, too, but was that all just made up? Joe certainly hadn't said anything that would alleviate her concerns. "You must have been out of touch with him for some time."

"Years," he admitted. "I had just planned to get away from work and go anywhere that a wolf could run for a bit, but when I saw your ad and…" He spread his hands as if expressing the sentiment: *What else is there to say?* He was game to spend time with a female who was free. Maybe he was hoping Hunter was out of the picture so he could see her without her brother's interference.

Her face warmed. Had she been so obvious about wanting to check out some alpha male prospects?

She'd have to ask Hunter about a friend named Joe as soon as she was able to reach him—about six hours from now—to see if Joe's story checked out.

"What do you do out here for fun?" Joe asked, then took a swallow of water.

"Hike. A river is located in the area where you can

go white-water rafting. Fishing. All kinds of outdoor stuff. Hunt, when it suits you." She wasn't about to mention a moonlight swim or a run through the woods with him now.

"And indoors?"

She couldn't help smiling just a hint, seeing where this conversation was headed. He seemed interested in her, although if he was a friend of Hunter's, that made her really wary. She motioned to her bookcase in the living area. "I've got a library of books, if you like to read."

"Books," he said under his breath, not looking all that interested.

"Books," she repeated, serious now that he was supposed to be a friend of Hunter's. Then figuring it was time to do something about the guy down the hall, she pushed the warning note to Joe about the possible intruder.

Watching carefully to see his reaction as he read the note, her hand shifted to the knife drawer in case this guy was also bad news.

Finn Emerson didn't recognize the voice of the man Meara was entertaining in the kitchen, nor did he know the guy he was remotely viewing on his cell phone. He'd sent the image of the man in an email to his friends to see if any of them could identify him.

Hell, Finn couldn't believe Hunter had left Meara alone to manage the cabin resort.

Just seeing Hunter's sister set Finn's heart racing. He wanted to say that was because he was concerned about her welfare, but he knew better. She was too damned enticing.

The sexy spitfire was bound to get herself into a hell of a lot of trouble if someone as capable as Hunter wasn't here to watch over her—or at the very least, one of his sub-leaders, as long as neither of them had designs on her that Hunter didn't approve of. But with a maniac on the loose, she was in even greater danger.

The guy talked about fishing and other mundane topics while Finn watched the two of them on the hidden camera, making sure the renter wasn't about to try anything. But when she passed the note to Joe Matheson, Finn suspected she must have smelled his scent, recalling the way she'd tilted her chin up and taken a deep breath earlier.

Matheson had also sampled the air, and Finn didn't think that was because of Meara's fragrance, but because of the other male wolf in the cabin. When Joe read the note that she'd passed to him, the guy didn't do anything but give a stiff nod and a small smile.

Matheson was definitely an alpha. Despite smelling another male wolf on the premises, he didn't make his excuses and leave for his own cabin. Instead, he was standing his ground. Finn assumed Matheson would come for him soon. Ready for the confrontation, Finn smiled sardonically.

He hadn't thought Meara would get home this soon, considering the distance her place was from the airport. She must have driven like the proverbial bat out of hell to get here in time to meet with Joe Matheson. And here Finn was, in the middle of bugging her room and home phone when she had arrived. Why the hell had she disclosed to the renter, whom she didn't know, where Hunter was and that she was alone?

Even though she'd mentioned the pack, none of them were hanging around her place, visible enough to show anyone who might threaten her that she had backup. Finn wondered if Matheson truly had been a friend of Hunter's. Finn's instincts told him Joe Matheson wasn't one of the bad guys, though. Except for making not-so-subtle moves on Meara.

Meara's voice sounded smooth as satin and silky with seduction as she talked to Joe. *Hell*. Finn had planned on waiting until this Joe character went to his cabin, but at this rate, the rental guest wasn't going anywhere any-time soon. And when Matheson asked what they could do inside? Finn didn't like it that the guy was making a play for her already—although Finn certainly couldn't blame him. If the roles were reversed and he hadn't had such close ties with Hunter and knew what trouble she could be, Finn would have been making the moves on Meara himself.

She tossed her hair back over her shoulders and spoke animatedly, while damn if Matheson wasn't eating her actions up.

It was time to take charge of the situation—and Meara.

Finn closed the bedroom door without making a sound, then yanked off his clothes again, littering them all over the floor. Afterward, he mussed up the sheets and comforter, inhaling Meara's appealing feminine scent. God, she was sexy, but under no circumstances did he want to tangle with her in that respect.

He figured the best way to get rid of the guy in the kitchen and protect her from the possible threat to her well-being was to lay claim to her—in a pretend way, of course. She and he had butted heads enough in the past

when he and Hunter had returned from missions that
he wasn't going down that vine-twisted path. She was
under the mistaken impression that *he* had always talked
Hunter into another mission after they had left the Navy.
But half the time, Hunter had sought *him* out to conduct
another privately contracted undercover operation.

Finn headed into the bathroom, started the shower,
and entered the glassed-in stall. He figured any scenario
would work to his advantage as he quickly soaped up,
using her vanilla-scented bath soap—wondering just
how enticing it would smell on *her* skin—rinsed off,
and grabbed a towel. The two of them had to have heard
him taking a shower. Either she would send Joe in to
investigate, or they'd both check him out. In any event,
they'd find her lover waiting for her—in the bedroom,
for better effect. If they didn't investigate, he'd quickly
remedy that.

He walked out of the bathroom towel-drying his hair,
naked, water droplets dribbling down his shoulders, his
chest, and his thighs, and found a slack-jawed Meara
staring at his body. Which made his loins react as if on
cue. Hell.

She was as beautiful as ever. Her dark hair curled
over her shoulders in a cascade of silk tresses. Black
denim fit her hips and legs in a seductive way, and a
turquoise satin blouse accentuated her pert breasts. He
finally managed to pull his gaze away from her and
consider the hulking black-haired man who was aiming
a rifle at him. Joe looked at home holding the rifle, as if
he'd used one in military operations, and as short as his
hair was, he did look like he was in the military. That
made Finn question who the guy really was. Although,

if Joe had been the assassin, he'd already have made his move.

"Meara," Finn said in a deeply seductive way, his gaze shifting back to hers as if the armed man didn't worry him in the least, "I didn't expect you back from the airport so soon after seeing Hunter and Tessa off. You must have missed me." He gave an inviting wink, telling her just how much he'd enjoyed being with her.

He slipped the towel around his waist as if it was an afterthought, but he noted that Meara had been taking her fill of his nakedness, her enticing lips still parted in surprise. Even though their kind shifted and it wasn't that big a deal to be seen naked by others in a pack, he wasn't of her pack, and he wasn't shifting. He thought that explained some of her reaction.

Then he turned his attention to Joe. In a dark way that left no doubt he was worried she was already throwing him over for someone else, Finn asked, "Who's *he*?"

Chapter 3

"Is this guy a close friend of yours, Meara?" Joe asked, still pointing the rifle at Finn, his brows furrowed with menace.

Despite Joe's alpha-wolf posturing, Finn swore that the man wasn't an assassin. But a hint of something else lurked beneath the surface. This guy truly was interested in Meara, Finn suspected.

Although he scoffed at himself. Why wouldn't Joe be? She was attractive, intelligent, and even a pack leader's sister. She was an unattached female, and if Joe was looking for a mate, she wouldn't be a bad prospect for someone who was willing to be tied down. That bothered Finn more than he was willing to allow.

Finally finding her voice, Meara asked Finn, "What are you doing here?"

Her words had a whispered, breathy quality, but they weren't dismissive. She chewed her bottom lip and appeared worried, maybe figuring the only reason he would be here was that something was wrong. He had considered that she might think he had another mission for Hunter, since she wouldn't let go of the notion that Finn, not Hunter, arranged them. Under normal circumstances, Finn would never have come on to her like this—even in a pretend way. Not only that, but if Hunter had initially contacted him for another undercover operation, Finn would have known Hunter wasn't here.

She had to realize the situation was really bad if he was putting on a show of being her lover. But she also had to know he wouldn't say what the trouble was in front of Joe.

"He's… Joe Matheson is renting the blue cottage," she said, answering Finn's question rather than Joe's.

"You didn't mention that last night…" Finn motioned to the disheveled bed. "…but then I must have distracted you." He cast a purely wicked smile at her.

Her flustered expression quickly changed from startled to worried and finally to the way he always remembered her whenever he dropped by to see Hunter about another mission—annoyed—as she crossed her arms beneath her breasts. His gaze lingered on the silk blouse she wore, and he swore her nipples were ripening into mouthwatering peaks right before his eyes.

She cleared her throat. "We need to talk."

"Just what I had in mind. As soon as you tell Joe where his cabin is and he settles in there, we'll have that little talk." He strode to the other side of the bed and lifted his duffel bag as if he'd already moved in. Which he had, whether she liked it or not. Setting the bag on the bed, he unzipped the zipper and then glanced at the two of them. Meara was still staring at him in disbelief, while Joe's expression indicated that he'd gotten to the party a little too late.

"The blue cabin is the closest to this one heading north, Joe," Finn said to get the ball rolling, having already scoped out all of the cabins and memorized their names and locations, according to the listings in Meara's notebook. All of them were empty, ready for occupancy. And he was past ready for Joe to move along.

Finn pulled out a fresh pair of boxer shorts, khaki shorts, a tank shirt, and a pair of flip-flops.

"Who is he?" Joe asked again, his voice rough with contempt, and yet Finn could have sworn he heard a ribbon of amusement in Joe's tone, as if his actions were all a show.

That didn't make sense. Or just *maybe*, the guy was so damned cocky that he figured Finn wasn't any competition.

"An old friend of the family's," Meara begrudgingly replied. "Come on, Joe." She sounded resigned, but Finn knew when she returned, she'd be anything but prepared to accept this arrangement.

Finn would deal with that the best he could. While Hunter was away, he felt it his responsibility to protect Hunter's sister. Mostly because the reason for the attack on their teammate, Allan, had probably been Finn's fault. *Damn it to hell.*

Their last mission had almost been a complete abortion. They had all suspected that someone had tampered with their explosive devices before they arrived on the island to rescue the hostages. Someone who had wanted the rescue to fail. Someone who had known their plan. But Finn was at fault for not checking the bag one last time before they hit the beach.

He listened while Meara tried to smooth things over in the hallway with who she probably hoped was a prospective mate. That curdled the remains of Finn's hastily eaten lunch, a fast-food burger consumed earlier in the day.

"I'll just show you to your cabin and—" she began as she walked Joe down the hall.

"No need," Joe said, sounding somewhat aggravated as Meara trailed along behind him.

"I'll get you the key. But your meal isn't ready, and well, don't mind him," she said, motioning back to the bedroom, her tone and actions dismissive.

Finn smiled and wiped off some droplets of water clinging to his chest. If Joe was here on vacation like he said he was, the guy had to realize that Meara wasn't going to dismiss Finn as insignificant.

Joe stalked down the hall toward the living area. "Sorry, Meara. I told you I was here on vacation. It looks like your friend has already staked a claim to the *territory*." His inference being that she was part of the territory.

She gave an audible snort at that. Finn smiled at her spunk.

Not to be dissuaded, Joe continued, "So I'll mind my own business and enjoy whatever else the area has to offer in the line of recreation in the meantime."

Meara sounded peeved when she said, "He's *not* staying. Here's the key to your cabin. If you need anything else, just let me know. There's just been some misunderstanding about the sleeping arrangements around here. That's all. We *weren't* together last night. And he's leaving as soon as I have a word with him."

Joe didn't say anything in response, and Finn wondered if the guy was reconsidering making a play for Meara. Finn would have to put a stop to that pronto. The man was too cool, too confident, too... Finn couldn't put his finger on it exactly. But he didn't entirely trust Joe.

The back door shut and for a moment silence ensued. Was Meara looking at the door where she'd lost her prey? Or considering the bedroom and what she'd say to Finn as soon as she got angry enough?

Finn had never known Meara to stomp. She'd always moved gracefully, sensually, more like a feline than a canine, even when she was irritated whenever Finn had showed up in Hunter's life after they'd left the Navy. This time she stomped down the hall toward her bedroom. He skipped getting dressed, climbed onto the bed, *her* bed, propped her pillows behind his head, and lay there, towel around his waist, legs stretched out, waiting for the explosion.

He didn't have to wait long. She stormed into the bedroom and saw him on her bed, totally relaxed and still not dressed, which again rendered her speechless. But she quickly overcame her surprise.

"What the hell are you doing here?"

"I came to see Hunter—"

"And you know he's not here." She crossed her arms underneath her breasts, which were rising and falling in rapid succession as she took steadying breaths. "If this is more private *consulting* work, Hunter isn't here to go on the job. He's mated now." She waved at the door. "You can leave now that you know he's not here. And for your information, he's not available to go with you on jobs any longer." Then she paused and narrowed her eyes at him. "You're not staying here and waiting for him to return while I'm running the resort either, if you had that notion in mind."

Wondering how Hunter would take it if he knew his sister was deciding what he would and would not do now that he was mated, Finn folded his arms across his bare chest.

Her gaze shifted to his towel. It wasn't big as bath towels went, and his legs were spread in a relaxed, invitational way. Not that he was inviting her in any way, but he hadn't crossed his legs at the ankles in a manner that suggested he was closed off to her. He swore that if she kept staring at the towel, it was going to begin to rise to the occasion. And he damn well would want to invite her for a closer engagement like the ones he'd only imagined having with her in their former encounters, which had been brief and heated—and not in a sexual way. Although he had to admit, any kind of interaction with her made him think of her in a sexual way.

"Hunter *shouldn't* have left you on your own," Finn said in a matter-of-fact tone.

He swore she stiffened even more regally at the comment. He loved it. Loved the way she was even more beautiful when her temper flared. Her eyes sparkled with heat, and her lips—even turned down—made him want to devour them with his own.

"I happen to be perfectly capable of taking care of myself, thank you very much. You still haven't explained why you're here." Her lips parted a little as if she'd come to a surprise conclusion. "You're not here at Hunter's request, are you? He didn't put you up to this, did he? Thinking you could baby-sit me while he was away? Afraid our pack sub-leaders couldn't keep me under their thumbs?"

The notion of his thumbs caressing her nipples instantly invaded Finn's thoughts.

"Baby-sitting you, Meara?" He gave a bitter laugh. "Guarding that sweet body of yours is more like it."

And he was definitely up to the task. He wouldn't want anyone else to have that job.

Her eyes widened fractionally. She had to know how hot she was.

Eyes quickly narrowing, she blew out her breath. "Get out of here. Hunter had no right…"

Time to set the story straight.

Finn slid from the bed and stalked toward her. She stood her ground.

He loved the challenge in her darkened eyes, the way she wouldn't back down, no matter how determined he was to take charge of this situation and of *her*. "Hunter doesn't know what this is about. By the time I reached California and discovered he had moved the pack here, it was already too late. Knowing he'd sometimes come to the resort to see his uncle, I chanced coming here. Or at least figured I'd get a location from your uncle as to where Hunter had relocated the pack.

"But then I learned the pack had settled here and I'd missed seeing Hunter before he took off for Hawaii. Although I've called him on his cell phone, he must have it turned off because of the flight. In any event, you have one of two choices. Either I stay with you until he gets back, or I send you packing to be with them."

"On their *honeymoon*?" The pitch of her voice rose with incredulity. "Are you kidding?"

But he knew she had to realize something was really the matter, something more than Hunter wanting him to baby-sit her.

"All right, so what is this all about?" she grudgingly asked.

"Someone tried to murder Allan Rappaport."

"Allan?" Her voice was unsteady and her face turned ghostly pale. "Sweet Allan?"

Before she collapsed, Finn seized her arm and made her sit on the end of the bed. "The assassin nearly succeeded. Just an inch or two lower, and Allan would have died from the bullet wound to his chest." Even though *lupus garous* healed faster than humans, a strike to a major artery could make them bleed out before their bodies could heal. "Thankfully, he received treatment right away and survived. We've got some SEALs watching over him now."

Finn didn't get why she would call the guy sweet, though. Allan was one of the roughest men on their team. At least he had been around the team members. Maybe he'd acted differently toward Meara when Finn hadn't been around. That notion gnawed at him. He thought Hunter had made it clear he didn't want any of his SEAL team members pursuing her. And Finn had been sure none of the guys had or he would have learned of it fairly quickly.

She sure as hell could make a man forget himself.

"And you thought... you thought the assassin was coming after Hunter?" she asked, very concerned now.

"Yeah. I've warned Paul Cunningham, the other of our teammates, and the only one who's left is Hunter."

"And you," she said softly, frowning up at him.

"True." Although Finn didn't really count himself as one of the hunted. *He* was the hunter. "I've ensured that one of your pack members, who's a former military man and currently on your police force, will take the next flight to Hawaii to warn Hunter and watch his back."

She motioned to Finn's clothes strewn on the floor

and to the unmade bed. "So what's this all supposed to be about?"

"I'm your lover for now, until we stop this bastard or until Hunter returns to keep track of you."

Her lips parted in a totally sexy way, but then she frowned and pursed them. "Oh, no you're not. No way am I going to let anyone think I'm mated with you."

"You'll have to do your mate selection some other time, Meara. This is serious business."

She studied him for a minute and then frowned more deeply. "What makes you so certain this guy intends to target all of the men on the team? Maybe it was a fluke, or maybe Allan provoked some guy but it has nothing to do with the team."

"He left a calling card. The Knight of Swords. And a cryptic note referring to the last mission we were involved in. But I can't say any more than that."

"The last mission," she whispered, looking at the floor and then shifting her gaze to Finn. "The one where Hunter was injured."

"Yes, he was badly injured. And so were Paul and Allan."

"But... but not you."

"No. Listen, I can't really discuss it. Only that I'm sure this has to do with a traitor in the ranks."

Her eyes grew huge. "Not among the members of your SEAL team."

"No. We've been like brothers. We're all *lupus garous*. Someone who..." He shook his head. "We don't know anything for certain. Suffice it to say, I'm staying here to protect you. Paul's watching his own back since he prefers it that way. We've got friends protecting

Allan. One of your pack members will be there to watch out for Hunter and Tessa, and Hunter will ensure he gets more coverage while he's on the island. As soon as I can get through to him, I'll call him again. But it would be too easy for whoever this is to target you and wait until Hunter returns, while using you as the perfect little hostage. Hunter would expect this of me."

Finn knew there'd be trouble, as defiant as she always was with him, as soon as she stubbornly lifted her chin. "*I* don't expect this of you! I've got two weeks to find a mate."

"Think of it as a vacation. Two weeks away from Hunter's rule, just taking it easy."

"So I can be under *your* rule? No way. I'm not *taking it easy* while Hunter's out of my hair. I've got the resort to run, and that's just what I'm going to damn well do. Once the meal is done, I'll take it to Joe and eat with him over there. You can…" She motioned to the front of the house. "…go back to wherever you came from."

"All right." His face turned hard as he gave up trying to reason with her. "Then I'm coming with you. I'll eat Joe's portion of the dinner, and you can share your portion with him." He gave her a derisive smile. "Take it or leave it. If you don't want my offer of protection, I'm packing you off to Hawaii, and I'll wait here for the assassin alone. I'm sure it would be a safer bet for you anyway."

She ground her teeth. "If you think I'm going to mess up their honeymoon… well, no way. Besides, what if whoever this is follows them there?"

"That's a distinct possibility. And the reason I sent your pack mate to Hawaii to watch out for Hunter. As for you, I could send you to your uncle in Florida." Finn was serious, too. Although he'd accompany her there if she decided she wanted to go to the Sunshine State.

"Ha! You're not sending me anywhere. And I'm going to do what I had planned on doing while Hunter is away. You can't tell me what to do!"

Hell. He sighed. "What if one of the men you've leased the cabins to is the assassin?"

She chewed on her bottom lip. "Okay, so we investigate each of them before they get here. You're the expert at that, aren't you? You must have a way to access personal records, and then once everyone looks all right, that's the end of it. Once we've eliminated them as suspects, I'll go about my business."

Considering they were *lupus garous* and records were changed over the years to hide their longevity, that would be the problem. Finn had known as soon as he learned Hunter was gone that this was one mission he shouldn't have signed up for. "Even this Joe Matheson could be one of them."

Her eyes widened and she looked in the direction of the blue cabin. "No."

"You don't really know a thing about him, Meara."

Pop! Pop!

"*Shit!*" Fearing gunfire, Finn lunged for Meara, shoving her to the carpeted floor as his body slammed into hers and losing his towel in the process.

Finn was planted firmly on top of Meara on her carpeted bedroom floor, listening for any sound that could mean danger as her heart and his beat at an accelerated pace, although she was barely breathing. He could tell by the expression on her face as she watched him that she also was listening for any sounds of an intruder.

Finn's towel was now draped across her pelvis, and he was naked again. But she was fully dressed, so no big deal. Except no matter how hard he tried not to think about the way their heated bodies were pressed together, he couldn't help becoming aroused.

"Gunfire?" she whispered, keeping very still.

"Might have been. Or not. Could have been a car backfiring."

"Way out here?"

"Maybe one of your other guests arrived."

Meara squirmed underneath Finn, and he fought groaning out loud as she pressed dangerously against his rapidly growing erection. "Well, let me up then. If you're not going to check it out, I will."

He knew Meara was headstrong. If he hadn't been worrying about her safety or what she might do that could put her at more risk, Finn would have already left the house and searched the area. He was rethinking the situation about either of them staying at her place, though. Looked like the money he'd paid and strings he'd pulled to move the renters out of his home farther south had been a good bet. He'd never thought he'd be taking Hunter's sister there *alone* to safeguard, rather that he might be moving both Hunter and Meara in.

"Well?" She wriggled some more. "We're not going to continue to lie here and do nothing, are we? I believe in being proactive."

"Quit moving, Meara," he ordered tightly. Hell, the woman was hot, particularly pinned beneath his body, and her squirming around was making him even hotter than he already was.

Her eyes widened as she undoubtedly felt his rigid

arousal. "How could you be thinking about stuff like that at a time like this?"

"I'm not thinking of anything of the sort. Just quit wiggling." At least he tried not to think of her wriggling beneath him and how hard it was making him. He grabbed the towel and got to his feet. "Haven't you ever heard of friction? That's all it is. Nothing more."

Friction, his ass. From the moment he'd seen her, remembering just how hot the woman was, and how she seemed so interested in the way he looked, had made him hard. But he hadn't meant for her to know how little control he had over his physical reaction to her.

She snorted. "I know a man doesn't need much encouragement, but give me a break."

He managed to control a smile. When he tossed the towel aside to shift, aware he was fully erect and that Meara was staring at him in... well, he wasn't sure about her reaction. Amusement? Wonderment? Maybe a little of both. And it wasn't helping.

Not liking that he seemed to have so little control over his libido when he was around her, he growled, intending to go look for the assassin, and summoned the urge to shift.

Chapter 4

ONCE FINN HAD SHIFTED INTO HIS WOLF FORM, HE CAST A long, hard look at Meara, as if he was trying to tell her to stay put. He was a beautiful, big gray wolf with a tan face framed by fur in a mixture of browns and black, giving him a distinguished appearance.

Exasperated, Meara waved her hand toward the wolf door. "Go. Protect me, oh hero of mine." She couldn't help it if her words sounded faintly sarcastic. She'd never gotten herself into a bind she couldn't get herself out of, given enough time. And she didn't feel this would be an exception.

Finn hesitated and even looked a little surprised.

She smiled, liking that he seemed a bit unsure for the first time since she'd met him six years earlier. Not that she had seen much of him since Hunter and the rest of the team had left the Navy. Most of the time, Finn would come to the door, usher Hunter outside for a super-secretive conversation, and then vanish without a word. Hunter would make arrangements with his sub-leaders, leaving shortly after that with duffel bag in hand.

Sure, she'd seen all of them together when they were still members of the SEAL team, but they were mostly part of the background. The guys aimed a few sly smiles in her direction, but none of them ever spoke to her except to greet her by name. They had remained subdued, standoffish, and secretive.

So she really didn't know Finn well, except that she'd had words with him on more than one occasion when the team returned from a mission. She was angry that he was always getting Hunter involved in something that could prove fatal. They had left the Navy once their commitments were up. Enough was enough. Hunter had done his duty for God and country.

Finn would listen patiently to her tirade and cast Hunter surreptitious looks as though commiserating with him for having a sister who couldn't leave well enough alone—and that had irritated her to no end.

Then Finn would depart and, several months later, turn up for another secretive mission, and they'd do what they intended without paying her any mind... *again*. She hoped that Hunter would give up the clandestine operations all together, now that he was mated.

But God, Finn had a body that wouldn't quit. If there was a werewolf calendar, he could be featured on every month—and women would be even more apt to buy it if he was featured for an additional couple of months the following year. A natural Scandinavian blond with hazel-green eyes, he was a real looker.

She thought of him without the towel, the way he had been drying his hair so *innocently*, acting as though he'd forgotten to cover himself in front of her. He'd only done that to pretend he'd been her lover the night before. And she had been determined to pretend right back that his nakedness had no effect on her, not wanting him to think he'd not only shocked but intrigued her. No matter how much she told herself she shouldn't, she couldn't quit giving his physique a few gaping looks. Even though she'd tried damn hard to refocus her gaze on his. But the way that his mouth curved up and his wickedly darkened eyes smiled back at her meant he knew the truth. She couldn't get her fill of him.

"Go. I mean it. I'll stay here," she said to Finn, nearly forgetting what he should be doing.

Seemingly reassured that she'd stay put, Finn loped out of the bedroom, and she went for her rifle.

As soon as Finn made certain the house was clear and no one was lurking inside, he used his nose to push through the wolf's door to check the perimeter of the house and its surroundings. Outside, he smelled Joe's scent coming from the direction of the blue cabin. Finn raced through the woods to the first of the cabins, circling around the outside, but he didn't see or hear any signs of life. Where was Joe?

As he made a broader search, Finn smelled that a male werewolf had been in the vicinity, but he saw no sign of the unknown wolf. He continued to search around each of the empty cabins but found nothing. The faint smell of gunfire rippled through the breeze, though. He hadn't been wrong about that.

Gnashing his canines in frustration, Finn didn't like that he had no leads, but not wanting to leave Meara alone and unprotected, he headed back to her cabin. He inspected the outside walls, looking for signs of a bullet hole in the windows or siding. *Nothing.*

He raced around to the back of the house and shoved his nose through the wolf door in the kitchen, praying she was still safe and secure, and came face to face with an armed Meara, who was aiming the same rifle that Joe had held on him earlier.

Relieved, he smiled, glad she'd had the sense to protect herself in case someone had tried to break into her place while he was away.

She lowered the muzzle of the rifle and frowned at Finn. "You didn't find anything." She sounded disappointed.

He shifted into his human form. Trying not to notice that she was staring at his nakedness again, he motioned to the rifle in her hands. "Do you even know how to use that thing?"

Her gaze shot up from eyeing his torso, and she snorted, raising the rifle parallel to her body. "You mean this?" She laid the rifle on the kitchen counter. "I'm just as accurate at shooting as you or any of the rest of your SEAL team. I'm surprised Hunter didn't tell you I'm an expert marksman at a range." She grabbed a pot holder shaped like a large red-hot chili pepper off the counter and handed it to Finn. "Cover yourself, will you?"

He gave her a small smile. He knew Meara was more than a little physically attracted to him. At least if the way her feminine pheromones were kicking his into high gear was any indication. As wolves, they sensed the pheromones in each other. If they'd been only human, the pheromones would still have played a role, but only subconsciously as the released pheromones sent signals to the hypothalamus region of the brain.

Her physical reaction to him—her increased heart rate, darkened eyes, and erect nipples poking at the silky fabric of her blouse—showed just how much her sexual response had heightened. But her female pheromones were also triggering his testosterone to surge, which meant he was getting damned horny around her again.

Otherwise, nudity between wolves shouldn't have mattered. Although he had to remind himself that playing with fire wasn't something he wanted to do.

He tossed the pot holder on the bar counter. "It's not big enough to do the job."

She laughed. But it was more of a haughty, give-me-a-break laugh than one of fun.

He chuckled under his breath as he strode down the hall to her bedroom. Her footfalls padded after him.

"So? Did you find any signs of a shooter?" she asked, sounding worried.

He glanced back at her and found her gaze riveted on his ass. Her eyes immediately rose to meet his, and to his amusement, her cheeks flushed crimson.

"We're leaving." He entered the bedroom, then grabbed his bag and dug around in it. He pulled out a different set of clothes—black denim, black T-shirt, and black boots, all more suited to the job he now had to do. But it was the pair of white boxers that caught her attention. They were strictly utilitarian so he wondered why she was so fixed on them. He quickly began to get dressed.

His words must have finally sunk in, because she shifted her gaze to his face and said, "What?" She sounded incredulous, which he figured was why she hadn't responded in the negative yet.

But he knew that was coming. "Tell your sub-leaders you're taking a trip. You can't tell them where you're going or how long you'll be gone."

She pursed her lips, eyeing him with irritation. "You listen here. I'm not going anywhere. I've leased the cabins, and it's my job to see to the guests' comforts."

He yanked on his shirt. This was nonnegotiable. Meara was not going to be "seeing to the guests' comforts."

Before he could say so, she said, "I'm staying here. You have no right ordering me about. If some assassin is after the members of the team, he'll be targeting you, not me. So *you* need to get as far away from *me* as possible." She quickly folded her arms underneath her breasts. Her face turned a hot red and her lips thinned as she scowled at him.

"Hunter is the only one of us who has family. You don't think they won't also target you?" He was trying for negotiator calm—an attempt to settle the crisis in a nonthreatening way. But her defensive posture said she wasn't falling for that, and although he tried his best to cover it up, his irritation was showing. "None of the rest of us has to worry about the assassin coming after our loved ones," he tried again, sitting on the bed to pull on his boots.

He would attempt to convince her in a reasonable way, but if he had to take unreasonable methods to protect her—like locking her away somewhere safe—he wouldn't hesitate. "Hunter won't want your life jeopardized while he's away. And you don't want to be a weapon used to draw him back home. So you and I are going to disappear for a while."

"My guests—"

"Can stay here *without* you comforting them." Without further delaying the inevitable, he pulled out his cell phone. "I'll take care of it."

"No. You won't." Meara stomped out of the bedroom. With fascination, he watched her butt jiggle as she hurried down the hallway. He had to move her quickly. And he was damned glad he was able to call in a favor if he'd needed it. Right now, he needed it.

He had laced his hiking boots and was repacking his duffel bag when he heard her speaking. "Hello, Chris? I've got to leave, and I need someone from the pack to check in my guests at the cabin resort."

Good, she was agreeing to Finn's terms—for now.

A significant pause followed, and she said irritably over the phone, "*No.* I don't know where I'm going." Another pause. "Listen, Finn's a Navy SEAL, as well you know. Undoubtedly, he knows what he's doing."

She must have considered that Finn was listening to her from down the hall when she added, "At least Hunter will believe so." Again silence. "No, of course I can't get through to Hunter yet to okay it. It's a done deal. Just have someone cover the cabin rentals until I can return."

She didn't say anything more so Finn assumed she'd finally convinced Chris that it was all right for her to go with Finn. He was sure Chris didn't like the friendship he and the other SEALs shared with Hunter, since they weren't part of the pack. But he had a sneaking suspicion there was more going on here than just a sub-leader's nose being out of joint because someone outside the pack was making decisions that affected the pack leader's sister. Chris had designs on Meara, whether she was aware of that or not, and her being alone with Finn was raising Chris's hackles.

Finn heard the oven door open and assumed Meara

was either removing the chicken or checking on it, but it couldn't have cooked long enough. She let out an exasperated sigh and turned her ire on Finn as he joined her in the kitchen. She still had the phone to her ear. Finn was right about the food, though. The chicken was only partially cooked—still pink and inedible.

"We can take it with us or finish baking it, then go," he offered, in an attempt to appease her somewhat. But at this point, Joe Matheson wasn't eating a bite of it.

She gave him an annoyed look, closed the oven door, and said over the phone, "Chris, I'm doing this. I'll be perfectly safe in Finn's hands."

Finn couldn't stop the sinful way he was thinking about that remark or the calculated smile he cast her.

She shook her head at Finn and said to Chris, "Just have one of the guys stay at my place to manage the resort. I'd appreciate it. Bye."

She ended the connection and scowled at Finn. "All right?"

He smiled. He couldn't help himself. When she was riled, Meara was even more striking, her color high and becoming.

"I'll get the ice chest and whatever else we might need." He headed for the garage.

"Don't tell me you know where my ice chest is."

"In the garage. When I searched the place earlier, it was hard to miss."

"Anything else you felt you needed to explore?"

He glanced over his shoulder at her, and he couldn't contain the slow, lazy smile curving his lips. "Ask me later, and I'd be happy to answer your question. Maybe even demonstrate."

~~~

Rourke Thornburg loved reporting the news when there was something interesting to report. In the news business, no news was *not* good news. But being a recently turned werewolf with Hunter Greymere's pack had its drawbacks. The pack wouldn't let him dig too deeply into a situation that could be considered newsworthy because they didn't want him getting that kind of attention. What if he shifted unexpectedly in the middle of a news story and *he* became the biggest news around?

He could see the headlines now: *Werewolf found on the Oregon coast! Will Bigfoot be located next?*

Some pack member was always following him around. That wouldn't have been so bad if the pack member had been a woman, but since there were fewer of them in Hunter's pack and most were mated, he was stuck nearly always being escorted by a male wolf.

Today, Chris Tarleton was sitting across the desk from him at the newspaper office, reading yesterday's paper and shaking his head. Chris was tall and strawberry blond, and Rourke had been told he was a red wolf, rather than a gray. In the wolf world, that meant he would be a smaller wolf. But in the werewolf world, the guy was just as lanky in wolf form as he was in human form. He was quiet most of the time. He preferred the quiet. Didn't care to chitchat. But he also didn't seem to care much for Rourke. Not for his occupation as a dealer in news nor as a newly turned werewolf who had to watch his step.

Rourke had been glad when Chris left to take care of business for a couple of days. He was hoping that the sub-leader would be gone a lot longer, leaving someone else to watch over Rourke, but fat chance of that. Late last night, Chris had come back again.

Chris's phone rang, startling him out of his reading. He set the paper aside, then answered his phone. "Meara," he said, sounding more than surprised. "Hell, no."

Rourke was dying to know what was being said between the two. Even though Hunter had long ago set Chris and Dave up as sub-leaders to watch the pack while he was away on missions, Meara, being his sister and an alpha, was always asked for input on anything that would have warranted Hunter's attention, had he been available.

But as far as Rourke knew, neither of the sub-leaders could tell her what to do and expect her to do it. Unless she was in agreement.

What was going on? Trying not to attract Chris's attention, because Rourke was afraid Chris would leave the office if he did, Rourke strained to hear Meara's voice over the phone. At times, she spoke so loudly that he heard bits and pieces. But nothing much that he could make sense of.

As controlled as his emotions were normally, Chris was livid, his face red and his breathing hard. He was incensed, which made Rourke even more curious about what was happening.

Rourke suspected that Chris had more than casual feelings for Meara. But Meara didn't seem to notice, and Chris was afraid to pursue it. Or maybe he thought Hunter wouldn't approve. Rourke liked Meara, but he knew he didn't stand a chance with her. Not when he was newly turned and she was a royal, having few human roots in her bloodline. She had only tolerated him in the pack, not disliking him but not really accepting him. For whatever reason, Rourke wanted her acceptance and respect. So he was glad Chris didn't seem to have what it took to get on her good side, either.

"Have you okayed this with Hunter first?" A hint of threat was in Chris's tone of voice. If she did whatever she planned to do—and Chris was sorely angered about it—Hunter would be furious if she hadn't discussed it with him first.

That worried Rourke. He hoped Chris was making a big deal out of nothing, but Rourke had never seen him so riled up with Meara before, and that concerned him.

Chris ground his teeth while he waited as she said something further, and then he said, "Damn it, Meara, you can't leave with him until Hunter okays it."

A potential mate? She was always looking for one, and now Rourke suspected Chris was so riled because he was still interested in her. As for himself, Rourke wanted a much more subdued woman than Meara. The woman needed someone who could match her fiery personality.

"Damn it to hell," Chris said, staring at his phone. Meara had hung up on him.

Chris quickly punched buttons to make a call, and for a moment, Rourke thought he was calling Meara back to try and talk some sense into her, but instead he said, "I need you to run over to Meara's place and rent the rental units." He scowled. "Hell, I know that! Don't you think I would know that? Meara's going to be gone for a little while. So you have the task of running the resort. Just get out there." He hung up.

Now that was odd that Meara would give up managing

the units, since everyone in the pack knew how much she was looking forward to running them while Hunter was gone. Rumor had it that all the guests for the next two weeks were alpha male bachelors, and she intended to find herself a mate.

After Chris finished his call, he stuck the phone in the pouch at his belt. He cleared his throat, leaned back in the chair, and stared at the floor for a moment as if deep in thought. He must have realized Rourke was watching him because he looked up with an annoyed expression. "You should be glad things are quiet around here for a change."

It didn't seem so quiet any longer—at least where Meara was concerned. Rourke sure would like to learn what that was all about. "Quiet doesn't sell newspapers."

Chris shrugged. "Make something up."

Rourke stared at him blankly. "Reporting the news means reporting the truth."

"Ah hell, that's a crock of…"

Chris's cell phone rang, and Rourke wondered, *What now?*

Chris slipped the phone off his belt. "Yeah?" His eyes narrowed as he shifted his gaze from the floor to Rourke.

What had Rourke done wrong this time? He'd really thought he had this werewolf business down fairly well, but he felt like he was living undercover and he was always afraid he'd blow his cover.

"Yeah." Chris looked at the floor again. "All right. I'll ask him. Thanks." He pocketed the phone and looked grimmer than Rourke had ever seen him.

"What's wrong?" Rourke asked.

"Nothing to write home about. In other words, nothing to report in your newspaper. But we've got a problem."

More than the one he'd just had with Meara? "What?"

"A man just washed up on one of the more isolated beaches, dead. He's one of us."

Rourke closed his gaping mouth. "But I can't report it."

"He's one of us... *our kind*," Chris said in a tone that sounded as if he was relaying the information to a two-year-old. But Chris was angry, too, his face red, his fingers curled into fists, his jaw clenched.

"I understand that. But no one can verify he's one of us, so what difference would it make if I reported it?" But Rourke could see from the hostile expression on Chris's face that he wasn't getting anywhere with this. "Who found him?"

"One of our teens was searching for sea life on the rocks. She realized he was one of our kind right away and reported it to Dave. He wanted to know if you might recognize the man."

"How would I know—"

Chris raised his hand to stop Rourke from asking anything further. "He had newspaper credentials. His name was Joe Matheson."

"Joe..." Rourke shook his head. "Never heard of him."

Chris frowned. "Are you sure?"

"Well, sure I'm sure. If he's from a community around here, I'd probably know him unless he was brand new on the job. If he's from somewhere else, that's another story. How did he die?"

"Fell from the cliffs. Even though we have pretty good healing abilities, a fall on the rocks at low tide could kill anyone."

"Was he pushed, did he commit suicide, or did he just accidentally fall?"

"Our police officer is looking into it. But he wants you to look at the man, just in case you might have known him, being that he's supposed to be in your line of work."

Rourke would have jumped at the chance if it meant a news story. But now it was just a viewing to ID the poor slob when he was sure he wouldn't recognize him and wouldn't be able to help the pack. Then his instincts for investigative reporting gave him pause. "The isolated beach where he was found wouldn't be near Meara's cabin, would it?"

Watching the fowl bake was like the old adage about observing a teakettle boil, Finn thought as he waited while Meara packed her bags. He was dishing out the finally cooked chicken when he heard Meara's phone ring.

A significant pause followed, and then she said, "Joe Matheson?" Her voice shook with unease.

Wondering what the hell had happened now, Finn turned off the oven, deposited the empty baking dish on the stove top, and then hurried to join her in the master bedroom.

Her face was pale and her knuckles white as she gripped the phone. He took the phone from her, and her mouth gaped as she stared at him in surprise. Then her surprise turned to a scowl, and she grabbed for the phone.

Finn deflected her grasping hand, determined to hear firsthand what the trouble was. "What's wrong?" he asked the caller.

"Who the hell is this?"

"Finn Emerson. Is this Dave? I talked to you earlier about sending a man after Hunter. What the hell's going on now?"

"I was just on my way to Meara's place. A Joe Matheson was found dead at the bottom of some cliffs north of Meara's cabin. He was carrying a card with her phone number on it, so I figured he was renting one of the cabins. He had a return plane ticket for Asheville, North Carolina, scheduled for a week from today."

Hell. "Have you retrieved the body?"

"Yeah. He's at the morgue. Can Meara ID him?"

If it was the assassin's work, why had the man killed Joe, not Finn, and not taken Meara hostage?

"We both can ID him. We'll be right there to check it out." Finn handed the phone to Meara, not liking where this was headed. "Where's the morgue? We have a body to ID."

Meara still couldn't believe the news about Joe Matheson. He'd been her first alpha-mate prospect and cabin renter. And now he was dead. She felt sick knowing that and now was certain all he'd said was true. He'd been Hunter's friend several years back, and she hadn't trusted him.

Her stomach roiling, she and Finn entered the morgue.

The mingling smells assaulted her—the strong odors of blood and decay and bleach. Even humans would have noticed the odors, but her finely tuned wolf's sense of smell made them worse. It didn't matter that she had hardly known Joe; she felt horrible that she'd thought ill of him and now he was dead.

She balked at going further into the room. Finn's steadying hand remained at her elbow, and she appreciated his strength. She would never have thought she'd need someone to help her confront something like this.

"You don't have to see him, Meara," Finn said. "I can ID him."

She shook her head. "I'll be all right." Although she felt anything but. She'd had to kill to save others before, so she'd seen dead bodies, but this was different. She had liked the guy and felt it was her fault that she'd encouraged him to come to her resort—for what? Relaxation, maybe a wolf mate? Not to be murdered.

White tile walls and fluorescent lights bathed the room in brightness, while the red floor masked any bloodstains. With a little more pressure on her elbow, Finn encouraged her to keep walking toward the sheet-covered body, where a police officer, Wes Caruthers—one of her pack, although a red wolf—and an attendant greeted her. She couldn't help the way her whole body tensed in anticipation of seeing Joe dead. And because of her concern that innocent and unsuspecting Joe had been murdered instead of her or Finn.

"I'm sorry I had to call you to identify the body, Meara. If you want to step outside, I'm sure Mr. Emerson would be able to ID him and you won't have to."

She shook her head, hating to see Joe in death, but it was her pack, and the man had had business with her, not Finn. But when the attendant pulled the sheet aside, she stared at an unfamiliar angular face, cold gray eyes, bushy red brows, and wet red-blond hair. A chill raced down her spine.

"This man isn't Joe." She meant to sound firm in her

statement, but the words came out in a rushed whisper of shocked surprise.

Then again, maybe this *was* Joe.

"Not the man we met at your place, in any event," Finn said, shaking his head at Caruthers but confirming what she'd suspected—that the dead man had been Joe, and the other had been an imposter. "Did he have any picture ID?" Finn asked, pulling out his phone and taking a picture of the man.

"No, sir. Just the return plane ticket and the note with Meara's phone number and address on it." Caruthers shoved his hands in his pockets, watching Finn and acting as though he was trying to decide whether to question Finn or remain silent. Caruthers had been a police officer up north, but when he'd learned that Hunter needed a couple of officers to help police his werewolves and others trickling into the area, Caruthers had jumped at the chance to bring his mate and join the force.

Some of the reason had to do with their werewolf longevity. As Caruthers put it, he'd been a Texas Ranger early on and then had moved farther west. He'd retired a few times and had had to die sometimes to avoid anyone becoming suspicious that he didn't grow old very fast and had lived so many years. He and his mate had been in the Portland area long enough when they left.

Finn rubbed his chin thoughtfully. She'd seen him do it before, deep in concentration, when Hunter had talked secretly to him about a mission, right before he'd ask her brother another question.

"Were any weapons found on or near the body?" Finn asked.

Knowingly, Caruthers shook his head. "We searched the area but didn't find any."

Finn nodded.

So what did that mean? No weapons meant this Joe was the good guy?

Meara noticed the damn worried look Caruthers sent her way. She knew he wouldn't want to do anything Hunter didn't want him to do, and being new in the pack, he was probably afraid he might jeopardize his pack ties and job.

"I'm taking care of her," Finn said, as if trying to reassure the officer.

"Hunter knows?" Caruthers quickly asked.

"No," Meara said, annoyed she was being left out of the conversation. The officer was part of *her* pack, not Finn's. He didn't have any jurisdiction here or any say in their pack politics. Typical that he would take charge in Hunter's absence as if he were the pack leader.

"But Hunter would approve of the arrangement," Finn said, giving Meara, a small knowing smile.

Caruthers looked from her to Finn and then gave a stiff nod. "Thanks, Miss Greymere, Mr. Emerson, for coming by."

She'd almost told the officer not to mention this murder to Hunter, but she knew it was Caruthers's duty to keep the pack leader informed, although what Hunter could do about it while he was on his honeymoon was beyond her. Learning of the man's death would only make him worry more about her safety. From where he was, he couldn't do anything about that, either. And she did *not* want him to give up his honeymoon to take care of things here when she was certain the pack and Finn were capable of dealing with the situation.

Finn took Meara by the elbow and was about to guide her out of the morgue, when Rourke and his *lupus garou* mentor, Chris, walked in. Chris looked annoyed that he had to baby-sit Rourke, but his green eyes brightened when he saw her. Even though Chris was one of Hunter's sub-leaders, he'd never appealed to her. Too quiet, too by the book, way too somber. He was a nice enough guy, but she liked a man who could laugh about things.

Finn eyed them both, his whole body tensing at once, and Meara hurried to introduce everyone. "Rourke Thornburg, a news reporter and friend of Tessa, Hunter's mate—" She paused and turned to Rourke. "No story on this, or Hunter will have your head."

Rourke gave her an exasperated look. "Apparently I'm supposed to make up the news," he said, turning his aggravated expression on Chris.

"Oh?" She motioned to Chris. "And that's Chris Tarleton, Rourke's... mentor and one of Hunter's sub-leaders."

"And you're at the morgue because...?" Finn asked Rourke, sounding suspicious.

Rourke frowned at him. "The dead man had newspaper credentials. Chris wanted me to check it out. Who are you?"

Finn gave him a wry smile. "Finn Emerson, friend and SEAL on Hunter's team." He waved toward the dead man. "Go ahead. See if it's anyone you recognize."

"Hell, you're a SEAL," Rourke said, looking impressed.

That was all Finn needed to do to impress Rourke. Ever since Hunter had told Rourke he was a Navy SEAL, Rourke had been proud to share the information—and even prouder to know Hunter.

Rourke sucked in a deep breath, then headed over to the dead body, studied him for a moment, and then shook his head. "No, I told Chris I'd never heard of the man. Probably someone new or he isn't from around here."

"He has a return ticket to North Carolina, but he might not be from there, either," the police officer suggested.

"Let's see if the Joe we met is still hanging around," Finn said to Meara.

The police officer hurried after them. "I'll follow you over there in case you need my help."

"We could help, too," Rourke added, looking hopeful, as if he was about to find the news story of the century.

"No." Meara knew that Rourke was still a reporter at heart, even if he tried to stay out of trouble as a newly turned wolf. She said to Chris, "Take him back to his office. I'm sure a story will come up, and here you'd be at my place, missing out on an article for your paper."

Rourke gave her a sour look. "Chris won't let me report on anything except the weather."

Meara smiled. Hunter had gotten himself into a mess of trouble when she had lost him for a time. She had figured that at the rate he was going, he might have turned half the population of Oregon. Good thing she had rejoined him in the nick of time. And he'd always worried about *her* turning someone on purpose or by accident.

"I'll meet you at your place," the police officer said.

Chris cast an icy glower at Finn, who just gave him a smug smile back.

Alpha males.

As she walked through the basement with Finn, Meara thought about the "Joe" who was supposedly renting her cabin and felt a tightening in her chest.

"I gave him my rifle," she whispered, feeling another chill. "If the man was an assassin, why didn't he take both of us out when he had the chance?"

"Maybe he's not the assassin. Maybe he's really Joe, and that guy…" Finn said, motioning to the morgue, "was the imposter. Also, the assassin would prefer using his own weapon, not someone else's untried gun."

She hadn't considered that. She had just assumed that the dead man was the good guy and that any weapon the bad guy could use would be sufficient.

"What's this business between you and Tarleton?" Finn asked once they were out of earshot of the others.

"What?" she asked, totally thrown off stride by the question.

"You heard me. He's clearly interested in you and hates me, thinking I'm one of your potential suitors."

Not believing Finn could think anything of the sort, she shook her head.

"Are you shaking your head because you don't think he's interested in you or because you don't think he believes I'm a potential suitor?"

"Get serious."

"I'm damned serious."

She cast him an annoyed expression. "According to you, everyone is interested in me. So why don't I have a mate?"

He gave her a conceited smile. "You're a handful."

She snorted, then added for his benefit, "Well, I'm not interested in him, if it's any of your business. Chris is the most humorless man I know. I could never get along with a man who doesn't have a sense of humor."

Her cell phone rang, and she jumped a little, her nerves

shattered. Then she yanked the phone out of her jeans pocket. Her heart beating faster, she checked the caller ID as they continued out of the basement and up the stairs. Then she felt a sliver of relief.

"Hunter." He had to be all right. "Hunter, are you and Tessa safe?"

"We're fine. Dave got hold of me about the danger you could be in and that Finn's there watching over you. I've arranged for a couple of men to watch our backs as soon as we arrive at our lodging. I'm more concerned about you."

"You should be more troubled that Finn is hanging around me, and some assassin might be targeting *him*."

Chapter 5

HUNTER DIDN'T SAY ANYTHING AT FIRST TO MEARA over the phone as she and Finn headed for her car, and she knew damn well he was siding with his SEAL partner instead of her, wanting her to go with Finn and not stay at the cabin alone.

Finn gave her a small smile as he opened the passenger door for her while he took over the driving and headed back to her place.

Hunter broke into her stormy thoughts, saying, "Finn believes you could be a target to get to me. I have to agree with him. So listen to Finn. He knows what he's doing. If that's not acceptable, you can join Tessa and me in Hawaii."

"On your honeymoon? No way." Meara sighed heavily, still thinking she could stay at the cabins and take care of the guests. Finn could check them out and make sure none of them were the bad guys. Even so, Finn seemed more likely to be a target than her, and he would therefore be bringing the bad guys to her place. On the other hand, if Finn was right and she could be a target, she wanted him to stay with her.

"Tell Finn I want to stay at the cabin. He can protect me there. We have paying guests scheduled to arrive soon." And prospective mates to check over at her leisure.

"Let me talk to Finn."

She frowned, not liking the way Hunter sounded—like

he and Finn would decide this for her and she had no
say whatsoever because she was just a civilian and they
were hotshot SEALs. "He's driving," she said tersely.

"Meara." The way he said her name meant she needed
to hand over the phone or else. She could just envision
Hunter giving the word, and Finn turning the car around,
then driving straight for the airport where he'd deposit
her on a plane bound for Hawaii, if he could find one
that wasn't already booked.

She shoved the phone at Finn. "My brother wants a
word with you. If you wreck the car, it's not my fault.
And the cost of repairs will come out of *his* wallet."
Although the pack shared expenses and income, so it
wasn't like everyone worked for himself or herself in
a pack. That wasn't what really concerned her, though.
She assumed Hunter would give Finn instructions concerning her, and that's what she didn't like.

Finn took the phone, a smug smile tilting his lips up-
ward a bit. "Yeah, Hunter?" He glanced at Meara and
then back at the road. "A tight leash. Got it."

If he wasn't so damned far away, she'd sock Hunter.
She had half a mind to slug Finn in Hunter's place because of the fun he was having at her expense. Although
doing so while he was driving wasn't a smart move.

Her brother wondered why he annoyed her sometimes. She folded her arms and scowled at Finn, not
about to be put on any "tight leash." Then she thought
of what putting *him* on a tight leash would be like. That
definitely appealed to her.

Finn gave her a brief smile, knowing she would
be testy with both him and Hunter after he ended the
call. But he grew serious as he watched the road and

concentrated on his talk with Hunter, having to clarify a couple of questions. "Did you know a guy named Joe Matheson?"

"Not that I can recall. Should I?" Hunter asked.

Hell. Finn was usually the best on the team at making character assessments. He hadn't believed the man who had spoken with Meara at her cabin, pretending to be a renter, was one of the bad guys. Or the man would have made his move already.

But now Finn wasn't so certain. "I overheard him tell Meara that you had gone to Mexico together and were friends."

Hunter didn't say anything for a moment. Then he asked, "When?"

"When you were a wild teen, I imagine."

"No. I don't know anyone by that name, and when I was a wild teen, I was a loner, not hooking up with any male."

Females would have been another story, Finn thought.

"Okay, well, we have one dead man who had paperwork saying he was Joe Matheson—no picture ID. And we have the man we met at Meara's cabin who stated that he was your friend and called himself by the same name. But they're two entirely different people. Both men wore military haircuts. Both were in great physical shape and looked like special ops types."

Finn knew Hunter's silence meant he was damned worried about his sister. So was Finn. He also knew Hunter was probably reevaluating whether she should join him in Hawaii so he could watch over her. But then he'd have both his mate and Meara to safeguard. And she'd have to travel all the way to Hawaii, although Finn would go with her if that was the case. Any choice they made could be a dangerous proposition. Better to leave Meara in Finn's care here, and he'd get her to the safe house as soon as he could.

Finn could protect Meara. He *would* protect her. Without waiting for Hunter's okay, Finn said, "We won't be in touch once we leave. Watch your back."

"Take care of her, Finn."

Finn glanced at her and knew she was trying to hear their whole conversation. "Yeah, like she was my own sister." He winked at her, and she rolled her eyes. He loved it.

"Be safe," Hunter said gruffly.

"Thanks. We will. I'll let you talk to her." Finn could just imagine her response to Hunter. She'd let him have it, just like she'd done in the past with Finn when she didn't like some mission he and Hunter had taken on.

In any other woman, her spunkiness might have been downright annoying. He admired Meara's lively determination and her courageousness without boundaries, but her penchant for getting into troublesome situations on her own, from what Hunter had told him, meant Finn would have to be doubly vigilant to keep her safe.

Irritated to the extreme, Meara grabbed her cell phone and snapped at Hunter, "Tight leash? I might as well go to Hawaii and bunk with you and Tessa. Forget what I said about being concerned that I might spoil your honeymoon."

She was about to tell him she'd sleep with Tessa and he could sleep on the sofa in the living room of their suite, since this all had to do with *his* having been in the SEALs, but she curbed her tongue. Knowing Hunter, he'd agree to it, and to keep from being thwarted on her honeymoon, Tessa would end up sleeping with Hunter in the living room. Then how would Meara feel? She'd be sleeping in *their* honeymoon suite... alone, and the honeymoon couple would be making do on a fold-down sofa.

She made a small disgruntled sound of disapproval. It wasn't *her* fault an assassin, who really had nothing to do with *her*, was ruining her life!

"It's up to you," Hunter said in a congenial way. She knew he wasn't going to make the decision for her. If he did and something bad happened to her, he'd never forgive himself. But he was also telling her that either he or Finn would ensure her safety. So make a choice.

She chewed on her bottom lip as she studied the pine trees zipping past the window. She thought of how much of an intrusion she'd be as Hunter worried about both her and Tessa's safety. The men who were watching their backs would remain unobtrusive and behind the scenes. But she was certain Hunter would make sure she stayed with him and Tessa in their suite. And he might even be the one to make her stay with Tessa in the bedroom.

No. Meara couldn't do it.

She let her breath out in a huff. Hell, all she wanted to do was find a mate. All her plans were falling apart just because of one visit from a SEAL. Damn their having to run around the world saving everyone and the trouble they were now in because of it.

"All right. I'll stick it out with Finn." She cast him the evil eye but saw his grim mouth ease up a bit. "But believe me, there's nothing sisterly or brotherly about this arrangement, despite what Finn says."

Finn glanced in her direction, looking a little sur-prised. And she thought he might even be concerned that Hunter would worry about her with his friend.

Hunter didn't say anything for a minute, and then he began laughing. "Hell, I knew Finn would get into hot water over this." Hunter burst into another fit of laughter.

She stared at the front windshield, startled at Hunter's reaction. She'd expected him to be worried or upset or something. But to *laugh* about the situation?

Irritated at her brother for thinking the situation was hilarious, she ended the call without saying another word and glared at Finn. "Don't you *dare* say a word."

Finn had known he'd be taking on a handful of trouble when he made the decision to protect her. But what was a SEAL to do when a wolf needed protection?

Bjornolf Jorgensen had known Hunter's SEAL team was in trouble the minute he'd heard via the grapevine that an attempt had been made on Allan Rappaport's life in Pompano Beach, Florida. Bjornolf had been too late to warn the rest of the team and should have let the whole thing go as soon as he discovered Finn Emerson was protecting Hunter's sister and the rest of the team had been alerted about Allan's injury. But damn, one look at Meara, and Bjornolf wanted to stick around. Finn had made it clear that he didn't want anyone else's help, and he was already staking a claim to the she-wolf, even if he was implying that this was a pretend affair.

Bjornolf knew better. He knew by the firestorm of pheromones triggering their senses that there was more to Finn's posturing than an obligation to protect his friend's sister. And damn if she wasn't responding to him in kind.

Bjornolf couldn't give up now, though. Not when he'd already had to kill one man to protect her. He was certain Finn could have done the job, but he had preferred for Finn to stay right where he was, protecting Meara in the bedroom, while Bjornolf targeted the shooter.

Joe Matheson had no more been a news reporter or business consultant than Bjornolf was. And that hadn't been the man's name, either. As soon as the assassin had arrived at Meara's place, Bjornolf had had to take him out. He sure as hell hadn't expected to find Finn Emerson scent-marking the territory and then showering in her master bedroom suite, though.

Bjornolf had almost wanted to shoot Finn with Meara's rifle, for God's sake! Standing there naked, speckled with water and towel-drying his hair, Finn had been smug as sin.

Thankfully, none of the team knew Bjornolf by sight or smell (well, until now, although because of his behind-the-scenes job, they still didn't know him), and he had finally gotten his own raging testosterone somewhat under control—enough so he could leave the place without feeling the need to protect Meara from Finn.

Even if Bjornolf couldn't have the girl—although depending on how that went, he still might have a chance—he was watching their backs. He owed it to the SEALs after the last disaster that broke the team up. He'd pay Hunter back and then he'd disappear again, and they'd never know he existed, just like before.

He watched from a safe distance as Finn drove his Hummer to Meara's cabin from an isolated turnout up

the road. But Finn hadn't been as clever as he thought he
was. Bjornolf had located Finn's vehicle once he realized
Finn had to have gotten to Meara's place by some form
of transportation. No public transportation way out here.

Finn packed Meara's bags into the Hummer and
then hauled an ice chest out to the vehicle. Along with
her rifle and a laptop, his duffel bag was the last to be
packed into the vehicle. It all looked very domestic—
except for her rifle. All they needed were a couple of
kids and, if they weren't werewolves, a family dog. Not
that some of their kind didn't have dogs or other pets,
but most that he knew didn't bother with them.

Bjornolf had planted a couple of tracking devices on
both Meara's and Finn's cars, so if Finn didn't search
for any on his Hummer, Bjornolf could easily follow
them. But he'd also surreptitiously left a couple in her
living room and kitchen when she was preoccupied and
before he knew they'd be leaving.

"Come on, Meara. Quit dawdling," Finn said as
he threw his duffel bag in the trunk and slammed the
lid closed.

Bjornolf had to smile when he saw Meara scowling
as she stalked out to the Hummer, backpack in hand.
"Quit... ordering... me... around." Every word had bite.

Why the hell hadn't Bjornolf checked Hunter's sister
out before? Way before all this went down? Yet, she
looked like the kind of woman who could really give a
man a hard time.

He smiled wryly as the possibilities tempted him.

Yeah, he could live with that.

Chapter 6

"SO WHERE ARE WE GOING?" MEARA ASKED, AS FINN drove south along the Oregon coast. She glanced back at the ice chest, the aroma of the freshly baked chicken making her stomach rumble, and she wished they'd had the chicken before they left her place. "Couldn't we at least have eaten at the house first?"

"Later. Or you can fish out the chicken and eat while I'm driving."

Hating that he was so in charge of their every move, she frowned at him. "When are we going to stop for the evening?"

He glanced at her. "Don't tell me you're going to ask that all night long."

"Don't tell me we're going to drive all night long."

He concentrated on the road again. "We'll drive until I say we stop."

She ground her teeth. Hell, he was ten times more controlling than Hunter.

"Great. Then I'm not waiting to eat." She reached back, pulled out napkins and a container of wet wipes, and opened the ice chest, digging around until she snagged a plastic bag filled with chicken thighs. "Want one?"

"Later. Thanks."

With napkins on her lap, she began eating a piece of chicken. "I can drive later so you can eat then," she said between bites.

He didn't say anything, but about twenty minutes down the road, he pulled into a car dealership.

She cleaned her hands with a wet wipe, stared at the new and used car lot, and said, "What are we…"

He put his finger to her lips to silence her, wrapped his hand around her head, and pulled her close to whisper in her ear. "We need to inspect our stuff for anything that might have tracking devices or bugs." He glanced at her clothes and then spoke in a hushed voice next to her ear again. "Either you can get a whole new set of duds and change, and I can look over what you've been wearing, or I can search them while you're still in them." His lips lifted in a small smile.

He was enjoying this espionage crap a little too much.

"I like what I'm wearing," she whispered back.

"Fine. I'll check you over," he said quietly.

She raised her brows at that. "Do you tell all the women you're protecting that you need to frisk them for electronic bugs?" she whispered. The feeling of his lips next to her ear and his hot, caressing breath made her burn up, and she imagined that her whispered breath on his ear was doing the same number on him.

"This is my first time."

"I bet." Her gaze swept over him. She asked in a hushed voice, "What about you? What if you have something hidden in *your* clothes?"

His eyes sparkled with a hint of mischievousness. "I *do* have something hidden in my clothes — although it won't remain hidden for long if we don't get this over with quickly. As far as bugs go, I've already swept my things. But if you want to give me a personal sweep of your own, *just to be certain*, I'm all yours."

Her face flushed over the sexual innuendo. "Thanks, but I'll pass."

He tilted his head forward in agreement. "Hope you're not too ticklish." He gave her another of the boyish grins that she was beginning to recognize as his trademark. "I love what you do to me," he said in a sexy, husky way that she was sure wasn't all put on as he pulled something out of his pocket. Then he began to move the device down her thighs and her calves, and over her tennis shoes.

His gaze shifted to hers. "Spread your legs for me, Meara," he said again in a lusty voice, somewhat hushed, but loud enough that if a *lupus garou* was listening in, he'd get an earful. And the lusty voice wasn't in the least bit faked.

She raised her brows.

"It's easier if you willingly open yourself up for me," he said when she didn't promptly comply.

She hoped she wasn't wearing a bug, but for all the humiliation she was going through, she hoped he would find one and she wouldn't have to clobber him.

She parted her legs for him, gave him a steely glower, and said in a sultry, sensuous way, "Is that wide enough for you?"

"Hmm, Meara, you sweet thing."

He ran the device between her legs, nearly touching her denim-covered crotch, and she swore he was going to give her an orgasm just from the way he was sliding the device between her legs and breathing so close to her. His heartbeat had kicked up a couple of notches to match hers, and she knew her damned pheromones were spreading the word that she had the hots for him.

They were making *her* feel as though she was about to be singed by the sun.

He positioned his free hand on the back of her head so he'd look like he was truly her lover if anyone happened to drive by and see, yet it was more to keep her in line if she balked and tried to slip out of his grasp. He brushed the detector over her crotch, and she wondered if he had to get it that close to detect a bug. Surely he didn't need to. Besides, how could anyone have stuck one in her clothes down *there* that she wouldn't have noticed?

She gave him an annoyed look, and he caught her expression and gave her a silkily satisfied smile.

He swept the device over her breasts next, grazing her nipples as it passed over them, and they tingled in traitorous response. She glanced at his face. His eyes darkened to midnight as he stared at her nipples, and she didn't think his actions or reactions had anything to do with finding a bug.

"Hot, huh?" she murmured, attempting to get him to focus on his mission before she was so hot and wet and aching that she'd force him to do something about it.

His lusty gaze quickly shifted to hers as if she'd awakened him from his hazy trance. He gave her a wicked half smile and then continued the sweep, maneuvering the detector over her stomach, under her arms, and around her neck and head.

"Turn around," he said, demanding, but his voice was already drenched with need.

"In the vehicle?" She couldn't help the squeak in her voice.

"You can do it," he whispered, his lips brushing her ear. Now she *knew* he didn't need to get *that* close.

In the confined space, she maneuvered around until she was on her knees.

"Hmm, Meara honey, bend over," he prompted, sounding horny as hell, and she was certain it wasn't an act as she bit back a hasty retort.

He slipped the device around the outside of her legs, and she shivered to think where it was going next. Then he slid it in between her legs, and if she wasn't so damned turned on and wanting him to rub her crotch until she came, she'd wonder why he thought she could have a listening device there! Like with her breasts, she felt he was searching the area way too methodically and had gotten lost in his thoughts or something. She cleared her throat, and he finally brushed the device over her back pockets in a sensuous slide, again concentrating a little too long on that part of her anatomy for her liking.

He suddenly stopped at her left back pocket and rested the device there. She barely breathed. He maneuvered around so he could slide his hand inside, his fingers groping her ass as if he thought his hand could do a better job in the search. She was about to make a remark to that effect when he pulled his hand out.

He patted her on the bottom with way more than an innocent touch. "Ah, Meara," he said, his voice as deep and rough as if he'd just climaxed. "We've got to get a room."

"Now you say so," she said, trying to sound as breathless and sexy as him, which wasn't hard to do with her hormones raging out of control.

She turned around and saw him holding up the small listening device between his fingers. Her heart did a triple somersault. How and when did it get there? And who had put it there and had been listening to everything they'd said? Hell, what *had* she said?

For a second, she had the idiotic notion that Finn had planted it there so she wouldn't think him a cad for feeling her up in the name of security. But despite her fleeting hope that it could be something so benign, she knew that wouldn't be the case.

He set the bug carefully on the console between them, then leaned over the seat to sweep the ice chest and other bags.

He shook his head at her when she watched to see if he'd found any others. The notion that someone had been listening to them—well, hell, had stuck a bug inside the back pocket of *her* jeans—really irritated the hell out of her. And then the notion struck her—had it been done while she was wearing the jeans or before that? And if it was before that, how would the culprit have known she was going to wear these particular jeans? Her skin chilled at that thought.

Before she could recall who'd been around that might have done so, she worried that whoever was listening might think they were on to him. She said in a sultry voice, "Was it as good for you as it was for me?"

Finn turned to look at her, his expression briefly astonished until she pointed at the bug. He grinned. "You have to ask?"

Her face flooded with heat that spread throughout her body. He was just too damn good at playing the seducer's role and making it sound genuine. She wondered how many women he had seduced in the name of keeping the nation secure. She quickly scolded herself for even going there.

He sat for some time, staring at the cars parked in the lot of the dealership. She wondered what he was waiting for, but she didn't dare ask because of the bug sitting on the console between them.

After what seemed an eternity, he finally grabbed the handle and opened his door. "Stay here."

Okay so she wasn't Miss Super Spy. She didn't have the training for covert military operations, or civilian ones either, and she didn't have a top-secret or even run-of-the-mill secret security clearance, but he could at least take her with him or tell her what he was doing. She glanced down at the bug. She kept feeling like it was a minicamera and that whoever had stuck it in her pocket was watching her every move.

She thought back to Imposter Joe and tried to remember when he had been close enough to slip the listening device into her pocket. Master thieves could do things like that, but they often used a distraction.

And then she had it. When Finn had exited the bathroom towel-drying his head, the rest of him dripping wet and naked, *that* had distracted her. Imposter Joe had slipped closer to her, one hand on the rifle, the other briefly brushing her backside as if reassuring her he'd take care of her.

He was taking care of her all right. *The bastard.*

Finn caught her eye as he stalked across the parking lot, waved at her or maybe at his Hummer, and then brought out a checkbook.

She frowned. What was he up to?

He came back to the vehicle, opened her door for her, and said, "Come on."

When she hesitated, he hauled her out of the car, shut

the door, and whispered into her ear, "We've got some new wheels."

"What?" She felt a chill cascade down her spine. Finn must know they were being followed.

He escorted her inside the dealership where his Hummer had been taken inside, she assumed for an inspection to give him a trade-in price.

"What? Why are you getting another car?"

"I like new cars." He held her hand as if they were married or seriously engaged and pulled her into the finance office where they took seats in front of a desk. An hour later, after Finn paid for the vehicle and transferred his car insurance to the new one, they were back on the road.

"I don't understand. The assassin knew what you were driving, right?"

"Yes."

She stared out the window of the new Hummer as he sped further south. "But you got the same kind of vehicle. Same color and everything."

"It doesn't have any of the bugs. The other could very well have had a tracking device in a couple of hidden locations and a couple of listening bugs that would take too damned long to find. Plus the one he stuck in your pocket is now on the visor. This one is bug- and tracker-free."

"Why didn't you tell me?"

"You might have let on. I wanted him to think we didn't know he had planted the devices on the Hummer. Besides, it was time I upgraded my vehicle."

"You could have told me. I can act, you know. I thought I'd put on a pretty good show already." She gave him an irritated look. She might not be one of them, a SEAL, but she could play games like these.

He wore a silly smirk. "Your acting is top-notch. In fact, I'd say it felt so real that it would have taken a miracle for anyone to know the difference."

She stared at him for a minute and then sat back in her fresh leather seat. That's why he had waited so long to leave the car after their "show." He probably could hardly walk until the blood that had all run south had finally returned to his brain.

"Why didn't you just remove the bugs?" she asked.

"He could've spotted me doing it. While they have my old Hummer inside the building, the man following us will think we had to have it repaired. At least that's a possibility. He would have been hanging back, not wanting to get too close. He'd think he could track us without any difficulty. And he did for nearly a half hour. Most likely, he'll suspect that if we got another car, it wouldn't look anything like the one I already had."

"You still could have told me. And you should have let me drive so you could get something to eat."

"We'll stop before long."

"But I thought you planned to drive all night."

"That's what I wanted our listener to think. We'll spend a few days at a furnished, unoccupied home just up the road. It has a garage and is off the main road. Hopefully, one of my friends had time to stock the refrigerator."

She could just see them getting arrested. "So now we're going to be house-sitting illegally?"

"I called in some favors once I arrived in this part of the country and before you came home. The house is ours for as long as we need it." He drove for another twenty minutes and then slowed down as they came upon a group of homes overlooking the ocean. Minutes later, he was driving into a walled-in estate with a circular drive, although it had no security gates.

Knowing how expensive homes on the coast were, and as large and new as this one looked, she figured it had to have cost a fortune. Why would anyone allow perfect strangers to stay here? "Whose place is this?"

"You don't need to know." He drove into the driveway of the whitewashed Cape Cod house. What shocked her next was that he pulled a garage door opener out of his pocket and punched the button. The garage door opened and he drove inside, then quickly closed the door again.

"I made arrangements to use it when I located Hunter and thought I was rescuing the two of you. It's a safe house of sorts. While no one knows where we are, it's safe."

"What if the guys were part of your secret society? Wouldn't they know where your safe houses are?" She shoved the car door open.

"No. This place isn't on the list of safe houses. It's strictly a friend of a friend of a friend's."

She eyed the oversized two-car garage: neat and orderly, but obviously in use as evidenced by the tools hanging on a wall, all neatly organized on pegboard. She was certain the owners would be unhappy if she and Finn messed the place up. On the other hand, they probably had maid service and gardeners, if they could afford a place this fancy on the coast.

"Now that we found the bug, do you think Imposter Joe was the assassin?" she asked, as she followed Finn across the garage, carrying her bag while he carried his duffel bag and her rifle.

"No."

She joined him at the door leading out of the garage to what she assumed was the house. "How can you be so sure?"

"He wanted you."

Her lips parted, and then she laughed. "Right."

"Yeah, he did." Finn sounded a little more disgruntled than she would expect him to be. "If he'd been a real assassin, he would have attempted to kill the both of us. No. This guy was someone else. As soon as I can get one of our men to check out the other Joe, we'll try to uncover just *who* this other guy really was." He opened the door, which revealed a sparkling tiled kitchen.

Everything was sunny yellow, from the floor tiles to the walls. The table and cabinets were all in a honey-oak wood, and the countertop had gold and yellow streaks running through the faux marble. A bay window offered a panoramic view of the ocean, and she paused to take a look at the pines rising far above the house from way down below and the frothy waves hitting the sandy beach and striking boulders scattered along the shore. Her scenic view was different—the beach smaller, the trees framing the house even more, which she preferred because it gave more of a woodsy feel—but she liked the bay window.

"He did lie about who he was. Then the other Joe ended up dead. I just don't see how the imposter could have been the good guy," she continued, wanting to explore the beach, to look for seashells, to feel the sand between her toes.

She watched with fascination the way the water swirled in little eddies at the edge, pulling the sand out and tossing it back inland again, exposing precious seashell treasures in its wake.

Finn glanced over his shoulder at her. "What I want to know is how he got the bug into your pants without you knowing about it."

She felt her face heat up all over again. "I was distracted."

"Oh?"

She couldn't believe Finn didn't realize that *he* had been the perfect distraction.

"Yeah. Some naked guy had just taken a shower in *my* bathroom. And Imposter Joe, *I believed*, was my protection. He sort of swept his hand over my back pocket, and I thought it was a gesture aimed at reassuring me."

Finn snorted. "The guy palmed your butt, and you don't think he's interested in you?"

"Right! He stuffs a bug in my pocket, and that shows how much he's intrigued with me?"

"If he didn't care for you, or if this was strictly a job, you would never have felt his hand on your ass."

She took a deep breath, trying to settle the way her stomach had tightened over Finn's irritation with her and what Imposter Joe had done. She would have argued with Finn further, but she suspected he would probably know better about matters like that. And that made her feel even more uncomfortable about Imposter Joe.

She glanced at the sunny living room off the kitchen, with its large picture windows letting in light and the walls covered in paintings of sunny daffodils, fields of sunflowers, drifts of daylilies, and the rising sun. The tile floor was yellow, too, continuing the yellow theme from the kitchen and dining area. She wondered if the bedrooms were all yellow also.

"Looks like someone didn't like the gloom of Oregon weather and tried to preserve the sun indoors."

"Probably someone from California."

She raised her eyes to the ceiling as if asking for divine intervention, and then headed for the deck door. "*I* lived in California, and I wouldn't decorate my place here in Oregon like it was one giant sunflower."

He smiled a little and then disappeared.

She glanced back, wondering what had happened to him. When he reappeared, she realized what he was up to. Checking out the place. Making sure they were alone. *Alone.* She'd hoped to find a mate in the next two weeks, and what had happened instead? She had been swept into a dangerous situation that Hunter and his team had been involved in, and now she was stuck alone with one of his teammates. One who was not on her list as an acceptable mate for her or any other she-wolf. Not in the line of work he was in, and as far as she knew, he wasn't on the mate mart.

"So where are you from originally?" she asked. She noted a very large doggy door for a wolf next to the regular door, and then she walked out onto the deck, leaving the door wide open.

The air was wet and heavy. She hadn't thought she'd ever get used to living next to the ocean after having lived in the redwoods for so long. She wasn't good at adapting to new locations, but she was beginning to really like coastal life.

She walked back into the kitchen as Finn hauled in the ice chest and set it on the floor next to the fridge.

Her rifle was already lying on the kitchen counter, and she figured later she would put it under the bed where she would sleep.

She opened the fridge and peered inside. *Empty*. Except for a few condiments. "Great. No food. Guess they cleaned it out before we arrived."

"My associate must not have had time to get here with the food," Finn said, pulling out the remainder of the baked chicken, potato salad, bottled water, and milk she'd brought with them in the ice chest. "We should have picked up something at the market. But I didn't want to get too much stuff in case we had to leave again. And I didn't want to chance him picking up our trail."

"I had intended to stay at your cabin and just watch you there in the event someone turned up to bother you. But with the gunfire we'd heard, a dead body, and a man who claimed to be another..." Finn shrugged. "Time for a change of plans. As to your question, I'm from southern California. I used to belong to a gray wolf pack that still lives down there."

"No siblings?"

He put a chicken thigh and leg in a microwave dish and heated them for a couple of minutes. When the microwave dinged, he offered her a piece of chicken.

"Thanks, but I had enough chicken to eat in the car."

"No siblings," he said, glancing out the window at the view and taking a bite of the chicken. "Hmm, good stuff."

"Thanks. It's all in the lemon and pepper spice I used." She tucked a curl of hair behind her ear and asked, "Do you ever wish you had any siblings?"

He grabbed a bottle of water, twisted off the cap, and

took a swig. "Nope. Look at the difficulty it causes." He motioned to Meara with the bottled water. "With no family, I don't have any worries about anyone targeting someone close to me."

"Ah. So you're a loner wolf."

"Yep. It's perfect for the kind of work I do."

That was just the way she'd had him pegged. She wasn't all that surprised. Hunter had never mentioned that Finn was looking for a mate, although her brother probably wouldn't have said anything to her about it anyway. Even though she hadn't meant to feel anything one way or another about it, a hint of disappointment formed at the edge of her awareness, until she watched Finn dish a huge amount of potato salad onto a plate.

He scarfed down the salad, then refilled the plate. She couldn't help but smile. The only one she knew who had that much of an appetite and loved her potato salad as much was Hunter.

Finn looked up at her, saw her smiling at the way he was eating her cooking, and grinned. "I didn't think you'd catch me getting seconds. Hunter didn't tell me you were this good of a cook."

"I doubt he would. He just eats second and third helpings, which clues me in." She pointed at the potato salad. "That's an old German family recipe passed down through the generations with a few minor changes."

"I have some German roots, too, but no one ever cooked anything that tasted this good." He finished his second plateful and eyed the container of potato salad. Looking reluctant, he finally replaced the lid and set the salad in the fridge.

"You could have more," she said.

"I will," he promised. "A little later."

She glanced out the window. "So what do we do now? The place is furnished, but there's no food. Are we just supposed to hole up here for a few days? What if the guy who died was the assassin? We wouldn't need to hide any more." She quickly backtracked. "But then the guy who killed him could be even worse trouble."

Finn nodded. "If someone else is pulling the strings, he most likely will still want the job done right. When the word gets out that the assassin is dead and we're alive, what do you think will happen?" He finished his chicken, washed his hands, and then punched in a number on his phone.

"Cheery thought. Aren't you supposed to be reassuring me instead of trying to frighten me out of my wits? I'm a civilian, if you recall. And not trained for all this deep-cover work."

He gave her a small smile and shook his head as if he didn't think she scared that easily. She didn't. But she was surprised he wasn't trying to whitewash the trouble they could be in. Or maybe he was smiling about her comment concerning the deep-cover work.

"When Hunter and I hooked up for missions this past year, you always wanted to know what was going on," Finn finally remarked. "In fact you insisted on it."

"I did. I was speaking tongue-in-cheek about wanting reassurance. I want to know the truth."

He frowned, undoubtedly not reaching his party, and then punched in another number.

She expected him to leave her alone, to take his call in private—for all this superspy stuff—but instead he remained in the kitchen with her. Watching her? Worried about her? She was ready to ask him more about what was going on when he lifted his head. The person he was calling must have answered the phone.

"Hi, it's me. I've got a situation. A man named Joe Matheson was found dead near Hunter's place," Finn said into his phone.

"*My* place," Meara cut in.

"Yeah," Finn said to the person on the phone, as he glanced Meara's way but didn't comment on what she'd said. "So I'm sending you the picture in an email. ID says he's a news reporter. Did you get anything on the other man I sent the picture of?"

The other Joe? When did Finn take a picture of him? Finn had been naked, wearing only a towel, for part of the time when Imposter Joe was in the room. She frowned at Finn.

His gaze locked onto hers, and he frowned back. "All right. Keep trying to track down anything you can on either of the men. We're holed up in a safe house for now. Get back with me when you can." He repocketed his phone.

"It's not Hunter's house. It's mine," Meara reiterated to Finn. Hunter might interfere in a lot of things in her life, but when he'd moved into Tessa's home, he'd given up the rights to owning their uncle's house. It was now *all* Meara's. Initially, she hadn't wanted to move to the Oregon coast, but she'd made the cabin her home, and she really enjoyed having her own place without any of Hunter's bossiness.

"My contact doesn't need to know that the house is now yours. Only that the dead body was in the vicinity of your brother's home. It shows intent to follow through with some master plan to hit all of us."

"Why? Why would anyone be doing this? What was going on with your last mission?"

"It's classified. We should be safe here."

She gave him a ladylike sound of annoyance. "Yeah but since I'm involved now, too—through no fault of my own, *I might add*—I should know what's going on."

He shook his head, and that was the end of the discussion.

But not quite. "When did you take a picture of Imposter Joe? I saw you take one of the dead man with your camera. But you were wearing only a towel and, for some time, not even that when you saw my pretend renter."

Finn hesitated to say but acted as if he'd come to a turning point in their relationship, moving beyond him being the protector and her the protected. He finally said, "I bugged your place and had placed cameras in various locations in the cabin."

Her mouth dropped open. Then she snapped it shut, glowered at him, and said, "In my bedroom and bathroom, too?"

"No. I hadn't gotten that far when you arrived, and then Joe came calling."

"When were you going to let me in on that secret?"

"I didn't think I'd need to since we'd have to leave your place anyway. Besides, it was only for your protection." He turned to open a cabinet and found food, canned and boxed. Tons of it. "Looks like we're not going to starve."

She was still thinking about what he'd seen on his camera while she had been talking to Imposter Joe—the way she had slipped him the note, all that she'd said to the guy and what he'd said back, and all the while Finn had been watching and listening—when Finn pulled out a package of marshmallows, a box of graham crackers, and chocolate bars.

"Want some s'mores?"

Her irritation instantly dissolving, she eyed the ingredients with a sudden wistful craving. "S'mores?"

Chapter 7

MEARA HAD EXPECTED SUPER-ESPIONAGE SPY STUFF—
locked doors, lights out, and whispered voices—as the
dark gripped the cliffside home. Instead, she was sitting
on a bench on the private beach, heating up marshmallows on a metal skewer while chocolate melted on graham crackers over the fire.

She and Finn had passed a gas grill situated on flag-
stones nearby, and she thought how much fun it would
be to eat a romantic dinner ocean side, something she
hadn't done since she'd moved to Oregon. Not that Finn
would be the one she wished to eat that kind of a dinner with. A dinner like that should be a purely romantic
affair, reserved for someone who suited her as a mate.

Yet she enjoyed the old-fashioned, roughing-it fire
pit. The heat from the flames and the way the ribbons of
fire licked at the air in oranges and reds made her feel
closer to nature than if they were cooking on a grill.

The dark waves rolled in, clashing with the rocks
and sandy beach in a melodic roar while the sea breeze
whipped her hair about. She pulled it back and wound
it into a knot, although misbehaving tendrils escaped
confinement and tickled her cheeks. She watched Finn
roasting the first of the marshmallows, two on the
skewer initially, and her stomach rumbled with delicious anticipation. She hadn't had s'mores in several
years, and they brought back memories of hikes in the

woods and backpacking to forested areas inaccessible any other way.

Even though she loved to camp, she and her pack mates had usually stuck to fishing as wolves and had hunted for wild blackberries and currants on outings like this. Strictly nature's provisions. Not graham crackers and marshmallows and chocolate. But one time her mother had sneaked the ingredients for s'mores into her pack, and Meara would never forget how much fun she'd had with the others when they'd fought over the last one.

She had to force herself to sit still on the bench and not lick her lips more than she'd already done, or to show just how interested she was in crunching down on that first mouthful of melted chocolate and marshmallow sandwiched between graham crackers.

Finn glanced over at her and smiled. "Won't be much longer now."

Did she look as eager as she felt? Or was he just guessing?

He slid the marshmallow onto the graham cracker and partially melted chocolate and handed it to her. "See what you think."

While she eagerly ate hers, not feeling any remorse that she got to sample the decadent dessert first, he fixed her another.

"What about yours?" she asked, still savoring every bite of s'more. She was in heaven, which almost made her forget she would have been trying to learn more about a potential mate tonight, if not for Finn's untimely arrival and news about an assassin. "Oh," she moaned with ecstasy. "Forget I intimated anything about you having the next one. That one's mine. You can have the next several." She reached to take the next one he'd fixed for her while he roasted a couple of new marshmallows.

When she looked up from taking another delicious bite, she found him watching her and not his marshmallows skewered over the fire. He smiled, the flames glistening off his eyes and making them glow green like a wolf's at night when light reflected off them. She'd never pictured him like this, cooking marshmallows over a campfire. Skinning and eating a snake, yes, as any survivalist might in a dire predicament. But s'mores? No.

She smiled.

"What?" he asked, sandwiching his own s'more, although he waved it at her in case she wanted another before he got one.

Admiring him for being so generous, she motioned for him to eat it. "You'll think I'm a little piggy instead of a wolf."

He laughed. "The way you're eyeing the s'mores makes me think you've been deprived for way too long."

"Hmm, I have been. I couldn't see you making them, either."

"What did you think I did at campouts? Strictly clambakes?"

"Grilled snake," she said, trying to keep a straight face. He grinned, and she laughed and then shrugged. "I thought all SEALs were hard core. I never thought one would make s'mores during a dangerous mission."

He sat next to her, leaned over, and licked her lips.

She sat stock still, staring at him in astonishment.

"No sense in letting the chocolate go to waste," he

said, winking. He was sitting so close to her on the bench that their legs touched.

Heat from the fire and from him touching her started a slow burn, warming her to the core. His actions might have been innocent enough, just leaning in close and licking the sweet chocolate off her mouth, but she sure as hell felt like something more was going on between them. Especially after he'd nearly made her come an hour or so earlier in his car when he was frisking her between her spread legs with the listening-device detector. And earlier still, when he'd thrown her to her bedroom floor when they thought they'd heard gunshots. He had protected her with his towel-covered body, but then lost the towel in the action-packed moment and then became hard as a steel rod as she squirmed to get free.

She thought again about what he'd told Hunter, that he saw her in a brotherly way. *Right*. Yet she didn't move away from him, seeking a safe distance, either.

The chill in the night air made her shiver, and she instinctively inched closer to Finn, seeking both the heat from his body and his protection from the breeze. She'd thought she might be walking along the beach with Joe tonight, if he hadn't said he'd known Hunter and turned out to be an imposter. But she'd never expected to be snuggling up to one of Hunter's SEAL mates and devouring melted chocolate-marshmallow creations beside him.

She glanced up and saw that his lips had remnants of chocolate and a couple of specks of marshmallow. She wanted to lick the chocolate and marshmallow off his lips, but she resisted. He watched her, and she suspected he knew just what she'd thought of doing.

Before she did anything stupid, she motioned for him to get back to cooking her marshmallows. "Some more."

He laughed in a deeply seductive way and then skewered another couple of marshmallows. "Hunter didn't tell me you had a real sweet tooth."

"Hmm, I'm sure Hunter didn't tell you a whole lot about me."

A smile lingered on Finn's lips as he turned away to watch the marshmallows melting, browning over the fire, and almost ready to eat.

"Well, he didn't, did he? I mean, maybe that I'm strong-willed."

Finn took a deep breath. "He told us you saved a human girl once who had fallen into a swollen river. Nearly drowned yourself in the process. And another time, you took on a pack of hunters who were killing deer out of season. That you chased a purse snatcher, faced down the knife he was armed with, and still got the woman's purse back intact without getting sliced to ribbons."

"It was instinctive." Meara didn't care for the way Finn was looking at her, just like Hunter would when he thought she'd done something foolhardy. She was a werewolf, and that meant she reacted instinctively. Well, because she was an alpha werewolf. A beta probably wouldn't have.

At least Hunter hadn't known about most of the situations she'd gotten involved in because he was away on missions, either serving in the Navy or working on contracts after that. She just wasn't the type of woman who could stand by and hope someone else would step in and save the day.

"I don't want you doing that here. While I'm protecting you, no heroics."

"Unless you're the one who's being heroic," she said.

"That's my job. I'm trained for it. So yeah, let me take care of the bad guys, if the time comes."

She smiled. "Suit yourself." But if Finn needed her help, she was not going to sit back and watch as if she was observing a gladiator fight and was strictly a spectator.

He looked like he didn't believe her. "I mean it, Meara."

If *that* didn't sound just like Hunter! "I heard you the first time."

"Yeah, but you have that intense look that says you're not going to mind."

She didn't respond, watching the shape of his mouth as it closed over the last bite of his s'more.

This time when he finished it, she boldly reached up and licked the chocolate off his lips. She could be just as brash as he was.

Only she didn't expect his next move. She ended up flat on her back in the sand as he maneuvered on top of her, devouring her lips, licking and kissing and gently biting as if he wanted to eat her all up. Ohmigod, she'd created a monster!

His hands slid up her silky blouse, the palms massaging her breasts with such finesse that she moaned against his mouth. His tongue entered her mouth, probing firmly, his fingers tweaking her nipples, her crotch wet with desire. This so wasn't happening.

Yet it was. And damned if she hadn't wanted it, too, from the first time she'd seen him leaving her bathroom, naked and towel-drying his hair.

Now, he was so aroused that his stiff penis poked at

her waist, his body thrusting at her as if it had a will of its own. She knew if she was naked now, he'd be inside her in a flash. She had the insane desire to let him in, to open herself up to his primal urges, to tame the sexy beast.

But that meant a permanent mating, and no way in hell were they going there.

He groaned and collapsed onto her. "You're not supposed to look or taste or feel this damned good," he said, his mouth brushing her throat, his thumbs still working magic on her swollen nipples. "Or encourage me the way you do." He shoved her blouse up, and then her bra, and nuzzled a nipple first with his mouth, then licked and kissed it. The cold breeze swept across it, making it tingle and ache with need even more as he licked and sucked on the other.

He was so incredibly hot as she ran her hands through his hair and savored the feel of his body thrusting against hers, making her come as he rubbed against her cleft. She hadn't believed anyone could make her orgasm like this, fully clothed and lying on a bed of sand under the cloudy sky at night, with the sound of the surf serenading them.

Feeling the climax hit, she cried out, her words caught on the breeze and washed out to sea, the orgasm rippling through her like a gigantic wave of pleasure.

He suddenly stilled as Meara thought she heard a footstep on the wooden stairs to the beach. Her heart nearly gave out.

"Hello?" a woman called out from up near the house, and Meara shoved at Finn to get him off her.

But he was already moving as fast as he could to distance himself from Meara.

Hell, Meara thought, what was I thinking? She hadn't been. And although she'd thought Finn was a fairly sensible guy, she was now thinking otherwise. *She* sure hadn't been in her right mind to allow it to go that far!

———∿———

"Down here," Finn said to Anna Johnson as she called to them from the cliff while he thought of taking a quick dip in the ocean to cool off his libido.

"Who is it?" Meara whispered, trying to get her bra and blouse back into place.

He could have kicked himself for what had happened between them. If Anna hadn't arrived, he wasn't sure just how far he would have taken this. Ever since he'd arrived at Meara's place, he'd had an overwhelming need to do more than just ensure her safety. He couldn't put his finger on what it was, although all the team members had been fascinated with her and none had dared cross Hunter by approaching her. But now?

She was his to protect, and somewhere along the line, that had turned into an uncontrollable need to possess. He brushed the sand off his trousers, not believing how easily he could lose control over himself when it came to her.

"It's Anna Johnson," he said to Meara, his lust-filled thoughts finally clearing enough to answer her. "She was supposed to stock the place with groceries. *Earlier*."

His contact ran down the stairs and then strolled across the sand.

"Well, I see *you* made yourself at home," Anna said to Finn, joining them on the beach, her auburn hair pulled back into a ponytail and swinging with her walk.

A black windbreaker hid her shoulder holster, while her matching trousers covered up a knife and a spare gun. The only part of her outfit that wasn't holding a weapon was a tight-fitting tank top clinging provocatively to well-rounded breasts that would easily distract any man from looking elsewhere.

Even with all her weaponry well hidden, she appeared dangerous, Finn thought. But maybe that was because he knew her so well. Knew how easily she could disarm a man. Knew how stealthily she could move. How deadly she could really be.

She looked Meara over, and he understood Anna well enough to recognize that she was checking to see if Meara looked as though she had been fooling around with Finn when he had a job to do and seduction wasn't part of the mission. Meara's hair had been knotted behind her head but was now half hanging out of the knot and draping over her shoulders as if she had indeed experienced a tumble with a man. Sand stuck to her clothes where it would not have collected if she had been sitting on the bench the whole time. And her expression and flushed cheeks indicated she was guilty as charged. Yeah, she looked as though they'd been making out.

Everyone knew Hunter wouldn't go for it if he learned the truth. Meara hooking up with one of the members of the team was too risky, Hunter would say. He wanted his sister to have a mate who lasted longer than any of them might if they continued to take care of dangerous business like they were bound to do. That was one of the reasons Finn was so surprised that Hunter had taken a mate of his own. Tessa had to be someone really special.

Picking up on what had happened, Anna quickly glanced at Finn, her gaze shifting to his trousers. She raised her brows and looked up at him. "Well, you really *did* make yourself at home." She motioned to the fire as if that was what she was referring to, but he knew better. "Have any more s'mores?" she asked.

"Help yourself. Anna, this is Meara, Hunter's twin sister."

"I gathered that."

"And, Meara, this is Anna, one of our operatives."

"I'd shake your hand," Meara said, "but I'm afraid mine is a little sticky."

Finn noted the distinct annoyance lacing her words. But Anna was acting like a smart-ass and riling up Meara.

"No need," Anna said, reaching for the bag of marshmallows.

"You two probably have business to discuss *alone*," Meara said and rose to get up. "I'm getting chilled anyway. See you in the morning, Finn. Nice meeting you, Anna." Before he could object, Meara headed through the sand to the steps that would take her to the house above.

Anna cooked her marshmallows as they both listened to Meara's footsteps on the wooden stairs until she reached the top, then walked across the deck to the house, opened the back door, and shut it.

Neither Anna nor Finn spoke for a moment, making sure they were alone. Then she said, "Wow."

"Don't. Say. Anything."

She shook her head and combined the chocolate, marshmallow, and graham crackers. "Wasn't going to say anything but 'wow.' Have you thought how Hunter will take this?"

"Anna." His voice was firm. He didn't want any discussion concerning his private affairs.

"All right, all right. Not a word. But you know how fiercely protective he is of her. When Paul said something that one time about how hot Meara looked, I swear Hunter was ready to tear him to shreds."

Finn raised his brows at her.

She threw her hands up in the air, one still clutching a half-eaten s'more. "All right. Okay, not another word. It's your ass that's at stake, not mine."

"Have you found out anything about the man who attacked Allan?"

"Not yet. But the guy they found dead on the cliffs? He was a contract assassin. Worked for anyone who would pay the bills."

"Hell. But who was paying the bill this time, and will they send another to find us?"

"They will, and they have."

Finn stared at her. She smiled with a look of pure innocence, and yet he recognized that look. She'd killed the assassin without blinking an eye. "He's dead. He found your car at the dealership up the road. I made sure he didn't learn where you went after that."

Finn cursed under his breath. Who the hell wanted them dead? "And you don't know who he worked for, either."

"Nope. You had to know this case wouldn't be easy. There was a second one, too. But I found him dead just a short distance from the other. I suspect he might have been killed by the same man who killed the assassin at Meara's beach. He has to be on our side, and I believe he lost you at the car dealership. So what do you want me to do next? Want me to baby-sit Hunter's sister?" Her eyes sparkled with amusement. She had to know his answer to that question. "You probably need some relief."

"No."

A small smile percolated as she made herself another s'more. "Because?"

"I've promised Hunter. He trusts me." Although after he said so, he chastised himself for giving her an explanation. And he realized that Hunter's trust didn't extend to Finn tackling his sister in the sand and rutting her—even though they were fully clothed—like some primeval beast.

"Hmm." Anna took a bite of her s'more. "Can't eat just one." She looked up at the house. "Better watch yourself."

He knew she didn't mean in regard to assassins, but to watch himself with one hot female gray.

"Hell, even if Hunter doesn't kill you for going after his sister, the other guys on the team will be waiting in line to wring your neck for not having the chance to pursue her."

"Anna."

She shrugged. "I'm just saying. You know how they all are. They'll all be p.o.'d if they learn you..." She smiled when she saw the scowl he was giving her. "Everyone said she was a handful. I just didn't know *that* was what they were referring to."

Finn stood and brushed the sand off his jeans. "Take care of the fire before you leave."

"As if you had to tell me."

"And I want you to track down this Joe who wasn't Joe. I have a hunch that if he killed the other man near the dealership, our Joe's still there searching for any clues of where we've gone. He's got to be trying to track us. He stuck a bug in Meara's jeans pocket. Standard issue. Anyone can pick them up anywhere."

"Was she wearing the jeans when he did it?"

Ignoring Anna's annoying comment, Finn gave her a warning look. "Be careful when you look for this guy. I don't think he's one of the bad guys, but he'll be watching for anyone who might be looking for him next. And I haven't a clue what his reaction would be if he got caught in his game. Or what his business is.

"Something tells me he's damn good at what he does—and like you, I'm pretty sure he killed the first of the assassins. No evidence of a crime, although a gun was most likely fired—which was what we heard, probably the assassin's gunshot—and this fake Joe was as cool as the breeze whipping off the ocean as he took care of the man. He's good, Anna. Don't let your guard down."

"I won't. Be careful yourself, Finn," Anna said, sincerely. Then she smiled. "With her, too."

"Watch yourself with this Joe character, Anna," he reiterated, not about to comment on her dig about Meara.

Finn really didn't like Anna ending up with the raw end of the deal where that guy was concerned. But he also knew she might succeed where the men on their team couldn't. He shook his head at her when she waggled her brows at him, and then he headed through the sand to the stairs, ran up them two at a time, and stalked across the deck.

When he pulled open the door to the dining room, he found the whole house dark. He walked inside and then locked everything up. Meara's rifle was no longer where he'd left it on the kitchen counter, so he figured she had hidden it underneath her bed.

The place had three furnished bedrooms, and the couch folded into a bed. He should have taken one of the beds. The one Meara wasn't sleeping in. He should have. But on the other hand, he told himself, what if someone broke into the house and he couldn't get to her in time?

That meant he really needed to sleep with her. After he'd kissed her in the sand, he wasn't sure how trustworthy he could be. And she sure as hell wasn't discouraging him.

He stalked into the bathroom to take a shower, breathed in the damp air where she'd taken one a few minutes earlier, and imagined what running soap over every delectable inch of her would be like. That made him hard all over again, and he quickly started the water—cold water. He took a Navy shower, lathering up with the water off and then turning it back on to rinse off. He'd never get used to a luxurious Hollywood shower. Then he smiled. Unless he was sharing it with one hot little gray female, and he wouldn't be taking it then cold, either.

Shaking his head at himself, he realized he didn't want to go there again. He wrapped a towel around his waist and headed down the hall to the bedrooms, breathing in the air and tracking her like a wolf hunting for his prey. He stopped at the first closed bedroom door and meant to rap on it, but he listened instead. The room was dark and quiet. She had to be in bed already. Probably asleep. He opened the door and stared at the empty bed. His heart did a triple flip. He swung the door wide. Unless she was hiding under the bed or in the closet, she wasn't here.

He stalked out of the room and down the hall to the next bedroom, barely registering that her scent was down, too. He realized she had probably checked out each of the rooms before she settled on the one to sleep in. He pushed the door open and stared at the bed. *Empty*.

Hell. He stormed down to the last room—the master bedroom suite, threw open the door, and stood frozen in the entryway for a split second, staring at the mattress. The bedcovers were still undisturbed, just like the others.

He whipped around and hurried for the kitchen, hoping to God she hadn't hot-wired the Hummer and taken off, that somehow Anna had gotten to her and she'd just said to hell with everything and—well, where in the world would she have gone? Back to her cabin? Or maybe to Hunter's place? Damn it to hell.

Movement in the living room caught his eye, and he turned and stared in the direction of the couch. There, curled up under a blue-and-yellow starred quilt, was Meara, her dark hair splayed out over a white pillow, her eyes shut in sleep, her breathing soft and sleepy.

Relieved didn't even touch the insurmountable way he felt at seeing her safe and secure. He just stood there watching her, unable to stop observing her, his heart still pumping up a storm. She looked like an angel, when he'd thought she'd been the devil, slipping away from him for some unknown reason. Or maybe not so unknown. Was she afraid he'd ravish her in the middle of the night? Was that why she preferred sleeping on the couch?

He walked over to the couch and touched her

shoulder. When she didn't stir, he lifted her into his arms, one hell of a soft bundle of woman, and carried her into the first of the three bedrooms. He wouldn't ravish her, and he had to prove he could be trusted, but he sure as hell was going to stick close to her. Two assassins had come for them. He wasn't going to risk her being in another room alone.

Not until this was all over.

Chapter 8

BEFORE FINN WENT TO SLEEP WITH MEARA, HE SET UP his laptop and checked email messages while monitoring the camera in her living area and kitchen. Although he had meant to use the cameras to monitor whoever came to Meara's home while she was living there, he'd continue to watch from time to time to see the new cabin renters as they came in, take pictures of them, and forward them to his associates. But he also wanted to see who was staying at her place to check in the renters. He heard movement down the hall in her home where he hadn't placed any cameras, footfalls getting closer, indicating the person was headed for the living room.

He tensed a little in anticipation of seeing who it was. Chris Tarleton, Hunter's sub-leader. Finn couldn't imagine Chris would be checking in renters, not when he was a sub-leader and had the additional duty of watching that newly turned reporter, Rourke. So Finn wondered why he was at Meara's place. Ensuring no one else was there? Or something more personal? Maybe whoever he had assigned on such short notice had to be relieved for a while to take care of other business and Chris was just filling in.

Chris peered around the room as if looking for something. Then he spied the notebook that Meara had written in and the notes she'd made about the renters. Finn suspected Chris wouldn't like it. Sure enough, he read a couple of pages and scowled. After he flipped through the rest to find nothing else but blank pages, he tossed the notebook on the counter with a mumbled curse.

Chris stalked out of the house and shut the door. No sense in watching an empty house any longer, Finn figured. So he did some looking into Imposter Joe himself, since he hadn't received word that anyone had been able to uncover who he was.

But after a good hour, Finn gave up the search and shut down his laptop.

Nothing. Not a known assassin. A phantom. Who the hell was he?

Bjornolf pulled into a service station, began filling his tank, and shook his head as he stared at the coast road, which was virtually deserted at this time of night. One minute he was tracking Finn and Meara and listening to them making out in the car. He figured that was a ruse, but damned if it didn't sound like the real thing—and all he could do was envision himself in Finn's place and ended up with a hard-on he couldn't do a thing about. The next minute, Bjornolf was pursuing an assassin. Well, two, but they'd split forces, and he had been obliged to track down one before he could go after the other. And then?

After he'd taken care of the one, the other had vanished, only to reappear dead in his own car a couple of miles from where Bjornolf had first spotted him. Bjornolf swore the contracted assassins they were hiring weren't half as well trained as in the good old days. Lucky for Bjornolf, the second one had been human, not *lupus garou*, and appeared to have died from a heart attack. What kind of idiot would hire assassins with weak hearts?

But he didn't think that actually was the case. Someone from Hunter's team must have gotten to the man. Worse, Bjornolf had lost Finn. His Hummer was at a dealership, where he'd traded it in for a new model. Now, Meara's and Finn's trails had grown cold.

Bjornolf shook his head as he again thought about the scene they'd played out for him—as if they were having sex in the vehicle. He knew Finn had to have been looking her over for bugs and found the one in her pocket. But hell, Bjornolf figured Finn wasn't faking the way he'd sounded so hot and bothered. Bjornolf smiled evilly, sure that Finn would be ticked off to know her cabin renter had slid his hand into her pocket, and she had let him without even a reproving look.

He finished filling his tank, climbed into his car, and wondered where to go next. He'd find them. He always did. He just hoped he wouldn't be too late this time.

A navy Dodge pickup truck drove by slowly. He wouldn't have thought anything of it except that he was damn sure he'd seen the vehicle headed in the direction of the second assassin who'd turned up dead with a heart attack shortly thereafter. Now the pickup was headed this way again?

Through the truck's darkened windows, he studied the petite driver, who appeared to be a woman. She didn't look in his direction, but she didn't have to. She could have spotted him way before he noticed the truck again. She continued on past without slowing down. The coincidence probably didn't mean anything.

But he had no other leads to pursue at the moment, and he wasn't ready to call it a night. He pulled onto the road and headed in her direction. If she wasn't anyone to worry about, he'd soon learn that. If she was, he'd discover that before long also. And if she was with Finn, eventually she'd lead Bjornolf to him and Meara.

There was something intrinsically satisfying about pursuing his prey when the object of his attention knew he was following him or her. Although hunting on the sly appealed as well, he loved to see the reaction of the one being pursued when he or she realized the pursuer was hot on the trail. Good guy, no reaction. Unless she was worried he might be stalking her.

He backed off on the accelerator.

Bad guy, he'd get a reaction sooner or later. The woman would try to ditch him or kill him. *Try* was the operative word.

He smiled. The night was still young, as far as a wolf's sense of timing went, and perfect for the hunt.

Anna Johnson didn't have to look at her rearview mirror to know she was being followed. She'd suspected something was off when she'd spied the silver four-door sedan sitting at the service station. The driver—male— had already finished filling the gas tank and was staring out the windshield as if he didn't know where to go next. Who wouldn't know that?

Unless he'd just broken up with his sweetheart, or received bad news or good news, and was lost deep in thought.

But the thing that had caught her eye most? His haircut.

Sure, men other than those in the military wore their hair short, but she bet he was military or had been. She would bet one of her contract fees that he was *the one* Finn had warned her about. Although on this mission, none of them were getting paid. It was more a rallying of the Musketeers in support of one of their own or, in this case, four of their own—a whole SEAL team.

The man had been headed in the same direction as Finn and Meara, and that made Anna suspicious. Maybe the guy in the sedan was sitting there wondering how to locate them, since Finn had successfully ditched his older Hummer at the dealership, bugs and tracking devices and all. Most of all, the man looked suspiciously like the one in the picture Finn had emailed to all the team members who were working this case.

Yeah, she'd just bet he was the one. He hadn't looked in her direction when she came upon him at first. Wolf types, particularly those in the business they were in, were always wary, always watchful. Then he'd turned his head to look at the vehicle she was driving, and she'd quickly refocused on the road, her skin prickling with worry heat. Had he made her? She feared he had.

The telltale sign he had was when he started the vehicle's engine and swung around to follow her instead of heading in the direction Finn and Meara had taken. All of a sudden, he had both a mission and a direction. And *she* was the focus.

He wasn't being sneaky about it, either. He wanted her to know he was after her, that he knew she was with Finn. Or assumed it. Or... maybe he thought she was one of the assassins after Finn. His actions told her that he was letting her know he could take her out whenever he wanted.

He didn't know *her* that well. Let him make the first mistake.

At first he was too close, his headlights pressed tightly against her back bumper. And she didn't like it. Even if he wasn't pursuing her and was just a man about town, she hated when someone crowded her. Probably that had to do with the time she was on a mission and had been shoved and pushed in an open market, arrested, and thrown into a South American jail on trumped-up charges. Before that, crowds hadn't bothered her. But since then, they made her leery, afraid of a repeat performance. She meant to keep her body relaxed and her mind cool to deal with the perceived threat like she had been trained, but her skin prickled with heat and every muscle was tightly wired.

And as far as keeping her thoughts collected and unperturbed? He was rattling her, damn it, as much as she hated to admit it.

But then he backed off, as if... as if he was worried he'd scare her. Maybe just in case she was a clueless civilian who might fear that he was stalking her. Maybe he realized she might not be someone who had the military training and the wherewithal to use her programmed senses of escape and evasion. She fished out her cell phone, not intending to speak into it because he'd see her and most likely realize she was calling in support. Instead, she attempted to covertly type a message to Finn, who would disseminate the information to the rest of the team.

Joe, 4 door sliva

Shit. How could she type and watch the road at the same time, while pretending not to be typing a message? She'd never tried to do that before, and her feeble attempts were proving to be too much to handle. Her palms were sweaty as she tried again.

Silver sedan 91

Her car tires hit gravel on the shoulder, spitting the bits of stone into the grass, and she snapped her attention from her rearview mirror back to the road, yanking the car back into her lane. Her heart pounded spastically, and her skin chilled with the fear of having nearly had an accident. Hell.

She wondered what her tail thought about her actions. Probably that she was overly tired and falling asleep at the wheel, or had too much to drink or was trying to text for backup.

She wished she had eyes in the back of her head. Maybe she could pull over and… too bad she couldn't take a picture of his license plate. His whole car at the same time. But as soon as she held up the phone, he'd see what she was doing. Even if a light didn't show from the phone, their wolf vision would allow him to see the phone, the movement of her holding it up catching his attention. He'd know she was taking a picture to pass along to others. Although, she wasn't sure if the camera would take a picture of anything more in the dark than glaring headlights.

Her hand shaking, she sent off the partial message,

hoping Finn would get it and make sense of it. She set the phone in the console and then tried to view Joe's license plate through the rearview mirror while still watching her driving. If she could memorize it…

She squinted. Mud covered the number on the plate. *Terrific*.

Where to go to next? Get a room at a hotel or a cozy little bread-and-breakfast up the road? Try to lose him? Losing him sounded like fun. But she hated to do that when, as long as he was in her sights, she wouldn't have to track him down later. Maybe she could get word out to the team about her location and others could join her in learning who he was.

Her phone played the little jingle, "Li'l Red Riding Hood," compliments of Sam the Sham and the Pharaohs. She held the phone up only so high, unable to lift it to her ear without alerting the guy on her tail that she'd contacted someone. She called out to the caller, "Shout to me!"

"Anna, are you all right?"

She'd expected it to be Finn. But Paul? Hunter's other SEAL teammate? He was supposed to be hiding in… well, wherever he was supposed to be hiding. No one knew for sure where.

"Yeah," she said. "Got a tail."

"Where?"

"Coastal road, heading north."

"What do you plan to do?"

"Get a room. Invite him in."

Paul didn't say anything for a while, then spoke again. "Need a bedmate?"

She chuckled. "Think I might already have one."

"I won't be there for another three hours or so. Can you sit tight?"

"Depends on what his next move will be. I don't want to lose track of this guy."

"I'll join you. Just don't do anything stupid."

"You mean like rash?" When the guys did something that she considered rash, they considered it heroic or necessary; they had no other choice. When she did something that she felt was heroic, they called her rash. "I'll watch myself. See you soon."

She disconnected and started to look for a place to stay, while Joe stuck to her like a shark after his next meal.

Initially, she'd thought Joe was trying to unsettle her. Normally, she wasn't the unsettled type. She still needed to get her nerves under control, which she attributed to the near accident, but if he wanted to play predator stalking prey, that was fine with her. Only she fully intended to be the predator.

Tension filling every muscle, Finn held his cell phone in hand, waiting for another text from Anna while he lay squished against a bunch of lace-trimmed, silk pillows on the guest mattress that formed a wall between him and Meara.

The phone jingled, indicating he had another text message, and he looked at it.

"Hmm, Finn," Meara sleepily muttered, her tone annoyed. "If you're going to have your phone jingling all night, find another bed to sleep in. You shouldn't be in here with me anyway. Or you should have left me on the couch in the first place."

Finn ignored her, his back to her. As soon as he'd woken her while checking his emails, she'd stuck the bunch of decorator pillows between them, clearly stating: your side, my side. And in case he hadn't gotten the point, she'd also told him.

The damn pillows took up so much room on the queen-sized mattress that he was getting ready to toss them.

He read the message from Paul, not liking Paul's explanation of Anna's situation, which he described in more detail than Anna's cryptic text message had. But Finn wasn't about to jeopardize Meara's safety by leaving her alone so that he could help Anna. She usually knew what she was doing. Meara wasn't trained to protect herself the way Anna was. Plus, this Joe didn't know where he and Meara were, and if Finn went to help Anna, this guy would know Anna was with him. And that would make it easier for Imposter Joe to locate Meara again.

Finn had texted Paul with the news about Anna and had asked how close Paul was, in case he could give her a hand. Paul had responded quickly that he was coming to the rescue, but he was three hours out. *Hell*.

Paul texted: I worry about her doing something stupid.

Finn responded: I know. We just have to trust her. I'll keep in touch.

Finn set his phone aside, his body protesting that he was attempting to sleep on the edge of the mattress and close to falling off at any moment. To hell with that. Meara was just going to have to put up with not having a barrier between them. He grabbed two armfuls of silky decorator pillows and tossed them over the edge of the bed. Two more handfuls to go, and no more barriers.

He smiled at Meara as she gave him a grumpy look over her shoulder. The way her dark hair fell over her bare shoulders, the tiny strap of the silky tank top dangling precariously down her arm, and with her tantalizing lips parted in surprise, she looked like an open invitation to sex.

That's when he knew he should concede and leave the bed, the room, and the sweet temptation behind.

But he had a job to do, and he was staying put.

She turned away from him, jerked the covers over her shoulder, and didn't say another word. He watched her and knew she wasn't sleeping, despite the way she was so still. He assumed she was wondering what all the text messaging was about. Questioning what the problem was.

He sighed and folded his arms behind his head, staring at the sparkly ceiling and wanting to get back to sleep, but he couldn't. Not until he knew Anna was safe and Paul had arrived to watch her back.

"Well?" Meara said, cranky as could be, her back still to him.

Knowing she couldn't leave well enough alone without asking what was up, he chuckled. But he wouldn't give her the satisfaction of telling her straight out. In fact, he was fairly sure it would be best for all concerned if he didn't say what was going on.

"Well, what?" he asked, as if that was a perfectly acceptable response to her query. And to him it was. Anna was his business, not Meara's.

He didn't see her reaction coming. Not in a million years. And he'd thought he was damned good at judging character. Meara moved so quickly that it didn't even register that the pillow her head had been resting on was now slamming into his face until it socked him.

In lightning-quick response, he jerked the pillow to the floor and tackled her. Before she could react, he pinned her on her back against the mattress, straddling her waist, his hands restraining her wrists on either side of her head. Her stomach was bare, as the soft pajama shorts she wore were slung low and the matching aqua tank top had ridden high during the flip. Her hair draped over her throat, and her breasts in the skimpy tank top rose and fell as her heartbeat quickened. Both straps were negligently resting halfway down her arms, pulling down the top edge of the top to expose more of her creamy breasts than he should be able to see.

Looking away from all that tantalizing skin, he focused on her flushed face, with eyes narrowed and lips provocatively parted as she breathed fast and hard. He should have talked to her—told her she didn't need to know the details of what was going on with the team, or told her something of what was going on to appease or reassure her.

But instead he did what his body willed him to do and kissed her.

Chapter 9

MEARA RESISTED FINN'S KISSES AT FIRST, TRYING TO wrest her wrists out of his iron grip and attempting to unseat him from her waist as she arched her back like a bronco endeavoring to throw off its rider. His masculine lips curved into a smile against hers as he buried his tongue in her mouth, silencing any objections she might have voiced, his oh-so-hard body quickly getting harder.

She feinted giving in, unclenching her fists and even tangling her tongue with his as he probed her in a hot and tantalizing way—and damned if she didn't enjoy it. She forced herself to relax the rest of her body as he remained crouched over her, the conqueror over the conquered. At least to his way of thinking, she was certain.

It wasn't that she didn't enjoy him kissing her—the heat of his mouth, the exploration of his tongue, the sweet taste of peppermint—and the way his desire for her was growing. A man had never pinned her down like this, and she found it rather exhilarating in a sensuously exciting way. If the circumstances were different, she would have liked the feeling of wrestling him right back.

But she did not like being kept in the dark as if she wasn't important enough to be given any details. And although she had to admit she had started it by impulsively socking him with the pillow, she thought he'd tackled her to keep from explaining what was wrong. She wasn't falling for his ploy.

When she thought she'd conned him into believing she was surrendering to his superior strength, she jerked her hands up to shove him off her, at the same time jamming her feet into the mattress and lifting with her hips to toss him aside. It worked for about a half second. She threw him aside just enough that she thought she could scurry free, but he swiftly regained his balance and pinned her, this time with the whole weight of his body. And smiled, his expression one of pure, unadulterated smug maleness.

Wearing only his cotton briefs, Finn pressed against her, his stiff rod sliding up her bare belly, and she groaned into his mouth as he began kissing her again.

She capitulated, giving herself to him and greedily kissing him back, unwilling to battle with him any longer or to fight her burgeoning desire to sample him further. She wound her hands around his neck, pulling him closer, her body writhing under his in a way that showed him just what she wanted—to be pleasured short of a mating. *When you can't beat them, join them* would became her new motto if it felt this damned good.

He knew it, too, when he felt her truly give in this time. He didn't have to ask, just reached down between their bodies and stroked her cleft through her soft cotton pajama shorts.

Her nipples tightened against the skimpy fabric of her tank top, stretching to him and sensitizing to his touch. She moaned against his mouth as he stroked her slowly and firmly. Without giving herself permission, she arched against his fingers, wanting them inside her *now*. But he only shifted for better access, still stroking her through the soft fabric.

Next time, if there was a next time, she was sleeping naked like she usually did. But she often lounged around in the tank top and shorts before she went to bed and then shucked them when she retired for the night. She'd thought she'd be safer not removing them while sharing a place with Finn. She hadn't expected to be in bed with him, and definitely wearing anything wasn't a guarantee she'd be safe from him or her own feelings about him.

Only now—she wanted his fingers inside her.

Then as if he read her mind, either that or her wriggling against his fingers clued him in, he slid them underneath the crotch of her shorts and pressed into her wet sheath. She groaned in pure ecstasy, hating that she sounded so needy, but the expression on his face made her think he was experiencing his own kind of sweet agony. Watching her writhing against him, wet and prepared for his entrance, his masculine scent and her feminine one mixing in a heady aphrodisiac, he looked like he wouldn't last.

So much for *him* being the conqueror. She smiled at the notion.

The fabric of his white cotton boxers was so translucent that they revealed the shadow of his rigid erection curved toward his belly. She wanted to touch him, to stroke him like he was stroking her, but his fingers pressing deep inside her stole her thoughts. She was powerless to do anything but arch against his questing fingers. Until she surged toward climax.

A cataclysmic flood of orgasmic pleasure swept over her, but before she could cry out, his mouth was on hers, kissing her, tasting her, nipping at her. Thrusting against her, he rubbed his penis between her legs. Like before, they were both clothed, yet as hard as he was and as forceful as his movements were, she envisioned him ripping out of his shorts and finding his way inside hers.

Wanting to ease his agony, she slid her hands around his waist and tugged at his waistband to pull his shorts down. "No," he groaned against her mouth. "It isn't safe."

She was certain he was honorable enough that he wouldn't put them in jeopardy by mating with her because of biological need but nothing more. And she wanted him to feel pleasure like he'd given her. "But..."

He shook his head. "You're too damned... *desirable*."

She loved his words, still coated with a throaty lustfulness, the sound so sexual and raw it made her moan for more. He simulated being inside her, rubbing his erection against her shorts-covered crotch, hard and fast and furious, making her come all over again. And this time, he did, too.

"God, Meara, you're too damned hot," he ground out with a final thrust against her.

She felt the wetness between them and knew he'd come in his shorts, but she was glad he'd been able to climax this time instead of just her. She'd never felt anything so wonderfully erotic, so sexually satisfying with a man.

And that was the problem. The only ones she had been with had been human, had to be, or if she'd taken the relationship too far, she would have been mated for life.

Finn Emerson was pure wolf. Sexy as the devil, and as much as she told herself that just her hormones were making her want more, that any wolf would do, she knew it wasn't so. There was something about the way he sought adventure and danger and confronted it like an alpha male that made her admire him. She couldn't forget how he'd saved Hunter and the rest of the team's lives when they'd been injured on the last mission. He would never have abandoned them to save his own neck, despite the ease with which he could have slipped away to do so.

Finn sank on top of her and nuzzled a breast, taking a taut nipple in his mouth, and only then did she realize that her tank top had slipped down, revealing one naked breast. "Scorching," was all he said, then pulled away, and left the bed and the room. Soon, the water pulsed in the shower down the hall.

She still didn't approve of how he continued to draw Hunter into risky assignments on a contract basis since they'd left the SEALs for the second time. The first time had been years earlier under different names, owing to the fact they lived such long lives. Hunter and the rest of his team members had been on the same team both times—all except Paul, who replaced a team member who had died. Paul had been in the same boat as them, so to speak, having been on a SEAL team some years earlier and having not had enough of the experience to suit him.

They enjoyed updating their training, loving that they were new at the job but already had years of experience behind them. But she hoped Hunter was done with that life now that he'd found Tessa.

When Finn returned to the bedroom, he was wearing a fresh *dry* set of boxers and smelled of vanilla soap. Her vanilla body wash? He smelled damned sexy wearing it.

He lay down on his back, pulling her against his chest in one fluid movement.

He was hot. She'd always thought all the SEALs on Hunter's team were pretty darned hot. Their physical conditioning kept their prime, hard bodies ready for any task, no matter how physically challenging. But because they were friends of Hunter's, she'd never looked beyond their sexy physiques, never wanted to think of them as men—or more appropriately wolves—who might be worthy of having as a mate. Not with the kinds of dangerous missions they were always involved in. Not when none of them seemed interested in settling down with a mate.

She let her breath out in a heavy sigh.

She wanted to ask him what the calls were about. She wanted to be kept informed—not treated like she was an outsider, a civilian, not one of the gang. Happily satiated, she snuggled against Finn. She was a pack animal, always had been, and despite not being a member of Hunter's world when he left for dangers unknown, she wished she had been with him and his loyal friends, taking care of the world's troubles.

He'd had two packs, his wolf pack and his SEAL pack, until they broke up the team. But even now, with the business they continued to do, his SEAL pack worked together as a team. They also had others who worked with them in their covert operations. Others like Anna.

Meara couldn't help feeling a ping of jealousy. She hadn't known that Hunter and his team worked with female operatives. How long had Finn known Anna? Just how deep undercover had *their* work gone?

Finn's hand shifted to Meara's ass. He pulled her leg between his and then began stroking the back of her upper thigh. She didn't want to think about anything but the way his big hand caressed her skin as if he cherished touching her. She sighed contentedly, listening to his heartbeat, nearly purring—if a wolf could purr—against his chest, and wondering why Finn hadn't ever made a move on her before this. Which she quickly summed up with one word that was a name.

Hunter.

~~~

Finn had known he was in trouble when he got a glimpse of Meara at her cabin and remembered how he'd always secretly found her one of the sexist women alive. She was a turn-on for him in so many ways. Her looks were only part of the package. The way she cared about others made him admire her—just like her concern for Hunter when Finn and he and the other guys went on a mission. Finn had always thought how nice it would have been to have a sister who worried about *him* so. On the other hand, he didn't want to think about *Meara* in a sisterly way.

Finn knew her tirades had been because of her concern for Hunter's and the rest of the men's safety—but he'd learned to read her a long time ago, despite the invisible protective armor she wore. She was rash sometimes, but when it came to righting wrongs, she wouldn't wait for anyone else to get there first to do the job.

He sighed deeply, stroking her leg until she fell sound asleep. He knew she was worried about his text messages. And he suspected that if he'd told her what they were about, she would have insisted that both she and Finn rescue Anna.

He smiled and kissed the top of her head. *He* was the undercover guy. He slipped the comforter over them. Then he let his breath out in exasperation. And what was *she* supposed to be? The hostess for the cliffside rental cabins? Free for any wolf to pursue? He didn't like that notion one bit.

Give it up, he told himself. He wasn't settling down. He liked his life of adventure, of feeling he was saving the world one mission at a time. He liked being in new places. He was sure he'd hate settling down and getting stuck in one place. And he knew how hard it was for Meara to move to new locations. Hunter had always said she never liked to leave a place once she'd set down roots.

Finn still couldn't believe that Hunter had found a mate without telling anyone on the team. How had Tessa convinced Hunter to go on a honeymoon? Their kind didn't marry or follow other human traditions like that.

Finn shook his head. No, mated life wasn't for him.

He listened to the ocean surging onto the beach, reminding him of his Navy days and his early SEAL training. As a part-time wolf, he'd had to fight wanting to shift and chew out of his restraints while being drownproofed. Being attacked by a trainer in a pool had also triggered the need to shift and eliminate his attacker. He'd had to keep reminding himself it was only part of the training.

He caressed Meara's arm, felt the way her satiny hair splayed across his chest, and luxuriated in the warmth of her soft body. He inhaled her tantalizing sexy fragrance, memorizing it for all time.

Hell, being in the Navy had never been like this.

———

Anna considered hotels and bed-and-breakfast accommodations, trying to figure out which would allow her to monitor Joe's movements more easily. Neither type of accommodation would be all that safe if an assassin wanted to get to her. But she thought a bigger place would protect lodging staff better. Too small a place and the people running it could get caught in the crossfire, if there was any.

She had to settle down and set her trap. She finally picked the Oceanview Hotel and parked. The hotel was situated cliffside with a sandy beach below, although beaches and ocean views weren't important to her mission. But her choice did make her appear to be on vacation, in case he wasn't quite sure if she was a civilian or on a job.

Fresh fruit and buttered popcorn greeted guests in the lobby, reminding Anna that she hadn't eaten in a long while. After she checked in, she grabbed a bag of popcorn to finish her I'm-on-vacation look before she headed up to the room.

The hotel advertised that it was pet friendly, and a short squat man who had been walking his short squat bulldog on a patch of grass out front entered the lobby. Would wolves be welcome? Only if guests thought the wolf was a nice doggy that looked rather wolf-like. If she wanted to go out on a walk as a wolf, she'd have to have a handler. *Handler.* As if anyone could handle *her*.

She glanced through the glass lobby doors and saw the faux Joe park his car. *A wolf.* Finn had said the man was a wolf. But the assassin she'd killed hadn't been. The other who'd fallen from the cliff near Meara's cabin had been a wolf. Which meant? Maybe the person who contracted the killings was limiting his pack losses, if the one on the cliff had been part of his pack, and trying out a few human assassins. And this guy? Maybe he was the one who had nearly gotten Hunter's team killed six months earlier.

After paying for a room, she rolled her bag to the elevator, catching a glimpse of the man whom she thought called himself Joe Matheson. His green eyes caught and held hers in the brief instant before the elevator door closed. His gaze stroked all the way down her body, *cad*, but he smiled a little when his focus settled on the bag of popcorn in her hand.

And she knew he knew she *wasn't* on vacation.

He followed me into Oceanview Hotel, 20 min north of you. Didn't come into elevator. I'm in my room, 601.

Anna texted Finn while he still reclined in the guest bed in the safe house, his arms folded around Meara. She stirred and Finn slipped out from under her, his heart in his throat as he padded down the hall to the living area and texted Anna back.

Paul there in hr and a half or so. Don't take unneeded risks. Bolt door.

Anna immediately responded.

I've sent Paul a message. Shit, lockpick in door...

But Imposter Joe couldn't get to her if she'd bolted the damn door. Finn waited a heartbeat for Anna to send another text to finish her statement, but when she didn't, he texted her. She didn't respond. Adrenaline surged through him as he tore into the guest bedroom, grabbed his trousers, and began yanking them on.

"What's wrong?" Meara asked, sitting up, and looking sleepy and well-loved as she stared at him.

Normally decisive, Finn was having a devil of a time trying to figure out what to do next. Rescue Anna and leave Meara behind, where he thought she'd be safer. Or let Anna take care of Joe on her own, while Finn stayed and protected Meara, which was the way he and Anna had been trained to accomplish such a mission. Or take Meara with him to rescue Anna, which was the *worst* possible scenario, as far as he was concerned.

Meara got out of bed and pulled on her shirt over her pajama tank top. "Is he here? At the house?" she asked. She tried to hide her anxiousness, but he saw it in her widened eyes and heard it in the slight tremor in her voice.

"No," Finn said abruptly, jerking on his boots. If he'd been alone, he would have already left to take care of Anna. He felt the guilt of letting her deal with the threat alone, while worrying about Meara's safety, too.

Meara narrowed her eyes and yanked on her pants. "But we're leaving."

"I am. *You* need to stay here."

"Alone?" she asked, sounding surprised.

"Joe, our imposter, may have gotten into Anna's hotel room. We're the closest she's got for backup. *I'm* the closest she's got for backup," he quickly amended.

"Ah." Meara wiggled her feet into her still-tied tennis shoes and headed toward the bedroom door. "What are we waiting for?"

"You are staying *here*," Finn repeated, strapping on his gun.

She passed him and headed for the garage. "Hunter would be ticked off if he knew you left me behind... *alone*." She gave Finn a crooked smile over her shoulder.

"Hunter would undoubtedly know you better than that," Finn said sarcastically. "But I doubt he would want to hear you tagged along, either."

Yet Finn hadn't wanted to enforce his decision to leave her. As much as he didn't want Meara with him and in harm's way, he really didn't feel comfortable leaving her behind.

"So where is Anna?" Meara asked, nearly to the garage.

"We passed it on the way here. It's the Oceanview Hotel, about twenty minutes up the road."

They didn't speak any further and were soon in Finn's Hummer and on the road. With his foot flooring the gas pedal, they barreled north toward the hotel. He hoped to hell no cops were on the road tonight. He wasn't stopping to get a ticket if an overzealous cop happened to catch him speeding.

"What's happened?" Meara asked softly.

"Anna began texting me a message that sounded as though he was picking her lock to get into her room, but she abruptly stopped in the middle of a sentence. She didn't respond when I tried to contact her again."

Meara paled a little at that. "She hadn't bolted the door in time."

"Sounded like it. When we reach the hotel, I want you to stay in the Hummer."

As soon as she stiffened her back, he realized Meara wasn't going for it.

"Why don't I sit in the lobby? Hotel staff and guests would be there, and I should be safe." Meara smiled sweetly when he continued to clench his teeth, his neck muscles taut and his grip on the steering wheel just as tight. "I can scream really loud, Finn," she added, trying to get him to concede.

Finn hesitated to say no, and his hesitation told Meara she was close to convincing him to allow her to stay with him, or at least not far away. She didn't think staying by herself in the semidark parking lot was a good idea. And she wasn't going to stay put, even if he told her to do so. Sure, he was a well-trained covert operator, but he didn't have a crystal ball to tell him where she should stay to remain safe.

"Here we are." His vehicle tore into the hotel parking lot. He jerked the car to a stop, raced around the other side of the Hummer, and hurried her out of the vehicle toward the lobby with a short, "Come on."

She might have objected to his rushing her when she could rush on her own very nicely, but she sensed his concern about Anna and went along with him tugging her. If she'd had legs longer than his, she would have hauled him instead.

Movement toward the wooden walk to the beach

caught her eye. When she turned to see what it was, she glimpsed a man shielded by a pine tree. She would have figured he was outside taking a smoke, collecting his thoughts, or something like that except that he looked like—no, couldn't be.

The guy Hunter hadn't let her date before the team went on that last SEAL mission, Cyn Iverson, wouldn't have just popped up here of all places. Too weird to consider.

She tried to see more of him, but he stepped behind the tree, and she missed her opportunity, especially with Finn tugging her toward the hotel at a sprinter's pace.

Finn threw open the door and hauled her inside.

"Stay here," he ordered, moving her to the lounge chair closest to the check-in counter in the plush lobby. Chandeliers sparkled above, dripping with crystal icicles, and beneath her feet was terra-cotta tile—warm and rustic looking, at odds with the formality of the light fixtures. She sat in the cushy chair, which was covered in floral pastel, and glanced up at Finn, who repeated, "Stay here," gave her a look that said, *Or else*, and then hurried toward the stairs.

Her gut tightened with tension as she watched his posture shift into offensive rescue mode. She knew Hunter had placed his trust in the right man when he'd said for her to stay with Finn. And she rather liked Finn, despite his bossy demeanor. But she worried about both him and Anna.

As soon as Finn disappeared into the stairwell, she noted how empty the lobby was. Just one clerk was at the front counter, dressed in a charcoal gray suit and a red tie that clashed with the tile floor and busy taking a reservation on the phone. She glanced back at the doorway, thinking of the man who'd looked vaguely like Cyn. If that had been him, he wouldn't like seeing her with another man, and she figured he wouldn't attempt to approach her. For all Cyn knew, she was mated to Finn, they had gotten a room, and he was in a hurry to take her there for a romantic night.

Since Hunter hadn't let her date Cyn, she knew Finn wouldn't allow her to meet with him, either, even if everything was all right upstairs and she had the opportunity. If not for Imposter Joe, who could still be on the premises, she would have left the hotel on her own to satisfy her curiosity—to set Cyn straight that she wasn't in a permanent relationship with Finn and to see if Cyn was still worth pursuing. She was beginning to have her doubts, since he hadn't gotten in touch with her since before Hunter's failed mission. Oh, and of course, she wanted to find out if the man even was Cyn.

That made her wonder if she'd seen someone else lurking, rather than enjoying the view and the great outdoors—someone like the assassin who had hit Allan. That made her decide to stay where she was.

But considering how devoid of guests the lobby was, she wondered if she should have remained in the dark in the Hummer. If she had stayed in the vehicle, she might have seen more of the man lurking by the tree without him noticing and discovered if he truly was Cyn.

But Joe was a wolf, too, and in the dark, he could have easily spied her sitting there all alone.

Just like here.

———

Finn dashed up the stairs to the sixth floor of the hotel and reached Anna's suite in record time. With his lock-pick, he quickly unlocked her door, which automatically shut and relocked itself behind him when he entered the suite. He hurried through the empty living area, noting a table overturned, a lamp lying on the floor, and a couch cushion askew—evidence of a major struggle. But no smell of blood.

His heart pounding thunderously, he cursed under his breath as he stalked to the bedroom, smelling Joe Matheson's and Anna's scent throughout the place while listening to a faint rustling sound in the bedroom.

Anna wasn't saying a word, and neither was Joe. Had they heard Finn? Most likely, despite how he was trying to move soundlessly across the carpeted floor. They couldn't have missed the door closing with a slight click.

Knowing it could be a trap, Finn pondered shifting into the wolf, but instead, with gun in hand, he rushed into the bedroom. And found Anna gagged, with her hands tied to the headboard, her legs spread-eagled, her ankles tied to the footboard, and her eyes wide with surprise. But appearing uninjured, thank God.

Snapping his gaping mouth shut, he did a quick search through the room, the closet, and the balcony, finding no one in the suite but Anna.

When Finn headed back to the bed, he tried to fight a smile and failed. Anna rolled her eyes at him. That's when he noted what Joe had used to confine her. A pair of her sheer black panty hose was tied around her mouth. Her wrists were tied to the headboard with another pair, and her ankles tied to the footboard with...

he squinted to identify the items. A black silk scarf and black net leggings. She was still fully clothed but he imagined she'd been stripped of her weapons, and she looked unharmed, just a little tussled.

He freed her mouth first, then quickly worked on her wrists while she scolded him. "Hell, Finn, where's the girl?"

The girl—Meara—was about the same age as Anna. His teammate's derogatory way of calling Meara "the girl" was probably because Anna knew Finn had a thing for Meara, like the rest of the guys on Hunter's team, and because Meara was a civilian and not "one of the guys" trained to use deadly force like Anna was. At least as a human. As a wolf? That was a different story. Their wolf instincts for self-preservation and protecting others came naturally to them. And from the stories Hunter had told about Meara, she didn't hesitate to use her wolf teeth to make her point with other wolves who gave her trouble.

He was already leaving the room, letting Anna free herself the rest of the way so he could make sure Meara was safe, when Anna called after him, "The fake Joe did this so he could find you again, Finn. And he wanted to make sure I was one of the good guys on your team."

"I take it he's one of us."

"Deep cover," she said, hurrying after him. "Or at least I assume he is. He didn't tell me. I just figured since he tied me up and didn't do anything else, he was waiting for you to come to my rescue. Which would prove we worked together."

He glanced back at her. "Lose your weapons?"

She gave him a withering look, opened a drawer in

the chest of drawers, yanked her guns and knife out of
it, and then quickly tucked them in the leather holsters
where she always kept them.

"He put them in the drawer?"

"Yes, of course. I *was* wearing them."

He could almost hear the "duh" after her statement.
"How'd he manage to overwhelm you? I thought you
were more capable than that."

His words were spoken with tight humor, more joking than critical, but he couldn't help worrying about
Meara's safety. Teasing Anna helped to diffuse the
tension he was feeling. He hurried out of the suite and
down the hall toward the stairs.

Anna snorted as she followed him to the stairs.
"You said he was good. You were right. And unlike at
least one of the assassins who came after you, he's a
wolf." She smiled. "Not bad looking, either." Then she
frowned. "But you shouldn't have risked coming after
me and leaving Meara to fend for herself. I could have
taken care of myself."

Racing down the stairs with Anna trying to keep
up with his lankier stride, Finn shook his head. "You
looked like you were doing a fine job of it."

In the lobby, Meara was watching the hallway to the
elevators and emergency stairs for any sign of Anna and
Finn, as well as the front door, half expecting the man
who looked vaguely like Cyn to come inside. The man
most likely had a room here.

Then movement from one of the hallways caught her
eye, and she turned. Her jaw dropped. Joe, or *whoever*

he really was, exited into the lobby. Her heart began skipping beats.

Now all dressed in black—trousers, boots, and T-shirt, but no weapons that she could see—he looked very spook-like, his expression hard and determined, his gait focused. He was definitely on the move. Nothing casual about him.

She hesitated to react, wanting to sink into the cushions before he spied her or to get up quickly and find another location where he couldn't see her. Even though she wasn't usually a coward, she was worried about Anna and Finn, and she didn't feel equipped to deal with this man.

The tension in her spine ratchetted up several notches as she watched Joe head toward the lobby. Before she could do anything, he saw her.

His eyes widened, and he changed course, heading straight in her direction.

Heart beating even harder, if that was possible, she stiffened and quickly pulled out her cell phone, scolding herself for not having done so the instant she'd seen him. Although she knew any movement on her part would have caught his eye. She had hoped he wouldn't see her. *Fat chance*. She was the *only* one sitting in the lobby. Even if she'd been a block of wood resting on a chair, he would have noticed.

Joe was smiling at her like a cat that had cornered a mouse, and she frowned back at him as she punched a button to automatically dial Hunter's number. She had no clue what he could do for her when he was in Hawaii. Maybe relay a message to Finn or Paul—who was on his way but would be too late to do her any good.

She hadn't thought to program her phone to include Finn's number. But Mr. Wolf-Man Spy hadn't, either.

Even so, she wasn't afraid of Joe, figuring he wouldn't risk trying to move her out of the lobby, considering the fight she'd put up. Maybe she should be more afraid. What if he shoved a gun in her ribs and told her to come with him or else? She'd be dead if she went with him. No matter what, she wasn't leaving here with him.

Would she have been better off in the Hummer? No. He could have forced her out of the vehicle, and no one would have even noticed. Except maybe the man by the pine tree. *If* he was still there.

She felt safer in the well-lit lobby, although at this late hour, it was empty. The same lone clerk stood behind the counter, speaking on the phone to yet another potential customer and oblivious to the menace approaching Meara.

"Meara! What's wrong?" Hunter asked over her cell phone. She gave a start when she realized he was speaking to her over the phone, having forgotten she'd punched in his number. How many times had he already asked her what was wrong without her hearing him?

Joe reached her in a couple of lengthy strides. Towering over her, he stretched out his hand, palm up, and silently asked her to give up her phone.

She hesitated to speak to her brother as Joe slowly shook his head at her, his eyes dark and his expression even darker, warning her not to say anything.

"Meara?" Hunter said again, only this time his voice was even harder and more anxious.

"What do you want?" she asked Joe, still not handing over her phone. "You can't take me hostage with all the

people hanging around here." There, she'd let Hunter
know what was happening. He was probably wondering
what had happened to Finn.

Joe smiled at the reference to the nonexistent people
hanging around the lobby. Maybe also because she'd
defied him by letting Hunter know what was going on,
although technically she hadn't spoken to her brother on
the phone. The man had to know she was warning someone about his threatening presence, yet he remained cool
and didn't seem the least bit worried about Finn arriving
to save the day.

A trickle of worry slid down her spine. What had
happened to Finn? Was he hurt or worse? And Anna?
What had Joe done to her?

Meara would not show how terrified she was that
they could be injured or worse. Already adrenaline
was shooting through her icy veins, preparing her to
do everything she could to fight him, should Joe try to
remove her bodily from the lobby.

Hunter was silent, and she knew he had to be worried
sick about her and Finn. Angry, too, that anyone might
be threatening either of them.

Joe pried the phone from her fingers, ended the call,
and handed the phone back to her. "Don't try to lose me
again." His words were spoken with dark emphasis.

Then as if he wanted to make sure he'd impressed
her with his serious intent, he crouched in front of her
with his hands on her knees, firm and caressing. When
she tried to jerk them free, he tightened his grip. As if
he could read her thoughts, he said, "I wouldn't need a
gun to encourage you to come with me." His eyes were
nearly black with promise.

Yet, something else flickered across them. Intrigue, sensual desire. She had to be mistaken.

Then without another word, he leaned forward and kissed her on the lips, soft and warm and honeyed. Not pressuring, just a sampling of what he could provide if she took him up on it.

Shocked, she didn't react to his impudence like she would have, had she been thinking clearly. He leaned back and smiled a little to see her lips parted in surprise. Then he stood, winked in a most maddeningly self-assured way, and strode off into the lounge.

It took her a moment to recover, to think of what to do. Hell, she didn't even know his name. Not that she figured he was going to give it to her. But she wanted something to call him other than Imposter Joe, should the need arise. And she hoped she could delay him long enough that Finn might catch up with him, if he was able to reach her anytime soon. From the way this man had treated her, she assumed he wouldn't have harmed Finn or Anna. Or maybe that was damned wishful thinking.

"Wait!" she called after Joe, standing, her legs surprisingly weak and her stomach weaker. "What's your name?"

But he didn't say a word or even glance in her direction, leaving her torn between chasing after him or finding Finn and Anna. She didn't have a clue which room Anna was staying in, though. She hurried after Joe. "Wait!"

He cast a knowing smile at her over his shoulder. Like a pied piper, he opened a dark door, luring her toward the darkened hotel lounge, which was filled with people, she noted with surprise as she drew closer. Joe was right. He hadn't needed a gun to get her to go with him. Although she wasn't going with him exactly, but rather following him. Maybe she could ID his car's license plate number, get the make of his vehicle, and learn more about him when he left. Not that she was going anywhere outside with him. She would peek out a window, though, and try to determine what his car looked like and its plate number.

Then she'd tell Finn what she'd learned.

The stairwell door opened with a loud thunk that resounded through the lobby. Meara whirled around. Finn hurried toward her, Anna on his heels, both looking like they were ready to have heart attacks, their gazes dark and worried. Relief flooded her that they were both okay.

"Hell, Meara, you're all right," Finn said, his voice threaded with concern. He frowned at her when he noticed she'd been headed away from her chair toward the lounge.

She quickly motioned at the door of the lounge, which was closed again. "Joe went that way."

"*Damn it*, Meara. What were you doing? Following him?" Finn turned to Anna and said harshly, "Stay with her."

Meara didn't like his tone of voice, as if she had been a disobedient child and he was leaving a keeper with her to make her mind.

"When I offered before, you didn't want me to watch her." Anna tilted her chin up, defying him to deny it and sounding testy.

Meara was surprised to hear Anna talk back to him, as harshly as he'd spoken. She figured both she and

Anna were in the proverbial doghouse. The notion was even more insulting to a wolf.

He gave Anna an irritated look, stormed off toward the lounge, and said over his shoulder, "That was before this Joe tied you up, and you thought he was pretty good looking."

Shocked, Meara switched her attention to Anna.

Anna raised her brows at Meara's questioning look. "He was handsome. Don't you think?" Anna asked Meara, giving a tiny shrug.

"He tied you up, and all you can say is that he was handsome?"

Chapter 10

"COME ON," ANNA SAID TO MEARA IN A RUSHED TONE AS Finn disappeared into the hotel lounge. "Let's go back up to the relative safety of my room. You never know when the real bad guys might show up again."

"Who was he?" Meara asked, hoping that Anna had learned more about Joe, although maybe not, considering the way he had tied Anna up. She glanced at the lobby door as she pondered asking if Anna was armed and if they could check out the pine tree where the man had been standing.

"Joe's a deep undercover operative, I figure. On our side—for now." Anna looked in the direction of the door and said, "What?"

"Are you armed?"

"Yes." Anna growled her response, and Meara wondered why. Then she realized Imposter Joe probably had disarmed her, and Anna was still sore about it.

"I saw someone outside and thought maybe… I might know him. Would you mind if we took a walk out there and checked?"

Anna gaped at her. "Seriously?" The way Anna said the word revealed her disbelief that Meara would consider anything of the sort. Then Anna raised her chin and narrowed her eyes a little. "He's not a former lover, is he?"

"Forget it," Meara said and headed toward the elevators in the hall.

Anna quickly joined her. "Well, is he?" She sounded more curious than annoyed.

"No."

She and Anna took the elevator to the sixth floor, and Meara appreciated the fact that Anna wasn't treating her with as much animosity as when they'd first met on the beach. But she got the distinct impression that Anna didn't like the idea that Meara might have a former lover hanging around outside the hotel.

Anna unlocked her door and pushed it open, then turned to Meara and said, "Why would your *friend* be here?"

"He might not be. I just wanted to see if it was him." Meara's lips parted as she saw the mess Anna's room was in—the overturned table, the lamp on the floor, and the upset seat cushions on the couch in the living area.

Meara's phone rang, and her heart seized. She jerked her phone out of her pocket, saw the caller ID, and her heart fluttered—*Hunter!*

"I'm all right," she hurried to say, instantly remorseful that she hadn't called him as soon as she knew she and the others were safe.

"What the hell happened?" His dark voice was strangled with worry.

"A man was following us, but he turned out to be one of the good guys. Well, kind of a good guy."

He *had* tied up Anna, and he *hadn't* allowed Meara to talk to Hunter to let him know what was going on, and he *had* kissed her *without* her permission, which made him kind of not a good guy.

"Let me talk to Finn. You're not making any sense, Meara."

"He's not here," she said, exasperated.

"You're alone?"

She envisioned Hunter wringing Finn's neck. "No. He's talking to the guy in the lounge downstairs. Anna's here with me in her hotel suite. Anna Johnson. I'm okay, all right?"

Silence.

Knowing he wasn't going to let this slide until he had every detail of what had happened, although no way was she going to mention to him or anyone else that Joe had kissed her, Meara let out her breath with a heavy sigh. "Hunter? I'm all right."

"Who is he? Why did you hang up on me?"

"He wouldn't let me talk to you and ended our call. Anna says she thinks he works as a deep undercover operative."

"*Hell*. You were alone? With him?"

"I was with him in the lobby. Full of people."

Anna smiled at Meara's little white lie.

"I didn't hear anyone conversing in the background, Meara. It's late there. The damned place was probably empty. Don't cover for him. Where was Finn?"

Meara should have realized that with his wolf's hearing, Hunter would have known the truth. "Finn was making sure Anna was safe," Meara said.

"Hell, he knows better than to leave you by yourself. I'm returning home on the next flight out of here."

"No! Hunter, you can't. It's your honeymoon. Enjoy it with Tessa. I'm fine. Anna's with me, and Finn will be back any minute. I won't hear of your ending your honeymoon over this. Stay there!"

Anna was chuckling to herself.

"Got to go, Hunter. It's late. Kiss Tessa for me, won't you?" Meara quickly said.

"Don't. Hang. Up. On. Me. Meara."

"'Night!" She ended the call, her pulse pounding.

She was certain he'd have words with her over this as soon as he came home. Then again, by the time he returned, his anger would have settled. She imagined Tessa would help calm him, too. At least Meara hoped she would.

Anna turned away, but not before Meara saw a glimmer of a smile on her lips. She was probably used to Hunter being in total charge and expected his sister to bow down to him like so many people did. Anna probably hadn't expected Meara to tell him what to do. Meara knew Hunter would call Finn next and give him hell about what had happened. She almost felt sorry for Finn, but she figured he was used to it and could stand up for himself.

"Did the man hurt you?" she asked Anna, wanting to think of something other than how angry her brother was.

"A bruise here or there, I'm sure," Anna said as she and Meara began righting the table and lamp. "A little roughhousing never hurt anyone, if neither was trying to kill the other."

"Weren't you? Trying to kill him, I mean?"

"Nah. At first, I reacted pretty violently, figuring he intended to kill me, and I planned to do it to him first. But I could tell by the way he forced me down, countering all my lethal moves with blocking maneuvers and attempting not to hurt me, that he didn't intend to harm me permanently. At least I didn't think so."

"But he tied you up." Meara righted the couch cushions.

"With… nothing that hurt. And he was trying to keep me from injuring him. I imagine he'll have a few bruises, but our werewolf genes heal them quickly." Anna grinned at her and headed for the bedroom.

Meara followed her in there. Anna probably considered the confrontation between herself and Imposter Joe to be nothing more than a good workout.

Meara stared at the two pairs of black sheer pantyhose lying in a pile on the bed and the black silk scarf near the footboard. "He tied you up with your own clothes?" But not just with Anna's own clothes. With her sexy, sheer panty hose.

Anna grabbed them and threw them in her suitcase, which was lying on the floor on the other side of the bed. Anna's clothes were strewn all over the pale blue carpet.

"I wasn't easy on him when he tried to confine me. We usually go into a situation packing light. If we can, we use the other's possessions like this so we don't leave any evidence behind." Anna began to gather her clothes: black lace panties, black leather miniskirt, strapless black heels, and a black negligee.

Meara would have thought Anna was goth because of all the black clothes, but she didn't have any piercings or heavy makeup, and her hair was a rich auburn color. Not that werewolves would have any piercings or wear heavy makeup. It just wasn't done. Meara could just imagine seeing one panting as a wolf—the only way to cool off since wolves don't sweat—with a miniature diamond barbell centered on the wolf's tongue.

That would be easy to explain to a hunter if one caught a werewolf in wolf form. *Not*.

Meara's gaze swung back to Anna, and she asked, "Did you… knee him in the crotch?"

Meara had intended to, or at least to swing her leg up between his to incapacitate him, until he'd kissed her and turned her to stone.

Anna harrumphed in a dark way. "Tried to, but he was damned quick and seemed to know what I was going to do before I attempted to retaliate."

Just like he seemed to know what Meara was thinking when she worried he might hold a gun on her and try to force her outside.

"Did *you* try to knee him in the crotch?" Anna asked, her brows raised.

Meara felt her face grow warm, which irritated her. She wasn't about to tell Anna that Joe had kissed her and that she hadn't done anything about it, like slap him or something. At the same time, she hadn't kissed him back.

"Hmm," Anna said, as if she'd just witnessed some deep, dark secret. The intense gaze of a wolf gave others the impression he or she had the ability to see into a person's soul—and right now, Meara felt as though Anna had done just that.

Anna finished resettling her clothes neatly in her bag and then set it on the luggage rack. "He didn't catch your interest, did he?" This time she eyed Meara with suspicion.

Was it because Anna was drawn to Joe and worried he might have a thing for Meara? Or was she concerned that Finn might be hurt if Meara threw him over for Joe?

"Of course not," Meara said too quickly and way too vehemently. Hell, she figured both Joe and Finn were in the same line of work, one where they wouldn't settle down and take mates. Anna didn't need to worry about her interest in either man.

"No," Meara said again, and wished she hadn't as Anna eyed her speculatively.

Anna pulled the desk chair around and sat down on it while motioning for Meara to sit on the end of the bed. "So then what exactly *did* happen between the two of you?"

Finn had expected to discover that Joe had slipped out a back door through the kitchen of the hotel lounge, but following the man's scent, Finn found him sitting at a booth in the lounge, watching for him.

Or most likely not for *him*, but for Meara. Damn it to hell. She had been headed in this direction, following the operative and unconcerned about her own safety, most likely hoping to learn more about him so she could share her findings with Finn. Her impulsiveness would be the death of him.

He blew out his breath and stalked toward the booth. He should have known she wouldn't stay put in the lobby like he'd told her to do. He should have left her at the safe house.

"I was expecting someone else," Joe said with a half smile, lifting a beer in greeting. His expression was pure predatory wolf, and Finn had to reign in his combative nature before he took out the bastard.

Finn had seen the way Joe had seemed fascinated with Meara at her cabin, and Joe hadn't hidden his animosity for Finn, either. He wouldn't easily forget that the man had stuck his hand in Meara's pocket, letting her know he was doing so as he left a bug there.

"She's not coming," Finn said abruptly.

"I gathered that when you showed up instead." Joe motioned with his free hand for Finn to join him, although Finn wasn't waiting for an invitation.

"At Meara's place, you told her that you didn't drink," Finn said, letting Joe know he'd had an eye on him the whole time he'd been in her house.

"I lied. Some women are wary of a man who drinks."

True enough. Sliding into the booth, Finn asked, "Who are you, and what's your business?"

"Bjornolf Jorgensen..." He bowed his head slightly. "...at your service." He gave Finn a look of conceited satisfaction when he saw Finn's expression change to instant awareness.

"Bjornolf," Finn said under his breath. *Bear-wolf.* The person known by that name served as a deep undercover operative, although many thought the man was a legend or a myth rather than someone real. No one was sure who the man really worked for. And he rarely revealed his identity. Many thought that those who bragged about knowing him were telling tales.

"That's me." Bjornolf waited for Finn to ask something further, then seeming to remember that Finn had asked what he was doing here, he added, "I'm here to watch your backs."

"Ours," Finn said softly.

"Yours, since you're here, and Hunter's sister's."

"And the others on the team?"

"They were merely a distraction."

Finn narrowed his eyes. "The assassin nearly killed

Allan Rappaport. How is that nothing more than
a distraction?"

Bjornolf shrugged. "Fatalities can cause a pretty
good distraction."

Finn's phone buzzed and he looked at it, noting that
Hunter was calling. Finn hoped he wasn't having trouble
in Hawaii—the only reason he could think of for Hunter
calling at this hour. He lifted the phone to his ear and
asked, "Hunter, can I call you back?"

"What the hell happened, and who's the guy you're
talking to?"

How in the hell had Hunter gotten word about this
already? *Meara had to have called him.*

Finn studied the man sitting across from him and said
to Hunter, "I'm talking with Bjornolf Jorgensen." He
figured Hunter would be just as surprised since the man
rarely revealed himself to anyone. Finn wondered who
Bjornolf was working for now. "I'll call you back in a
bit. Meara's safe with Anna Johnson."

"Call me back ASAP," Hunter said, his tone short
and angry, and hung up on him.

Finn knew Hunter was incensed about the way he had
handled the situation with Meara and Anna. It wasn't
the first time Hunter hadn't liked the way Finn dealt
with a situation, nor would it be the last. But there were
times when Finn had felt the same way about Hunter's
handling of a mission.

Bjornolf was watching him with an amused expression, and Finn wanted to wipe the arrogant look off his
face. Bjornolf was the whole reason Finn would have
words with Hunter over this mess. "What if I send
Meara to Hawaii to join Hunter?" Finn asked.

Without hesitation, Bjornolf said, "They'll go after her there."

Finn couldn't believe it. "Why her?"

"She's Hunter's sister."

Finn scowled at the operative. "I already got that part. But why go after Meara?" he repeated.

"You would have all been dead on your last mission if it hadn't been for Meara. Didn't you know that? That's what this sick bastard intended. But when Meara thwarted him, he vowed revenge. At least I assume that's the case.

"The fires that burned down Meara and Hunter's home and those of their pack members? Who do you think set them? Neither Meara nor Hunter were supposed to have escaped that. As luck would have it, the winds were in Meara and Hunter and their pack's favor. After Hunter and his pack relocated to the Oregon coast, they ran into all kinds of trouble. On top of that, a red pack leader named Leidolf was poking his nose into their business. The man in charge waited for a more opportune time to strike again—a time when fewer pack leaders could cause him trouble."

Finn straightened taller. "Did Hunter know the fire was set on purpose by someone out to get them?"

"Yes. But he didn't let Meara know it. Several in the know have been investigating, trying to find a link to the arsonists."

Finn scowled at Bjornolf. "Meara should have been told. How did Hunter think she could protect herself if she wasn't aware of the danger to them both?"

"None of us thought it would be carried any further. Possibly it had just been a way of getting back at them.

Destroying their homes. Hunter's pack even mutinied. Quite effectively, the arsonist wreaked havoc on
Hunter and his pack, more so than if he'd just eliminated Hunter and Meara. But then, maybe the arsonist
didn't believe they'd been punished enough. Maybe he
saw how nicely Hunter and Meara were doing in their
new home in Oregon, how Hunter had located a mate
and Meara was happily looking for one through renting
the cabins."

"Hell," Finn said, rubbing his chin and feeling a
shadow of a beard making its appearance because of
the late hour. He wanted to know what was going on,
but he still felt apprehensive about leaving Meara alone,
despite Anna being with her.

"As soon as Hunter flew off on his honeymoon, we
figure the man in charge made his move, striking at
Allan as a distraction, figuring you and Paul would go to
his aid and assume he was after the team. Hunter was already out of the picture. I'm sure the head honcho never
considered any of you would think to protect Meara. She
wasn't part of the SEAL team.

"Even I was surprised to see you join her here.
Thinking none of you would consider Meara as a possible target, I came here. To protect her. Then here you
are, claiming the territory for your own—both the land
and the woman." At that revelation, Bjornolf looked and
sounded annoyed.

Momentarily stupefied, Finn stared at him. Bjornolf
had to be either highly misinformed about their mission
and how Meara fit into the scheme of things or pulling his leg. But worse, he wondered just what lengths
Bjornolf had planned to go to while protecting Meara.

Pretend he truly was Joe Matheson, a guest, interested in finding a mate?

Until he'd discovered Finn had beaten him to it. Well, not as a guest interested in finding a mate, but as her close protection. "They haven't caught the arsonist who set the fires in the redwoods, but you're sure he's connected to Allan's attack?"

Bjornolf took another swig of his beer, set the mug down, and leaned back against his seat. "No, the arsonist hasn't been apprehended. But the threat to their lives is too coincidental not to be suspect. Particularly when Allan was hit next."

Still not believing that Meara could have saved them in any way, shape, or form, Finn said, "Meara had nothing to do with our missions."

Bjornolf gave a dark laugh. "Oh, really. She fought with Hunter over every job he went on, worried that she'd lose her twin brother and her pack leader at the same time. She berated you every time you returned with Hunter, thinking you were the one who got the contracts for the missions after your team left the Navy."

Hell, how long had Bjornolf been watching the team behind the scenes? Then a darker thought occurred to Finn. Just how long had he been watching Meara?

Bjornolf continued, "She's not the sweet little innocent that you think she is. She's devious, if she thinks she might be able to save Hunter from harm." A gleam shown in Bjornolf's darkened eyes. "Or possibly you know that already. She tends to leap into a frothing river to rescue someone from drowning before fully thinking the situation over."

So, he even knew about that incident in Meara's past.

Finn's mind raced over the events of the past, of their final doomed mission, the explosive devices that had been tampered with, and Meara's angry words over their operations. Sure, she was impetuous and would face down danger to protect those in need. But she couldn't have been involved in their final assignment or any other. Their assignments were classified.

He stared at Bjornolf. "I don't believe you."

Bjornolf shrugged. "Believe what you will."

Finn didn't like it. He didn't want to believe Meara had had anything to do with their last mission, that she might have saved their lives, that she could have been endangered because of it, and that she might now be in danger because of something she had done. Was it inadvertent?

He couldn't believe it.

Bjornolf finished his beer. "If she wasn't so head-strong, she'd make a good operative. But she's too stubborn and way too impulsive. She'd be a team all unto her own and happy for it."

Finn could call her stubborn and too impulsive, and often thought that of her, but he didn't like Bjornolf doing so. He knew she loved being part of a pack and wasn't a loner in the least. But he thought Bjornolf was right about her being her own one-man team. She did *not* take orders well. And for the most part, she didn't seem to give them, either. So in that regard, she seemed to run the show all on her own, not waiting for anyone else to help.

"What's your interest in her?" Finn asked gruffly, wanting to get the truth out in the open.

"Suffice it to say I like my women like that."

His voice low and cold, Finn said, "You leave her alone."

Bjornolf gave an irritated grunt. "Why? Are you going to settle down and take her as a mate? The great adventurer? The savior of lost causes? She needs someone who warms her bed at night, keeps her content and happy. She's not the one for you."

"You think you're the one for her? Hell, you're cut from the same cloth as me, from what I've heard."

"Ah," Bjornolf said, waving away the waitress who'd noticed his mug was empty. "I've been thinking of settling down." He cast Finn a wry smile.

"Like hell you are." Finn didn't believe the man. From everything he'd heard, the operative was a loner who preferred undercover work. Settling down wasn't in the picture.

Then Bjornolf's expression turned icy. "I was supposed to be watching your backs on your last mission, but I was surprised as hell when Meara got involved, and I missed doing my job. You can't imagine how much that bothered me when a woman—*a civilian*—distracted me. Nothing like that has ever happened to me before. I've been pondering what occurred for these past few months. Maybe there's something to the way she sidetracked me so thoroughly. What do you think?"

Finn wasn't sure what to think, wondering if Bjornolf was just leading him on and trying to rile him over Meara. Maybe get him to reveal how intrigued he was with the woman.

Bjornolf didn't wait for Finn to respond but added, "I regret that the mission was botched and everyone but you was injured in the process."

Finn raised a brow and Bjornolf chuckled evilly. "I didn't mean that as it sounded. I was glad you weren't injured, but no one else should have been hurt, either. I'm not going to let any harm come to her because I owe that to Hunter and to Meara."

Finn was glad to have Bjornolf on their side—as long as he didn't try to seduce Meara—but he wondered about the other Joe they'd seen at the morgue. "Did you kill the man near Meara's house?"

"Yeah. Took his identity before he arrived. He was pretending to rent one of the cabins, but that wasn't his identity, either. When he spied me heading for the blue cabin to lie in wait for his arrival—assuming whoever had paid for the contract would eventually learn where Hunter and Meara were—he tried to fire a round at me, and I threw him off the cliff. He still got a couple of rounds off as he made his backward dive. His gun must have found a watery grave."

For that, Finn was grateful. "No evidence of any foul play."

Bjornolf gave Finn a sly smile. "That's what they pay me for. Getting rid of assassins without leaving any trace of wrongdoing." He leaned back in his seat and changed the focus. "The woman working with you isn't half bad."

Not sure what Bjornolf's intentions were concerning Anna, Finn scowled at him. Anna could handle herself, but Finn still didn't like that Bjornolf had bested her and then was talking about her like she was someone he might pursue as a side hobby.

Bjornolf added, "She did a good job of taking out the assassin that I'd lost while I tailed another."

"But you still bested her in her hotel room."

Bjornolf chuckled. "She's dangerous. Has killer

knees. If I hadn't moved quickly enough, I'd be singing soprano."

At that, Finn almost smiled, knowing from workout
sessions with her just how dangerous her knees could
be. Thankfully, he'd managed to outmaneuver her at
every turn. But he still didn't know Bjornolf's intentions
toward either Anna or Meara. And that bothered him.

"Why has the bastard waited six months to take revenge?" Finn asked.

"For one, he hasn't waited that long. The fire, remember? And for another, I believe he was injured during the
incident when your team was hit or out of the country.
Or both. So that slowed him down a bit. Not only that,
but some take their time planning revenge. Maybe he's
not the kind who jumps into a situation without mapping
every move. Who really knows?"

Finn mulled that over, then nodded. "So what now?"

"Let your female operative know—"

"Anna," Finn said, perturbed.

Bjornolf smiled a little. "...*Anna* know that I'm on
your side. As much as she fought me, I didn't figure
she'd believe anything I had to say. As for Meara, I'll
be behind the scenes, watching over her."

"All right." Finn rose, but Bjornolf remained seated.
"Paul will be here shortly," Finn said, half in warning.
Paul wouldn't like Bjornolf anymore than he did.

Bjornolf pulled out a twenty. "Hell, that's what these
guys want. The team all back together in one place,
easier to hit."

Finn cast him a thin smile. "Maybe that's how we
need to take them out. Do you know who they are?"

"If I knew that, I wouldn't be sitting here chatting

with you. I'd have taken out the one responsible, and without a buyer, no more deals."

"The Knight of Swords," Finn said under his breath.

Bjornolf gave him a solemn nod. "He's the one. Whoever he is."

Finn was surprised to find Meara sitting cross-legged on Anna's bed in her hotel room while Anna leaned back in a chair, feet propped up on the mattress, as if the two had been pajama-party buddies for years. Not that either of them was wearing PJs, but that's what this reminded him of. The thought of seeing Meara in her pajama shorts set stirred him up all over again.

With a ragged breath, he explained as much as he could to Anna with Meara listening in. He told them who Joe really was, and when Anna's eyes grew huge, he turned to Meara and said, "Bjornolf gets rid of assassins, leaving no trace, making it look as though they died of natural causes. At least that's one of his jobs. No one really knows who he works for or what else he does. But I will tell you that his name means 'bearwolf.' And from what I've heard, he earned the name for a reason. He's not one to tangle with unless you know what you're doing."

Meara looked sufficiently shocked, and he thought—and hoped—she wouldn't pay Bjornolf any attention now that she knew what he did for a living, if that was Bjornolf's intention. But Finn was beginning to wonder if hiding his real objective was part of Bjornolf's chameleon persona. Finn noted that Anna appeared just as surprised to learn who "Joe" was, and he thought she wouldn't see anything good in the man now, either.

Having covertly made eye contact with Finn, Anna looked as though she wanted to talk privately about something. From the way she wouldn't sequester him in the living area of her suite, he assumed the something was about Meara. He wondered what Meara had done now. Finn had given Anna ample opportunity to speak with him privately, but she didn't seem to want to alert Meara that she needed to talk to him about her. Hell.

When Anna still didn't say anything about it, he finally decided to call it a night. Whatever it was couldn't be too bad, or Anna would have made more of an effort to speak with him secretly.

Feeling smug about Bjornolf not having a chance at seducing the women, he said good night to Anna, knowing Paul would arrive momentarily and watch her back as she did his. The time had come to take Meara back to the safe house. He assumed they'd have a tail, Bjornolf again, only Finn didn't plan to try and lose him this time. But he damn well wanted to know what was bothering Anna.

Meara was quiet on the drive back. He figured she was frazzled and tired, so he didn't push the issue of her following Bjornolf to the lounge when he'd instructed her to stay in the lobby.

But when they arrived back at the safe house and Meara went straight to the kitchen to grab a stash of graham crackers, chocolate, and marshmallows, he studied her in surprise.

"What are you doing, Meara?" Finn figured as late as it was and as little sleep as they'd had, she'd want to return to bed. Like he did. He hadn't planned to do anything more than hold her close, thank the merciful heavens that she and Anna were safe for the time being, and sleep.

He had every intention of questioning Meara about the SEALs' last mission the next morning after they'd both had sufficient sleep. He wanted to learn how she had become involved and what exactly she'd done that none of them had known of.

"I'm having some more s'mores," Meara said matter-of-factly and pulled open the door to the deck. "You and Bjornolf and Anna worried me sick. I need some chocolate to help me get back to sleep." She sounded drained by the experience as she left the house and walked down the wooden stairs to the beach.

Finn stared after her for a moment, then shook his head and followed her. There was no figuring women—especially *this* woman.

He'd never paid much attention to a woman walking on a beach before, but when he reached the sand and saw the way Meara was trying to navigate through the sifting particles and the way her hips were swaying, he found himself mesmerized. She soon broke the spell when she turned and motioned to the fire pit.

"Why don't you start the fire? I'll hold on to the fixings." She possessively held the packages to her breast, and he noted again how beautiful but tired she looked.

He wasn't used to a woman giving him orders, and he would have preferred that she tell him to carry her off to bed, rather than start a fire and roast more marshmallows. But he silently did what she'd requested.

His thoughts slipped to what Bjornolf had said

concerning how she'd saved their lives, and despite the hour, Finn couldn't wait for morning to have this discussion. If they'd gone to bed, that would have been another story. He started the fire, then glanced over at Meara as she settled on the bench, quietly observing the ocean, her expression one of peace, tendrils of dark curls tickling her cheeks in the cool breeze.

She looked at home on the beach with the pine trees behind her rising on the hillside and stretching ponderously over the house. When he'd seen her in the redwoods of California, he'd thought she was at home there as well. He realized then that she was the kind of woman who suited the great outdoors, no matter what the environment. Well, maybe not the desert. He couldn't see her living there.

Unless it was a desert island. And he was shipwrecked on it with her. But there wouldn't be any s'mores to share with her then. Oysters could work wonders, though.

He sighed. His need to know what had happened during their last mission nagged at him, and he wanted to ask her what she'd done to save Hunter and the rest of the men. Yet for an instant, he didn't want to spoil the moment. He had to ask her, though.

He cleared his throat, drawing her attention. "Meara, Bjornolf said you saved our lives on our last mission."

Her eyes widened, and then she smiled a little. "How'd he know I made my special homemade soup for the rest of the guys after Hunter and the others were injured? Did you know that family recipe had been passed down for generations? It works, though. It truly helps to encourage healing."

Soup?

Finn reached for the bag of marshmallows and skewered a couple. "I thought he meant something more... directly related to the mission."

"Like what?" She snorted. "I didn't even know where you were going to be." She frowned. "What did Bjornolf say I did?"

"He said you saved us. That we would have all been dead if it hadn't been for you."

Meara looked back out to sea. "He's making it up."

Finn thought he saw a niggling worry line etched across her forehead. Maybe from trying to recall something that might have happened. Had she done something inadvertently and didn't even realize what she'd done?

"Maybe it seemed insignificant to you at the time, but it was really important. Can you remember anything to do with that last mission?" Finn asked.

"Yeah. I fought with Hunter. I was going out with this guy..."

Finn couldn't help that he was scowling. What did he care about some guy she was dating?

She frantically waved at the marshmallows. "Hey! You're burning them!"

"Hell." He shook them off the stick into the sand, the marshmallows covered in flames and the white quickly turning black. Concentrating on the task at hand, he poked two fresh marshmallows on the stick.

"Hunter didn't care for the guy," Meara continued.

Finn didn't want to hear this. He was certain he wouldn't have cared for the guy either, no matter who he was. But what did that have to do with their mission? Since she seemed focused on that instead of with his real question, he might as well let her get it out of her system first. "Was he wolf or human?"

"Wolf."

Finn tried to appear neutral, despite not liking that she was seeing wolves, assuming she wouldn't want to talk about it with him if he seemed to feel the same way as Hunter.

She concentrated on the marshmallows. "Don't burn them this time."

"Why didn't Hunter like this guy?" Hunter's instincts had always been good about keeping Meara from making a mistake so Finn trusted Hunter's judgment over hers. He wondered if she actively sought problem males just to provoke Hunter.

"Here, let me have the marshmallows. Your mind is elsewhere." She pulled off the melted ones and let him have them. "Next two are mine." She poked the marshmallows on the stick, her fingers inadvertently sliding down the length, and he thought of how she had wanted to put her hand on him earlier that evening and stroke him like he'd stroked her.

He closed his eyes and shook the notion loose, then looked back at her and prompted, "He didn't like this guy you wanted to date. Why?"

"He never liked any of the guys I wanted to see, Finn. *Period*. None of them were good enough for me, so he said."

"He was right, too, wasn't he?"

She grunted and sandwiched the chocolate and the gooey marshmallow between the graham crackers. "He wouldn't like you seeing me in that way either, you know."

Finn snorted. "We're not talking about me. Why did Hunter not like this guy in particular?"

"It was right when you were going on your last mission. Hunter was adamant that I not see the man while he was away. He was afraid something might happen between us, and he wouldn't be able to stop it before it was too late. I wasn't planning on mating the guy, just dating him.

"It wouldn't have mattered who he was, at least I don't believe so. All he had to be was an unmated alpha male and that was it. Hunter…" She sucked the marshmallow and chocolate off her fingers, one after another. "…had an uncanny ability to know when someone wasn't right for me. Or at least he thought he had. I really think he was wrong about this guy. That's all."

Finn stared at the way she sucked her fingers, wanting to be the one licking them, and then at her lips, thinking of how he'd kissed her in the sand and wanting to repeat the performance.

But damn it, he was not a moonstruck teen. And he had to get his raging testosterone under control. "What happened between you and the guy?"

"Nothing. He left. I figured that Hunter must have had words with him, and I never heard from him again."

All right. Finn could see Hunter doing that. And anyone who wasn't alpha enough would have backed down, tucked tail, and left. "What happened between you and Bjornolf at Anna's hotel?"

"What do you mean?"

Her question struck Finn as odd. Why not say nothing had happened? *If* nothing had occurred between them.

She was watching Finn with an alpha's challenging

gaze, but he swore her armor had slipped when he heard the nearly imperceptible hitch in her voice and observed the way she stood a little straighter, stiffening her back, the way her eyes were wide with feigned innocence, as if she was hiding a guilty conscience.

Hell. "He was seated in a booth in the lounge, drinking a beer and waiting for you. Why?"

Meara looked genuinely surprised. "He said he didn't drink."

Taken aback by her response, Finn paused. "He said he lied," he growled. And that was *not* what Finn was concerned about.

Her lips were parted in a way that offered an invitation to a kiss—at least to his way of thinking. Then she smiled a little. Finn frowned at her.

She shrugged. "I thought he'd left through the lounge and was headed outside to his vehicle. I was going to look through a window and would have gotten his license-plate number and then shared it with you. I never expected him to be waiting for me in the lounge. He had to have known you and Anna would come soon for me. I don't know what kind of a game he was playing."

"He stuck his hand in your pocket and felt you up." He couldn't help still being irritated by Bjornolf's earlier action.

"He put a bug in there," she countered, her face reddening slightly.

"You felt his hand on your ass, Meara." He couldn't help the frustration he felt at Bjornolf's luring her toward the lounge and her plan to follow him blindly into the dark recesses.

Would she have had a drink with Bjornolf, if Finn

hadn't arrived as soon as he did? A couple of drinks? Would she have left with him if he had promised to keep her safe?

"Well?" Finn challenged, wanting to know what the hell she'd been thinking. She was just like Hunter had said she was—impulsive and putting herself in danger when it wasn't warranted.

"He kissed me, too, damn it! So what?" Meara froze after the words spilled from her lips.

Chapter 11

FINN STARED AT MEARA IN DISBELIEF, AND HE INSTANTLY wanted to pummel Bjornolf.

"Bjornolf kissing me didn't mean anything," Meara said to Finn, her face red, as she slumped on the bench, grabbed a stick, and began poking it in the sand. "Hell, Finn. I wasn't going to tell you that part."

"That he kissed you? Why the hell not?" He couldn't help how angry he felt, partly because she hadn't planned to tell him what had happened between her and Bjornolf. She'd only blurted the truth because Finn had ticked her off. Was that what Anna had known and had wanted to warn him about?

He still couldn't believe the bastard had actually kissed Meara. When? No wonder the man had been so damned smug when Finn had seen him in the lounge. First, Bjornolf had felt her up and she didn't do anything to indicate she didn't like it, and then she'd let him kiss her?

"I figured you might want to kill him," she said, her voice soft with regret.

"And you wanted to keep him alive."

"No!" Her face blossomed with color anew. "I mean, of course I didn't want you to kill him. I didn't kiss him back. I was shocked. That's all."

"Shocked." When did a woman like Meara not react to such an intrusion of her space? If she secretly wanted it! *Damn it*. "When in the hell did he kiss you?"

She poked the stick deeper into the sand. "In the lobby."

"*When?*" he asked more gruffly.

"When you were rescuing Anna!"

He unclenched his fists. He should have left her here at the safe house—safe from the likes of someone like Bjornolf. "And then you went to meet him in the lounge. Why? To share a drink? Another kiss? Kiss him back this time?"

"You're an ass."

That was the Meara he knew. He smiled a little at that, but then his smile faded. Yeah, he was an ass. If Meara was intrigued with Bjornolf, who was he to say the man wouldn't be right for her? She was *Hunter's* responsibility, and *he* could have dealt with her falling for a deep-cover operative.

Finn settled on the bench next to her and took a deep breath. They didn't speak for what seemed like forever. She kept poking the damn stick into the sand, and he kept stewing over Bjornolf's intentions toward her. Finally he said, "I'm not a romantic, Meara. I don't believe in giving flowers or chocolate or mushy cards or any of that sentimental stuff."

She pointed to the chocolate bars and softly said, "Might not be a date, but I haven't had a nicer outing with a man than I've had with you."

Surprised she'd feel that way, he stared at her for a moment for any indication that she was teasing him, but she seemed sincere.

"I'm talking candy hearts filled with chocolates." He was talking real dating. And he couldn't do it. He just wasn't made that way. It all seemed fake, part of some ritual he didn't believe in. And he wasn't about to fall into that trap.

—◆◆◆—

At first, Meara didn't know where this conversation was going. She assumed he was trying to let her down gently—that he wasn't the mating type. But she hadn't meant to say a thing about Bjornolf kissing her until Finn had riled her. She realized afterward what the matter was. He was jealous!

And that had both surprised and tickled her. She already knew he wasn't the mating type. But she also wanted Finn to know that was okay. That she enjoyed being with him, no matter what the circumstances. And that no matter what macho game Bjornolf was playing with Finn, the operative didn't mean anything to her.

She tried to keep the conversation less serious, more lighthearted. She'd been truly scared that Finn or Anna might have been injured or worse. And her intention had only been to learn more about Bjornolf so she could help Finn discover who he was, not to see more of the man.

She needed quiet time to enjoy the beauty of the beach and ocean, and to unwind before she collapsed in bed so that she wouldn't keep replaying what might have happened if Bjornolf had been one of the bad guys.

What she didn't need was any more discussion about Bjornolf and that stolen kiss.

"Hmm, never thought you'd be the type who would be into flowers and the like. So what *are* you into?" She envisioned a woman reloading a musket for her man during the American Revolution. Someone who was

stout of heart, a real outdoorswoman not bothered by
sharing a snake bake on the beach. Someone probably
like Anna. "A woman who reloads your weapon without
being told to?" Meara asked, when he didn't respond
right away.

Finn didn't say anything for a moment, as if he was
considering that scenario. Then his mouth curved up,
and the skin beneath his eyes crinkled. "My *weapon* is
always loaded."

She hesitated to respond, then getting his double en-
tendre, she felt herself blush and she frowned. "Geez,
Finn. Do you ever think of anything but that? Here I'm
envisioning a woman reloading her husband's musket
during the American Revolution, and you're... well,
you're incorrigible."

He laughed, and she was glad to see him lighten up.
He didn't have to be jealous of Bjornolf, but she figured
telling him that wouldn't have any impact on him. He
had to see for himself.

"It's important that I'm always armed. Comes with
the job," Finn said, trying to put on a serious counte-
nance but failing.

She snorted. "Your dates must think you're loads
of fun."

He stared out at the ocean and appeared serious for
the moment, contemplative even. "I'm not the settling-
down type." He motioned to the water. "This is the only
life for me. It's in the genes. My ancestor was a descen-
dant of Leif Erikson, if Hunter didn't mention it."

"The Viking explorer?"

"Yeah."

"Oh."

Finn glanced at her. "Hunter told us you were strong-willed, and he worried about you. Especially when we were away on missions. He didn't trust the pack to watch over you like he could."

"I suppose he said a lot of things about me," she remarked as she looked out to sea, not liking that Hunter had talked about her to his men behind her back.

"He warned us to stay away from you."

She looked back at Finn. "What?" She couldn't believe Hunter would do that. Then again, she could. Not that she had planned on chasing after any of them.

Finn gave her a decidedly boyish grin that was more charming than anything. "The guys were curious about you, since you're unmated and Hunter's twin sister, and knowing him the way we do."

She just stared at Finn in incredulity. Was that why Hunter had never left her alone with any of the guys during the brief times she'd seen them over the years? Because one of them might have shown some interest in her? Was it for her protection or theirs?

Here she'd thought he was worried she'd learn too much about their secret missions!

But she remembered how the men would mill around in the background as Hunter gave her last-minute instructions that she would listen to only if she agreed with them. The men would watch her, not Hunter, as if waiting to see her reaction. She had always figured they were amused to see him giving his sister orders and not just them. Now she wondered if there was more to it. Maybe they wondered if she'd be as much trouble as Hunter no doubt had told them she would be if they thought of her as a prospective mate.

She growled. Hunter had no right to interfere in her life to that degree.

Then she reconsidered Finn's words: *The guys were curious about you, since you're unmated and Hunter's twin sister.*

The guys. Not just one or two of them. But the guys. And that meant this guy, too—Finn.

She felt her face flush, and she quickly looked back at the ocean. So what did that mean? The guys had been too afraid to check her out? To go behind Hunter's back? She'd thought they were all too alpha and would have stood up to him if the circumstances warranted. Then again, he'd been their team leader, and they did respect him.

She took a deep breath. *SEALs.* The fact that they were friends of Hunters and had been his teammates in the Navy had made them off limits, despite the fact she had been intrigued by them. Who wouldn't have been? Rugged, healthy, muscular, fascinating. And brainy. All were skilled in the operations they had to conduct. All were dedicated to the mission and to each other. Loyalty like that was hard to find. But still, she wouldn't have shown any real interest and caused trouble between Hunter and his men.

She and Finn sat in silence for a long time, listening to the waves crashing on the beach in a lulling, hypnotic way and the sound of crabs scurrying about the sand some distance off. She wasn't used to being at a loss for words, but for once, she really didn't know what to say. And for once, she felt truly uncomfortable being with Finn.

Up until now, she had brushed off any sexual interest he had exhibited toward her as being a matter of wolfish prowess. And since she'd wanted the intimacy as much as he had, she'd assumed he'd needed to satisfy some feral desire, nothing more. That didn't necessarily mean he wanted her. It was just a way of showing how hot he thought he was while taking care of baser instincts. And being a SEAL on top of that? Alpha to the max.

But now? He'd revealed that he truly *had* been interested in her all those years, and that made her feel—*differently*.

That's when the oddest feeling washed over her. Hunter had been saying for years how she was too choosey. That she'd never find the right mate. And that's when she realized it. Deep down, she was afraid of men. Well, not any man, but specifically alpha males. She couldn't take up with a beta because she couldn't see having a mate who wasn't up to the challenge. But she was afraid an alpha would quash her own natural alpha tendencies. She wanted—and feared—an alpha male.

She let out her breath with a heavy sigh and noticed Finn turn his head in her direction.

"What are you thinking?" he asked, his tone gentle, not pushy.

She shook her head. No way would she tell him or anyone else how she felt about alpha males. She'd successfully hidden her feelings all these years—from herself, even, it seemed. No sense in letting anyone else know how she truly felt. Awkwardly uncomfortable, she started to poke the stick into the sand some more, digging until she had a deep, narrow hole. Doing something physical helped her control her unwanted nervousness.

"If Hunter didn't want me around you guys, why did he leave me in your protective custody now?" she asked, figuring her brother hadn't any choice this time.

"He knows any one of us would protect you better than someone who wasn't one of our team. I just happened to be the only one available for the job."

Just happened to be? What about Paul? He could have come for her. Unless he had been busy. Maybe he'd been somewhere more inaccessible so he couldn't get there in time to warn Hunter.

She wanted to know what the guys had really said about her, if they'd bothered to speak about her at all. They'd have to have done it in private, she imagined, when Hunter hadn't been around. He could be annoyingly protective, even when she didn't need or certainly want his protection. He'd broken up more potential dates than she could remember.

She poked her stick even deeper, annoyed at Hunter for messing up what might have been a possible mating in several instances if she'd only been able to go her own course without his interference. Now she had Finn watching her every move and no chance to return to her cabin to manage the rental units until this was over. And then? Hunter would be back.

She glanced over at Finn, expecting him to be watching the ocean again as if he were his ancestor Leif Erikson, looking at his real home in the deep blue sea and wanting to sail away to new lands, when instead he was stuck protecting Meara on the beach. He was actually watching her poke the stick into the hole she had made in the sand. He caught her eye, raised his brows, and gave her the most wickedly evil grin. He clasped his hand over hers and pulled the stick out of the hole.

He held her hand firmly and leaning closer to her, his

whole posture stating that he was in charge. She frowned at him, not knowing what his problem was.

"Hunter didn't say *how* much trouble you could be," he said, and winked. "We ought to go inside now."

Her lips parted in protest as she narrowed her eyes at him. But he just gave her a small crocodile smile back and raised his brows a hair.

Heat filled her whole being when he didn't release her hand. She glanced down at his fingers wrapped around hers, the stick poking at the tip of the hole in the sand.

"I'll follow you up in a minute," he said quietly.

She noticed then that his voice was downright husky with sexual overtones. Her gaze quickly shifted to his jeans. Ohmigod, he was fully aroused. As if he knew what she'd realized, he grinned at her. "Follow you up in a minute?" he asked this time.

Hell, he probably couldn't walk with a boner like that.

Then she wondered what had brought that on? His hand squeezed hers, bringing her attention to the stick in her hand and the hole she'd made in the sand. Her mouth dropped open for a second. Her poking the stick in the hole had given him ideas?

Men were absolutely incorrigible. At least *this* SEAL was.

―――――

Meara would be the death of him, Finn thought glumly as he waited for her to enter the house while he attempted to reign in his raging erection. He'd tried to let her down gently, to explain that he couldn't be the one for her. Yet if he hadn't been a thrill seeker, Meara would have been just the wolf he wouldn't have minded settling down with.

He shook his head at himself and glanced at the dark hillside, wondering if Bjornolf had been watching them. He was sure the lone wolf had been, which was the only reason Finn hadn't given into his more wolfish desires and kissed Meara again on the beach. He couldn't do that when his mission was protecting her, not ravishing her.

After a few minutes, he put out the fire and headed to the stairs, unable to set aside the thought of Bjornolf kissing her in the lobby. The overwhelming question was: why had he done it?

To goad Finn into action? To announce his claim? Or was that just his usual MO with a woman he found attractive? What the hell was Bjornolf trying to say?

Finn ran up the stairs and entered the house, then locked the door behind him.

Meara was still in the bathroom showering when Finn walked down the hall. He breathed in the sweet, tangy fragrance of tangerines, fresh water, and Meara. He paused to take his fill and thought of her soaping up all that silky soft skin of hers. Then, with the utmost difficulty, he finally let go of thinking of her and entered the bedroom. For an instant, he wanted to haul her into his bedroom, the master bedroom suite of the house, and take her to bed. He sighed. Best to leave things the way they were. If he ever took her to *his* bed, trying to keep his distance would be a lost cause. As long as they stayed in one of the guest rooms, it felt as though they were more on equal footing.

He stripped out of everything but his boxers and

climbed under the covers of the guest bed, then waited expectantly for Meara to return to the bedroom. He should have gone right to sleep. He shouldn't have been anticipating wrapping his arms around her and snuggling until they both fell asleep. But no matter how hard he tried to see this as just a mission—protect Hunter's sister at all costs—somehow the demarcation line between what he should be doing and what he wanted to do was blurring.

He'd expected her to be wearing her skimpy pajama shorts set when she walked into the room, but instead, a long terry cloth robe covered her body, and her feet were bare while she towel-dried her hair. She hadn't seen him in the bed as she moved to the chair where he finally noticed her pajamas were set out. She hung the towel over the back of the chair and then began to untie the robe.

She should have known he was here. Smelled him. Even heard his heart beating at an increased rate. But barring that, he should have made an audible sound, cleared his throat, done something to let her know he was in bed already and watching her with feral desire.

Unable to move, he observed her with fascination as she peeled the robe off her shoulders until she was standing naked and dropped the robe onto the chair. She was turned so he could see her profile, the lovely curve of her breast, the peak of a dusky nipple, her hip, her shapely leg. She moved dreamily as if she was already half asleep, lulled by the heat of the shower, as she pulled the skimpy tank top over her head, the rest of her naked still.

She reached for her shorts, but something made her

turn to look at the bed, as if she'd finally realized he might already be there. Her eyes widened and her luscious lips parted, but she didn't say anything. Expecting her to scold him for being so quiet and watching her in silence, he was surprised when her mouth curved up fractionally, her eyes matching her amusement.

"I don't imagine this is what Hunter had in mind when he said he wanted you to watch me."

Finn smiled, and he was certain his wolfish grin looked as needy as he felt.

She slipped on her shorts and sauntered to the bed in a sultry, sexy way. He pulled the covers aside, inviting her to join him—close, and she obliged, her back to him, his body comfortably spooning hers. He should have left well enough alone. Snuggled with her. Enjoyed the heat, the softness, the fragrance that was Meara, yet he couldn't let go of the niggling exasperation he felt over Bjornolf kissing her in the lobby of Anna's hotel. And her letting him.

"Why did he kiss you, Meara?" Finn asked, wrapping her in his arms.

Meara sighed heavily and didn't say anything for the longest time. Finn caressed her shoulder, sweeping her hair aside, and then nuzzled her neck, enjoying her sweet fragrance but wanting to know what Bjornolf's reasoning was, even though he didn't expect Meara to have the answer.

She was barely breathing as she relaxed more deeply against him and then finally said, "Why does any man kiss a woman? He just wants to." She sounded sleepy and… slightly amused.

"He didn't kiss *Anna*." His answer was short and

quick and to the point. And annoyed. No matter how much he tried to keep this unemotional, he couldn't.

He toyed with the thin strap of Meara's pajama top, his fingers caressing her bare skin, itching to push the straps down and feel her creamy breasts in his hands.

"Did you ask her?"

He stopped what he was doing and considered what she'd said. Meara had a point. Maybe that's why Anna thought Bjornolf was handsome. Maybe he'd kissed her first and then Meara later.

Finn didn't say anything in response, but then he released her. She groaned as if wishing she hadn't asked. He pulled away from her, reached over to the bedside table, and grabbed his cell phone. After pushing the autodial for Anna's number, he let out his breath, curbing the urge to pace across the floor while he waited for Anna to answer the blasted phone. It didn't matter that everyone who had any sense should be sleeping.

After what seemed like an eternity, Anna answered, asking, "Finn, what's wrong?" Her voice was half asleep but anxious.

He could hear her getting dressed in the background, drawers slamming, her breath ragged. Not wanting her to think they were in trouble, he quickly asked, "Did Bjornolf kiss you?"

A brief pause followed before she growled, "You called to wake me up for *this*? I thought you were dealing with another assassin. Hell, Finn, what's going on?"

"Forget it." He'd be the laughingstock if she told the rest of the gang why he'd called her in the middle of the night like this. And despite desperately wanting to know the answer to his question, he wished he hadn't phoned her.

He was about to hang up when she hollered, "Wait!" Then her tone softened. "What's this about, Finn?"

"Nothing."

He could hear the mattress creak in her hotel room and assumed she was lying back down.

"No, he didn't kiss me." Anna let out her breath. "But that's not what's bothering you, is it?"

"'Night, Anna."

"You'd better let Hunter know what's going on."

"*Nothing* is going on."

Anna snorted. "Right. Don't tell me you're not hooked on her, Finn. I know you better than that."

"Later. Get some sleep." He shook his head and terminated the call. Then he set the phone back on the bedside table, turned, and pulled Meara back into his arms. "He didn't kiss Anna."

Meara didn't say anything, and for a moment, he thought she'd fallen asleep. But then he figured she couldn't have. She would have fought sleeping to hear if Bjornolf had also kissed Anna.

"So why did he kiss *you*?" Finn asked quietly.

"Because he wanted to see what it would be like?" Meara stiffened. "How would I know? I'm not Bjornolf, and I didn't encourage him, if that's what you're thinking."

"He did it to see if you would kiss him back." At least if Finn had been interested in a woman like Meara, that's the reason *he* would have done so.

"Well, I *didn't* kiss him back. And I wouldn't have, even if I hadn't been so stunned. Not only that, if I hadn't been so shocked, I would have hit him or something."

Somewhat mollified that she hadn't kissed him back, Finn grunted. "Why did you call Hunter instead of me when Bjornolf approached you? Hunter was in Hawaii. What was he supposed to have done?"

"I would have gone to Anna's room to make sure you both were all right, but I didn't know her room number. As for calling you, I didn't have your cell number."

"I had already added it to your address book."

Wide eyed, she turned to look at him. "You did? Where?"

"Where you couldn't fail to miss it."

She grumpily rose from the bed, retrieved her phone from her jeans, and looked at her address book.

The name *SEAL* snagged her attention. When Bjornolf had shaken her up, she'd just punched the number one for Hunter's number, not even reading who else was listed in the name field. She harrumphed. "SEAL," she said, and climbed back into bed.

Finn pulled her back tight against his chest and moved his hand over her tank-top-covered breast, the cotton fabric sliding over the protruding nipple that was already sensitive to his touch. "Once a SEAL, always a SEAL," he whispered against her ear. "We specialize in deep undercover operations."

"Is that a promise or a threat?" she asked just as quietly. The way he was touching her was making her hot with desire. She was glad he seemed to have given up on being angry about Bjornolf kissing her. God, what a mistake it was to have let that slip.

"It depends entirely on what you want," he said.

She smiled and reached back to touch his crotch and stroked his rigid length covered in the cotton boxers.

He ground out, "You are *seriously* asking for trouble."

She laughed and turned around to get a better grip.
But as soon as she smoothed her hand over the length
of him, he ran his hands up her bare thighs, his thumbs
dangerously close to the center of her, gliding over her
skin and setting it afire. His eyes were smoky with lust,
and his mouth curved up decadently. Here she was planning on seducing him, but the male wolf was already
making her wet for him.

She only thought to have sex with him to get him out
of her system so they could sleep the rest of the night
without any further interruption—no emotional com-
mitment, just pure physical sex. But she couldn't with
Finn. Not with the way he caressed her skin so tenderly,
the way he pulled her down for a kiss. His mouth was
gently pressing hers, questing for a response, and when
she gave it to him, when she moved her mouth over
his, intending the same gentle caress, he plundered her
mouth roughly, belying his true feelings as if he had
been holding back the storm, keeping himself in abey-
ance. Until she responded. Once she showed she was
willing, that she wanted this as much as he did, he pulled
out all the stops.

His hands slid up her waist underneath her top, cupping her breasts as he tongued her mouth, his thumbs
rasping over her nipples, her core aching as she perched
over his erection. She was torn between wanting him
inside her and wishing consummated sex didn't mean a
mating between the werewolf kind. Although she wondered what being mated to him would be like.

She ran her hand over his hair, telling herself there
was no likelihood of that, so she'd just better damn well

get that notion out of her head and enjoy him like he was enjoying her. And hope that someday some alpha male would be as good at pleasuring her as Finn was. Hell, all he had to do was look askance, raise a brow a little, and give her one of his devilish grins, and she was ready to roll onto her back and beg him to ravish her.

As if he knew just what she'd been thinking, he lifted her by the waist and set her aside, at first making her think he'd had second thoughts. But he quickly pulled off her top and slid her shorts off, making her feel vulnerable. A whole lot naked. And a little wary. Worried he might be thinking of taking it too far.

But he only smiled in that arrogant way of his and then pressed himself against her, kissing and rubbing his length against her thigh, his hands deftly feeling her breasts, his mouth nuzzling her throat, and she arched her hips in response. God, how she wanted him inside!

He grumbled something about how hard she was making him. He slipped his fingers into her tight sheath, smiled when he discovered just how wet she was, and began to stroke her until she was ready to burst into flames with pleasure and only feeling slightly guilty that she'd forgotten about pleasuring him. Until he made a final thrust against her hip and she felt his shorts wet against her skin. She smiled as he thrust a couple more times, and then he made a slightly disgruntled sound.

"We'll have to do a wash pretty soon," she said, cupping his buttocks through the boxers.

He grunted, then kissed her forehead and slid off her, finally heading down the hall to the bathroom. She sighed, then grabbed her pajama short set and headed for the master bedroom and bath to wash up.

Finn's assignment to watch over her was going to kill her desire for anyone else, if they didn't quit letting the situation get out of control.

After she washed up and pulled on her shorts set, she turned and nearly had a heart attack. Finn was standing in the entryway wearing a fresh set of boxers, brows raised and arms folded across his muscular chest, and watching her grimly. "Ready to sleep?"

Something about his posture made her think he believed she was leaving him to sleep in the master bedroom because they couldn't keep their hands off each other. But she'd thought maybe this was beginning to mean something to him, and he wanted her with him in bed—not just so he could watch her and keep her safe from assassins and the like.

She stalked past him and cast over her shoulder, "I wasn't intending to sleep in the master bedroom, you know."

"Good, because I wasn't planning on letting you." But his eyes and expression were darker than usual.

This time she grunted back at him. And he laughed!

Chapter 12

MEARA WASN'T SURE WHAT WOKE HER IN THE MIDDLE of the night while she slept with Finn in the guest bedroom, but she somehow managed to extricate herself from his arms without waking him—worn-out wolf—and got up to check out the house. She slipped her rifle out from under the bed and left the room. The house was dark and quiet except for the wind ruffling the tree branches and the waves striking the rocks and beach as her bare feet padded along the carpeted floor.

Yet something had woken—*her phone*. In the bathroom. She'd been so tired that she must have left her clothes in there when she'd taken her shower earlier. Her phone was in her jeans pocket underneath the rest of her things, lying on one corner of the bathroom counter.

She hurried to answer before whoever it was hung up. Just as she reached into her jeans pocket, the phone jingle quit. Typical. But when she pulled the phone out, she found the missed call was from Chris, the pack subleader. She worried something had gone wrong with Rourke, since Chris was tasked with baby-sitting him and would have to let her know if that was the case.

She pushed the button to redial Chris's number. As soon as he answered, she asked, "Chris, is Rourke all right?"

For a moment, Chris didn't say anything, and she was afraid something else was wrong and her question had thrown him.

"No," he said in a grouchy way, reminding her how much he didn't like Hunter having given him the baby-sitting job, even though it showed how much he trusted Chris.

"What's wrong?" Now *she* was grumpy and tired, and she didn't appreciate being woken up for nothing.

Chris's attitude toward Rourke had irritated her, once she'd gotten over the fact that Hunter had added Rourke to the pack by accident. If she could accept Rourke, everybody in the pack should. He was a nice enough guy, and he tried damned hard to fit in, readily acknowledging that he was a werewolf once the deed had been done. At least as far as she'd seen.

"Did that Cyn Iverson get in touch with you?"

She stared at the bathroom mirror, barely seeing her disheveled appearance because her mind was trying to sort out what Chris was saying. "Cyn Iverson?" she finally asked. Instantly, she thought of the figure by the pine tree at the hotel where Anna was staying.

"Yeah, he said he'd been out of the country on a job and had just gotten back in, and he wanted to hook up with you. Once he learned you'd left California, he traced the pack here. I told him you were staying somewhere but didn't know the exact address. He said he'd find you."

She felt a slight chill. "How?"

"How should I know? I thought maybe you'd kept in touch with him. I have no idea who you're seeing, or whether Hunter approves or not."

She parted her lips, then closed them. Okay, so Chris was still irritated about her having gone out to dinner with Cyn. Hunter had chewed Chris out royally for letting her get away from him during her shopping trip to

Sacramento. She hadn't apologized to Chris about it, either. Why should she have? She had every right to eat out with Cyn, and she wasn't the one who had forced Chris to get hung up in a video store, perusing the merchandise.

"I'm worried about you," Chris finally said, and this time her jaw dropped. "Hell," he continued, "I just wanted to warn you that the guy is looking for you and—"

"Did you tell Hunter?"

"No. I figured you could. I didn't tell the guy where you were. Hell, I don't know where you are."

"In a safe house. And perfectly safe. Thanks for telling me." Now she felt bad because even though she'd speculated that Chris had a secret affection for her, he'd always acted annoyed with her because she was looking for a mate and not giving him the time of day. If he'd teased her about it, maybe, or handled it some other way, his behavior might not have irritated her so much. "Finn will keep me safe."

Dead silence.

Was that what was eating at Chris? That he hadn't gotten the job of protecting her? That an outsider like Finn, a good and loyal friend of Hunter's, would get the job instead of a trusted sub-leader within the pack?

She sighed. "You've got your hands full, Chris. You're doing a great job."

"Baby-sitting Rourke, sure." The bitterness was back.

Yeah, he was irritated all right. He had to watch over Rourke instead of protecting her.

She was going to say she'd tell Finn that the guy she had wanted to see was trying to locate her, but she thought better of it. She knew Finn would want to know all about this man, and there wasn't anything to say about him. Besides, now that Hunter was no longer in the Navy, maybe he wouldn't be so against her seeing the guy. Finn certainly wasn't interested in her long-term. And all in all, she wanted a mate.

"I'm going back to bed. 'Night, Chris."

"Meara…"

His hesitation told her he wanted to say something more. She assumed he wanted to smooth things over between them, but she wasn't interested in him as a prospective mate. Never had been and never would be.

"'Night," he finally said, sounding resigned. And hung up.

She'd be glad when Hunter returned home to continue mentoring Rourke. She hoped her brother didn't plan on leaving Chris with the job because he'd be impossible to live with.

With that thought, she grabbed her clothes from the bathroom counter and wondered if Cyn had taken a room at the hotel where Anna was. It had been late, and the cabin resort would still have been an hour away. Besides, Meara would have been in bed by then. Seeing Finn with her had stopped Cyn from approaching her. She'd just bet he called the pack sub-leaders, or at least one of them, to learn if she was mated before he wasted his effort on trying to see her further.

Since Cyn was still trying to locate her, Chris must have said that Finn was staying with her to keep her out of trouble, not that he was a potential mate.

Maybe she still could see if Cyn might be her kind of wolf.

⁓⁓⁓

Meara sure as hell knew how to make him hard in a hurry, Finn thought. He had finally managed to sleep a few hours but woke wanting her again. She couldn't know how much he'd fought the desire to haul her into his bed in the master bedroom the night before when he'd found her in the bathroom freshening up. If she'd thought to sleep in his bed, away from him, she'd have never managed it.

Daylight was dawning as he breathed in her sweet fragrance and then frowned to smell the aroma of coffee brewing in the kitchen. That's what had awakened him. As light a sleeper as he was, he was fairly certain he would have noticed if the sultry siren still wrapped in his arms had awakened and left to make the coffee, even for a moment.

Intent on ensuring that the person who'd started the coffee was one of their operatives and not someone dangerous—although he couldn't imagine anyone wanting to do them harm who would brew coffee first—Finn slipped out from under Meara, trying not to disturb her slumber. He grabbed his gun off the bedside table and moved down the hall in stealth mode.

Upon reaching the dining area, he glimpsed Bjornolf watching out the back porch window, studying the ocean as he waited for the coffee to finish brewing. Still angered about the man kissing Meara without her permission and now breaking into the safe house without permission, Finn stormed toward Bjornolf.

He moved so quickly and silently, like a stealthy SEAL and a wolf combined, that he caught the intruder off guard. Bjornolf turned, as if suddenly aware of Finn's approach. But Bjornolf reacted too late.

Finn's fist smacked him in the jaw, throwing the startled deep-cover operative off balance, and he went down.

Sitting on his butt on the tile floor, his back resting against a kitchen cabinet, Bjornolf rubbed his reddening jaw and stared up at Finn. "What the hell was that for?"

"You know what the hell that was for." Finn set his gun on the kitchen counter and poured himself a mug of coffee.

Realization apparently dawning, Bjornolf's mouth curved up some. "She didn't kiss me back, if that's what you're pissed off about. But I didn't think she'd tell you about it."

Bjornolf's gaze shifted to the dining room, and Finn turned to see Meara observing the two of them, slack jawed.

She wore only that skimpy damned pajama shorts set, which was fine for Finn's eye, but not for Bjornolf's.

"Want some coffee?" Finn asked Meara, pulling another mug from the cupboard. He wanted to hustle her back to the bedroom to get dressed, but he figured if he made a fuss about it, he would draw Meara's ire and no doubt earn Bjornolf's amusement.

"Why is Bjornolf here?" she asked, her voice almost inaudible, making him suspect that she had just walked in and hadn't seen him hit Bjornolf—or even realized Bjornolf was here at first.

"Apparently, he decided to come and make us some early-morning coffee." Finn cast Bjornolf an irritated look.

Frowning, she asked, "Why is he sitting on the floor?"

Finn glanced down at him, and Bjornolf grinned at her as he rose to his feet, rubbing his jaw again. "Finn packs quite a punch. Seems you told him I kissed you last night in the lobby, and he was defending your honor."

"He hit you?" She gave Finn a severe look, then set his phone on the counter and turned her attention back to Bjornolf. "Finn didn't need to. My honor is quite intact." Motioning to Finn's phone, she said to him, "Anna called and said Paul had arrived safely last night. I thought you might want to know that."

Glad that Paul and Anna could watch each other's backs, Finn said, "Good." He poured Meara a cup of coffee, although he still wanted her to return to the bedroom and put more clothes on. But when he handed the mug to her, she shook her head and marched past him.

"Give it to Bjornolf. I'll drink some green tea, if they've got any."

Finn silently handed Bjornolf the second cup of coffee, which he accepted with a polite nod.

Meara pulled out a box of green tea flavored with mandarin oranges. "We're all on the same side so I expect you both to play nice." She started a kettle of water and turned to Bjornolf. "But you really should have been more careful when you came here. You should have knocked on the front door or something first. You could have been shot sneaking into the house. At least I assume that's what you did."

"No place around here to get a decent cup of coffee." Bjornolf smiled at her. "As to my getting injured? Finn's too good at his job. He would have known it was just me."

She eyed Finn, but he didn't make a comment. Meara was right, he thought. He might have shot Bjornolf, but he had picked up Bjornolf's scent as he'd drawn closer to the kitchen. Then again, the way he was feeling about Bjornolf kissing Meara, he still might have shot him, just on principle. He smiled at the thought, and Bjornolf gave him a hint of a knowing smile in return.

Meara poured the hot water in a teacup, dipped the bag a few times, then tossed it in the trash and headed out of the kitchen without another word to them.

"Truce?" Bjornolf asked Finn before she disappeared down the hall.

Finn grunted in response.

Bjornolf eyed Meara with intrigue. When he caught Finn's look, he raised his free hand in surrender but then said, "I'll get her permission next time."

"There won't be a next time."

"Fat chance of that, Finn."

Finn's fist shot out so quickly that Bjornolf didn't expect it this time, either. As soon as Finn's fist connected with the man's eye, Bjornolf dropped his coffee mug on the tile floor, breaking it and splattering the remaining coffee at his feet before he hit the counter with his backside. And grinned.

"Hell, no one told me you were a professional boxer."

"You didn't uncover that when you were checking up on us?" Finn asked, sipping his coffee. He wasn't a professional boxer, but he'd had the training, which came in handy for situations just like this.

*

Meara finished dressing in a pair of khaki pants and an emerald-green tank top, leaving her feet bare. She slumped in a chair in the bedroom after hearing the sound of a mug breaking on the kitchen floor. She suspected Finn had socked Bjornolf again after telling him that next time he'd need to get permission before he kissed her. She should have objected to Finn's treatment of Bjornolf. After all, Bjornolf hadn't really done anything to warrant getting another fist in his face, or at least she figured that's where Finn had aimed. Bjornolf did say he'd ask next time.

And she'd say no. He was handsome and sexy as all get out but way too smooth a talker for her. From past experience, she didn't trust the type. On the other hand, Bjornolf had taken the punch good-humoredly the first time. Maybe he wasn't such a bad sort after all.

She took another sip of her hot tea. Either Finn thought he was taking her brother's place in making sure someone who wasn't right for her didn't take advantage of her, or he was more than jealous of Bjornolf's attentions toward her. Taking great satisfaction in the notion that he was jealous, she smiled.

She ought to let them deal with this on their own, but it was all about her, and she didn't want them fighting each other over nothing. Especially since she knew neither was interested in settling down with a mate. And she was afraid that this time Bjornolf would be quite angry if Finn hit him again.

She sighed and set her teacup on the dresser, then headed back down the hall. She intended to get them both ice packs to help reduce the bruising and swelling that she sure would have resulted. Finn's hand had to hurt, and Bjornolf's face, too.

But what she found surprised her. Both men were sitting in lounge chairs on the back deck, watching the ocean and drinking mugs of coffee, neither talking, just enjoying the view. Well, she guessed they didn't need her to help them sort out their differences.

Good. It was best she stay out of it.

She was about to return to the bedroom to get her tea-cup and fix some more tea when she heard someone in the garage. Before she could warn Finn or Bjornolf to check it out, the door flung open, and she let out a squawk.

Finn was the first one barging into the kitchen from the deck with gun drawn to protect her. Bjornolf raced in on Finn's heels, armed in the same manner.

"Paul, hell," Finn exclaimed. "You should have warned me you were on your way over here from Anna's hotel."

"Sorry, Paul," Meara said, studying the blond-bearded man, whose brown eyes were focused on her. He was as tall as Bjornolf and Finn, but he was thinner, wirier, less muscled. "I didn't recognize you wearing a beard, and you scared me when you, barged in so suddenly."

Paul shook his head. "Sorry, Meara. I hadn't meant to frighten you."

Heart still palpitating, Meara sat on a kitchen bar stool and hid her shaking hands in her lap. She had been sure the man was another assassin out to get her and Finn. "No problem."

Paul turned to scowl at Finn. "Hunter said hands off, damn it, Finn. *You* can watch Anna's back in the future. I'll stay with Meara and watch hers from now on."

Meara's mouth dropped open. She couldn't believe what she was hearing. She'd thought Paul had word that an assassin's attack was imminent. But she'd never have thought he'd be worried about Finn's intentions toward her.

"You don't have to worry about Finn," she said so-berly. "Hunter's got him shaking in his combat boots. He won't take advantage of me." At least not if she didn't approve first. But as far as wanting a mating, no chance at that. She cast a glance in Bjornolf's direction.

He held his hands up in surrender, his eye and jaw discoloring. "I'm keeping out of this one. Finn's all yours, Paul."

Finn was looking amused about Meara's comment, though. She was sure no one had ever described him as shaking in his combat boots.

Finn shook his head at Paul. "What did Anna say to get you all riled up?"

"Enough." Paul's eyes turned stormy, and his lips thinned with anger as he regarded Finn with hostility. He was wearing blue jeans and a Hawaiian shirt with eye-hurting pink palm trees and green flamingoes, which didn't make him look as lethal as she knew he could be.

She wondered where he'd been staying before he'd arrived on the coast. She didn't want to ask him what Anna had said about her and Finn in case Anna had seen what they had been doing on the beach before she'd joined them.

But what she really wanted to know was why Anna was watching out for Meara's welfare. Trying to make brownie points with Hunter? Or was Anna more interested in Finn than Meara had thought and wanted to get everyone worked up? Whatever her reasoning, she'd stirred up a hornet's nest.

It also made her wonder about Paul's motivation. Was he truly jealous that Finn had gone beyond the call of duty when Paul himself hadn't had a chance? Or was Paul more concerned that he hadn't stepped in soon enough on Hunter's behalf?

"Hunter called me and said you'd left his sister alone,

and then this guy…" Paul jerked his thumb at Bjornolf, "…could have taken advantage of her. But Anna said you've also been overstepping your boundaries with Meara and that needs to be stopped, or she'll tell Hunter."

Meara frowned, not liking that Anna had threatened such a thing. That made her think Anna secretly did have a fondness for Finn that he might not even be aware of.

At that, Finn gave Paul a disgruntled look. "For everyone's information, Meara's a big girl and can make her own decisions."

"Hallelujah," Meara said. "Someone finally recognizes that."

"Did you ask Hunter for permission?" Paul persisted as if he hadn't heard what Finn had said.

"I don't need permission," Finn continued. "Only Meara's."

"That's not what Hunter says."

"He's changed his mind."

Ha! When the hell had that happened? Finn ought to know he'd get caught in the lie.

Paul's eyes narrowed with suspicion. "You're mating her?"

Meara could have laughed at the shocked expression on Finn's face. She gave him a moment to allow him to backpedal, but when he still didn't respond, she figured she'd put him out of his misery and take control of the situation. Like an alpha female would. "No, he's not mating me. I wouldn't have him. Or you, or Bjornolf, either. Allan, now he's a different story."

Not Allan either, but since he had been wounded, wasn't here, and couldn't defend himself, he sounded like the perfect scapegoat.

She didn't give anyone the chance to respond to her statement, figuring they were all too surprised. Allan was the least likely to catch her attention because he reminded her of a gruff bear at times, rather than a wolf. But if they told him that she thought he was an acceptable mate, he might show up unexpectedly on her doorstep looking to date her. That wouldn't do. Before anyone could say anything, she turned on her heel and stalked toward the back door leading out to the deck. Once outside, she ran down the wooden stairs and then walked across the warming sand, her toes squishing through the soft sifting grains.

A couple of boats motored past, and she had the greatest urge to swim. Well, actually, shift.

She *really* wanted to shift, which made her feel so attuned to nature, to the wilderness, to her wild side. She glanced at the woods surrounding the cliff and made the decision right then and there. If she ran into any assassin, she'd take care of the menace on her own.

She could hear Paul still arguing with Finn inside the house, but she couldn't make out what they were saying. Bjornolf had turned to watch her out the window. The way his eyes widened and he reached for the door handle, she knew he realized she was up to something. And he planned to stop her. Tired of everyone controlling her movements, she stalked up the hillside to where the terrain and trees hid her from the bay window's view.

Then she stripped out of her clothes—feeling free and natural and gloriously naked—and left her clothes in a pile under a tree. With heat filling every cell, a nice quick stretch, and a quick blurring of forms, she shifted.

The door opened, slamming against the wall, and

then frantic footfalls raced down the steps. They were too late.

~~~

"Hell, Meara!" Finn shouted, ahead of the pack as he raced down the stairs.

"She's shifting," Bjornolf said. "I saw the way she looked back at the house to make sure none of us was observing her. When she saw me watching her, she headed for the hill north of the house and out of sight."

"There!" Finn pointed at her clothes next to a pine and began stripping off his clothes. When Paul began to yank off his shirt, Finn shook his head. "Just me. We can't have a whole pack of wolves running through the area."

"Then I'll go after her," Paul said brusquely.

Ignoring him, Finn shifted, welcoming the warmth of the fur covering his bare skin and the length of the four legs that would propel him through the forest and take him to her. He sniffed the air with his long snout and breathed in her scent, adrenaline racing through his blood as the urge to hunt compelled him to climb the steep hill and bolt into the woods.

"You were saying?" Bjornolf said to Paul, sarcasm in his voice.

"Damn it, Finn," Paul said. "You bring her straight back here!"

"Are you going to tell Hunter what Finn said?" Bjornolf asked.

Finn wondered what Paul *would* do.

Paul growled. "Why don't you just crawl back under the rock where you came from?"

Bjornolf laughed, and in his wolf form, Finn smiled.

Meara wanted to run miles away—just for the fun of it. Not because she wanted to run away from the men or cause trouble. Running was in their wolf blood. She loved stretching her legs, exercising, smelling the smells, and collecting them in her wolf fur and taking them back to the den, so to speak, to relive the memories when she returned to the human-built home. The freedom she felt was so part of being a wolf.

She often ran when she felt like it, but especially when she felt stressed, tense, or confined. She really hated all this spy stuff and having to stay out of an assassin's sights, although she wondered if the assassins they had already killed had been enough of a warning to the others that she and Finn weren't easy targets and no one else would bother them.

At least that's what she hoped.

But then she heard him—a wolf tracking her. No, two. One to her flank and one from behind. She'd never seen Hunter's team members in their wolf coats, except for Finn back at her house, and not Bjornolf either, so she wouldn't recognize them on sight unless one was Finn. And she wasn't facing the wind the right way to catch their scents, but they would be getting a fill of hers.

She halfway assumed they would be Paul and Finn. Bjornolf was too cocky to stoop so low as to chase her down.

But when the first of the wolves suddenly shot out from behind some trees, she darted away to avoid being tackled. He was larger than she thought any of the men might be, a dark gray with barely any markings. Just a little bit of black fur over his eyes to make him appear as though he were frowning. Maybe he was.

Probably he was.

But he wasn't Finn. The worst of it was that his legs were much longer than hers, and he ran faster so that even though she had dodged out of his path, he was now following her and quickly catching up. And then he lunged. She sensed, rather than saw, that he would jump to catch her from behind, and he did. The weight of his body and the violent impact effectively brought her down, and she yipped in surprise.

But the way he growled at her in a sinister manner that made her suspect he wasn't one of the good guys.

She tried to get out from under the wolf, but she couldn't move an inch with his weight pressing her to the pine-needle floor.

She feared he'd bite her in the spine to kill her, but a growling from behind them warned that another wolf was approaching in a hurry. Before the one on her back could move, the other jumped. She felt the impact of his mass striking the wolf pinning her down and causing the additional body weight to crash into her, too. Buried under the two wolves, she yelped again.

The newly arrived wolf's teeth clashed with those of the wolf on top of her as he lay on his side, squishing her. But he couldn't move away, either, as the new-comer viciously attacked, tooth enamel clashing against tooth enamel, throats growling, and the heavy smell of testosterone in the air as the two wolves tangled.

The term "top dog" came to mind, even though that was an insult to their wolf kind. The one on top did have the advantage, and he wasn't giving it up. The one

beneath him struggled to get free, all the while fighting for his life, his mouth wide open, teeth bared as he
fought the one on top. Attempting to keep the attacking
wolf's teeth from sinking into his neck, he was effectively keeping Meara pinned in place. His struggles and
massive weight pressed against her painfully bruised
her, and she could barely suck in air.

As much as she hated being confined beneath a
couple of roughhousing wolves with no way to help or
retaliate or run, she tried to calm her panic and concen-
trate on any move between the two wolves that would
indicate she had a little wiggle room to free herself.

The wolf on top of her made a momentous effort to
ditch the attacking wolf, and the increased pressure of
his massive body against her made her yelp again.

That made the one on top growl more deeply and tear
into the other even more fiercely. Despite the noise they
were making, she heard two more wolves racing across
the ground. Her ear picked up the sound and vibration of
their footfalls where her head was resting against the earth.

With a strangled bark, the one on top of her collapsed,
and she knew the attacking wolf, her avenging wolf had
killed the other one. Once she was able to lift her head
and look, she saw that her protector was Finn. Teeth
sinking into the massive wolf, Finn yanked him away.
Then panting, he leaned over and licked Meara's face
as she struggled to sit up. So much for a nice wilderness
run and the thought that she would kill any assassin that
threatened her on her trek. She had never expected a
wolf to come after her.

The other two wolves finally appeared, and from the
way her savior looked at them, she knew they had to be

Bjornolf and Paul. Finn shifted and stood before her, naked, sweaty, glorious. As a wolf, he was just as striking, but as a man, he was utterly gorgeous.

And from the scowl on his face, he was furious with her. She narrowed her eyes at him. She was sorry for the fight that had ensued, but she wasn't sorry about taking a run to get out of the house for a while.

"Are you all right, Meara?" Finn asked, already crouching beside her, feeling her ribs with his fingertips, and touching gently to keep from hurting her.

But the bruises hurt, and where the wolves had pressed hard against her, her muscles were sore. She winced, and he quickly pulled his fingers away and said with genuine concern, "I'm sorry. The good news is you appear to have no broken ribs." His gaze returned to hers. "He didn't have time to bite you?"

She shook her head, and despite trying to justify her actions to herself, she felt unworthy of Finn's kindness.

Still wearing their wolf coats, Bjornolf and Paul watched her, but then the one directed the other with a nod of his head toward the naked dead man—a heavyset blond with large bones, fair skin, and lifeless amber eyes. The two wolves took hold of his arms with their teeth and dragged him deeper into the woods.

She only hoped that however they disposed of him, their wolf kind wouldn't be held accountable for the man's untimely death.

"Are you ready to return to the beach house? Do you need for me to carry you?" Finn asked.

She stumbled to get to her feet, feeling sore and bruised, but unless she passed out, she wasn't going to make Finn carry her all the way back to the house.

Finn's dark expression was unreadable now, although she surmised he was upset with her. Trying not to look as sheepish as she felt, she headed back to the house, head held high, ears twisting back and forth, as she listened for sounds of the other wolves as they conducted their business with the dead man or of anyone else who might be prowling the woods.

Proudly, she held her tail high like an alpha wolf. She might feel badly for having alarmed everyone, but she wasn't going to skulk back with her tail tucked between her legs like a beta over it. And as reluctant as she was to have to concede her recklessness—although she still felt that dealing with stress by running as a wolf was only natural—she would apologize to Finn and the other men.

She didn't have to look back to see Finn following her. Having shape-shifted again, he quickly joined her, running close beside her as if he were her mate.

He had to know she wasn't planning to tear off for parts unknown. But then again, maybe he was just trying to ensure she was protected in case another wolf showed up with deadly intent.

When they finally reached where they'd ditched their clothes, Finn offered to help Meara dress. At first, she was reluctant, but then feeling bad again about running off, she acquiesced. When she was dressed, she waited for him to dress, and then he took her by the hand as if they were on their first date and walked her across the sand to the stairs leading to the beach house's deck.

"Are you all right, Meara?" Finn asked tenderly.

She nodded, and then he took her inside, making her wait in the kitchen where she took a seat on one of the bar stools. He hurried through the house, checking it, she surmised, for anyone who might have slipped in when they were all out running as wolves.

When he came back and stood before her, she looked up at his tender gaze and said, "I'm so sorry. I—"

"Don't be, Meara." He kissed the top of her head and rested his hands on her shoulders. "Why should you be sorry? Hell, Paul and I were fighting with each other like a couple of damned teens instead of watching the area for any sign of an assassin."

"But—"

"You drew him out, distracting him, just so I could get the advantage."

She rolled her eyes. "You can't be serious. Hunter would have been furious with me."

Finn touched her cheek with a gentle caress. "I'm not your brother." He pulled her from the bar stool and, with his hand wrapped around hers, guided her to the master bedroom.

"What...?"

"A soak will do you a world of good for the sore muscles." He smiled at her, and when he took her into the master bathroom with its whirlpool tub built for two, he stretched his arms above his head a little.

In that instant, she wondered if he planned on joining her in the bath. But what if Paul and Bjornolf learned about it? The word would definitely get back to Hunter, and she was certain he wouldn't like it.

Chapter 13

FINN LOCKED THE DOOR TO THE MASTER BATHROOM AND started the bathwater for Meara, but she still wasn't certain what he intended to do.

"Is Anna jealous of you with me?" Meara asked, still bothered by the notion because she'd felt like she was beginning to bond with Anna like she had with her brother's mate, Tessa. She didn't often develop relationships with other women. Partly, she figured, because she'd never had a sister. "Is that why she sent Paul after you?"

"She's afraid of what Hunter will do to me if he learns what I've been doing with his sister." Finn barely concealed a smirk.

"I'm a grown woman," Meara said caustically, hating how much her brother tried to take charge of her life.

Finn helped her out of her tank top and pressed his mouth against her bare shoulder. "As well I know."

"You don't think I really have a thing for Allan, do you?" she asked, hoping Finn didn't think so as he helped her step out of her khakis.

She groaned with the effort as her sore legs and the bruise on her hip reminded her how it felt to be at the bottom of the heap when two alpha male wolves fought.

Finn's expression turned concerned as he gave her a hand into the tub. "No, I'm not worried about you and Allan. He's only the one for you for the moment because he's not here. I'll be right back." Finn gave her a knowing wink, then headed out of the bathroom and closed the door.

She turned on the jets in the tub and noticed a container of lavender bubble bath that must have been left behind by the people who'd had to leave in a hurry so Finn could move her in. She'd never had a bubble bath because they seemed too prissy and pampering. Eyeing it, she finally gave in, seized the bottle, and poured some of the bubble bath into the heated water. Nothing much happened, so she kept pouring until the bubbles began to surface.

"How is she?" Meara heard Paul ask Finn from the living room a couple of minutes later.

"Bruised and sore, but she'll be fine."

"Is she mad at us?"

She couldn't believe that Paul would be worried how she felt about them and not angry with her for causing all the trouble by taking a run on the wolf side. She realized then that they didn't consider her as a civilian but part of the extended family, so to speak. That made her appreciate Hunter's team members all the more.

The water from the jets was stirring up the lavender bubbles something fierce, and the cloud of bubbles was growing and growing and growing. She stared at the massive, building foam and hoped it would stop any second now.

"I'm going to look around the area and make sure the guy didn't have a buddy or two with him," Meara could hear Bjornolf saying. "And take care of the body."

"Good idea," Finn agreed.

The back door closed with a clunk as Bjornolf headed out.

"No, she's not mad at us," Finn assured Paul. "Is Anna all right?"

"Yeah, she's making a sweep of the area in her car." Paul let out a harried sigh. "Hell, man, you know we all were interested in Meara. But none of us would approach her because of how much we respect Hunter."

"I'm protecting her," Finn said, as if defending his honor.

Paul snorted. "Yeah, well, if I hadn't been in southern Florida, *I* would have been protecting that sweet body of hers, not you."

Now Meara knew why Paul had been wearing the palm-tree shirt. She quickly turned off the jets, but the foot-high bubbles were stretching over the tub walls and boiling onto the tile floor. She groaned.

"Watch the place, will you?" Finn said, sounding more like he was giving an order than asking a question.

"What are you going to do?"

"Take Meara some Epsom salt. The brute strained her muscles and bruised her, making her pretty sore."

"Oh."

Epsom salt. Would it mix well with the bubble bath? She really didn't want Finn to see the mountains of lavender she'd created. Footfalls headed down the hall toward the bathroom, and Meara sank under the foam still bubbling to the surface of the warm water, hating that he would see the mess she'd made.

"Finn?" Paul said.

Finn stopped in the hallway halfway to the bedroom. "Yeah?"

"You know Hunter's going to be pissed with all the attention you've been paying her, don't you?"

Finn harrumphed and headed back down the hall toward the master bedroom.

Meara assumed her brother wouldn't like how cozy she and Finn had become when there was no way a mating would follow. But then again, Finn was keeping her safe, and Hunter would have to appreciate that. Nothing else would happen between Finn and her. Once they discovered whoever was ordering the hits on them, he'd go back to his secret missions, and she'd work on bringing alpha males to the cabin rentals again. End of story.

Missing the feel of the jets, she turned them on again, closed her eyes, leaned back against the numbing pulses of water aimed at strategic parts of her back, and purred.

"I love it when you do that," Finn said, closing the bathroom door behind him, a slight smile on his lips as he stared at the huge mound of bubbles half hiding her.

Her eyes shot open. "You love it when I do what?" she asked innocently. She had no idea what he meant.

"Purr." He mixed some Epsom salt into the water. Testing the warmth, he dipped his hand lower until he found her thigh and then ran his fingers not so innocently over her skin, and nodded. "Just the right temperature. But you could probably use some more bubbles."

"You're so funny," she said sarcastically.

He chuckled and stood. She thought he might join her, but he probably wasn't interested in smelling like lavender. The scent had a calming effect, though, and smelled divine.

He handed her a washcloth. "If you need me for anything, just holler. I'll be talking with Paul in the living room, trying to sort out what's going on."

Then after one more longing look at the water—she

wasn't sure if it was because he wished he could see the part of her buried under the bubbles or if he just wished he could soak his muscles in the warm water, too—he left and closed the door behind him.

She figured that Paul had made Finn come to his senses. That Finn realized he shouldn't have been with her like he'd been. She knew Paul was right, but she couldn't help feeling a bone-deep disappointment.

She wasn't sure what she liked so much about Finn. Maybe how after she'd expected him to really be angry with her, he had acted chivalrously instead by taking the blame for not protecting her better. Or how he'd been ashamed that he hadn't been doing what he was supposed to while watching her. Or maybe the way he had come for her last night, worried that she was leaving him and sleeping in another room, and he wasn't having any of it. She still didn't know if he had wanted to make sure she was well protected or to prove to her he could keep his hands off her the rest of the night. Not that he had, but at least they had slept the rest of the evening and hadn't pleasured each other again.

But even so, she had dreamed a fantasy scenario of having him all over again in the middle of the night, only that time he was fully inside her. She sighed. All good things must come to an end, she told herself.

With that disconcerting thought, she closed her eyes and considered what she might have done that would make anyone think she'd somehow managed to save Hunter and his team on their last mission. That could be the root of all the trouble they were in now, she thought as the jets continued to shoot pulsating columns of water at her tender muscles.

All she could think of was Hunter's leaving, and how he wouldn't let her date Cyn Iverson while he was away on that final SEAL mission.

What had Finn said? Only that Bjornolf had told him she'd saved them. But what had she done? She envisioned the day the men had left. Hunter packing his gear. Her glowering at him. Probably having a heated word or two. She knew he was obligated to do the mission, but she hated that he was trying to control her life so much, whether he was off on a mission or home on leave. The man she was supposed to have a date with had been such a gentleman that she couldn't understand Hunter's objection to her seeing him. Cyn hadn't done one thing to make Hunter dislike him so.

Bubbles popped under her chin as she sank deeper into the bathwater, wishing it would stay hot longer. Her cell phone rang, startling her. She turned off the jets and reached over the tub to snag the phone from her pants pocket. Expecting Hunter to be calling her, she yanked the phone out, and without looking to see the caller ID, said, "Hello?"

"It's Rourke."

At first she was so surprised he'd called that she just sat there staring at the phone. Then, regaining her wits, she asked, "Rourke, why are you calling me?"

Since Rourke was newly turned, normally his handler, Chris, would have called her. If *anything* was going on with the pack that she should know about, one of her long-term pack members would have gotten in touch with her. Rourke should have gone through Chris.

"I'm a reporter," he said, sounding annoyed, as if he knew just what she had been thinking.

"So?"

The bathwater was beginning to grow uncomfortably cool, and she was starting to wrinkle, so she had intended to get out and wanted him to get to the point.

Rourke said hotly, "An *investigative* reporter. Nobody in the pack will let me write about anything but the most unimportant drivel. But one of my watchdogs—"

"Watch*dogs*?" Meara said, annoyed.

"Watch-wolves, whatever. I can't believe *lupus garous* have such a hang-up about being referred to in any way as dogs. They are loyal and man's best—"

"Rourke, what do you have to tell me that's so important you didn't wait to tell Chris?"

A heavy pause followed as if Rourke was trying to forget the issue of being referred to as dogs or wolves. Then he said, "Chris mentioned something about a card being left with one of Hunter's SEAL team members, Allan, when he was wounded in Pompano Beach. The card was the Knight of Swords. I asked if Chris had talked to you, and he said he didn't want to bother you with it. Do you know what it means?"

"No, I've never heard of it." Why hadn't Chris wanted to tell *her* about it? Even if she didn't know what it meant, if a sub-leader of the pack knew, then she should have been informed.

"It's a tarot card picturing a young man riding a white horse, sword raised, as he's charging into battle. The card symbolizes taking risk, rushing headlong into danger. It represents an impulsive reaction, without a lot of thought given to the course of action that needs to be taken. The individual is full of passion, nearly blinded with the drive to accomplish the mission without regard for his own safety."

All of a sudden Meara felt as though Rourke was talking about her. "We *are* talking about whoever left the calling card, right?"

"Yes. If the card is turned upside down, it means becoming a loner—taking risk, trying to show one's own independence."

Hell, it still sounded like Rourke was talking about her. "So which way was it turned?"

"When Allan was discovered in his injured state, the card had been inadvertently turned sideways. One of your pack members said that if the man was acting alone, the card was probably turned upside down. If he enlisted a pack, the card was probably turned right side up."

Meara considered the way she took risks, impulsively and determinedly. She'd never endangered anyone but herself. So where was the wrong in that? Immediate action had been needed to protect lives in peril. Well, the lady whose purse had been snatched hadn't been in danger, unless she'd had nitroglycerin pills in her bag for a heart condition. But she might have!

Meara lifted her chin higher. If she was like the Knight of Swords and whoever was in charge of this operation was also, he'd met his match.

Rourke continued to speak. "Hunter feels it has to do with his final SEAL mission, the botched rescue mission. With three of the hostages dying before Finn pulled two others to safety."

She stared at the bubbles covering the water, trying to envision Finn rescuing two of the hostages alone while the others on the team were injured and unable to help. She hadn't thought any of the hostages had made it, and a mixture of disbelief and relief filled her. "Are you certain?"

"It's classified."

"But *you* have knowledge of the details!" She only knew that Hunter and the others had been wounded, that Finn had managed to avoid any injury, and that he'd helped them all to safety. A Navy SEAL buddy never left his own behind. But still, she hadn't known he'd accomplished part of their mission. That he alone had further risked his life to save the remaining hostages. She'd thought the whole thing had been a total disaster.

"I told you. I'm an investigative reporter and a damned good one at that."

"What happened that day?"

He was quiet, then before she could demand that he tell her, he said, "One of the women who'd been taken hostage and died during the rescue mission had a brother who was in the Navy."

"A Navy SEAL," Meara whispered, guessing at the truth.

"Yeah," he said darkly.

"What was his name?" she asked, barely able to get the words out, her skin chilled with anticipation at hearing what it was, figuring the man was on some kind of vendetta now.

"Cyn Iverson."

"Cyn Iverson," she said, choking on the words, never in a million years having thought it would be someone she'd known, albeit briefly. Or that he was the same man who had wanted to date her but Hunter had said no. Or that he was trying to track her down now. A chill swept over her wet skin.

She'd never considered that he might be a Navy SEAL. Did he hold a grudge against Hunter and the team for his sister's death? He must have cared very much for her.

"Did you know him?" Rourke asked.

"Ah, briefly." And then Meara's lower lip dropped. Did Cyn mean to kill her because Hunter hadn't saved Cyn's sister in time? For revenge?

"What's this all about?" Rourke prompted.

"He seemed so mild-mannered, not in the least bit impulsive or headstrong. Not like the Knight of Swords, if he was supposed to fit the description from what you've told me. Unless he was a chameleon, acting one way but hiding his true character. Still, from what I've seen of him, I can't imagine he might be involved in any of this."

Rourke made a scoffing noise. "Someone sure as hell is involved in this. And from the sound of it, he could feel he has a very good reason."

She thought back to the day she'd met Cyn. He had acted impulsively by taking her out, realizing that she was with a pack and that they wouldn't like her going to dinner with a wolf they knew nothing about. What if he had taken her to dinner with some other nefarious intent…

What if he'd wanted to be on the team that had tried to rescue the hostages? What if he resented not being allowed to go and felt that his not being there had meant his sister's death? What if Meara hadn't been Cyn's real interest at all? And now he was hunting her down. Thank God, Chris hadn't known where she was and couldn't have let Cyn know, not realizing he might be behind all this.

Her stomach tied in knots, she took a deep, settling breath. "He met me in Sacramento, and we had a dinner date. You probably heard about it."

Rourke didn't say anything for a minute as if he was thinking about it. Then he said, "The time Chris was supposed to be watching you at a bookstore, and you got away from him, and Hunter chewed Chris out?"

"That's the time."

"Yeah, I heard about it. A couple of guys were saying what a handful you were and they were glad they didn't have the job."

Knowing that word had probably spread among the pack members and was still juicy gossip months later, she shook her head. "Thanks, Rourke. If you learn anything more, let me know."

"I will. I meant to tell Hunter, but I can't reach him. And no one thinks I'm important enough to be allowed to call that guy who's watching over you, even though I attempted to locate his number anyway."

"Finn."

"Yeah. Chris won't let me talk to you, saying everything has to go through him. But I thought you should know, and you could pass the information along to Hunter and whoever else has a need to know."

"No one else knows but you and me?"

"No. I dug up the information on my own. Cyn's sister had been married three times, changing names each time, so it took some digging to learn her birth name. She wasn't a wolf."

Meara stared sightlessly at the bubbles in her bath. "He was a wolf."

"Yeah, well, she wasn't. He was changed a few years back, but she was still human."

That didn't make sense. Either Cyn hadn't had the heart to change her or he had felt she wouldn't want to be a wolf. In Tessa's case, she'd refused to leave her brother the way he was, as close to him as she was. Meara knew that despite her differences with Hunter, if she'd been turned, she would have turned him, too.

"I'll... I'll pass along the information. And, Rourke, even if I haven't said it before, you've been a welcome addition to the pack. No trouble at all."

And she meant it from the bottom of her heart. When she'd learned Hunter had turned the reporter by accident, she knew it would be a disaster. But Rourke had readily accepted his role, and even shape-shifting hadn't seemed to be much of a problem for him. *Most of the time*. Still, he had to be watched over, like any recently turned, mateless werewolf, to ensure he didn't make a mistake, and if he did, so it could be rectified quickly.

Rourke was quiet and then said, "Thank you."

In that small bit of thanks, she heard a world of appreciation for what she'd said. That made her wish she'd said it earlier. She wasn't in a habit of doling out praise for any little thing, which would make the praise not worth giving or receiving. Still, she should have said something before this.

She'd make it up to Rourke and show her appreciation to him somehow later, when assassins weren't out to get her. She frowned. If Cyn *was* behind this, was it because Hunter's sister was alive when his own was dead? But if he had been that close to his sister, Meara couldn't understand why he hadn't bitten and changed her. As a human, she would grow old and die, and he'd lose her eventually while he'd live on for eons. Something wasn't right.

Goose flesh erupted on her arms, and she felt another chill race through her.

"I'll talk to you later. I've got to tell Finn what you've learned. Thanks again." She ended the call, but before she could lift the phone over the tub and set it on the floor away from the bubbles, the phone slipped from her soapy hand and landed in the bathwater.

Frantically, she grabbed for it, searching for the phone at the bottom of the tub. She grasped it, fished it out, and tried to turn it on. No sign of life. "Damn it all, anyway." She dropped the dead phone on her pants outside the tub.

"Finn!" she called out, trying to get out of the tub. Oh, oh, oh. Her muscles reacted with twinges of pain in her hip and thigh when she tried to stand, reminding her that she was still sore and bruised.

She was reaching for a towel, her skin dripping with water and soap bubbles, when Finn and Paul barged into the bathroom with guns drawn. She gave a startled squeak, not expecting to see Paul with Finn, or that Finn would come that quickly. As she drew the sunny yellow towel around her, she said, "I'm all right. I just think I might know who was involved in that fiasco of a last mission of yours."

"Who?" Finn asked, holstering his gun, while Paul took in way too much of her towel-clad but mostly naked body.

"The guy Hunter wouldn't let me date when he was going on the mission. Although the card that was left behind with Allan doesn't seem to represent Cyn's behavior in the least."

"*Sin?*" both Finn and Paul said at once.

"Do you know him?" she asked, climbing out of the tub and the much-too-cool water as Finn quickly grabbed her arm to steady her.

"No," Finn said with a snort. "I just wondered how he ever came up with the name 'Sin,' and how anyone let him get near you. For that matter, how the hell do you know about the tarot card?"

"Cyn. C-Y-N, Cyn, short for Cynric, which he said comes from his Anglo-Saxon roots. He said it means powerful."

Finn narrowed his eyes at her.

"Well, I thought he was referring to…" She gave a slight cough. "You know, the way he gave me this wickedly sinful look, like… well…" She couldn't help the blush warming her cheeks and sliding all the way down her skin. "But then he explained his name was Anglo-Saxon in origin and…" She shrugged.

Finn's expression was still rigid as ice, and Paul was staring at her just as hard.

"Who told you about the card?" Finn asked.

"Rourke, the reporter, newly turned. You met him at the morgue."

"How the hell did *he* know?"

"Well, hell, Finn, it seems everyone in the pack knew about that but me. Chris told him." She glowered at Finn.

"And you know what it means?"

"Of course." Rourke had told her, but she wasn't letting Finn know that she hadn't had a clue before that.

Finn gave her an elusive smile. "When I learned the meaning of the Knight of Swords, someone came immediately to mind."

"Let me guess." She looked at the sparkly ceiling and then eyed Finn with annoyance. "You?"

He chuckled and shook his head. "What did he look like?"

"Let me get dressed, and I'll describe him the best I can."

Finn and Paul didn't budge from the bathroom as Finn asked, "Did Hunter see him?"

"No."

"Then why didn't he want you seeing the man?" Finn asked, frowning again at her.

She gave him the same annoyed look back, not caring for his harsh tone. "He didn't like his name, or what he said it meant, if you have to know."

The way Finn was scowling at her, she could tell he didn't like Cyn, either. Although she thought there was a deeper reason for Hunter not liking Cyn, but he wouldn't disclose it.

"If you'll both *leave*, I'll get dressed, and then I'll tell you more."

"Tell me what, Meara?"

"He was a Navy SEAL, one of you guys. His sister was one of the hostages that died on the island during your last mission."

Finn stared at her in disbelief, but she figured he was coming to his own conclusions about what that might mean. Paul was looking just as stunned.

"Go," she said, motioning to the door with her free hand. "I'll tell you what else I know after I get dressed."

Finn gave her a stiff nod, fearing the worst—Bjornolf had been right. Meara was the one the assassin had been targeting, and now they might just have the reason.

He ushered Paul toward the door, already pulling his phone out and punching in a button. "Hunter?" he said, closing the bathroom door behind him. "What do you know about the guy Meara wanted to date named Cynric

Iverson, Cyn for short. Yeah, besides that you didn't like his damn name or what he said it stood for."

"He called me and wanted to be on our team before I asked Allan to join us, and I said no to Iverson."

"So what was the problem?"

"He wanted Meara, and he wasn't good enough for her. But I suspected he was just using her to make points with me, thinking that if she fell in love with him and vouched for him, I'd let him join my team. He didn't have the training that we needed to get the mission done. Hell, if this has to do with him, I'll kill the son of a bitch." Hunter didn't say anything for a couple of heartbeats as Finn wondered how close Cyn had gotten with Meara before Hunter put an end to it.

"Did you know that Cyn's sister was one of the hostages that died during our last mission?"

More silence, then Hunter asked, "Who told you that?"

"Rourke, your resident reporter, newly turned."

Hunter let out his breath. "How the hell did he learn of it?"

"He's a reporter," Finn said, guessing Rourke was used to doing investigations.

"Hell. Then if Cyn is the one behind this, it's damned personal."

"Yeah, that's just what I thought," Finn agreed, not liking the scenario one bit.

"How's Meara holding up?"

"She's doing fine. I'll make sure she's taken care of."

"I'm coming home," Hunter abruptly said.

At first, Finn thought Hunter didn't trust him to protect her, maybe even thinking that the incident with Bjornolf at the inn proved that. But then Anna's warning that she'd tell Hunter what Finn had been up to with Meara flashed through Finn's mind. "Don't believe everything Anna has to say."

A significant pause followed. Then Hunter said, "What has Anna got to do with anything?"

Finn was totally thrown off kilter by Hunter's question, certain that Anna had already talked to Hunter about Finn's relationship with Meara. "Didn't Anna call you?"

"No," Hunter said tersely.

Finn rubbed the stubble on his chin. *Shit*.

"What was Anna going to tell me?" Hunter asked in none too friendly a manner.

"Nothing. Why are you coming home then?"

Hunter said, "Bjornolf just called me."

"Hell."

Hunter waited for Finn to say something more, but when he didn't, Hunter said, "So is there something *you* want to get off your chest with me?"

"No. What the hell did *he* call you about?" Finn really hadn't expected Bjornolf to stoop so low as to inform Hunter of Finn's business with Meara, but well, hell. Finn knew the bastard was more than a little interested in Meara.

"He thinks Meara is the focus of this operation. That she's the one the assassins are targeting. And if this is true about Cyn's sister dying during our mission, I believe Bjornolf is right. Which is why I'm coming home."

Finn's mouth dropped open. Hell, chalk it up to feeling damned guilty about his handling of the situation between him and Meara when Hunter's plan to return home didn't have a thing to do with that.

"Yeah, so what did you think Bjornolf was calling me about? The same thing you thought Anna might be reporting back to me about?" Hunter asked, his tone stony.

"Hell, Hunter, she's a grown woman."

"You'd damn well better be talking about Anna, Finn. Meara is my *sister*. And grown or not, the same rules don't apply."

Finn wasn't sure why, maybe because of the respect and admiration he'd always felt for Hunter, but at that moment, he felt like a schoolboy who was in serious shit and standing before a stern-faced, pissed-off principal.

A prolonged silence lapsed between them. Then Hunter said, "I'm boarding the flight now. I take it you want to talk to me about joining the family. If not, just let this be a warning."

The phone clicked off and Finn found himself listening to dead air space.

Damn it all. Finn would have taken Meara for a mate in a heartbeat if he'd been wired differently. She was fun and courageous and a treasure for any male who could win her hand. Even if she was very much like the Knight of Swords. Maybe that was what he liked so much about her.

When he was all in the planning, considering every possible action and reaction like a chess player contemplating his next move, Meara would have lunged forward and played the move without regard to what could happen. In a way, he wished he was more impulsive like that. Actually, he had to admit he had been more spontaneous in dealing with Meara. He realized that she was rubbing off on him—which he found wasn't a bad thing.

But if they became mated, she'd throw a conniption

as soon as he told her he was going on a dangerous mission. He didn't need the aggravation, and he wasn't willing to give up that lifestyle yet.

He glanced up to see Paul watching him, looking like he knew just what had happened and truly sympathized with Finn. Paul threw up his hands and said, "I didn't call Hunter, either. I wouldn't have. Maybe threatened to a few more times to make you come to your senses. But I wouldn't have actually done it, knowing how angry Hunter could get." He tried to look like he felt Finn's pain, but somehow the effect wasn't quite sincere. "So what happens now?"

"We keep Meara safe and catch the bad guys while we're at it." Finn's personal life wasn't the issue at the moment. Or shouldn't be anyway.

"What about you and Hunter?" Paul persisted. "What are you going to do when he gets here?"

Finn let out his breath. "We'll work out our differences. We always do."

"And Meara?"

Finn didn't have a ready answer for that. The problem was that he liked Meara too damned much. The thought that any other male would have her didn't set well with him. But more than that? He just didn't want to give her up.

Paul stared at him in disbelief, and then the corners of his mouth rose. "My God, you've fallen for her. *Hard*." He shook his head. "I don't want to be you when Hunter returns. But I have to admit I'm glad it's you that fell for her and not someone who wasn't one of the team."

Now what was Finn supposed to do? Tell Meara that Hunter knew about them or suspected something had gone on between them? Or just drop the subject and keep this on a strictly professional basis for the rest of the mission like he should have done from the start? When this was over, Meara could shop for her perfect mate again. Finn would stay far away from the temptation that was Meara and the whole Oregon coast where he might run into her anytime and want to take up where they had left off. "Might" wasn't the word for it. He knew if he saw her again after having a taste of her, he could never go back to the way they'd been.

Anna shoved the back door open, her face red with annoyance, and fisted her hands on her hips. "Hunter just called me. He said you thought I'd phoned him about something that was going on between you and Meara. And he wanted to know what *that* was all about. Care to explain?"

"I'm going to check the perimeter of the house for a while," Paul said, smiling at Finn. He took off by way of the back deck, leaving Finn to dig himself out of the deepening quicksand he found himself in.

"Yeah, well, it was a misunderstanding," Finn said, hating to have to explain himself further to anyone else.

"We both figured that, but I don't like having to lie to Hunter to protect your ass, even though you and Meara are a big boy and girl. Hunter is still her brother."

"He reminded me of that. All right?"

Anna shook her head. "Fine, but the game plans have been changed, and now Hunter's setting the rules. I told you I should have stayed with Meara. Now that's just what's going to happen. And you get outdoor patrol."

Finn heard movement behind him and turned to see Meara walking down the hall toward them. Her eyes were wide, and her sexy mouth was parted in surprise, her cheeks lightly flushed. He wondered how much of the conversation she'd heard before she'd let them know she was joining them.

"I have to hear what Meara has to say about the 'date' she nearly had with Cyn," he said to Anna without taking his eyes off Meara.

"A date with sin? That should be an interesting tale." Anna shook her head. "Hunter said I should talk with her and pass the info along."

Finn stood firm. He was the one who'd come to warn Hunter and his sister about the danger, and Paul, too, and had arranged for Anna to be here to help watch their backs. He wasn't giving up protecting Meara for anything or anyone.

"Hunter learned about us, didn't he?" Meara asked softly.

As reluctant as Finn was to admit it, he did. "Yeah."

She shot an accusing glance in Anna's direction, but Finn quickly said, "By my admission, Meara. No one else told Hunter."

"Oh, well, terrific. So you went and told him all the sordid details?" Meara said, her tone of voice caustic.

Anna's eyes grew big.

"Well, just fine. Do as Hunter ordered," Meara snapped at Finn, her eyes fiery with indignation. "I'll talk to Anna, and she can relay what little I know to whomever she's working for."

"Hell, Meara, I…" Finn ran his hands over his head in frustration. "It was a mistake."

"A mistake?" she asked shrilly. "Oh yeah, how well I know. That's how it always ends up—one big mistake.

Do me a favor and don't make it any worse than it already is, okay?" She strode past him, her delectable scent piquing his hormones, and he wondered how any woman could smell as mouthwatering as she did, making him want her as much as he did, when she was ready to bite his head off.

She entered the kitchen and started heating water in the teakettle.

"Fine." He hadn't wanted a mate. He had told her he wasn't into romance or anything of the sort. He wasn't ready to give up his work.

He stormed out of the house. This was the kind of job he knew how to do well. Going after the bad guys and protecting the innocents.

Dealing with relationships? He totally sucked at that.

"Hey, if it's any consolation," Paul said, joining him out front, "you're the first SEAL on the team that Meara's ever shown any real interest in. If you ever decide to settle down, I'm sure she'd go for you."

The way she'd looked at Finn in the house with that hurt expression once she'd learned he'd told Hunter what was going on between them—not in so many words, but Hunter had to have known what had happened—Finn imagined she'd just as soon feed this SEAL to the sharks than do anything as foolish as consider him for her mate.

Yep, on the list of prospective mates back at her cabin, his name would definitely have been crossed off with big letters stating "NO WAY in hell!" written beside it.

—〰—

"Are you all right?" Anna asked Meara as they sat down at the kitchen table over steaming mugs of mandarin-orange-flavored tea.

Meara frowned. "Sure."

"Finn didn't do it on purpose, by the way. He didn't talk to Hunter about the two of you. I imagine it was more of a case of feeling guilty about your relationship and letting it slip with Hunter when Finn hadn't meant to."

Meara still couldn't help feeling perturbed about it. She'd thought they could keep what had happened between them secret from Hunter so he wouldn't throw a fit. Deep down, she didn't want Finn to lose his longtime friendship with Hunter over the situation. "I thought you wanted to talk about Cyn," she said curtly, not mad at Anna, but she couldn't quash her annoyance with Finn for letting the situation slip.

Anna took a deep breath. "I've known Finn for six months now and worked really closely with him on a few missions, and I've never seen him so wrapped up in a woman. Kind of nice to see. I was beginning to think he was a eunuch."

"Finn?"

Anna smiled. "Yeah, really. Because of the kind of work he does and not wanting to worry about a bad guy grabbing someone he cares for, Finn just hasn't bothered with relationships. So when I saw him with you and the way he was acting all smitten, I figured something more was going on."

"A big mistake," Meara said. "Sure."

Anna studied her for a moment, then said, "I wouldn't let your brother come between you and Finn."

Meara let out her breath. "My brother has nothing to do with this."

"Oh yeah, he does. He means well. And he's got your best interests at heart. But this is truly between you and Finn. For the first time, I believe he's considering giving up this line of work."

Meara sipped some of her hot tea. "Don't be absurd."

"No, really. I'm not very good at relationship issues, either. When I get mad at a man, I'm ready to use my whole arsenal of weapons on him."

Meara finally smiled. "I like you, Anna."

"The feeling's mutual or I wouldn't say any of this to you." Anna reached over and patted Meara's hand. "Give Finn a chance. Believe me, if I don't let him in the house to watch over you tonight, he'll be some wolf to deal with by morning. And I'm not about to put my ass on the line. Now, what do you know about... *sin*?"

Chapter 14

As a wolf, Finn concentrated on searching for any clues to the assassin's whereabouts before he'd tackled Meara, and Finn had had to end his miserable life. He assumed the wolf had parked somewhere in the area, although considering how much territory they could cover as wolves, he might have traveled a long distance in that form without tiring.

But with all the searching Finn had done, he hadn't located a vehicle that the wolf might have driven. Finn also checked the area where the wolf had been before he attacked Meara and discovered his trail, but still no clothes. Looking out to sea, Finn wondered if the man had come from that direction. As a SEAL.

It reminded him of earlier SEAL operations when he and his teammates had shifted into wolves to go in as a reconnaissance team, although no one else knew that Hunter's team took on the form of wolves when conducting some missions. With their noses to the ground, they were able to sniff out mines, locate cadavers, and find the hostages much more quickly.

In forested regions, they'd take out the lookouts before anyone realized a pack of wolves was upon them. And in one case when the guard called out about wolves attacking when they didn't exist in the region, the enemy thought the guard was drunk on duty, which worked well when another man was sent to relieve him of his job.

Exasperated, Finn loped back to the house where Paul waited for him on the porch, maintaining an outside vigil. It had been several hours since Finn had started on his run on the wild side. Bjornolf was conducting his deeper cover surveillance and hadn't been seen in all that time.

Finn quickly shifted, then grabbed his pants and tugged them on. He pulled out his phone, saw that he hadn't missed any messages, and frowned. It was time he spoke with Meara about this Cyn person, since Anna hadn't bothered to contact him with any word about the man, which irritated Finn no end. He was not going to be relegated to outside guard duty for the duration of this mission.

Paul nodded at him in greeting at the front of the house.

"Did Anna talk to you about this Cyn character while I was running as a wolf?" Finn asked, his tone of voice couched in annoyance.

"Nope. She was waiting for you to return, figuring there wasn't much news anyway, and I wouldn't be able to do anything with the information. Hunter's still on the plane, so we can't call him and give him any update."

Finn finished dressing and looked back at the house.

"No word from either of them," Paul offered. "It's been real quiet."

"They're all right, aren't they?" Finn didn't wait for Paul's answer as he suddenly feared the worse. Heart thundering, Finn realized that while Paul had been watching the front of the house and Bjornolf was who knew where, someone could have sneaked in the back, taken the women by surprise and...

He slammed the front door open and rushed into the living room. Spying Meara curled up on the couch under a yellow quilt, he stopped abruptly. Paul ran into his back and quickly retreated a couple of steps.

Meara's eyes were shut tight in sleep. A book rested on her lap, featuring a Highlander in kilt, his chest bare, wolf eyes glowing above. *Heart of the Highland Wolf?*

Finn stared at Meara in surprise, his heart nearly beating out of his chest, while his mind was still unable to reconcile what he thought might have happened with the serene scene.

Anna frowned at him as she sat on a recliner, sipping a cup of tea. "You wore her out," she whispered, one brow arched. "All those late-night activities."

Not wanting to go there, he asked quietly, "What did she say about Cyn?"

Anna smiled.

He gave her a disgruntled look and motioned for her to go with him to the privacy of the back deck. Paul had remained standing where he was, but seeing there wasn't any trouble, he quietly closed the door and returned to his guard duty out front.

When Finn and Anna were settled on lounge chairs on the deck with the back door closed, Finn asked again, "What did she say about Cyn?"

"He was a SEAL, although she didn't know that when she first met him. Hunter confirmed that with me. Cyn wanted to use her to get on Hunter's team. Hunter didn't like him for that reason alone, but something else bothered him about that man. He wasn't as highly trained as the rest of you guys. And something else, maybe just some bad vibes. Hunter figured that was the end of it when Meara agreed, albeit reluctantly, not to see the man any further."

An attack of possessiveness grabbed hold of Finn again. "Had she been seeing him?"

"According to Meara, she had met him at a bookstore in Sacramento. She recognized he was a wolf right away. He seemed real interested in her, and she liked his attention. She said Hunter kept her under his thumb so much that men were often afraid to approach her."

Finn snorted. "Good thing, too."

Anna rolled her eyes, definitely seeing the situation from a woman's perspective.

"That weekend, she'd gone to Sacramento to shop, and while a couple of the pack members got sidetracked in a video-game shop, she met Cyn in the bookstore."

Finn interrupted Anna before she got any further. "I'd think Hunter would have ensured that only his most reliable wolves stayed with her."

"Chris Tarleton was in charge. He's one of Hunter's sub-leaders."

"I met him at the morgue. He's the one who is mentoring Rourke. And I imagine if she got away from Chris to see another man, he was pretty ticked off. Hunter would have chewed his ass also."

"Right. Well, normally Chris is as responsible as can be, according to Hunter. Very serious-minded. But Meara took so long to read every back-cover blurb on the romance books before she picked the ones she wanted that he figured she'd be there for hours and no one would even notice her. How likely would it be for an alpha male wolf to spot her in the romance section of a bookstore?

Anyway, Cyn bought her dinner right after that and was a bona fide gentleman. He wanted to see her further so she mentioned him to Hunter the next morning, but Hunter threw a fit. Not only that, but he was furious she had gotten away from the pack members who were supposed to be watching her. He was especially angry with Chris because he's a sub-leader and should have known better. So I'm sure Hunter gave Chris hell, as you suspected."

Finn could imagine Hunter being that way. Not that he blamed him. Hunter had a pack to run, but he had been away a lot and had to rely on sub-leaders who wouldn't let him down. "Hunter didn't tell Meara why he suspected the guy wasn't trustworthy?"

"No. Hunter didn't want to hurt her feelings. He was afraid she'd feel bad if she knew Cyn was only trying to get into the family so he could be on Hunter's SEAL team. That he truly wasn't interested in her."

Finn leaned back in the chair and stared out at the ocean swells making their way to the shore in constant rolling waves, white foam capping each like thick lace. "Why would he have wanted to be on our team so badly? Was it because he wanted to rescue his sister? He had to have known that his emotions would have been involved and could have adversely affected the mission. And why did Hunter have a bad feeling about him?"

"I don't know. You know how he is sometimes. He just has a wolf's intuition that something's not right. Paul told me Hunter felt that way about the mission before you all landed on the beach, and then his instincts were confirmed when so many of the team were shot to hell." Anna tapped her fingers on the arm of the lounger. "You're not going to give her up, are you, Finn?"

He glanced over at Anna, surprised at the question when all along she'd acted as though he shouldn't have anything to do with Meara.

She snorted. "Don't give me that damned innocent look. You're dying to have her, as much as she's dying to have you. Even though Hunter told me to stay with her until he gets back, in essence to protect her from you and to protect her from herself, I'm not standing in your way. Not when I know what you'll be like to live with in the morning. And I'm not even mentioning how Meara will be."

He'd always liked Anna. She'd been a great asset to their team, but he appreciated her all the more now, glad he didn't have to set her in her place if she hinted that he shouldn't stay with Meara.

She gave Finn a thin smile. "Tessa called me on the sly after Hunter left on the plane to return to Portland. She said that Meara doesn't share her room with just anyone. Male or female. When I asked Meara if she minded if I stayed in the same room with her, she politely declined. If I had insisted, I'm sure her wolfish blood would have fired up. So you see, you've made some headway where no one else has. And Tessa said if you didn't stand up for Meara, *she'd* have a word with you."

Finn shook his head. "I don't even know Tessa. How in the world did a wolf convince Hunter to go on a honeymoon?"

"She wasn't all wolf, exactly."

"If she's not all wolf, exactly, why does she think

she can talk to me as if she is one?" He raised a brow at Anna.

"Maybe she has her own arsenal of weapons," Anna said, patting her waist, "like I do."

The door opened behind them. Finn turned to see Meara standing in the doorway, pushing straggles of dark hair out of her sleepy face. He damn well wanted to take her straight back to bed and have his way with her. Hell, the woman would be the death of him.

"So Cyn took you to dinner and was a gentleman, and you wanted him after that?" Finn growled at Meara, unable to stop the words as they spilled out of his mouth. What was it with him when it came to other men's interest in her?

Anna rolled her eyes and vacated her seat. "I'm getting some sleep while the two of you talk about Cyn so I can take the night shift." She gave Finn a look like she could strangle him, and then she shut the door as Meara glowered at him.

"Yeah, he was a gentleman," Meara said.

"And that's what you wanted. Some gentleman. Someone who would keep his hands off you. Who would say good night without a kiss or offer you one so benign that it wouldn't scare you off. I know you only thought you liked him because he seemed safe."

Meara glared daggers at him, but she didn't deny it.

"You wanted a gentleman who was sin in name only. But he was using you to get on Hunter's team, Meara. Only your brother didn't tell you that, not wanting to hurt your feelings."

Meara stared at Finn. "You're lying."

"No, I'm not lying. Hunter should have told you. We

don't know why Cyn wanted to be on the team so badly.
Maybe it was so he could help to rescue his sister. Or…"
Finn paused. "…maybe he planned some criminal act of
sabotage. The reason is still unknown to us. But since
that fiasco, several scenarios have come to mind. He
wants revenge for Hunter saying no to both his being on
the team and making something more of a relationship
with you or maybe losing his sister. Maybe Cyn thinks
you were the one who said no to seeing him further and
hurt his efforts at joining the team. We don't know. But
Hunter shouldn't have kept you in the dark about Cyn
being a Navy SEAL and wanting to be on the team."

"So… so you're saying he followed me to the bookstore? Offered to take me to dinner? Made me believe
he was genuinely interested in me so that he could get
to Hunter?"

He hated making her face the facts, but the guy was
no good for her. "Yeah, that's exactly what I'm saying. He might have been following you, waiting for the
chance to get you alone. As soon as he saw that your
escort had left you by yourself, he made his move." Finn
thought back to the book she'd had on her lap while
she'd been sleeping in the living room. "Were you looking for romance books?"

"How did you…" She glanced back at the house.

"You were reading one before you fell asleep on
the sofa. At least I figured that's what it was since the
cover featured a bare-chested man with a six-pack. So
where did Cyn meet up with you? In the romance section? Looking to buy a book?" From what Anna had told
Finn, that's where Meara had been, but he had to hear
the details from her and not just secondhand.

She parted her lips to speak, hesitated, and then said softly, "He said he was looking for science fiction and fantasy. I told him they were in the next aisle over."

"Most likely clearly marked, too." Finn gentled his tone. "Did he buy any books?"

"No. We got to talking and… well, I bought six romance books, but I didn't even remember he was there to look for a book. After I paid for my purchases, he escorted me across the street to a steak restaurant. I guess I was so wrapped up in the notion of a wolf wanting to dine with me—and I didn't have Hunter or one of his men watching out for me, knowing they might be checking up on me any second—so I jumped at the chance."

She turned and looked out at the ocean and harrumphed. "And here I always thought that of all the men Hunter chased away, Cyn was the only one who wouldn't have backed down. I thought he would eventually learn I was in Oregon and come to see me because he really did feel something for me," she said in a silky, sultry way, her arms crossed beneath her breasts, raising them in an inviting manner.

Finn placed his hands on her shoulders and caressed lightly, still concerned she might be bruised from the earlier fight he'd had with the assassin on top of her. She tilted her chin up, her brown eyes challenging him. He leaned his mouth down to brush her lips with an unassuming kiss, barely skimming the softness, the taste of the orange-flavored tea on her lips, her light breath coming quickly as her heartbeat picked up its pace.

His hand caressed her neck with the barest of touches, and she shivered, her eyes misting with tears. Then he lowered his face to kiss her throat, to lick her soft skin, to sample her sweet lavender fragrance. That reminded him of when she had been buried in lavender-tinted bubbles and how much he had wanted to join her—and would have, if Paul hadn't been around.

She stiffened slightly, and he captured her hands, unwrapping her arms from beneath her breasts and setting them around his neck so his hands could feel her breasts underneath the cotton tank top she wore. She moaned into his mouth as he stroked the soft mounds and felt the nipples extend. He touched and teased and captured one between his lips through the light fabric.

"God, Finn," she breathed out.

He nuzzled her cheek tenderly. She caressed the nape of his neck and swallowed hard. He lifted her face and kissed her mouth, touching her lips with his tongue and probing until she opened her mouth to him, gave herself to him, and clutched at his neck to keep from slipping to the floor as the stiffness in her posture melted away.

Finn wrapped his arms around her and held her lightly against his body, which without his permission—as he only intended to comfort her in a damned gentlemanly way—was hardening with feral need. "I'm the only one who won't back down from Hunter when it comes to you," he said against her ear.

"Yeah, well, you talk big, but when you have to face him down…"

He smiled. "I have faced him down… on other issues, Meara. We don't always see eye to eye."

"But you're not giving up your job, and well, it just wouldn't work out between us."

"Hmm, you may be right, but I'm staying in your bed tonight."

She looked up at him, tears in her eyes.

"All right?" he asked in a more appeasing manner, stroking her cheek, wanting her more than he had ever wanted a woman, and feeling tenderness toward her that he had never felt for any other woman. He sure as hell didn't want her to be upset, but she had to know that Cyn most likely had ulterior motives for wanting to see her.

"And if Hunter arrives here in the middle of the night?"

"Only two people will fit in that bed. He'll have to find his own bed to sleep in."

She groaned, and he kissed her cheek. "Want something to eat?"

Hunter would arrive in the middle of the night. They might as well make the most of the time they had left with each other before Hunter interfered.

She twisted her mouth for a second, and then she smiled, her whole expression brightening.

Suspecting just what she had in mind, he shook his head. "S'mores later. You have to eat something more substantial first." He took her hand and led her back into the house.

He wasn't sure why he asked Meara what he did next, but the words were out of his mouth before he could stop them. "So what do you plan to do when you find your mate?"

She didn't hesitate to respond. "Run the cabin resort. Maybe focus on finding a single female for poor Rourke. You know, the reporter who learned about Cyn's sister. He needs a mate for certain."

Finn stiffened.

"*Not me*. And well, when I find my mate, he'll take me on a nice long cruise."

"A cruise?"

"Yeah. Like Tessa's idea of going to Hawaii for a honeymoon. We may not have church weddings, but I think honeymoons are the way to go. I've never been on a cruise before, and that's where I want my mate to take me."

"What if you get seasick?"

"I'll just take something for it and stay in the cabin with my mate, curled up in bed with him so he can take my mind off the waves—or we can make our own waves."

Finn had been on a lot of ships in his lifetime, but never a cruise ship. To think he could be on the high seas with Meara, sequestered away in a cabin for two. The scenario definitely played into his fantasies.

He looked into the fridge and smiled at all the steak. "Anna brought us some groceries."

Moving in behind him, Meara slipped her arms around Finn's waist and peeked around his shoulder. "Hmm, shrimp," she said.

"And steak."

"You and Hunter."

He looked down at her. "You don't like steak?"

"Of course I do." She ran her hand over his hard stomach. "Beefsteak is my favorite. But I love shrimp, too. Do you want to grill it by the ocean? We could use that gas grill down below."

"Yeah. I'll let Paul know we'll be down there, and he can watch our backs."

She studied the bottle of wine Anna had gotten them and set it aside, then looked for a couple of wineglasses. Once she'd found them, she fished out a couple of plates and sighed. "Too bad we have to have an audience."

Finn shook his head and pulled out his phone to call Paul. Having an audience was good, or he was bound to forget what he was here for—*again*.

———

Meara set an old comforter Finn said he'd found in the garage on the sand. Like a pro, he prepared the steak and vegetables, which she hadn't thought he'd go for. Hunter liked to grill, never bothering with the vegetables, but she didn't figure that meant Finn would grill, too. At least half of their male pack members didn't cook.

She loved watching Finn flip the steaks with finesse as if she was in a fancy Japanese restaurant. Then she poured them some wine, thankful to Anna for being so thoughtful, and stood next to Finn as the breeze tugged at the collar of his shirt.

"Do you vacuum?" she asked, teasing in a casual way.

"Vacuum?"

She shrugged, thinking how even more perfect he would be if he wasn't running off on deadly missions. Not only could he grill great impromptu meals, but he was a damned sexy lover. But if he also vacuumed, the chore she hated most, he would be a woman's dream come true. It wasn't the vacuuming, particularly, that she hated so much. It was that the vacuum spit out more than it sucked up.

"Never was part of my SEAL training." He gave her an elusive smile.

"Hmm, well, maybe it should have been. Every man needs to know how to vacuum."

"What about Hunter?"

She sighed. "I'm afraid he didn't get any training, either." But then she brightly added, "I'm sure Tessa has him vacuuming up a storm now, though."

Finn flipped the steaks and said with a smile, "I can't imagine Hunter vacuuming, sweeping, or mopping floors. He'd be good at giving the orders, though, pointing out spots that needed further work, a little more polish, a little more sweeping and vacuuming."

She laughed. "Yeah, that's Hunter all right. He's also good at building fires to keep Tessa warm."

Finn gave her a devilish look, and Meara felt her body warm considerably. "I'm talking about wood fires. The electricity was out during a snowstorm, and he had to keep them warm."

Finn grinned broadly and nodded his head.

"By keeping the fire going."

He chuckled.

She shook her head. She'd never known a man who was better at taking what she said innocently and turning it into sexual innuendo. She gave up trying. But then she began to think of what it would be like if her electricity went out in the middle of a snowstorm and Finn was with her. Would he spend a lot of time trudging down to the beach to gather firewood?

For certain, he'd take her to bed and ply her with hot kisses designed to thaw her out, his body rubbing against hers in the heat of passion.

Her cheeks warmed again, and he cast her a questioning glance. "Anything you want to share with me?"

"No. I'm ready to eat, though."

He still looked like he was more interested in knowing what she'd been thinking about.

Within minutes the meat was browned, along with potatoes, zucchini, yellow summer squash, onions, and carrots. The steaks and shrimp had perfect grill stripes and had been seasoned with thyme, rosemary, and lime rind after being lightly coated with olive oil.

"Rare, right?" Meara asked, watching the steak as it sizzled.

Finn gave her a sexy smile. "Steak seared on the outside, nice and red and juicy on the inside."

"Hmm, just the way I like mine." She carried their drinks to the blanket as he brought their dinner plates.

To her surprise, he brought up the vacuuming issue again. "I take it you don't care for the chore of vacuuming." He sat down beside her as the sky over the ocean blossomed with pink and orange, the white clouds thinly stretched behind the setting sun, rays stroking the dark water.

"It's just that my vacuum cleaner doesn't pick up well. I end up moving the dirt around the floor as the vacuum sucks it up and spits it back out." She took a deep breath and raised her glass to Finn's. "To sunsets over the water, and to peace and prosperity everywhere."

He drank some of his wine and raised his glass to hers. "To a beautiful wolf on a golden night. May you find happiness always."

"Thanks. I try to." Once she found the perfect mate to share it with, she would. Of course there would be bumps on the road to bliss, but still…

She watched the sun set as she ate the steak and shrimp and vegetables, also enjoying apple slices and red and green grapes, and washing it all down with sips of red wine. To top it off, they shared bars of chocolate, no s'mores this time. The meal couldn't have been more perfect. And the company and the setting.

She thought about Finn and his declaration that he wasn't into dating. Did he mean dating as in eating out at restaurants? They were nice, but she didn't need five-star restaurant service to enjoy a night out. In fact, this was better than most dinners she'd had where she was waited on hand and foot. More relaxing. More atmospheric and appealing to a wolf. More conducive to a romantic liaison without tons of people in attendance. With Paul watching them, protecting them, she figured Finn wouldn't kiss her at all.

She hadn't had any nicer dates with a man than these impromptu affairs with Finn.

When Finn took the empty wineglass and plate from her and set them aside, she envisioned another kiss, hoping that he'd ignore Paul for the moment.

He didn't give her a kiss, not at first. He gazed into her eyes as if he was doing some real soul-searching. Then he sighed and pulled at her to join him. When she did, he made sure she was nestled between his legs as they sat on the blanket and watched the last of the fireball sun melt away beneath the waves. She imagined it sizzling as the heat of the sun hit the water and the night air grew cooler.

Finn rested his chin on the top of her head and held her gently in his arms. When the last of the light was gone, he nuzzled her bare neck with his face and then caressed her cheek with his mouth, his hands shifting to her breasts. That made her wish they really were alone with the sound of the waves washing over the sand and the night breeze swirling around them.

"What did you think of us? The team?" Finn asked, his voice low and husky.

"I was too busy giving Hunter a hard time about the missions you all were going on after you left the Navy."

"Paul swore up and down you favored him," Finn persisted, "because you were always giving him a coy smile."

"That's not true. I didn't pay any attention to him." She felt her cheeks heat. Had everyone believed Paul's teasing?

"Allan said you blushed whenever he caught your eye."

She shook her head. "Not me. Ever." When Finn didn't say anything further, she looked over her shoulder at him. "Well, what did you say to the other guys about me?"

Finn smiled reminiscently. "That only I stood a chance with you because only I riled you so that you'd speak with me. Sure sign of love. I knew it was only a ploy to get me alone."

"Yeah, right. So that I could have my wicked way with you? I'm sure they believed it as much as you did."

For a long moment, he said nothing but caressed her neck and shoulders with his large hands. And then he chuckled. "If they didn't before, they'll believe so now."

Later that night, as Finn relaxed with a sleeping Meara in his arms in the guest bedroom, he thought about the fun he'd had with her on the beach. Cooking the steaks and shrimp and watching the surf with the breeze in their hair had made him feel as if he hadn't a care in the world. Like when he'd been a young man just out to have some fun.

He'd wanted to kiss her and hold her close, and he finally had allowed himself to do so, despite knowing Paul had to be watching them. He had tried to keep it just a sweetheart's kiss, nothing too sensual, but with the way she'd leaned back in his arms and tilted her face up for more, he couldn't help himself. He could never get enough of her.

Hunter would be on a rampage for sure as soon as he arrived.

After thinking how much he had enjoyed being with Meara, Finn closed his eyes and slept for a short while until Anna yanked open the guest bedroom door and said in a rush, "Hunter just drove into the driveway in case you want to make yourself presentable and... put some distance between you and Meara."

Finn was torn between staying with Meara and seeing to Hunter.

"Stay," Meara coaxed. Her voice had a sultry, sleepy quality as she tightened her arm around his as if intending to keep him in the bed with her by force if he thought otherwise.

"We're sleeping," Finn said firmly to Anna, tucking Meara tighter in his arms. "Close the door on your way out."

"It's your funeral," Anna said cheerfully.

"I won't let him kill you," Meara whispered to Finn as the door clunked closed.

"Good." He kissed her hair, the sweet fragrance of her shampoo tantalizing him. "I don't care for funerals."

He really didn't think he could fall asleep, what with Hunter's impending arrival, but as soon as he heard voices, he knew he couldn't doze again.

"Where's Finn?" Hunter asked gruffly from the direction of the living room.

"In the first guest bedroom on the right down that hall," Anna offered.

"And Meara?"

"She was afraid of the dark," Anna said very seriously.

"She's with Finn?" Hunter asked, his voice irritated but with a hint of surprise.

Meara moaned. "She would have to tell him I was with you," she said quietly to Finn.

He squeezed her in a warm embrace. "Good thing you're afraid of the dark."

"I'm not. And Hunter knows it."

Finn shook his head. "We'll have to come up with another story then."

Meara sighed. "I'll protect you."

"Hmm." Finn kissed her head and snuggled close with her. "Not to worry."

Anna said to Hunter in a cheerful voice, "The master bedroom's free if you want to sleep in there."

"That's all right," Hunter said with dark promise. "I'll just wait to hear the good news when my new *brother-in-mating* wakes to tell me."

Finn let out his breath in a heavy exhale. This wasn't going to be easy, because hell, he wasn't even sure he knew what he was going to say to Meara's brother when the time came.

When Finn finally decided he'd had enough of a rest and it was time to face Hunter, he left Meara to sleep longer in the bedroom or to hide away from Hunter while he had to deal with him. Finn took a shower, dressed casually in jeans and a plain blue T-shirt and a pair of sandals, and then walked down the hall to the living room to see a brooding Hunter.

He was the only one of the SEAL team who had let his hair grow long, and the windswept coffee-colored strands hanging to his collar softened his stern look. But his eyes, normally dark brown, were nearly black as he waited for Finn to make an appearance. His gaze had been focused on the front picture window but quickly shifted to Finn as he approached.

Finn noted that Anna must have gone to bed, and Paul was nowhere to be seen.

"We've got a bigger problem than dealing with my being with Meara," Finn said, broaching the subject first, hoping to get the attention off him and Meara.

Hunter scowled at him. "My sister needs a mate. You're leading her astray."

Finn shrugged and remained standing, wanting to get a cup of coffee before he had any weighty, lengthy discussions about Meara or anything else. "Call it the courtship phase. If we decide we don't get along well enough, no harm's done."

For a brief moment, Hunter seemed taken aback, as if he couldn't see Finn courting any woman. Maybe because Finn never had.

"You aren't right for her. She needs someone who'll stay with her and keep her in line, not someone who is gallivanting around the continents, saving the whole wide world."

"What about you and Tessa?"

"That's different."

"Really? I suppose time will tell since we haven't been contacted for a mission since you got hitched. Then we'll see if you'll go or not. Then again, maybe it's time for me to settle down."

Hunter eyed him suspiciously. "Are you?"

Finn shrugged. "Maybe. I don't know. She sure makes a man lose his sense of what's important and what's not."

For the first time, Hunter gave him a sinister smile. Then it faded. "You haven't met my mate. You might think I'll run roughshod over you if you upset Meara, but you haven't seen Tessa. She's like a wolf with a mission when she's got it in mind to right a wrong."

"Anna said she wasn't all wolf."

"Believe me, she is." Hunter took a deep breath and didn't say anything for a moment as if he was coming to some conclusions of his own. Then he said, "All right, so what do we have concerning this case?"

"Two assassins who were human—run-of-the-mill guns for hire. Two others that were wolves."

"I got a look at them. I didn't recognize any of them, but Bjornolf's running some prints on them." Hunter frowned. "Because of the bruised eye and jaw that Bjornolf was sporting, I asked if he'd gotten injured when he took down one of the assassins, but he said he hadn't. Some madly jealous wolf caught him unaware. Want to elaborate?"

"No." Finn headed for the kitchen. "I'm getting a cup of coffee. Want one?"

Hunter followed him into the kitchen. "Sure. So what did Bjornolf do to Meara that you popped him twice for it?"

Finn knew Hunter wouldn't take no for an answer about Bjornolf's black eye. "He kissed her without her permission. Then he said he'd do it again with her permission."

"Hell, Finn," Hunter said, rubbing his hand over his jaw. "His regular job is killing assassins. And you socked him over Meara?" He shook his head, but he looked half amused and half pleased.

"Somebody had to do it."

Hunter chuckled, and Finn figured he'd gotten into Hunter's good graces to some extent. Hunter's phone jingled, and he lifted it off his belt. "Hey, honey. Yeah, I got here just fine." He looked at Finn. "No, I haven't killed him yet. I need him still. And Meara likes him. What can I say?" He listened for some time, smiled a whole hell of a lot, looked up at Finn, and then said, "I'll tell him. Call you later. Get some sleep. I'll return as soon as I can. Love you, too. Bye."

Finn handed Hunter a cup of black coffee. "Was it Tessa?"

Hunter took a swig from his mug. "Yep."

"Did she have a word for me?"

Hunter looked sternly at him. "Yep."

"And it was?"

"If you're sleeping with Meara, you're mated to her. No going back on the deal. Tessa's words."

"Ah."

"Tessa's serious." Hunter finished his coffee, walked over to the coffeemaker, and poured himself another cup. "Her words have merit. In the old days, Meara would be a ruined woman, and to be honorable, you would have to mate her."

"If we both wanted the same thing, yeah. In this day

and age? No. That's saying Meara even wants me. She has issues, you know."

Looking damned surprised, Hunter stared at Finn. "Oh?"

"Yeah. Nothing that she'd talk about, but deep down she's afraid of an alpha male who might exercise too much control over her. She would never do well with a beta who would roll over and play dead at her feet, but…" Finn shrugged.

Hunter sat down on the bar stool. "Is that what her problem has been all these years? I always thought she needed a beta to boss around."

Finn straightened and looked Hunter in the eye. "Bjornolf said he was interested in her." Finn studied Hunter's expression, glad to see his eyes darkening with irritation.

"Over my dead body," Hunter growled. "He'd be ten times worse than you."

Amused at the comparison, Finn smiled.

"I mean, as far as his work goes."

"I knew what you meant." Finn refilled his coffee mug. "Bjornolf said he'd try to track down Cyn and see where he's been these past six months. If he was in the SEALs, we should be able to come up with something."

They heard someone walking through the living room. Hunter turned at the bar and looked to see Meara approach. Her chin was tilted up in defiance, but she still looked a bit unsure.

If Hunter took her to task for what had happened between Finn and her, Finn would give him hell right back.

Chapter 15

To Finn's consternation, Meara looked snappish, probably waiting for Hunter to give her hell. And she'd give it right back to him—forget about Finn getting the chance. But she looked a little worried, too, as she shot a glance Finn's way, most likely looking to see if he was wearing bruises now like Bjornolf was.

"Hey, Hunter," Meara said, trying for a casual greeting, but Finn noted the tension in her voice as she walked into the kitchen, twisting her hair into a knot that looked damned sexy, and then leaned over to give her brother a light, sisterly hug.

Hunter looked just as tense but gave her a perfunctory hug back. She tried to shrug off his mechanical reaction to her, but Finn noted she was bothered by it.

Finn filled the teakettle with water and started heating it for her tea, knowing she'd want some first thing and that it might make her feel more at ease. Hunter gave her a disgruntled look but then watched Finn in amusement as if he thought that a lot more was going on between Meara and Finn than his teammate had revealed.

"You didn't have to come here and protect me, Hunter." Meara inserted a finger though Finn's belt loop and gave a tiny tug that made him want to haul her right back to the damned bed. But he got the distinct impression she wanted him close by to stand up for her if she needed him. Or maybe she was trying to protect him from Hunter if her brother showed hostility toward him. It would be like her to do so.

He slipped his hand into her back pocket and smiled down at her. She looked up in surprise at him, her face warming like soft sunlight on a sunny day.

"Finn's doing a great job. Except…" She pulled his phone out of her front pocket and waved it at him. "…he keeps forgetting to take his phone with him." She tried to hide it, but she bit her lip slightly with anxiousness. "Bjornolf wanted to talk to you."

"*Bjornolf?*" Finn said, astonished. He figured Hunter was again running the show, and Bjornolf would have called him with any news.

"Yeah, he wanted to know if Hunter had killed you yet."

Hunter chuckled darkly in amusement.

Smiling, Finn took the phone, kissed her cheek, and set a tea bag in a floral cup for her. He redialed Bjornolf's number, and when he answered, Finn said, "Meara told me you called."

"Yeah, did she tell you what about? I thought maybe I had a chance with her if you were gone now." Bjornolf sounded like he was only half joking.

Finn chuckled. "Yeah. Hunter said he'd let you near her only over his dead body."

Meara glanced at Hunter who gave her a small shrug. "It's true."

Bjornolf laughed over the phone. "Okay, well, although I told Hunter I'd get back to him, since you're still around, you can give him the news."

In that instant, if Finn wasn't reading too much into the situation, Bjornolf was acknowledging that Finn was still in charge of Meara's safety? He wondered if the way to impress Bjornolf was to catch him unaware and sock him. Or if it had to do with Finn getting the woman. Maybe a little of both.

He looked down at Meara. Hell, she'd sure hooked him. And he wasn't letting her go. But as far as a mating, this wasn't the time to propose it. No matter how much Hunter might think he should have a say, this was strictly between Meara and Finn.

"Cyn formed a team of four men, who, from what I could learn, were from his own home pack in Georgia. The one you killed when he attacked Meara in his wolf form was one of them. I assumed Cyn was hiring any old assassins off the street, in addition to using his wolf team, to see if he could eliminate anyone protecting Meara without jeopardizing his own people too much.

"He and the other three men had been SEALs. They quit the Navy right before you attempted your mission but *after* Hunter told him no about joining his team. Apparently, Cyn had the notion that Hunter was the top wolf and that working for him would be the pinnacle of Cyn's career. But Cyn knew Hunter handpicked his own men and figured he might need an in, so he went after Meara first. Which was probably his first big mistake."

"So he thought Meara had kept him from his chance at being on Hunter's team?" Finn asked, running his hand over her arm in a soft caress as she watched him, still possessively holding onto his belt loop. "But what about his sister? Didn't he want on the team to rescue her?"

"Not sure. I doubt we'll know the truth until we catch up to Cyn. From the looks of it, he and his men sabotaged Hunter's mission, hoping to destroy the team in the process. Not sure if they'd planned for all of the team members to die or just to curtail the mission to give Hunter and all of you a black eye, but the situation got out of hand."

"But his sister… how does she fit into the equation, if Cyn had anything to do with the sabotage and had hoped everyone on the team would die? His sister could have been killed that way."

Meara broke in and said, "What if he was involved in the hostage taking?"

Not having considered that, Finn stared at her with awakening pride, glad she had come up with a new angle. "Bjornolf, did you hear what Meara asked?"

"Yeah. Hell, if he was involved, he probably wanted a share of the ransom money and maybe even intended to be the sole survivor of the team, had Hunter agreed to allow him to be on it. Then he would have sent the women safely home, having earned all the glory and the money."

Finn shook his head at the idea that anyone could have sold out the team and risked his own sister's life. But then another thought nagged at him, one that Bjornolf had set him to thinking about in the inn's lounge. "How did Meara save us?"

"Ask her about the coded message she intercepted that was meant for Hunter. That she consequently destroyed. She probably thought it was about another dangerous mission and wanted to save him from going on it. Instead, it was a message changing the location of the meet. If Hunter and his team had gone there, all of you would have been dead."

Finn frowned at Meara. He wondered if Hunter knew about the coded message she'd gotten ahold of.

Thinking back to the way she had been pondering his question on the beach about how she had saved their lives, he assumed she'd recalled something about deleting the message.

"One other thing, your formerly wounded team member, Allan, is on the move, headed in your direction. Paul told him where you all are."

"*Shit.*"

"Yeah, I told you the whole team would be in one spot and then they'd come for you."

"Fine with me." Except that Finn didn't want Meara here when the fighting went down. But sending her to some other location where he couldn't protect her wasn't a viable option, either.

Finn wrapped his arm around Meara and held her close.

"A little birdie told him Meara was interested in mating him," Bjornolf said. "So apparently, he wants to stake his claim before he's too late. He was in a real rush to join all of you."

Finn frowned down at Meara. She raised her brows in question. "He's too late," Finn said but wouldn't elaborate.

The moment he'd seen her in her cabin making small talk with Bjornolf, Finn had known the only real choice he had was to send her packing to Hunter in Hawaii. So what did he do? Pretended to be her lover so he could protect her instead. And now? He didn't want to give her up. But he was certain she wouldn't go along with him going on dangerous missions any more than she wanted Hunter to do so.

"Hmm, I figured Allan was too late where Meara is concerned. Does Hunter know about the two of you?" Bjornolf asked, a hint of dark amusement in his voice.

"He will." But only after Finn discussed the conditions with Meara.

Bjornolf didn't say anything for a moment, then added, "With the team all coming together again, I think you can handle this. I've got a job elsewhere that's of national importance. If I'm not there to avert this new crisis, God knows what a mess it'll be."

Finn was surprised to hear that Bjornolf planned to leave them behind to take on another mission when this one wasn't quite resolved. Although he suspected the other paid and this one didn't. He wondered if Bjornolf's leaving had anything to do with Finn's declaration that Meara would be his mate. But he appreciated all that Bjornolf had done for them up until now.

"Thanks for helping us out, Bjornolf." He stopped short of saying they couldn't have done it without him, as he still felt testy about Bjornolf's kissing Meara and feeling her up before that. "Do you want to talk to Hunter?"

"No. That's all, except, hell, if you decide not to mate Meara, let me know, all right?" Then there was a click, and Finn realized the phone line had been disconnected.

Finn stared at the phone for a minute, then slipped it into his pocket. He didn't know if Bjornolf had really meant want he'd said about Meara or if he'd only wanted to push Finn into making a decision concerning her. On the other hand, Bjornolf had kissed her, and the way he'd slid his hand in her pocket, yeah, the bastard was damned interested. But he must have known he'd have a real fight on his hands if he went after Meara when Finn wanted her.

Turning his attention to Hunter, Finn said, "We're on

our own. Bjornolf's got another assignment, and Allan's on his way here. Cyn's got at least two other wolves left on his team."

Hunter swore under his breath. "Okay, I want Meara safely away from here. Tessa's home. You take her and you watch over her."

"There's Anna and me," Meara said, objecting to Hunter's wanting her out of the way. "We can help. And you'll need Finn."

Finn could tell from Hunter's expression how much he didn't want her here or involved.

"Tessa's home, south of Meara's. An hour and a half away. That'll work," Finn said, agreeing with Hunter. He handed the cup of tea to Meara. Trying to lighten the mood, he said to her, "Somehow Allan must have gotten word you want him for a mate, Meara."

Meara's eyes widened. "Who would have said such a thing to him?"

Finn shrugged. "You told everyone that. Maybe Paul joked with him about it. Who knows?"

Hunter shook his head at Meara. "I knew I shouldn't have left you alone. As soon as I was gone, you led my whole former team astray."

"That'll teach you to tell them to stay away from me." She smiled mischievously in the way only she could, looking halfway innocent and a whole lot devilish, and then she took a sip of her tea.

So that Hunter and the others could discuss among themselves what they intended to do about the impending threat—and knowing they didn't want her in on the discussion since she wasn't a highly trained operative like them, only she wished they'd let her help if she could—Meara retired to the master bath to take another long soak, without the bubbles this time.

After turning into a near prune, she dried off, wrapped her soft terry cloth robe around her, and rested in bed while reading a Highland werewolf tale to relax. Her favorite author, Julia Wildthorn, had switched from writing contemporary stories to historical tales of Highland werewolves and had even picked up a castle in Scotland, a wolf pack—at least Meara assumed—and a handsome Highland laird of her own to sweeten the deal. Meara sighed, wishing she could have such a romance.

Then she thought back to what was inevitable about her situation here. She hated that her brother and the others would be risking their necks while she hid at Tessa's house. At the very least, she could resort to using her rifle or revert to her wolf form and use her wickedly lethal teeth.

She was still thinking along those lines when she heard the door to the master bedroom suite open. She looked up from her book and saw Finn enter the room. He closed the door behind him with finality. His predatory gaze took in her robed figure with the comforter covering her lap. If he'd thought they'd make sweet love while her brother was in the house and they weren't mated—

"Meara, we've got to talk."

He looked deadly serious. She guessed this wasn't about making love then. She figured he was going to tell her that she had to leave the safe house without further delay. Had they gotten some more news?

She set her book beside her on the mattress and folded her arms, attempting not to look cross, except she didn't feel anything but. "I could help the cause, you know. You don't all have to treat me like some innocent bystander." Hunter knew damn well how capable she was in dealing wolf-to-wolf when the circumstances warranted. Just because one gray wolf had tackled her in the woods near here and then Finn had wrestled him on top of her didn't mean she was always that disadvantaged. She had been unaware of the menace. That was all.

This time she would be prepared for any eventuality.

He shook his head. "That's not what I want to talk about."

That surprised her even more. Before she could come up with another reason for his dark mood, he moved in close to the bed and towered over her.

As much as she hated to admit it, the effect was intimidating. He stood taller than her anyway, but while she sat on the bed, the difference was astronomical. She patted the mattress and scooted over so he could sit down. He'd still be taller but not quite so daunting. Not that she wouldn't stand her ground; it was just the principle of the thing. How would he feel if he sat on the floor beside the bed and she talked down to him? That brought a smile to her lips.

He frowned at her and the smile quickly faded. No, this was to be a serious discussion, nothing amusing about it.

He remained standing. *Damn him*.

Fine. She glowered up at him. "What?" she snapped, whatever thread of patience she had breaking.

"Bjornolf said you intercepted a coded message for Hunter and deleted it. How did you access it, and whatever possessed you to do such a thing?"

Her lips parted without her express permission as she gaped at Finn in surprise. "What... what coded message?"

His expression took on a darker cast. "Don't try to hide the truth from me, Meara. It's up to you to tell Hunter what you had done. But in the meantime, you'll tell me how you did it and why."

She cleared her throat, frowned furiously at him, and said, "If I had done something so dastardly and wished to own up to it, I would speak with Hunter about it, *not* you. If the message had been for Hunter, he's the only one I'd feel obligated to apologize to for my actions. Bjornolf is wrong. I wouldn't have done anything so despicable. What do you take me for anyway?"

Finn ground his teeth, and then he said in an even voice, "Someone who wants to protect her brother at all costs. I understand the underlying reason for doing what you did, but don't you realize how disastrous the consequences could have been?"

She snapped her gaping mouth shut. Didn't she just tell him she hadn't done anything of the sort?

"Listen, you..." she said, jerking the comforter aside, ready to end the discussion here and now. But as soon as she moved the comforter, her robe slipped open, exposing her belly all the way down to her toes.

She grabbed her robe to yank it shut and then planned to shove him out of the way as he blocked her in while standing close to the mattress. He seized her arm, forcing her to stay right where she was, and then yanked the comforter back over her lap.

"You're not going anywhere until you tell me the truth."

There was something about a man—or a woman, for that matter—telling her what to do when they had no right, that stoked her ire to blue-flame level. "I told you," she said with barely controlled anger, "that I did nothing with Hunter's messages."

Finn stared her down as if trying to read the vast inner workings of her mind. "All right." He pushed at her thigh buried under the comforter, indicating he wanted her to move over.

Now he was going to sit beside her? She didn't want him to *now*!

Yet she realized that whatever had happened must have been grave enough to warrant his concern so she set her annoyance aside—barely, let out her breath, and shifted over on the mattress. He sat next to her, facing her, his eyes still dark.

"I concede you may have inadvertently deleted a message meant for Hunter and—"

"Damn you, Finn! I didn't delete anything of Hunter's! On purpose or otherwise."

A shadow of a smile flickered across his face and then was gone. If she hadn't been glowering at him, staring him in the eyes like a wolf who was not about to back down, she would have missed the subtle reaction.

"If you *inadvertently* did it," he repeated, "you might not even realize you had done so."

That gave her pause.

His hard expression softened somewhat, and she felt as though he was taking several steps back from his initial reaction concerning what he thought she'd done. If she had carried out something like that by mistake, how could he fault her? At least that's what she thought he was thinking.

When he backed off, she considered any time she might have come across a message and deleted it by accident if she'd had Hunter's phone for some reason. Which, when she considered it, could have been the case. Maybe. But on his computer? She didn't think so.

"What was the message?" she asked quietly, figuring it had to be damned important or Finn wouldn't be making such a big deal of it.

"The contents gave new coordinates to where Hunter and the rest of us were to land on the beach."

"The final mission?" Tears filled her eyes.

She couldn't help it. If she had deleted something that vital to the team, she would have been responsible for them having been wounded and the mission being such a failure, resulting in hostage deaths even. They could have all died because of her. But then she attempted to shake loose of that notion because she hadn't ever done anything with Hunter's computer except to check her own emails a few times when hers was down. And she'd used Hunter's phone whenever her battery was dead and she needed to call about something important. But she didn't think she'd deleted any of his phone messages by mistake.

Finn managed a humorless smile. "By deleting the message, you ensured we went to our original landing coordinates, thereby saving our lives."

Her mouth dropped open, but she quickly narrowed her eyes and slugged him in the arm. "Damn you, Finn. I thought… I thought…" She wiped away several tears, trying her damnedest to get her emotions under control.

He wiped away a couple more tears with a gentle sweep of his fingers against her cheeks and then pulled her into his arms. "I had to know you didn't somehow get into Hunter's coded messages and get rid of one on purpose. In this case, it most likely saved our lives, but the situation could have been a lot different if the message had been some other."

She struggled to get out of his grip, but he held on tight, kissing her hair and sending tingles of need up her spine. No matter how much she hated that he thought she could have done something so underhanded, she wanted Finn's caresses, his whispered breath against her ear, the feel of his fingers rubbing her back through the soft robe.

"I… didn't… do… it." She tilted her head up to glower at him, her eyes still misting with detestable tears.

He took a deep breath. "When I asked you on the beach if you recalled anything you had done that might have saved us on that mission—"

"I said no."

"But you seemed to think of something."

She frowned, not at Finn this time, but in concentration as she tried to recall that nagging memory lingering in the recesses of her mind.

"Paul can hypnotize some people."

"Mindless sheep," Meara retorted.

"He might be able to pull the memory from your subconscious."

"No."

Finn let out his breath and kissed her forehead. "All right, we'll think of another way."

"I didn't ever get into Hunter's computer or phone email," she said, still not letting go of this issue. "That I recall."

"Someone had to have."

"I don't have Hunter's password for his emails, and I'm not a hacker. How does Bjornolf know about the message if it had been deleted? And yes, sometimes, I'd use Hunter's phone, but I don't recall any message on it that I might have mistakenly erased. Besides, how did Bjornolf know that *I* had deleted it?"

Finn stiffened and said, "An email was sent, confirming receipt."

She shook her head. "I don't understand."

"The message was still in the sent file. The original message emailed to Hunter had been deleted, but the sent message from *Hunter* showed the contents of the original note."

"How did Bjornolf know all this?"

"While you were taking a bath, I called him back and talked with him privately to find out more details. After the team had been hit, Bjornolf was trying to learn what had gone wrong. On a hunch, he hacked into all the team's emails to see if he could learn anything."

"All right, but how does that make *me* the suspect?"

"He said it had your signature all over it."

She snorted. "So what did I say that made him feel that was the case?"

"It didn't look like the kind of message Hunter would have sent."

"Why not?"

"He would have gotten in touch with the sender another way to ensure that it wasn't a hacker's hoax. And you've always been extremely vocal about not wanting Hunter to go on missions."

"And of course Bjornolf questioned Hunter about it first and my brother agreed I had to have done it."

Finn didn't say anything for a moment as his gaze studied hers.

She narrowed her eyes at him. How in the hell had Bjornolf come up with this notion if he hadn't already talked to Hunter? "Well?"

"Bjornolf wanted you to—"

"To confess to something I didn't do?" she said, her voice rising with barely controlled rage. "We'll clear this matter with Hunter right now."

Finn hesitated to move off the bed. *Fine*. She couldn't move the mountain, but she could get around him. She scooted to the other side of the bed and got up, then headed for the bathroom to dress.

"Hunter's not going to be happy about this," Finn warned, still sitting where she'd left him.

"*I'm* not happy about this."

Dressed in jeans and a tank top, Meara stalked out of the bathroom and headed for the door. With a slow, reluctant manner, Finn stood, crossed the floor, and followed her out of the room.

When she reached the living room, she found the place empty—no sign of Hunter in the kitchen, on the back deck, or out front.

"Great," she said under her breath, wanting to get this matter cleared up immediately. That's how she did things—jumped right in and tackled an issue. She didn't believe in letting a situation simmer, hoping it would go away. She thought to call Hunter on her cell phone but belatedly remembered that hers had met a watery grave.

"Cell phone?" she asked, palm outstretched to Finn.

He fished his out of his pocket and handed it to her.

She punched in Hunter's number, and when he answered, she asked, "Did you get a message changing the coordinates on the beach where you were to meet during that last mission?"

Hunter didn't say anything for a moment, probably trying to figure out how she knew about it and why she was asking him.

"Bjornolf said he hacked into the team's emails and located a sent message concerning the email," she added, trying to get Hunter to respond.

"Hell, why did he tell you that?"

She chewed on her bottom lip, giving Finn a sardonic look. "He told Finn who told me. And now I'm supposed to apologize for both deleting the message and sending a response. Except for one problem with that scenario."

Finn was so rigid that he looked like he was made from marble as he waited to see her reaction.

"*I* deleted the message and sent a response to the sender," Hunter said gloomily. "But there wasn't any reason you should ever have learned of the situation."

Shocked at the news, Meara stared at Finn's shirt but didn't say anything. Then finally she frowned and said, "Say that again, Hunter."

"I received the message and instantly realized it wasn't from anyone who should have been changing our coordinates. So that the bastard who sent it would think I believed it and would take my team to the new location, I sent him a confirmation email. Then I deleted the original notice in case anyone happened to see it and went to the other location. We would have been massacred had we done so."

Still not believing her ears, she said, "*You* did it?"

"Yeah, Meara, so don't think anything more about it. It had nothing to do with you."

It might not have, but now she was feeling ill at ease again. Someone had deliberately tried to have her brother, Finn, and the other SEAL team members killed. "But you never learned who did it?"

"No. I sent the information to another operative to look into it, but then we were hit on the beach. I figured whoever set us up realized too late that we weren't going to meet at the new coordinates and missed his chance to destroy us. Even so, they hit the location where we were, not quite as successfully as they'd imagined, though. We never did learn who sent the message. Why are you calling me on Finn's phone?"

"I drowned mine. Maybe you could tell Finn what had happened so he'll stop thinking the worst of me," she said with an edge to her voice. She gave Finn one more heated glower, then hit him in the chest with his phone.

He grabbed for it before she released it. His brows rose as he watched her while listening intently to whatever Hunter told him. She had to get a breath of fresh air to calm her anger so she turned around in a huff, walked out onto the back deck, and closed the door.

It didn't take long before Finn opened the back door, shut it, and walked across the deck, every footfall growing closer. She breathed in the fresh sea breeze and tried to settle her frustration, not knowing what to expect from Finn and attempting to ignore the way he was closing in on her. But she couldn't. She realized just how much it meant for him to believe in her.

"I'm sorry," Finn said, which surprised the hell out of her. Hardly any of the men she knew ever admitted to being wrong, nor would they ever apologize for it. Hunter was top of the list. Her father and uncle had been also.

Finn's hands covered her shoulders in a gentle grasp. If he had stood next to her, speaking softly like he did now, that wouldn't have had half the effect that his caressing her shoulders did. Or the way his body pressed against her back. Or the way his warm breath fanned the straggles of hair dangling next to her cheek, his mouth nuzzling her neck with an insistent need to make amends.

"I told you," she said grumpily. "I hadn't done anything."

He shifted his hands to her tank top, then slid them under her shirt and caressed her breasts. "Let's go back inside," he said, his cheek sliding along hers like that of a wolf who was trying to get her attention, his hands stopping their sexy assault.

"And?"

"I'll make it up to you. I promise." His voice was already low and husky and rampant with need.

"Hunter's around here somewhere," she warned, not exactly telling Finn she didn't want to go with him. She couldn't, damn it, when she wanted this as much as he did.

"Yeah, well, that's why I want to take you back inside."

She shook her head. "Next time I tell you something…"

"I'll listen."

"Yeah." She believed that as much as that she wouldn't have the urge to shift to her wolf form ever again.

She didn't move from her spot on the deck, trying to make up her mind whether she should prolong this torture or give up her annoyance and return to bed with him. But her reluctance to agree didn't stop him.

She gasped in surprise as he swept her up in his arms and then strode back into the house with purpose in his long stride. "Hunter might not be here right now, but he'll be back. It's time that you and I have a real heart-to-heart talk."

Chapter 16

BJORNOLF WAS SURPRISED AS HELL WHEN HUNTER called sounding as if he was ready to roast him alive for upsetting his sister.

"Why in the hell did you call Finn and accuse Meara of deleting my messages?" Hunter growled.

Bjornolf never—at least that he would admit to—made mistakes. And he still was damned sure Meara has been involved in the message fiasco, despite what Hunter said. But then again, maybe he was wrong.

"My mistake," Bjornolf said, without meaning it and unable to let go of what he thought was the truth.

"Next time you have an opinion about something that concerns her or me, bring it to *my* attention." Hunter hung up.

Not expecting the confrontation to end so quickly, Bjornolf was reminded of a squall abruptly appearing on the ocean during one of their SEAL missions and then disappearing just as suddenly. Bjornolf didn't care much about most people's opinions, but Hunter and the rest of his team had long ago earned the deep-cover operative's respect because of all their successful missions. And although Bjornolf didn't like admitting that he'd done anything wrong, he felt unsettled.

Then again, that might have had something to do with watching Finn standing on the deck with Meara as he slipped his hands up her shirt and began to caress her breasts, speaking low in her ear, his body pressed provocatively against her backside, and undoubtedly trying to win her favor.

Observing them through the screen of pine trees, Bjornolf frowned. Meara was softening under Finn's touch, but when he said something more to her, she balked. Bjornolf smiled cynically. She wouldn't be won over easily. Finn wasn't as charming a talker as he thought he was. Meara definitely wasn't buying his attempts to smooth things over with her.

Finn suddenly grabbed her up in his arms without her permission and headed for the house like some damned medieval warrior bent on taking the woman for his own whether she approved or not.

Bjornolf scowled. They were just the moves he would have made if he'd had the chance and a soft touch wasn't working.

Hell, it was a mating for sure.

―᜕᜕᜕―

For the first time since he'd been turned, Rourke was truly enjoying himself. Not that he had a news story to report, but he was really getting into investigating what he could concerning Hunter's final SEAL mission. One thing he thought odd: quiet, unassuming Chris Tarleton had seemed unduly on edge when Rourke talked to Meara about the Knight of Swords. It wasn't like the information was top secret or anything. And she had a right to know what was going on. Then he realized what it was all about. Chris didn't want Meara looking into the matter because she was known for lunging into situations that could get her into real trouble. Hell, now he wished he hadn't told her about it.

Rourke did another search on the Internet, breaking into areas that were classified but that he had a knack for getting into. Purely for research. If he'd wanted to be one of the bad guys, he probably could have made a lot of money at it. But he was cursed with wanting to do what was right—even down to stopping at a yellow light because it might turn red when he was in the middle of the intersection.

Thankfully, Hunter had enough faith in Rourke to allow him to remain unsupervised in his own apartment. And if Rourke could, he'd break this case for Hunter and stop whoever it was from trying to harm any of the rest of the SEALs or Meara. He wanted in the worst way to be an important pack member, someone others could rely on.

He chewed on his bottom lip and scrolled down the page some more. And then he figured he was going about this all wrong.

He called Dave, the other sub-leader, and when he answered the phone, Rourke said, "Chris gave me some of the information about the hit on Allan and the Knight of Swords card left behind. What do you know about any of it?"

Dave gave a grunt. "That's Chris's business. He's the one who's been looking into it. I've been busy with all the other pack troubles that come up. Don't know a thing about any Knight of Swords card. Why would you need to know, Rourke? You're not working on a new story, are you?"

"No. But this is what I do. Investigative reporting.

Except the only reporting I intend to do is finding out who is behind this and giving Hunter the news so he can deal with it."

Dave didn't say anything for a moment. Then he let out his breath with a heavy sigh. "Really can't help you with that. With petty wolf squabbles and one teen runaway, I have my hands full. Talk to Chris. If he believes he can trust that you're not going to put this in the paper, he'll fill you in. Good luck."

"Thanks, Dave. I want to help solve this if I can."

"You're all right in my book, Rourke, and don't let anyone tell you any differently." Then the phone clicked dead.

Rourke was so surprised Dave would say so that he just sat staring at his computer monitor, absorbing the praise for a moment. Then he smiled—and then he frowned.

He wouldn't get anywhere questioning Chris. If Chris wanted him to know something, he'd tell him. Otherwise, he'd say nothing to Rourke. If Chris had been taking notes about the investigation concerning the hit on Allan, where would they most likely be? His desk at home? Bedroom?

Chris didn't have a human job. Running the pack with Dave kept him busy. Now he had to oversee renting Hunter and Meara's cabins. That was where he was right now, dealing with two disgruntled renters.

Hunter would give Rourke hell if he knew the reporter had left the apartment without Chris's okay, and even worse if he learned that Rourke had searched Chris's house for evidence about the crimes against Hunter's team without permission. But Chris wasn't an investigative reporter. He might be sitting on the evidence that could prove who the mastermind of the whole operation was and never know what he was holding onto.

Rourke turned off his computer and grabbed his keys. If he could prove who was behind this, he had to do so. Lives were at stake. And this was a job he could do.

Meara couldn't believe what she thought Finn had in mind as he carried her to the master bedroom. "But we've been staying in the guest bedroom. Shouldn't we use the same room? Someone else should use this room."

"No. You belong in here *with me*." He smiled down at her as he put her on the bed.

"You said you wanted a heart-to-heart talk." She was fairly sure that if they didn't begin a conversation soon, it would quickly dissolve into something else.

"The chemistry between us is remarkable."

"The chemistry." If this was just about the sex…

"I'm not a romantic kind of guy."

She smiled, not thinking that was true in the least. There was romance in castles with brawny Highlanders, and then there was romancing a SEAL. They were two entirely different scenarios, and she was over the moon with the SEAL.

"You've said so already. Although I'd have to graciously disagree with your claim."

"I can't compete with the heroes in your romance novels," he said.

"Hmm, you're right."

He raised a brow, and she got the distinct impression he thought she should have argued with him over that.

"You make a passable hero," she said, staring up at him with wide innocent eyes, although inside she was smiling with amusement as he towered over her next to the bed.

"Passable." He snorted. "You want a mate, someone who's an alpha. I'm not giving you up to anyone else, Meara. So that means—"

"Wait a minute," she said, sitting up on the bed and figuring they'd better get the real issue out in the open before lust ruled their minds and bodies. "You would be just about right for my mate except for one thing. Your job."

He didn't look worried that she'd object to his line of work, which thoroughly puzzled her. But she wasn't going to let that stop them any longer. She continued, "So here's the deal—if you want to be mine, you'll have to—"

"Give up my job?"

She wasn't certain she wanted him to. That was one of the things she loved about him. His adventurous spirit and his desire to save the world and right wrongs where he could. How could he do that sitting on a beach with her for the rest of his life? She just couldn't see him helping her with renting out the cabins. He'd feel chained to her, obligated to give up his life for her.

She shook her head. "No, I was actually thinking of—" She sighed, sure he wouldn't go along with her idea.

"Of…?" he prompted.

"Well, you could still go on your missions, only I'd go with you. As your wife."

A slow smile spread across his face.

She frowned at him. "I'm serious."

"You're not trained."

"I could be. I could be as good as Anna. Maybe even better. And I'd be your mate, so we could be a team."

"I'm tired of living out of a suitcase, Meara. I'm tired of sleeping out in the open or in rundown motel rooms, of waking in the middle of the night and not even knowing where I am."

"I like to go camping and sleep out in the open," she said, looking up at him, seeing the sincerity in his expression, and loving him. "I'm really an outdoors kind of girl."

"Now that kind of camping, I can do. Snuggling in a sleeping bag built for two, watching the stars sparkle like white crystals on a midnight backdrop, and lots more s'mores... yeah, I could definitely get into that kind of camping. Steaks... and shrimp on the grill. It could work."

"You wouldn't miss all the danger and adventures?"

"From what Hunter told me while you were taking a bath, he had a whole truckload of danger right here on the Oregon coast once he moved the pack up here. And you were right in the middle of it." Finn shrugged. "Danger and adventure are what you make of them. I'm sure I can find all kinds of trouble to get into right here."

"You're really serious?"

"I couldn't be more so. But I want you to know one thing—Hunter is the one who contracted most of our missions after we left the Navy, not me."

She gave him a slow smile. "I know."

He frowned at her. "You were always giving me hell for getting the contracts."

"Yep."

Then he smiled evilly. "I told the guys you were only giving me a hard time so you could have a final word with me. That was the only way Hunter would permit you to see me. And he always give me a sinister smile afterward, glad you gave me hell instead of him."

"Men are so—*clueless*," she said.

"Clueless, eh?" He laughed and began removing her clothes.

"There's no going back for us." Meara pulled off her shirt as he tugged her pants off.

"There isn't going to be."

She enjoyed the way his breathing quickened, his pheromones stirred with lust.

His muscles tightened like a wolf ready to take down its prey. She gazed up at him and recognized the heat in his eyes. The testosterone filling his blood made him want her so badly that if she put a hand to his chest right now, she was sure she'd have a devil of a time convincing him she wanted to wait any longer.

"You're thinking too much," he said, yanking off his jeans and shirt and another pair of those semitransparent boxers. Did he know just how sexy those things were? Then he slid into bed next to her, his body warming hers instantly. He grabbed a handful of her hair and took a deep breath, lowering his body on top of hers, his mouth hovering over her lips.

She lifted her head to capture his tantalizing mouth, annoyed that he'd withhold the kiss, but he only smiled and brushed her lips quickly, then nudged her face over to kiss her ear and whisper, "I want to touch and taste every inch of you. I want to fill you and love you and make you mine."

His mouth caressed her ear and her neck, all the way down to her throat, awakening a feverish desire to have him deep inside her, every nerve ending thrumming with need.

"Hmm," she said and took his face in her hands and studied his heated gaze. "I want more." And with that, she pulled his face down to hers and kissed him. It was a tempestuous, heady kiss of yearning and passion, of pressed lips and tongues fusing, of heated breaths that left them panting.

"Damn, Meara," he said grinning, and she laughed.

But she didn't let up the assault and wrapped her arms around him, preparing for even more.

His hands slipped around her buttocks and she spread her thighs with willing anticipation. He pressed against her heat, hard and eager, rubbing her with incessant need, infusing her with a desire so strong that she didn't think she could last.

Hunger mobilized her to explore every inch of his taut muscles as her fingers felt his back and buttocks and thighs. His mouth moved from hers to a breast and he suckled lightly, then more vigorously, and she writhed against him, wanting him to enter her now. Every inch of her was filled with fire as she moaned against the sweet things his mouth was doing to her breasts.

Until he moved away and his hand replaced his body, cupping her between her legs. His fingers stroking the outside made her crave his penetration even more. But she wouldn't beg, fearing he'd just make her want more. Without permission, her body arched, forcing him to spread her feminine lips, enticing him to sink his fingers deep, making him smile just a little.

He was so maddeningly smug. Before he knew what she was up to, she reached between them and gave him a little back, stroking his penis with a firm, steady grip, and for a time, he allowed it. She could tell from the expression on his face that he was fighting giving in too quickly, and then he was pulling away and stroking her as if he was afraid she'd dissolve into an Oregon mist and fade away before he could finish this.

She closed her eyes, reveling in the feel of his fingers dipping inside her and stroking her outside until she had climbed so high, aching for the end, undulating to his touch, that the only thing that kept her from crying out when the climax hit was his mouth against hers, swallowing the sounds of joy.

Then he was inside her in one fell swoop, his hand lifting her legs around his buttocks for even deeper penetration. He was wolf-sized, the perfect fit, stretching her, filling her, the only one for her. Her mate, now and forever. And she knew the time had finally been right for the two of them, surrounded by unknown dangers but joined for life.

Finn had never thought it could get better than the sexual pleasure that he'd shared with Meara up until now. But this was something even he hadn't expected. To see her aglow with their lovemaking and know that he'd brought her to climax, to see her desire it so much yet fight the urge to beg him to finish her off, when he knew that's just what she was doing. He loved her actions; he loved her.

She nipped at his chin as he looked at her with wonderment. And then he gave her a smile and nuzzled her cheek, but his mouth soon reclaimed hers with rapaciousness as the fire in him burned. She was so incredibly desirable.

He still couldn't believe she had been free until now to mate. He kissed her and deepened his thrusts, wanting to bring the mating to completion, to feel the heart-thudding bonding between mates, to glory in the mounting passion. And then with a burst of raw sexual completion, he filled her with his seed, barely aware that her hands were grasping his hips and she was moving against him with wicked delight.

"Damn, Meara, you're good."

"We're good," she said, licking his whiskery chin. "Damned good—together."

He gathered her into his arms and pulled the covers over them. "*Together*," he agreed, a kind of bliss he'd never truly felt surrounding him completely. "Hell, I should have retired and sought you out long ago."

She chuckled against his chest. "You're absolutely right. But I doubt either of us would have been ready before this." And then they snuggled like two wolves, not caring for the moment what lay beyond their self-proclaimed den.

Although in the back of his thoughts, he knew he would be moving her to Hunter's house before long to keep her safe.

———✻———

When Meara finally woke again, she found that Finn had left the bed, probably worried what the others would think if they were alone together in a bedroom again before they announced they were mated. She shook her head when she saw his cell phone sitting on the bedside table. After she got dressed, she pocketed his phone and returned to the living room where she heard a heated discussion in the kitchen.

"Come on, Anna," Paul was saying. "Everyone knows women make the best coffee."

Meara laughed to herself. She'd made a pot on occasion, but since she didn't drink it normally, Hunter had to make his own. She wondered if Tessa made coffee now for Hunter.

Anna said, "I. Don't. Make. Coffee. I. Don't. Cook. Either."

Paul shook his head. "It just isn't natural—a woman who doesn't cook."

Meara was certain Paul was teasing Anna. And she was just having some fun back. Finn rummaged around in the drawers, then pulled out an instruction booklet. "Here are the directions."

"Don't you know how to make a pot of coffee?" Anna asked, sounding surprised.

Finn gave Hunter a conspiratorial look, then shook his head. "Bjornolf made it earlier."

"But," Meara said, looking from Finn to her brother, "I thought the two of you were having coffee earlier. And Hunter's always trying to get me to fix it. He only makes it when he's camping, using a saucepan and stirring instant coffee into a mug of hot water."

Ignoring the directions Finn offered, Paul scooped coffee into the machine.

Anna smiled and folded her arms as Paul added water. Meara imagined that Anna refused to fix coffee for the men because to her way of thinking that made her less of an equal. Meara wouldn't make it either, since she didn't drink it, while Paul seemed to be guessing at getting the proportions right.

She figured Finn wished Bjornolf was here to make the coffee. Especially when she saw the puckered faces as Hunter and Finn took their first sips. Anna drank hers as if she didn't see anything wrong with it. Meara was glad she liked tea, which she made for herself.

But just as they all walked into the living room to take seats, where Meara planned to ask what would happen next, a key turned in the front-door lock.

Anna immediately set her cup of coffee on a table beside a high-backed chair to free her hands and pulled out a gun. Finn moved to stand in front of Meara, his endearing posture one of protection. She'd never seen this side of him in earlier years. When he was getting ready for a mission with Hunter, he'd been all business. Although now that she thought about it, he had acted a little funny around her at times. Like he wanted to get the hell out of there before he'd seen too much of her yet enjoyed the way she tore into him about setting up the contracts and didn't want to leave.

Hunter was his indomitable self. Meara swore he could look at a man and make him cower like a beta when the stranger had thought himself a steadfast alpha before the encounter. She imagined Finn was not much different in the way he affected people.

Pulling out his concealed gun, Paul moved into a position where Anna wouldn't block his aim.

The door opened and Allan smiled grimly at the assembled group.

"Oh my God, Allan, you're here!" Anna said, hurrying to the door while she quickly holstered her gun.

Meara relaxed, as did the guys. She had to admire Allan for coming to help his team.

His pale green eyes were assessing her and Finn, his broad shoulders wide and his back straight, as if he was going to confront Finn over her. He scanned the room, his gaze taking in everyone gathered there. Hunter, Paul, Finn. But then he focused again on Meara, half hidden by Finn's tall frame. A smile cheered Allan's face.

She smiled back at him, glad to see him so well after his recent injury.

"Meara, I've come for you," he said, his voice bear-like, and he gave Finn an annoyed look as if he was in the way.

Her mouth gaped. Hunter shook his head as if declaring again that his sister had led his team members off course.

Anna glanced worriedly at Finn. But Finn didn't seem bothered by the declaration. Maybe because he'd moved behind Meara, stuck his hand in her back pocket, and was groping her as if to say she was not anyone else's but his. She didn't mind, since no one else could see his action and she rather liked where his hand was. But what was good for him was good for her. She slipped her hand in his back pocket and gave his buttock a warm squeeze. He shifted his gaze from Allan to give her a seductively heated smile that told her if they hadn't had company, he would have hauled her right back to bed.

Paul chuckled. "Welcome back from the dead, Allan."

"Good to see you," Hunter said. "Just like the old days."

"I wouldn't have been left out of the action, no matter what. What would you guys do without me?" Allan said. "So what's the plan?"

"Finn's taking Meara to my place, and he'll keep her safe there. We're getting the word out that the team is all gathered here."

When Allan took a seat on the couch, Paul offered, "Airline food sucks. What can I get you to drink? Eat?"

"Glass of brandy, if you've got any."

"It's not even noon," Finn said, teasing him dryly.

"We've got wine," Meara said, hoping Allan wouldn't mind and wishing that they had what he truly wanted to drink.

But everyone else looked to Finn as if he could conjure a bottle of brandy out of thin air. He finally pulled his hand out of Meara's pocket and said, "I'll get it."

Surprised Finn knew that the owners had any, she assumed he'd taken more of an inventory of their food supply than she had realized. A SEAL *would* take stock of provisions for a prolonged stay, she reminded herself.

Finn walked back into the living room with a glass and a bottle of brandy.

With a pointed glance in Finn's direction, Allan said, "Actually, the sooner we mate, the better, before anyone else gets any ideas."

Casting Paul an annoyed look, Finn poured some brandy for Allan, then handed him the glass, and set the bottle on the coffee table before him. "Meara was giving Paul and me a hard time and didn't mean anything by it."

Meara couldn't tell if Finn and Allan were serious. Nor could she tell by the others' expressions.

"I was teasing," she said, trying to clarify her comments. "Paul and Finn were arguing over me, and well, since you weren't here, I just said I wasn't interested in either of them. Just you."

Allan smiled again. "Ah." He took a swig of the brandy and sank back on the couch. "Sounds like a Freudian slip to me, Meara."

"You wish."

"Actually," Finn said, glancing at Hunter, "I wanted to tell you that Meara and I are mated, so no more bachelor alpha males will be signing up to rent the cabins."

Hunter gave him a slow smile. "Tessa will be real glad to hear that. What about undercover contracts? Have you and Meara come to some sort of agreement concerning your work?"

"I'm retired," Finn said, slipping his hand around Meara's waist.

"At least for a while. If he decides he wants to do more contract work, he's going to take me with him as his wife, and I'll help him." Meara smiled sweetly.

Everyone looked from Meara to Hunter to see his take on it. He shook his head. "She's all yours, Finn. Take good care of her."

"She wants to run the cabin resort," Finn said.

Hunter gave him an agreeable nod. "My gift to the two of you."

Meara beamed at him. "Thank you, Hunter. You won't regret it."

Finn gave Meara a warm embrace. "After you and Tessa finish your honeymoon in Hawaii once this business is over with, Meara and I are going on a cruise to the Caribbean."

"A cruise?" Hunter said.

Meara smiled up at Finn, thankful he'd really been listening to her when she talked of a honeymoon cruise. "I've heard they have lots of great food."

Hunter frowned at them. "What about shifting?"

"We'll time it right. Besides, we have more control over it than that," Meara said, annoyed. "At least I'm a royal, so with fewer human roots, I can change when I want to." She looked at Finn.

He nodded. "Me, too."

Hunter stood taller. "Even so, I can see a forced life-boat drill, and here you are in your wolf forms in the cabin and…"

Meara snuggled closer to Finn. "He's always like this. Didn't I tell you?"

Finn kissed her cheek. "We'll be fine, Hunter. Two weeks max, which will be plenty of time before the moon is full and the urge is stronger."

Not looking surprised, Allan leaned back in the chair. "I take it I came to the party a little too late."

"Yeah, me, too," Paul said. Then he jerked his thumb at Anna. "She's still available."

Allan laughed. "Hell, she takes her weapons to bed. She's a dangerous wolf for a man to have around. Especially, I imagine, in bed."

"You better believe it." Anna smiled deviously.

"And she doesn't cook," Paul reminded them.

"But she could save your hide if you needed it." Meara smiled at Anna.

"Speaking of saving hides," Finn said, "Meara and I need to leave."

"With my blessing. Keep her safe, Finn," Hunter said gruffly.

"Will do."

"And I'll take care of him, too." Meara wasn't going to be left out.

"Just don't distract him, Meara," her brother warned.

Paul and Allan looked like they wished they were in Finn's shoes.

"Speaking of cooking, anyone up for lunch?" Hunter asked, giving Meara a hug before she and Finn left, and headed for the kitchen.

Finn grabbed his and Meara's bags while she took the rifle. Anna nodded. "I can see what her priorities are. She could be one of us if she got some training. Never know."

Meara gave her a hug. "Keep yourself safe."

"You, too." Then Anna entered the kitchen. "Here, let me help you with that. Poor Tessa. Hasn't she trained you how to cook chicken right yet? The temperature's wrong. The timer is wrong. Did you season it first?"

Sounded to Meara like Anna knew very well how to cook.

Allan and Paul looked like they also wanted hugs from Meara as they stood in the living room waiting. Finn's expression told them not to even consider it. They laughed at him, slapped him on the back, and then joined Hunter in the kitchen.

"Ready to leave, Meara?" Finn asked.

"Yeah, I'm ready." She hated leaving the team and her brother behind while she and Finn were safe and sound. Especially when the team could have used Finn's help. But she knew Hunter and Finn wouldn't have it any other way. "Let's go."

Chapter 17

ROURKE ARRIVED AT CHRIS'S PLACE READY TO FIND ANY clue he could to help Hunter and his team. He just wished Chris would have been more open to sharing the information he had on the case so Rourke wouldn't have had to resort to more extreme measures. He really could be helpful if the pack members would give him a chance.

Taking a deep breath, he pulled out a set of lockpicks. He'd used them after Hunter had given them to him as part of his *lupus garou* indoctrination, and he'd already practiced with them a number of times. But this was the first time he'd put them to practical use.

He slipped around the back of the ranch-style brick house, not wanting neighbors to think anything of him playing with the front lock. And then he was inside, standing in the perfectly neat kitchen with no dishes on the gray slate countertop and the chrome sink sparkling. The guy was a neat freak on top of everything else.

Rourke quickly shut the back door, hoping that Hunter and Chris wouldn't be too angry with him if they discovered he'd sneaked into the sub-leader's house without permission. Rourke had to find the connection to Allan's attempted killing or he was toast.

As soon as he entered Chris's dining room, where the table's glass top was just as sparkling clean and the chrome chairs perfectly aligned underneath the table, he smelled Chris's scent all over the place. Rourke realized then that Chris would smell that he had been there also. There was no hiding the fact now.

With rigid determination, Rourke stalked into the living room and spied the morning's neatly folded paper on the coffee table. He wondered if Chris only read it to ensure that Rourke hadn't slipped in something that Chris would object to or if he really read the news on a regular basis.

Shaking his head, Rourke quickly located Chris's office down the hall and searched through all the desk drawers. He found a drawer full of pictures of Meara, as well as some that appeared to have been of Meara and others, but the others had been cut away and discarded, leaving just Meara. So Chris had *more* than a small obsession with her.

He pulled out another picture that he thought odd. Meara was dining with Cyn Iverson, seated at a window in a restaurant. The picture was taken from outside the restaurant. Why would Chris have a picture of Meara and Cyn conversing over dinner when he had denied to Hunter that he had known about it? According to two of the pack members who'd told Rourke how difficult Meara could be to watch over, she'd slipped away and had dinner with the wolf while Chris thought she was shopping for romance books.

Still pondering that bit of odd news, Rourke continued to search for the notes Chris must be gathering on the case about the SEAL team, but he found nothing. Rourke was beginning to think he was on a wild-goose chase, only his goose would be cooked if he didn't discover something important that could be used to uncover the mastermind of all this.

He thought that odd also. If Dave was right in assuming that Chris had been checking into this business with the Knight of Swords, why wouldn't he have notes about it somewhere? He wouldn't have a reason to keep his investigation secret.

Having looked through everything—even a file cabinet that had notes on various pack members and personal financial files—but finding nothing that would help with his quest, Rourke left the office with a heavy heart.

He would be in so much trouble and have nothing to show for it.

He glanced in the bathroom, but everything was neat, and nothing would help him there. He continued down the hallway until he came to what looked like the master bedroom, a sitting-room combination with an attached bathroom and walk-in closet.

His gaze shot straight to a black spiral notebook sitting on a bedside table, closed with a black pen lying on top.

Hope renewed, Rourke rushed to the bedside table and jerked the journal up, flipping it open to that morning's notes.

Nothing. He flipped through earlier notes. Just pack business.

He started rummaging through Chris's bureau and saw the corner of what looked to be a card in a sweater drawer. He moved the stack of sweaters aside and stared at the set of tarot cards.

His hands were shaking and his heart pounding as he quickly looked through the cards, searching for the Knight of Swords. It had to be there. It had to be a complete set of cards. These couldn't have anything to do with the one that had been found on the wounded SEAL team member.

The card wasn't there. Rourke sorted through them more slowly this time, studying each, certain he'd just overlooked it, hoping he'd just overlooked it.

But no. The card portraying the Knight of Swords wasn't among them.

Which meant?

Coincidence that Chris would have a set of tarot cards and the only one missing would be that particular card?

Rourke began searching the other drawers but didn't find anything else that might connect Chris with the hit on Allan. He moved to the closet, rifling through clothes and pockets, and found nothing. Then he spied a couple of suitcases on a shelf and a bag tucked on a shelf below. He pulled out the bag and unzipped it. Nothing inside. But then he checked the outside of the bag, slipping his hand in one zippered pocket, then another. And felt something. A couple of pieces of paper. He pulled the items out. A plane-ticket receipt and an itinerary.

He quickly read the date and time of the departure and arrival. It was the same time Chris had to leave town on an important errand, right before Finn arrived to protect Meara and Hunter.

But most of all, the destination was Pompano Beach, Florida, the same city where Allan Rappaport had been shot.

Rourke had to get out of Chris's house and share this information with Hunter as soon as humanly possible.

But he didn't know where Hunter was staying, and what if Chris discovered Rourke had been snooping around in his place before Rourke could share what he suspected with Hunter? He couldn't return to his own apartment. Chris was supposed to meet him there in a couple of hours so he could accompany Rourke to the newspaper office.

Rourke couldn't go to the office by himself, either, in case Chris tried to find him there. Somehow, Rourke needed to reach Hunter and Dave before Chris discovered Rourke's scent in his house. Quiet Chris would kill Rourke as soon as he found out.

Grabbing the airline-ticket receipt and itinerary, and stopping in Chris's office for the photo of Meara and Cyn, Rourke pondered whether this was enough evidence to show Chris was involved in Allan's shooting and a connection between him and Cyn.

He suspected that Chris had helped set up the situation where Meara would be alone so Cyn could meet her and have dinner. But if that was the case, what was the motive? Chris obviously felt something for Meara. Why would he willingly make it easy for Cyn to have dinner with her?

On a hunch, Rourke returned to the file cabinet and opened the drawer containing Chris's personal financial files. He began systematically going through the sub-leader's bank and credit card statements.

He found the charge for the plane ticket to Pompano Beach and a check made out to Cyn Iverson in the amount of $50,000. What the hell?

Not wanting to risk staying any longer and chance being discovered, he grabbed the additional paperwork and hurried out to his vehicle. He drove north, thinking to go to Dave's place, but then changed his mind and turned his vehicle around to head south. What if

Dave was also involved? The pack had mutinied once on Hunter. What if his sub-leaders both had been involved?

He'd go to Hunter and Tessa's house. It was only about a mile south of Meara's, where Chris was checking into the cabin-renter squabbles, but Chris would never suspect that Rourke would stow away in the pack leader's vacated house.

Rourke pulled out his phone as he drove down the coast road, intending to warn Hunter of Chris's involvement, although Rourke only had circumstantial evidence. When his phone rang in his hand, he nearly dropped it on the floorboard.

He glanced at the caller ID. *Unknown number*.

"Yeah?" he said evasively. Might be a wrong number. He hoped to hell Chris wasn't already on to him. But he knew it would be too soon. His nerves were frayed.

"It's Meara," the caller said, and Rourke sighed with relief. "I'm using Finn's phone because my own is out of commission, but Dave called and said you wanted to look more into the attempt on Allan's life. Dave tried to call Hunter to get his okay on it, but his line was busy. So Dave called me. What is this all about?"

Dave must be one of the good guys, which relieved Rourke no end. "Chris is involved," Rourke said. He tried to keep his voice on an even keel, but the repercussions of learning such a thing made his heart race and his voice sound desperate. "I found tarot cards at Chris's house, but the Knight of Swords was missing," he quickly added. "And I discovered a plane ticket that put him in Pompano Beach, Florida, at the same time that Allan was shot. I'm on my way to Hunter's house. This whole situation with Allan has to do with Chris."

Meara didn't say anything. Had the mountains cut their reception?

"Meara? Are you still there?"

"Are you sure?" she asked, sounding shocked.

"Yeah. I've got the plane-ticket receipt and the remaining tarot cards right here," he said, relieved she'd heard him right. He patted them resting on the console, feeling like he'd just discovered a case as big as Watergate, at least as far as the pack was concerned.

"What exactly did he say?"

"He's in it with Cyn Iverson, Meara. The guy Hunter didn't want you to date. Chris took a photo of you dining with Cyn at that restaurant when you were supposed to be shopping for romance books in Sacramento. He lied about it. He told Hunter he hadn't a clue you'd been with the guy."

Silence.

"Meara, are you okay?"

She cursed under her breath. "Anything else?" she asked. This time her voice was hard.

"He paid Cyn $50,000."

She didn't say anything for a moment, then asked, "How far are you from Hunter's place?"

"Twenty minutes."

"Finn and I will be there in thirty. Was anybody else in the pack involved?"

"I don't know. As soon as I picked up the evidence at Chris's place, I took off."

"All right, all right. I'll get hold of Hunter. Stay low until we get there. Don't call anyone else. I don't want to tip off the other pack members if anyone else is involved."

"I'm sorry, Meara."

"Yeah, so am I." Meara ended the call. She tried to get hold of Hunter but only got a busy signal.

"What's up?" Finn asked, his voice dark with threat.

"Rourke, the new guy, found evidence at Chris's house." Meara set his phone in the cup holder.

Finn's brows rose.

"Apparently Chris is involved in this whole sordid mess."

"Where's the evidence?"

"Rourke's got it. He's bringing it to Hunter and Tessa's house."

Finn let out his breath and reached over to rub Meara's arm. "Are you okay?"

She shook her head. "Chris has been with our pack since the early years. How could he be involved in something so hideous?"

"I don't know. Right incentive, maybe mad at Hunter over some slight? I don't know."

Meara grabbed the phone and tried calling Hunter again. No luck. "Can you drive faster?"

"What exactly was the evidence?"

"Rourke has the tarot cards, minus the Knight of Swords that was left with Allan. And he discovered a plane-ticket receipt for Pompano Beach."

"Pompano Beach? Hell, don't tell me it was around the time that Allan got shot."

"Yeah, same time. Then, too, Chris wasn't supposed to know that I was having dinner with Cyn that time I was shopping in Sacramento. But Rourke found a picture of me eating dinner at the restaurant with Cyn."

"So Chris knew all about it."

"Yeah. Rourke left Chris's place in a hurry before he was discovered."

"So Chris was the one who shot Allan? I'll kill the SOB myself. How did Rourke even begin digging into this stuff?"

"He's an investigative reporter."

Finn smiled. "Sounds like he's a good addition to the pack."

"Yeah," she said, still fuming about Chris and wishing that they'd trusted Rourke more to do what was right. "Sounds like you're right. Chris is a dead man, though," Meara promised.

"Where is Chris now?"

Meara looked at Finn. "My house."

"That's not far from Hunter's place."

"A little more than a mile. He won't suspect any of us are there. Hunter's supposed to be wherever we are at some safe house, as far as Chris knows."

"Yeah, but you know how well-laid plans can go awry."

―⁓―

Rourke parked some distance down the road south of Hunter and Tessa's house, hiding the car in the woods since the place didn't have a garage. He could just envision Chris driving by the pack leader's place, seeing Rourke's vehicle parked in front, and wondering what the hell he was doing there since Hunter wasn't home.

Rourke locked his car doors. Then with the evidence tucked under his arm, he bolted through the trees to reach the house. When he got there, he went around to the back door and picked the lock, memories flooding him of when he'd stayed there to help Hunter protect Tessa during a winter storm, electrical outages, and fights with bad guys. And how he'd wanted Tessa, but the SEAL had won out. Who could compete with a SEAL who was a wolf on top of that?

Now Rourke would help Finn to protect Meara, which was almost the same scenario. Only Rourke wasn't interested in Meara the way he'd had a crush on Tessa. Meara was too... *unpredictable* for him.

He locked the door to the place.

Rourke glanced at his wrist and then remembered he no longer wore a watch as a werewolf. It was one of the hardest things he'd had to get used to. At first, he'd fought the idea—until he'd stripped out of his clothes, forgot his watch, shifted, and lost his prized watch in the woods.

Meara and Finn should be here by now. They were probably hiding their vehicle like he had done and were on foot in the woods, headed in this direction.

He was damned thankful his need to investigate the situation had prompted him to search Chris's house. Never in a millennium would Rourke have believed that Chris had been involved. Without the evidence, they all might have been clueless about Chris's involvement until it was too late.

He heard a noise on the back patio, and thinking Meara and Finn were trying to get in, Rourke headed for the back door to open it for them.

His heart thundering, Rourke stared at Chris, who stood at the back door looking in through the kitchen window. When Chris caught Rourke's eye, he cast him an evil smile. Chris walked over to the back door and tried to unlock it with a lockpick.

"You know, Rourke, you're supposed to be at your apartment," Chris said through the door.

The lockpick twisted some more. Rourke's skin chilled.

"You're not supposed to be driving your vehicle, either."

Twist, grind, twist.

"You're supposed to be waiting for me until I pick you up to take you to the newspaper office."

Click.

"Why are you here at Hunter's house? Don't you know that's illegal? Breaking and entering? Hunter will not be pleased."

Rourke raced back into the living room and shoved the incriminating papers underneath the couch cushion. Should he shift? He had no weapon on him.

"So, what are you doing here? Dave said you wanted to speak to me about investigating this situation further concerning Allan's shooter. What was it you wished to ask me?"

Rourke bolted for the guest bedroom where he'd slept before and locked the door behind him. He was beginning to shuck his clothes when he heard the back door squeak open.

He should have brought the evidence of Chris's involvement in here.

"You're not hiding from me, are you?" Chris asked. "You're supposed to be a big bad wolf now, not a rabbit, Rourke. Are you still a rabbit?"

Rourke swore under his breath as he stood naked in the guest room, unable to the shift.

"Are you in one of the bedrooms?" Chris asked, heading down the hall. "Hmm, only one door closed. Are you hiding behind Door Number 1? The big question is why?"

"How did you know I was here?" Rourke asked, hoping that he could delay the inevitable so that Finn and Meara would have a chance to arrive.

"I just happened to be leaving Meara's house when who should I see roar lickety-split down the road in his truck past the place but my buddy Rourke, who was supposed to still be at his apartment. So I followed you here. Found where you hid your vehicle and gave the order to disable it, if you thought to leave again anytime soon. You weren't supposed to be driving, you know."

Someone else was with Chris? Hell, he'd never get out of this alive. "You said that already, Chris."

"Yeah, well, you seem to need more direction. So why are you here, and why, when you saw me at the door, didn't you let me in? You didn't think I'd just go away, did you?"

"Hunter's on his way here."

"Really. Well, a little birdie told me he's having a rough day of it on his own. I'd planned to oversee operations at the safe house, but… well, this seemed like something that needed looking into right away."

Rourke's heart was beating so hard that he figured Chris could hear it through the door. But no matter how many times he tried to tell himself to shift, it wasn't having any effect. "How did you learn where Hunter is?"

"That's the wonder of a mate who wasn't a wolf. She was worried about Hunter and called Dave to see if he could check on him. Since Dave is in the middle of a crisis, trying to track down a runaway teen, he asked me to look into it. That's all I needed to wrap this up. The location of the safe house."

If Chris managed to kill Hunter because of Tessa's mistake, she'd never be able to live with herself.

Again, Rourke tried to will himself to shift. Nothing. Hell, why was it that just when he thought he had the shifting down pat, it eluded him?

"So exactly *why* are we having this scene?" Chris asked with an odd tone to his voice. Like he was ready to end this now. But Rourke figured Chris was dying to know what Rourke had learned and possibly who he had told.

A lockpick was shoved in the bedroom door lock, and Rourke glanced from the door to the window, wondering what he could do even if he escaped that way when he was naked, when he heard the familiar click that told him the door was unlocked and ready to open.

Rourke expected Chris to open the door by throwing it aside. But instead, he did it in his usual quiet manner, slowly, no doubt listening to see if Rourke was a wolf ready to pounce. Rourke figured Chris probably hadn't shifted himself yet.

"Rourke," Chris said, his voice low and cold, testing to see if Rourke could still respond as a human.

But Rourke wouldn't ease Chris's mind one bit and kept silent, while he kept praying he'd shift.

Chris didn't push the door open wide enough to allow Rourke to see him. Then Chris moved away from the door. "Just for your information, Cyn should be here any minute now. The supposed squabble that cabin renters were having at Meara's place? Really just me and Cyn making some last-minute plans. He's the one who is sabotaging your vehicle. He wanted a piece of you, too. He doesn't like newly turned wolves at all and reporters in general, but I've waited long enough for this, and you're all mine."

Rourke heard Chris's zipper slide down. Chris was going to strip and shift.

Rourke cursed his inability to shift at will. He really loved being a werewolf, but he wouldn't be one for very much longer if he couldn't summon the ability to become a wolf like—now!

A tingling started rushing through his veins, heating him to the marrow of his bones, the muscles stretching, welcoming the wolf side of him, and for a moment, he felt relief. But just as he shifted and looked up from the floor, Rourke saw Chris standing in the doorway, a wolf ready to rip him to shreds, his amber eyes and mouth wickedly smiling.

His fur standing on end, his heart thundering, Rourke figured maybe he should have thought this out a little more. While he'd still had the chance, maybe he should have attempted to flee out the window, and then shifted and run like hell until Finn showed up.

It was now or never. Chris growled with a second of warning, then lunged at him.

~~~

Finn figured the reason Meara couldn't reach Hunter, Anna, or the rest of the SEAL team on the phone was because they had shifted into their wolf forms and were possibly in a fight. Meara was trying not to show how anxious she was, but he was certain she was even more worried about Rourke than she was about her brother or the others. They were trained in combat. Rourke was not. And he was alone.

"Does he still have problems shifting?" Finn asked, not having been around newly turned wolves much.

"Yes. That's why he's always got to have a mentor when he's out. He's not supposed to be driving until he can prove he's got this shifting business under control."

Finn hadn't even thought of that. He could just imagine a newly turned wolf trying to drive, getting the urge to strip and shift, and veering off the coast road into the Pacific Ocean.

Meara suddenly stopped, and Finn grabbed her arm as he heard a man's voice at the house.

"Chris," she whispered, her voice fearful.

"Stay here, Meara. I'll take care of it."

"No." She pursed her lips. "I'll speak with him. He supposedly wants me. I'll distract him. Then you can get the drop on him. But if you just go in, he could kill Rourke first."

"It's too risky. Stay here."

She ground her teeth, knowing that Finn was used to operations like this, but she still thought her plan had merit.

Finn stripped off his clothes shifted in record time, and looked back at Meara as if doubting his decision to leave her alone. When she motioned for him to go, he turned and raced through the woods toward Hunter's home.

As soon as he was nearly out of sight, a twig snapped behind Meara, and she swung around and gasped.

"You want me to shoot Finn, I will, Meara," Cyn warned, his hair longer than she'd remembered it, his amber eyes gleaming with power, his voice threatening. "Come here," he growled.

She moved away from the cliff and toward Cyn as slowly as she could without aggravating him further.

"You and your damned brother ruined everything for me," he said, his voice low and menacing.

"I don't understand," she said. "I thought you wanted to date me. But I guess that wasn't the master plan, was it?"

He snorted. "As if it would ever have worked out with your brother running things. My sister wasn't supposed to die the way she did."

She knew it. He would kill her for revenge because his sister was dead. But why would someone have changed the location of the meeting on the beach? If the team had gone to the other location, they would have all died and so would have the hostages.

Knowing the answer to the question, she asked anyway, wanting to hear him say it. "Why do you want me dead?"

"Hell, Meara, I wanted you. Period. I genuinely liked you. But you told Hunter you didn't wish to see me. That I wasn't good enough for you like I wasn't good enough for Hunter's precious team."

She scowled at him and folded her arms at her waist. "That's not true. I told Hunter I wanted to see you."

He turned to look in the direction of Hunter's house where they could hear the sound of growling wolves. "Damn your brother for lying to me." He looked back at Meara. "I thought you decided I wasn't worthy to see you. Hunter told me as much and then said the same thing about including me on his team."

"It wasn't so." And knowing Hunter, he wouldn't have said anything so cruel. She figured that Cyn had heard what he wanted to hear. "Why did you want to be on the team so badly? To save your sister?"

He laughed mercilessly. "She was human, you know. And she'd overheard my plans as I was talking to one of my men over the phone. She was suspicious of me. Knew something was different about me after I was turned. So we used her as one of the hostages. She was worth a hell of a lot more than a ransom to me.

"When she died, I'd inherit everything that she was to get. And you know how it is. When a human learns of our existence, they either have to be turned or die. It's our way. No way in hell was I making her one of us. So it was the perfect solution. Kill her off in a hostage-taking situation, and I would get the inheritance."

Meara stared at him in disbelief, unable to fathom how someone could hate a sibling that much. "So you planned the whole affair? Had the women taken as hostages so you could get the money? But you didn't intend their release?"

"That's about the gist of it."

She couldn't imagine anyone so unfeeling that he would kill for a handful of money. "What did your sister ever do to you?"

Cyn narrowed his eyes at her. "My parents didn't like me, didn't like what I was doing, and when they died, they left every bit of their million-dollar estate to my sister. Hell, I received a dollar to show they hadn't forgotten me in the will. A frigging dollar!"

Meara took a deep breath, wondering how his parents had died and what he had done to deserve being cut from the will. "Why did you send the message to Hunter to change the location of the beach landing?"

"Hell, I didn't do that. I certainly didn't have his email address. One of your own pack members did that. Chris Tarleton was the defector."

She still had a tough time believing Chris could be behind all this. Chris had always been quiet and had absolutely no sense of humor, but he did a good job as one of Hunter's sub-leaders. "Why had he been involved in all of this?"

"Hell, Meara, think about it. Hunter hasn't been around that much over the years, off fighting one cause or another. Chris is tired of playing second fiddle, so to speak. He kept thinking Hunter would get killed on a mission, and that would solve that, but the Navy SEAL just wouldn't die. And then when the fire destroyed your home in California, Chris had the perfect opportunity to convince a bunch of the pack to mutiny and—"

"Chris did that? He split the pack up completely! Damn him." Even now the pack was split up, with some living in southern California without any plans to return.

"Yeah, well, he hadn't exactly meant for that to happen. Those who went to southern California weren't supposed to. Chris would have succeeded with the group he took off with if they hadn't wound up in a red wolf's territory in Portland. Leidolf, I think the pack leader's name was, wasn't about to put up with your pack's encroachment. Chris was forced to return to the coast with the rest of the pack. Then Hunter had the trouble with that gray pack, and Chris thought that would be the end of him."

"But Hunter survived."

"Yeah. He always managed to survive. And he took up with that woman photographer. It looked as though he was giving up his contract work and staying here with her for good. No more missions. No more leaving the pack under Chris's control. And that wouldn't do. So Chris contacted me. Said he'd pay me again to gather a group of men and get rid of Hunter and his team for good."

"So this wasn't about me."

"Hell, yeah, it's about you."

About revenge for her not wishing to see him further, so he thought. "The two of you concocted the hostage crisis?" she asked.

"Me and my own team and Chris. We wanted the money. Chris wanted your pack. You were up for grabs."

Right. As if she'd go along with it.

"What about the Knight of Swords?"

"The what?"

She narrowed her eyes at him. Although she suspected that Chris was the Knight of Swords, she wanted to know if Cyn knew for certain. "Someone left the tarot card as a calling card of sorts with Allan when he was shot."

"I don't know anything about that."

Feeling chilled with the cool ocean breeze whipping across her skin, she asked, "Didn't you have Allan shot?"

"No, Chris did."

Finn would kill Chris if Hunter didn't do the job. She felt nauseated all over again. How could they have missed the signs that one of their own pack members had been a traitor? "So you hadn't intended for Hunter and his team to die on the beach?"

"Hell, yeah, we had. If I'd been with the team, I would have been the only survivor. Somehow I don't see Hunter as the kind of guy who would have allowed me to take the ransom money after making sure my sister was dead. Some of the women would have made it out with me, so I would have gotten all the honors. I would have been a team leader instead of just a team member, and the ransom would have been paid to the bad guys. Which would have been me and my men.

"Only it didn't work out as planned. And we didn't get any of the ransom money. My sister had changed her will so that charity would get every dime of her inheritance, should she die. I hadn't planned on that. Not only that, but she left a message that if she died an accidental death, the investigating officer should check me out because she suspected I had killed our parents."

"Had you?"

He smiled. "In any event, she was killed in a terrorist activity, and no one suspected me. Although you can't imagine how angry I was that she had changed her will and I didn't receive anything from it."

He waved his weapon at the trees. "During the operation, Finn returned fire and hit me in the leg, although he didn't know it, and then rescued the women who were still alive. It took me a while to recuperate, devise the forest-fire plan, and then come after you and Hunter."

"And Chris?"

He shrugged. "What can I say? He couldn't fight Hunter fair and square as a wolf, but he has been running the pack. Then Hunter mated, planning to settle down and really run the pack full time. The last straw was when Hunter accidentally turned that reporter, decided to go on a honeymoon with his mate, and stuck Chris with baby-sitting Rourke. You don't even want to know how mad Chris was about that."

"Hunter would have continued to watch over

Rourke. He really likes the guy. He wouldn't have given the job to anyone else in the pack except someone he really respected."

Cyn shook his head. "Maybe so, but Chris didn't see it that way."

"Who set the fire?"

Cyn ground his teeth and looked in the direction of the wolves growling. He turned back to Meara and said, "I meant to get Hunter and his whole blasted pack that time. I came to get you, and then some wolf was skulking around after a woman who was taking pictures of the fire—the woman who became Hunter's mate. When the wolf saw me in the vicinity, he chased me off. So I missed my opportunity."

"But Chris couldn't have wanted you to set the fire that destroyed all of the pack members' homes."

"No, he didn't know I'd set it. But he did take advantage of the calamity and convinced Hunter's pack to mutiny."

Bastard. "So this all started with coveting money, wanting your sister to die because she'd learned your plans and gotten all of your parents' inheritance, and wanting to get even with Hunter for not taking you on his team. And revenge against me because you thought I chose not to see you any longer."

"That about wraps it up."

"So now what?"

His eyes took on a maniacal gleam. "You come with me, or you die here."

Meara didn't have a choice. She couldn't strip and shift and have a chance against an armed man. She couldn't run away. She couldn't fight him for the gun and wrest it away from him. Not when he was a SEAL, trained for any kind of confrontation.

"Come on, Meara, you really don't have a choice here."

She knew that, damn it. All but one. She'd never believed she'd need someone as much as she needed Finn now. Nor that she'd do what she was about to do. Not when she was a wolf. The pack leader's sister. A woman who had rescued others when they had needed her help. But it was her only choice. And if she could, she'd kill Cyn herself for making her do this.

She filled her lungs with air and screamed.

Finn had tried to poke his nose through the wolf door to Hunter's house, but it was locked. *Damn it*. He could hear the growling inside, two wolves fighting, and he feared for Rourke's life. But when Hunter and his mate had gone on their honeymoon, he must have locked the wolf door. And Finn couldn't get in.

Finn suspected that Chris hadn't locked the door after he most likely picked the lock. So wasting more time, Finn shifted into his human form and grabbed the door handle, twisted, and found the door locked.

Without a lockpick, and seeing nothing on the patio that wasn't bolted down, Finn was fresh out of luck.

"Hold on, Rourke," he muttered under his breath, naked as the day he was born and headed down the path to the beach to locate a good-sized rock he could use to break a window.

His heart racing with concern, he was at the bottom of the steep incline before he found a rock he thought might do.

Rock in hand, he headed back up the steep path. Halfway up it, he heard a woman's blood-curdling scream. He froze. His first thought was that it couldn't be Meara. Never in a million years would she scream about anything. But there was no one else out here. He shifted into his wolf form, silently apologized to Rourke and prayed he'd last until Finn could return, and dashed back to where he'd left Meara all alone.

Meara's heart was still beating a million miles a minute as she screamed and ran into the woods, shoving aside branches, climbing over a fallen tree trunk, and traversing limbs torn from trees in a recent storm. Okay, so she didn't think she could run away from an armed nutcase, but she did think that Cyn might just chase after her and not shoot her.

She was right. The only sounds were his heavy boots clomping on the woodland floor, his heavy breathing, and his heartbeat accelerating as he quickly closed the gap between them way too fast. He was six-two, and his lengthy stride was gobbling up the ground in a hurry, nearly giving her heart palpitations.

In the horror movies, the woman always looked back just before whatever was chasing her got her. She wouldn't look back. She was afraid he'd strike her in the head with the butt of his weapon, knock her out cold, and then haul her off to some undisclosed location. But she wouldn't look back.

Not until she heard the sound of a wolf in rapid pursuit of Cyn. He was quiet, but still she knew the sound of a wolf running on four padded feet, knew the way he moved when he was chasing his prey, knew beyond a doubt that he would kill Cyn before he had a chance to turn and fire off a shot.

But if Finn didn't reach him in time, Meara had to ensure that the shot Cyn tried to fire went wild.

She looked back and saw Finn racing to her aid, his fur swept backward from the breeze and the run as he tore toward her. Or toward Cyn. Finn's gaze met hers for a second, as if making sure she wasn't injured, as if telling her she had nothing to worry about, his tongue hanging out of his mouth, panting hard, his eyes narrowed with anger.

Cyn had stopped and rapidly turned and, in a SEAL way, readied his weapon to kill his pursuer.

Meara had to stop him. She couldn't slam into his hard body and make any difference, she didn't think. She grabbed a sturdy branch lying on the ground, probably torn off in the last big storm they'd had, and ran up behind him. He heard her, but he ignored her, knowing the real threat was the wolf in front of him.

She swung the branch at Cyn's head with all her might, connected with his ear and head, and distracted him just enough to make him miss his shot.

She was sure he wanted to kill her now, but one pissed-off wolf lunged at him, and Cyn didn't have a chance.

Finn's jump knocked Cyn on his back, and Cyn dropped his weapon. He reached for a sheathed knife, but Finn was too quick, biting him in the throat, and ending his murderous reign. For a moment, he sat panting over the body, but then he looked at Meara and then again at Hunter's house.

"Rourke," she said.

She raced toward the house, but Finn woofed, then headed to where his clothes were. She turned and watched him, confused. He poked at his pants, and she ran back to where he stood over his clothes. When she found his lockpick, he bowed his head and raced back to the house. She ran after him, trying to catch up and fearing Rourke would never make it on his own. She was damned glad to hear the growling in the house, which meant he was fighting for his life but still alive.

Chris bit Rourke in the cheek, causing sharp pain to rip through his face and pissing him off. What if he was disfigured for life?

He snarled and growled and fought tooth to tooth with the sub-leader. He tasted blood, his blood and Chris's.

That made him even angrier. What if he chipped a tooth or, worse, lost one?

He hadn't fought wolf-to-wolf much, but thankfully, the instinct came to him naturally. When Chris growled at him again, Rourke gave an even lower, deeper bass-sounding growl, rumbling from low in the belly. He pulled back his lips and bared his sharp canines. And when Chris clashed with him, the two stood on their hind legs, forelegs thrashing for a better hold, heads swiveling to get a bite in where it would count.

This was not a game, like he'd played with the other wolves, which had just been a practice for a real hunt. This was a battle to the finish.

Oh, if only he could be the victor and write about it in a news story!

Rourke bullheadedly shoved Chris out of the bedroom

where he'd been confined by the bed and dresser. Now in the more open living room, they bumped into a table, sending a candy dish and pale-pink and green candy squares flying. Next, they upset another table and sent a lamp to the floor where it broke with a loud crash. Rourke realized now how important having a place of his own could be, not an apartment where next-door neighbors could hear the disturbance, if he ever again had the chance to get into another wolf fight, and call the police.

Chris was a tenacious bulldog of a wolf, though. He kept going for Rourke's throat, and Rourke kept twisting his head around to counter the attack, biting and snarling even more aggressively than Chris. He thought it was because Chris was always quieter. But the growling made Rourke feel more at home with being a wolf, more in control of his situation, better equipped to fight another wolf who wanted him dead.

They both banged into the couch and then the coffee table. Rourke kept trying to get hold of Chris's throat, but the wolf was as adamant about keeping him from doing so as Rourke was about protecting his own throat. They danced again on their hind quarters, sparring and fighting, then down again with Rourke persisting, pushing, and trying to wear Chris out. But Chris wasn't wearing out, damn him. Rourke was.

Somehow they'd ended up back in the bedroom.

But then Rourke got a lucky break. Chris backed into a clothes tree, and it began to fall on him. When he turned his head slightly to see what he'd run into and probably where to go next to continue the fight, Rourke had his chance. And took it.

With Chris's head turned, Rourke grabbed for the sub-leader's neck and bit down hard.

—◆◆◆—

Meara reached the back door where Finn circled her, anxious to get inside Hunter's house to rescue Rourke. She was so nervous that she fumbled with the pick, finally managing to unlock the door and shove it open. Finn rushed into the house, both of them expecting the worst. Finn would have to kill Chris, and Rourke would already be dead.

The place was a wreck: end tables on their sides, a candy dish broken to pieces, and the remnants of pastel after-dinner mints scattered all over the carpet. Chris and Rourke's scents and the smell of blood wafted into the living area as soon as they entered. But there were no sounds of anything. The place was quiet as death.

Then Finn ran down the hallway and entered a guest room. Meara waited, expecting to hear more growling as Finn fought with Chris. But then Finn poked his nose out of the room, smiling like only a wolf could.

"Rourke," she cried. He had to be all right. She rushed to the guest room as Finn headed through the living room and exited the house. As a wolf, Rourke was panting on the carpeted bedroom floor, while Chris's dead body lay near the bedroom window, a clothes tree on top of him.

She wiped away annoying tears and wrapped her arms around Rourke, pressing her face against his cheek. His tail thwapped enthusiastically against the floor. She didn't want to give him ideas and finally released him. She also didn't want Finn to see her hugging Rourke when he returned and get any wrong ideas.

She wiped away more tears and smiled at Rourke. "Thanks for learning the truth, and..." She choked on the words and gave him another hug. She was still hugging him soundly, so grateful he was alive, that she didn't even hear Finn come into the room.

But Rourke saw him and immediately rose, as if getting ready for a new confrontation.

"Where's the evidence, Rourke?" Finn asked, fully dressed and looking relieved that Rourke was alive but angry about Chris and his evil doings.

The papers. She'd forgotten all about them. Rourke licked her hand, then hurried out of the bedroom and down the hall to the living room. She suspected he couldn't shift back.

He poked a paw at the couch, and Finn shoved his hand between the cushions and pulled out a handful of evidence—plane ticket, tarot cards, photo, financial statements. He handed them to Meara, but she shook her head. "Let Hunter see them."

Then with new worry, she ground her teeth. "Hunter."

"They're fine." Finn pulled his phone out of his pocket and handed it to her. "Hunter said two men hit them at the house, but everyone's fine. Except for the two men. And the house."

"What happened to the house?"

"The two men were demolition experts. They blew it up."

Meara gaped at Finn.

"Of course, Hunter's more than furious that Chris

was involved. He and the others are driving up here—all but Bjornolf—and Hunter will take it from there."

"Bjornolf had already left, I thought."

"Apparently not. He hung around to make sure the guys didn't need his help. And then he heard there was a runaway teen in the pack and he wanted to look into the kid's disappearance."

Meara's mouth gaped again. "Bjornolf?"

"Don't start getting ideas that he's a nice guy, Meara." Finn pulled her into his arms and kissed her cheek. "If you were afraid Rourke was going to have a time finding a mate, after they learn what he did here today, the un-mated females will be flocking to him, wanting a chance to be that mate."

Rourke grinned with a silly, wolfish smile. Meara gave him a small, weepy smile back. Now she knew why Tessa had a fondness for the man who was now a wolf. He truly was a welcome addition to the pack.

Finn and Meara returned to her place and discussed all that Chris and Cyn had been responsible for—the fire that had destroyed their homes, the mutiny Chris had en-couraged, the murders of innocent victims—all so Chris could be a pack leader when he didn't have the courage to fight Hunter wolf to wolf for the position. And so Cyn could pocket a bundle of blood money.

Meara continued to obsess about all that had hap-pened as they entered her home. "The safe house was demolished," she said, shaking her head. "What will the owners say?"

Finn ushered her into her living room, sat her down

on the couch, and pulled a throw she had hanging over the arm of the couch onto her lap. Then he went into the kitchen and began making her a mug of mint tea. "The owners will say that the home can be rebuilt. That none of us could have been replaced. Nothing else really matters, you know."

"They won't care anything about us, except to be furious that we brought this down on them," Meara moaned. "Even if insurance covered it, which I highly doubt, the home would still need to be rebuilt."

"I'll just sell off the property. The location and land will still bring a good deal of money. Prime oceanfront property, worth a mint."

"You? You said it was owned by a friend of a friend of a friend."

"That's how I had to buy it to keep the ownership hidden so we could use it as a safe house."

"It was *your* home? You mean, here I made the remark about whoever the owner was must have decorated in all yellow to chase away the Oregon gloom, and all along it was *your* home?"

He carried out a cup of hot tea for her and tucked a straggle of hair behind her ear. "And I said the owner must be from California. To which you looked to the ceiling as if unable to believe I would say such a thing because you are from northern California. But it was my interior decorator's idea. She's from southern California like me and said yellow would help brighten the place."

Her lips parted, then she frowned. "That's why you knew where the brandy was located. And the master bedroom. It was yours."

"Ours. Was ours."

"Who was staying there before we arrived?"

"A Navy SEAL and his new bride—I reimbursed them sufficiently so that they were able to pay for an island adventure."

"Your poor home." Then she managed a smile with a gleam in her eyes. "So just how much will the land be worth if you sell off the property?"

———~~~———

Two days later, confident the pack would be secure without his being there, Hunter returned to Hawaii to be with Tessa while Finn and Meara settled into her house before they took off on their own honeymoon. Allan, Paul, and Anna had left for places unknown. And Bjornolf had run down the runaway teen. Seemed the runaway had wanted to start his own wolf pack—teen only—but couldn't get any takers. Bjornolf had talked him into SEAL training when he was old enough. Bjornolf was now taking a break somewhere in the South Pacific, or so he said. But for all they knew, Bjornolf could be lurking just down the road.

Rourke was the hero of the pack, and at least three of the females had taken notice of him. They all wanted to mentor him, and he didn't mind being mentored any longer in the least.

All that was left was a Caribbean cruise that Meara and Finn would take when Hunter and Tessa returned, only they'd extended their trip to three weeks instead of two. That left Meara and Finn exploring the coast close to home and each other.

After a brisk swim in the Pacific, Meara and Finn returned to the house for a hot shower. Meara was glad that Hunter had always watched out for her and that she hadn't ended up with the wrong wolf before Finn showed up to steal her heart.

She hadn't thought of showering with Finn, given the economical ones he always took, quick and over with in no time, and although she didn't like to waste water, she enjoyed the heat and steam or a simulated rain shower for a relaxing time. Water-tile body sprays in the wall provided an adjustable massage, working wonders on taut muscles, too.

But once she headed for the glassed-in shower stall, Finn walked into the bathroom to join her. Admiringly, she slid her gaze over his sculpted nude body, his skin salty from the sea just like a SEAL's should be.

"What happened to taking a brief shower?" she asked, hoping that he didn't think she would want to do the same.

"Hmm," Finn said, "I like to conserve water, and sharing a shower with you sounds like a good deal."

She smiled and switched on the digital interface, mixing water, light, and sound into a pleasing symphony of pleasurable sensations, and then stepped into the shower. "But," she warned him, "I don't believe in turning off the water while I'm soaping my body."

Finn entered the stall and pulled the door closed, then gathered her into his arms under the heat of the running water and kissed her upturned face. "I'll be the one soaping that gorgeous body of yours. And the water stays on."

Releasing her briefly while she shampooed her hair, he poured vanilla-scented body wash into his hands and began a careful and methodical soaping ritual. His large hands started at her throat, spreading the scented wash all around her neck, down her shoulders and breasts, pausing to lift and massage. Then he worked in tiny circles over and around her nipples while she made a mountain of soapy curls on top of her head and chuckled at the diligence he showed in making sure her breasts were thoroughly cleaned.

He smiled at her as she began to thoroughly wash him, too, her fingers massaging his neck and shoulders, lathering the soap all over him as the water continued to rain down on them, taking the soap with it.

She gave him the same attention to detail, her forefingers running over his nipples with delicate precision, making them as sensitive as hers, she was certain, from the way his erection poked her in the belly. He hugged her against his body to reach her back and soap all the way down to her buttocks. She found his rubbing against her like this more erotic than she could imagine. She tried to reach around to soap his back, but he was too tall and broad.

He laughed at her futile efforts.

Then he added more soap to his hands and shifted to her waist and down between her legs. "Hmm, Meara," he said, kissing her cheek, sounding as though he'd found wolf heaven, a version of SEAL heaven, as the hot water forced streams into their backs or sides, depending on which way they moved.

And then he was leaning down, soaping her legs as she lathered his head. That gave him pause as she used her fingers to massage his scalp from the hairline to the back in tight little circles and then did the same thing on the sides until every inch of his scalp was stimulated, the blood flowing freely to every follicle.

When she was done, he rose and slid his hands into the mountain of soapy hair she'd created on top of her head. Then he began to give the same delicious massage to her scalp, his fingers working her into a relaxed state of bliss, only she was also hot and needy and wanted him inside of her now. She soaped her hands again, wrapped her fingers around his erection, and slid up and down, up and down, watching the way his eyes darkened to midnight, hoping he would not be able to resist taking this to the next step.

"You're melting," his voice rasped, and she *was*, under his ministrations, ready to slide down onto the shower floor, spread her legs, and beg for him to finish her off.

Then he was rinsing her hair and the rest of her body and himself until they were squeaky clean and free of soap suds. But he didn't stop there as he slipped his fingers between her legs as if making sure she was soap-free there, too. His fingers gently assaulted her, ratchetting up the strokes over her clit until her body was shaking with need and wanting fulfillment, the desire so rampant that she'd do anything to reach the pinnacle.

Before she could demand that he hurry, she felt the uplift as the climax hit, and he knowingly smiled but didn't wait for her to come back down. In one swift movement, he lifted her and penetrated her deeply. Her body held him tight, contractions wrapping her in a cloak of heated bliss. Then he began the steady thrusts, deeper, his mouth on hers, their tongues and bodies wet and slippery and beautiful.

"Oh, Finn," she mouthed against his throat as another wave of orgasm drew over her.

But it wasn't until he gave one last thrust and she felt his hot seed fill her that he finally whispered in her wet hair, "You are a Viking's treasure."

"Conquest, you mean," she said, breathlessly.

"Yeah." He kissed her cheek and set her on the shower floor. "I always knew my mate would live by the sea."

She raised her brows. "What would you have done if I had still lived in the forests of California?"

"Moved you to a home by the sea."

She sighed and turned off the water. "I'm so sorry about your home."

He grabbed a towel and began drying her. "It didn't have the amenities that this one does."

"Since it was so luxurious, I'm surprised that you didn't have the fancy showerheads and all."

"I meant you," he said, wrapping the towel around her back like a sling and pulling her to his hard body. His mouth pressed against hers until her tongue played with his, and she slipped her arms around his waist and held on tight.

"I thought you weren't a romantic, but, Finn, you've got them all beat."

He finished drying her and grabbed a towel to dry off his body while she wrapped one around her hair in a turban. "Damn right I have," he said.

She chuckled and slipped into a strapless terry cloth dress, the smocked bodice fitting tightly over her breasts, the length of the skirt high thigh.

He wrapped the towel around his waist, smiled down at her, and cupped her breasts in his hands. "I like this."

"Thank you. It's meant to be a beach cover-up, but I

like to wear it when I get out of the shower sometimes before going to bed. I'm going to fix some roast beef hash from the leftovers—old family recipe. Want some?"

"Yeah, but…" he said, pulling her close, "I thought maybe we could lie down for a bit first."

"Not now. Afterward. I'm starving." She pressed his lips with a quick kiss, but when his hands went to her hips and he locked onto her mouth with a penetrating kiss, she quickly broke free. And smiled at him. "You'll have me barefoot and pregnant before long if we keep this up."

"Hmm, Meara, I like that idea." He reached for her shoulders, but she quickly dodged his hands, tossed the towel from her head into the clothes basket, slipped out of the bedroom, and headed for the door. "More *after* we eat."

Smiling, she hurried down the hall to the kitchen, thinking how much her uncle's place was really a home to her now that Finn was her mate. And wondering if he was through taking Navy showers for the rest of his life.

A knock on the back door had her nearly jumping out of her skin.

She walked to the door and opened it to see a tanned, attractive man with obsidian eyes and hair and a smile that brightened his whole expression as he looked her over from the wet tangled hair dangling over her shoulders to the short terry cloth dress she wore and her bare feet. "*Well*, I believe this little resort is just the place I needed to be for the first vacation I've had in years. You must be Meara Greymere. I'm—"

She didn't have a chance to say anything before Finn stalked into the room, silent as a SEAL and a wolf combined, still wearing only a towel around his torso as he closed in on her and pulled her against his chest in an overwhelmingly flagrant show of alpha male possessiveness. He kissed the top of her head.

In no uncertain terms, he was making it clear to any other male wolf, this one in particular, that Meara might be renting the cabins to single alpha males, but she'd already made her selection and Finn was one damn lucky wolf. But it also reminded her of how he had first claimed her in front of Bjornolf.

The man stood his ground, typical alpha male, but smiled a little unevenly. "Guess I booked my reservation a little too late."

"Reservation." She had totally forgotten about the incoming guests this week. "No," she quickly said, wanting to make the resort a success since Hunter had given her full rein over it now that he didn't have to worry about her because she was Finn's problem. She smiled at the notion. "You'll have a wonderful time. And Finn's a SEAL, so if you need a running partner or someone to show you the best places to swim, he won't mind going with you."

"And you?" he asked.

"For an extra cost, I cook meals." She caressed Finn's arm still wrapped around her waist. "Finn does a great job making s'mores, though."

"S'mores?" The guest chuckled. "Looks like I made the right choice for a vacation after all. Only I still wish I'd come a little sooner."

Meara smiled. "Things were a little... hectic earlier. And you would have had to come a long time ago, if you were looking for more than a vacation."

He looked at Finn and said, "Long drive to get here, and I need to work out some kinks before I retire for the night. Want to show me the area and take a little run?"

Finn smiled and tightened his hold on Meara. "We've got the night booked. Tomorrow, first thing, I can show you around the place."

She sighed. "You must be Hugh Sutherland."

"Yes, I am."

Thrill seeker, she recalled that she'd noted about him. But if he sought anything of the sort, he'd have to find it on his own. "There's your key. You have the cabin farthest from this one." She waved her hand toward the north.

Hugh nodded and took the key in hand, then said to Finn, "Tomorrow then. But I won't disturb you." He gave Meara a meaningful look, then refocused his attention on Finn. "Just drop by when it's convenient. Hell, I'm on vacation, so no appointments for anything. Oh, and someone delivered something on the back porch." He bowed his head to the two of them and closed the back door.

"Hmm, you're supposed to help market the resort, too," Meara said, as Finn slid his hands around her breasts and began to massage them, his face nuzzling her neck. "And sending away our guests without accommodating them further probably won't give us four-star rating."

"I'll make it up to him tomorrow," Finn said, seductively licking her ear.

She groaned and whispered, "I'm hungry."

"Me, too."

She headed for the back door to check out the

package, but when she opened the door, she frowned at the tall box. And then as she read the label, she shook her head. Turning, she saw Finn smiling broadly at her.

"Well? You told me you needed a new vacuum," he said smugly.

"A *vacuumer*. As in someone who vacuums. Hmm, I guess I did say that I needed a new vacuum also. And you know what? I know just who to teach how to use it."

He stalked forward to carry the box inside, then locked the door, and pulled her into his arms. "So, what do you think of the wedding present?"

"Oh, Finn, I think it's a great wedding present for you," she said, sliding her hands across his nipples in a provocative way.

His hands went to her breasts again, and he was about to kiss her when his phone rang in her pocket.

Uh-oh.

He slipped his hand into Meara's front right pocket. "Got my phone again?"

"Yeah, just in case you get any unwanted calls."

He snorted. "Like from old flames or anyone contacting me about any *dangerous missions*?"

He glanced at the caller ID, and she waited, barely breathing. He took a deep breath and patted her on the rump. "Fix dinner. I'll make a salad."

"Salad?" She couldn't believe he'd eat a salad, considering all the times when she'd had to force Hunter to.

Finn shrugged. "My mother taught me to eat my greens. It just became a habit."

"That's good, Finn." She frowned at the ringing phone in his hand. "Aren't you going to answer the call?"

He slipped his hand around hers and hauled her to

the kitchen. "What for? It's probably another of those damned dangerous missions Paul wants me to go on now that Hunter won't leave Tessa alone. I've got enough of one right here. First, I've got to make sure all these bachelor males that made arrangements to stay at the resort know you're not available, and second, I've got to keep you satisfied."

God, he was the only wolfish SEAL-man for her. And she loved him for it.

She touched the top edge of his towel with her fingertip. "Maybe we *could* eat afterward." She yanked off his towel, dropped it to the floor, and dashed around him for the bedroom.

Finn tackled Meara before she got far and swept her up in his arms, loving this aspect of her also—her playfulness. She tossed back her head and laughed. She was the most beautiful thing that had happened in his life, and he couldn't see how he'd even considered which option to choose—deadly contracts or... *this*.

Plus after the shower they'd just shared, he was never going back to Navy showers.

The SEAL had caught his wolf and his only mission now was making her happy, proving to her that he had no intention of quashing her alpha tendencies, and loving her just the way she was—every sexy damned bit of her.

While keeping her out of trouble.

LOOK FOR THE FIRST BOOK IN TERRY SPEAR'S
HOT NEW SHAPE-SHIFTER SERIES:

A SAVAGE HUNGER

AVAILABLE OCTOBER 2012 FROM
SOURCEBOOKS CASABLANCA

READ ON FOR EXCERPTS FROM

LEGEND *of the* WHITE WOLF

SEDUCED *by the* WOLF

WOLF FEVER

From *Legend of the White Wolf*

THE BLACK BEAR WAS RUNNING AWAY A HELL OF A LOT
faster than Owen Nottingham and his P.I. partner David
Davis thought capable. Their hunting guide, Trevor
Hodges, yelled at them to keep up, but at the rate the
bear was going, Owen and David would never last.
Already Owen had shin splints, and his side was aching something fierce. Damn, here he thought he was in
good shape.

They couldn't use dogs on the bear this late in the year
in Maine, but the owner of Back Country Tours, Kintail
Silverman, got around that by sending his pet wolves on
the hunt. The sleek white-furred creatures made Owen
feel like he was part of a wolf pack, hunting for survival,
diving around snow-laden firs, blending in, exhilarated,
hunting together as a cooperative team. The experience
would have been more pleasurable if his other partners
were with them—Cameron MacPherson, who wouldn't
hunt for anything other than criminals, and Gavin
Summerfield, who'd rather stay in Seattle and work than
fly anywhere. But the four of them were like a wolf pack,
solving crimes together as a collective unit and socializing
as the best of friends throughout the good times and bad.

So Owen wished they could share hunting excursions
together, too.

He noticed then that there were only snowy woods in
front of them. The wolves and the bear were lost in the

forest ahead as the chilly wind howled through the trees. Trevor was still keeping a good pace in the distance. For a white-haired old guy, he was lean and in incredibly great shape.

David had dropped way behind, but Owen was too busy trying to keep up the chase to wait for him to catch up. One last day before their hunt ended. And, hell, they'd tried to bag a bear for the last four years without any luck. The way the bear was outdistancing them in a hurry in the Maine wilderness; Owen was beginning to lose hope they'd make it this time either. But it was the closest they'd come.

When Owen didn't hear David's heavy breathing behind him, or his size ten boots trudging through the deep snow, he turned and looked to see how far behind he was. David was holding his thighs, leaning over, gasping for breath.

"David, you all right?" Owen asked, knowing it was a dumb question, when he figured David was trying to catch his second wind and couldn't answer anyway.

David motioned him on, wheezing, his face red and pinched with pain. "Get the bear! I'm fine. Go. I'll catch up."

But it wasn't like David not to keep up on a hunt and Owen ran back to check on him. "What's wrong?" Owen asked, grabbing his arm to steady him.

"Go. You'll... never... forgive... me... if... we..." David clutched his chest.

The wolves and Trevor circled back and joined them. The old man shook his head. "Chest pains?"

Through clenched teeth, David growled, "From... running... damn it."

David was the oldest of the four partners in their private investigator practice, but at thirty-five, David couldn't be having a heart attack.

With millions of acres of forest land all around them, they were too deep into the wilderness to get help. Cell phones wouldn't work out here. Owen knew CPR, but...

He helped David to sit. "What are you feeling?" he asked, trying to disguise the anxiety in his voice, although he couldn't hide a deepening frown, and David noticed.

"Don't be a... worry..." David clutched his chest even harder, his face sweating in the frigid air.

"We can't get any help to him way out here," Trevor said quietly. "If he's having a heart attack, it's not a bad way to go. Quick, no lingering illness."

"No!" Owen snapped. "Do you have any aspirin?" How could he let his friend from childhood and one of the best partners he'd had in law enforcement before they'd left the force die on him? He couldn't. "I know CPR."

"It won't be enough." Trevor sounded like the voice of reason, but Owen didn't want to hear it.

The image of David lunging in front of him, taking a bullet in the shoulder two years ago, flashed across Owen's mind. He wouldn't let him go. He couldn't.

The wolves watched silently, almost sympathetically as if one of their pack members was in trouble, their ears perked, their tongues hanging out, panting after the long run.

His hand clutching David's shoulder, Owen clenched his teeth to bite back the overwhelming feeling of hopelessness. "Can't we do something? Anything?"

"Possibly," Trevor said, "but it will change his life and yours, forever."

"I'd do anything to save my friend's life," Owen said, figuring Trevor was thinking in terms of if he had enough money, they could air-evac him out somewhere, maybe in a clearing where the loggers had been.

Trevor put a hand on Owen's shoulder. "You sure?"

"Anything, damn it. However much it costs, it's worth it."

Trevor looked back at the wolves. The biggest one bowed its head slightly, then bared his teeth and lunged.

Before Owen could fathom what was happening, the wolf bit David in the arm. He cried out in pain.

As Owen swung his rifle to his shoulder to shoot the beast, he caught a blur of white fur in his peripheral vision, right before one of the other wolves pounced on him.

From *Seduced by the Wolf*

EXCEPT FOR A COUPLE OF CARS PARKED OUTSIDE THE town hall, the lot was empty, and it appeared the wolf biologist speaking here tonight wouldn't have much of an audience to lecture to.

The Oregon air surrounding him felt damp and cool, not like the drier, much sunnier weather Leidolf Wildhaven had left behind in Colorado. He kept telling himself he'd get used to it. Old-time brass lanterns cast a golden glow over the sidewalk. A steady breeze stirred the spring leaves of the massive white oaks that lined the brick walk leading to the two-story building. An antiquated clock chimed seven times in the center of the tower on top, announcing to everyone in the listening area that the time had arrived for the lecture to begin.

He let out his breath and headed for the building. Anything to do with wolves concerned him, and even though the "doctor" couldn't say anything that he didn't already know, he wanted to see how others reacted to her talk concerning them. At this rate, it looked as though no one was going to show.

He took two steps at a time up the brick stairs and strode into the building, his gaze focusing on the empty chairs and the speakerless podium.

Dressed in a gray suit, Millie Meekle, the woman in charge of tourism and special events in the area, wrung her hands nearby and shook her head, her stiff, glued-together silver hair not moving a fraction out of place.

"Oh, Mr. Wildhaven, this is a disaster. Dr. Roux had a flat tire at the place she's staying, and my husband dropped me off here, so I haven't any vehicle to go get her." She waved at the empty seats. "And no one has even shown up yet."

"Where's she staying?"

Several men sauntered into the town hall, their boots tromping on the wooden floor, their expressions annoyed. "Where's the doc?" one of the men asked gruffly.

Millie quickly spoke up. "She's stuck at the Cranberry Top Bed and Breakfast. Mr. Wildhaven's kind enough to offer to get her. She's staying in the Blue Room, first door on the left down the hall from the entryway," she directed Leidolf.

The man snorted. "We don't need no damned wolf biologist telling us how we should reintroduce wolves into the wild out here."

"Now, Mr. Hollis," Millie said.

"Don't 'Now, Mr. Hollis' me, Millie. You know I raise sheep, and if any damn wolf slinks onto my land, I'll kill him dead. That's what I'll do."

"I'll go get her," Leidolf said. He stalked out of the building with its oppressive heat and back into the cool out-of-doors. He hadn't figured any of the livestock owners would bother to come to the meeting, but after seeing the burly men, he was afraid the professor was bound for trouble.

Climbing into his Humvee, he assumed the woman probably wouldn't get a whole lot of lecturing done but instead would be faced with a barrage of condemning remarks. He still couldn't figure out why in the world she'd come here instead of lecturing to a more intellectual crowd in the city of Portland, two hours away.

Putting the vehicle in drive, he headed to the Cranberry Top, a quaint little red-roofed home with white siding and a white picket fence. Like many of the homes in the area, the place had been turned into a bed-and-breakfast inn because it was situated on a creek perfect for fishing and picturesque Mount Hood could be seen way off in the distance. Great for a Portland getaway.

When Leidolf arrived at the inn, he saw the vehicle in question, a green pickup with California plates that was tilting to one side. *Women.* Probably didn't know how to change a tire or call for someone to come and fix a flat.

He'd barely opened the door to his Humvee when a woman hurried out, red hair in curls down to her shoulders and bouncing with her every step, eyes sea green and wide and hopeful, brow furrowed as she clutched a leather satchel tightly against her chest and headed straight for him. *Dr. Roux?* At least he presumed that's who she was, only he'd expected someone a lot less leggy and less stunning to look at.

What he'd figured he'd see was a gray-haired older woman, her hair swept back in a bun, with oval gold-rimmed glasses perched on her nose. Instead, this woman looked to be in her midtwenties and in terrific form, with shapely legs and a body to match. He envisioned her hiking through woods on wilderness treks to observe wolves, dispelling the notion that she was strictly a classroom lecturer.

"Dr. Roux?" he asked, feeling more like a knight in shining armor now.

She didn't smile but looked worried as hell as she chewed a glossy lip and then gave a stiff nod. "Did Millie send you for me?" She didn't wait for him to answer and motioned to the truck. "I changed the tire already."

He frowned and glanced back at the flat tire.

"Someone was nice enough to ruin the spare also when I ran inside to clean up," she added, her tone peeved. "It was too late to have the spare fixed before the meeting."

Irritated that any of the townspeople would treat her that way, he bit back a curse. Yet he couldn't help being surprised for a second time. First, by her appearance. Now, by how capable the little woman was.

He motioned to his Humvee. "I'm Leidolf Wildhaven, rancher south of town. I'll take you to the meeting and have one of my men fix the tires while you're lecturing."

"A rancher," she said softly, her voice slightly condemning.

He cast her a smidgen of a smile. "Yeah, but cougars are the only animals that bother me of late. Wolves? They're my kind of animal. Protective, loyal—you know, like a dog, man's best friend."

"They're wild, Mr.—"

"I'd prefer you call me Leidolf."

"I'm Cassie. Never met a rancher before who liked wolves." She sounded as though she didn't believe he would care for wolves. Maybe even worried that he might cause her trouble when she lectured.

From *Wolf Fever*

THE WAXING MOON WAS CALLING TO HER. *AGAIN*. Lying on the soft mattress in Darien Silver's guest room early that spring evening, Carol Wood tried to sleep. But she felt the growing white sphere begging her to shed her human frailties and run with the magnificent grace of the wolf, strong and agile, with purpose in every stride in the crisp, cold Colorado night air.

She did *not* wish to be one of them — at least as far as being a part-time wolf — no matter how much several in the pack had encouraged her to embrace this new side of herself. The moon would soon be whole, but deep down she rebelled against the werewolf's curse. Because it *was* a curse to her, just the way her premonitions and psychic touch often were.

She'd grown up with her revved senses and had realized she couldn't do anything about that aspect of her life, once she'd learned it wasn't normal to have the abilities she did. But now to be — she squeezed her eyes tighter and rolled onto her back — a *werewolf*... No matter how much she wished the truth could be changed, she knew she'd have to deal with it before long.

With all her heart, she prayed to keep her newly acquired bizarre condition — shape-shifting — at bay. Her body tingled with heat and her mind with apprehension. Even in the darkness of her half-asleep mind, she fought the change, fought the feeling she was losing control of

her physical form. Fresh tension made every nerve ending prickle while she clutched the comforter underneath
her chin.

The heat, like the sun shining on a bright and warm
Caribbean afternoon, invaded every pore, signaling the unwanted craving to shift. She moaned, tightening her hold
on the comforter, her nails digging into the white eyelet.
The moon was growing day by day, just like the damnable
desire to shape-shift. No, not desire. *Compulsion.*

Then, as if her psychic side finally gained some
ground against the wolf, her second sight kicked in. The
room and the need to shift dissolved into blackness, and
the wolf in her vision appeared again like a lucid dream.

*As big as it was, with massive shoulders, broad
muzzle and forehead, and long legs, the wolf had to
be a male, standing proud and tall, watching her from
the edge of the spring-green forest. Cloaked in rich
bluish-silver fur with a lighter mask, and with his ears
perked like an alpha male's would be, he panted until
he caught her gaze. His amber eyes focused on hers:
the wolf wanted her. Beckoned her to come to him. But
not as a human.*

As a wolf.

Even in her visions, the scene was one of cajoling,
begging her to recognize her destiny, to give in to her
wolf's half. At least that's the way she viewed him.

*Carol refused the wolf's alluring gaze and the moon's
sensuous serenade.*

But the moon *commanded* her! Aroused her to do its
bidding through its seductive pull, yanking her abruptly
from the vision.

The heat invading her body intensified now, like a

fever that couldn't be squelched. Never had the shift overtaken a vision in progress. The urge was growing. Yet she knew she still had some influence over the shift, like those born as *lupus garous* had an inborn ability to prevent humans from catching them during the conversion. Like them, if she wanted to change, the shift happened in a flash. And since she hadn't just automatically shifted, she must have some control.

Still, her muscles twitched with need as she shrugged off the comforter and blankets. She lay in her silky gown on the soft mattress in the pack leader's chilly guest room, ready to yank off her garment before the transformation took over in case she couldn't stop it. She envisioned the horrifying image of getting hung up in her gown as a wolf. Trapped, snarling, and growling, she'd try to free herself until she woke someone in the household. He or she would find her struggling in a cocoon of silk—furry legs kicking and sharp, wicked canines snapping.

She gritted her teeth and pressed the palms of her hands flat against the soft mattress, battling the moon's domination. She would not give up control and shapeshift! Not when she couldn't rule her paranormal abilities. Not when she would now have to relinquish control over her physical form as well.

But more than that, she feared the shift would change her forever. *Forever!* Doomed to live life as a wolf with the conscience of a human. Even a single moment as a wolf could permanently seal her fate. At least that's what she thought a new vision was telling her, yet she couldn't know for certain. That's why fear consumed her to a greater degree every time the damnable shift threatened to overtake her.

Cursing her fate, she ground her teeth and clenched her hands into fists, her fingernails biting into the palms of her hands, and attempted to think of anything that would halt the raging need to shift.

She visualized Lelandi, the pack leader's mate, throwing a first-ever All Girls' Night Extravaganza the previous week exclusively for women in the pack—complete with werewolf-romance writer Julia Wildthorn's latest novel made into a feature film, *Wolfly Desires*, popcorn, margaritas, and lots of laughter. They were still finding popcorn underneath cushions and beneath the couch in little clusters. Carol smiled at the memory, hoping they could repeat an activity like that soon.

But then the heat rushed through her body again with a new wave of warning. Every muscle tightened, preparing for the fight. As if she'd called to the gods of psychic phenomena and they'd taken pity on her, her thoughts began to blur, and she knew her psychic sense was trying to take control again.

Holding her thoughts hostage, the dreamlike image showed an out-of-focus man, dressed in red and white stripes, who had knocked her down and was holding her there. Instantly, her blood cooled, the need to shape-shift withdrawing. A scrap of relief trickled through her. She focused, trying to see the mental picture more clearly, attempting to determine who had tackled her and why. Annoyance was the driving feeling she experienced from the encounter. Not fear. Loss of control, maybe. But the strongest emotion was definitely annoyance.

Acknowledgments

Thanks to my Rebel Romance critique partners who always help me to smooth out the story—Vonda, Judy, Pam, Tammy, Randy, Carol, and Betty. I appreciate Deb Werksman for making my books shine, for loving my wolves, and for being wonderful to work with. And Danielle Jackson, my publicist, who keeps me straight on blog tours. I'd be lost without you! And the incomparable art department that make winning covers for each and every book. But most of all, thanks to my fans, who give me ideas for new stories, share with me true stories about wolves—sometimes about raising their own wolf and wolf dogs—and visit with me all over the blogosphere. Your inspiring comments make my day!

About the Author

An award-winning author of urban fantasy and medieval historical romantic suspense, Terry Spear also writes true stories for adult and young adult audiences. She's a retired lieutenant colonel in the U.S. Army Reserves and has an MBA from Monmouth University. She also creates award-winning teddy bears, Wilde & Woolly Bears, to include personalized bears designed to commemorate authors' books.

When she's not writing, gardening, or making bears, she's teaching online writing courses. Originally from California, she's lived in eight states and now resides in the heart of Texas. She is the author of *Heart of the Wolf, Destiny of the Wolf, To Tempt the Wolf, Legend of the White Wolf, Seduced by the Wolf, Wolf Fever, Heart of the Highland Wolf, Dreaming of the Wolf, Winning the Highlander's Heart, The Accidental Highland Hero, Deadly Liaisons*, and numerous articles and short stories for magazines.